CAPTAIN

USA Today and International bestselling author
Lauren Rowe

Prologue
Tessa

I grip the handwritten letter in my trembling hand, my eyes drifting with disbelief over the familiar, sloping script, my vision blurred by tears.

If I hadn't read these incomprehensible words with my own eyes, I never would have believed them possible.

If I hadn't seen them for myself, I would have defended the immutability of his devotion with my dying breath.

And, now, everything I thought I knew about love is shattered.

The love I aspired to have in this life is no more.

What is love?

I thought I knew.

But as it turns out, I have no fucking idea.

Chapter 1
Ryan

"So far so good," I say to my little brother, Keane. "I'm in no rush with her, though—we're just taking things slow."

My brother and I are sitting in a rented rowboat on Green Lake, just outside Seattle, drinking beer and fishing for trout (though not very well, apparently, since we haven't had a single bite all day), and I've been telling my brother about Olivia, the woman I've been seeing casually for about a month.

"You batten down the hatches with her yet?" Keane asks.

I chuckle. Gotta love my brother's bizarre Keane-speak. "Nah, Olivia and I haven't talked about exclusivity yet. We're just keeping it casual, you know? No pressure. No labels."

"Hold up," Keane says. "You're telling me you've been bonin' the fuck outta this chick for a month, Lionel-Richie-style, and she hasn't so much as dropped a *hint* she'd prefer you not stick your dick inside another chick?"

"Well, I currently have no desire to 'stick my dick' inside another woman, regardless—not every guy burns through 'chicks' as quickly as you do, Peen—I genuinely like focusing all my energies on one woman at a time. But it doesn't matter, anyway, because, so far, Olivia doesn't want exclusivity, either. Honestly, she doesn't seem to have a jealous bone in her body."

"Bullshit. Every woman's got at least thirty-seven jealous bones in her body. If this chick isn't showing you hers, she's just gaming you."

"Nah, Olivia's an open book. Super chill. Honestly, from what I've seen so far, there doesn't seem to be anything wrong with her."

"Ooph. Say it ain't so, Rummy-o. Gigantic red flag, dude. You best be finding at least a couple things wrong with this girl, *pronto*, or

3

two months from now, you're gonna find out every damned thing wrong with her, all at once, in a flash flood of batshit-crazy."

I open my mouth to tell my brother he's a dumbshit, but before I can say a word, the tip of Keane's rod bends and jerks sharply, instantly drawing our mutual attention.

"Fish on!" Keane exclaims, leaning forward excitedly.

"Reel him in slowly," I caution.

"We're not nine and fifteen, Ry. You don't have to coach me through this anymore."

"You're gonna lose him, Peen. You haven't set the hook."

"I know what I'm doing. Watch and learn, son: I'm fucking Ahab."

Keane continues reeling, but after a few seconds, the tip of his rod straightens and his line goes visibly slack. "Fuck!" Keane shouts. He raises his fist to the sky dramatically. "Damn you, fish gods!"

I laugh my ass off. "Maybe don't compare yourself to Ahab next time, *son*. I hate to spoil the ending for you, but Ahab never actually catches the whale."

"What?" Keane says, looking genuinely shocked. "But the book's called *Moby Dick*. What's the point in calling a book *Moby Dick* if no one ever catches Moby Dick? That'd be like *Jaws* if Roy Scheider doesn't blow up the shark but instead says, 'Oh well, I guess we just won't swim in the ocean anymore.'"

I laugh.

Keane continues, "Or *Finding Nemo* if no one ever finds Nemo and the dad-fish goes, 'Meh, I never liked that annoying clown-fish anyway.'"

"Or maybe it'd be like *Titanic*," I offer, "if, at the end, a big ship called *Titanic* sinks?"

"Aaah," Keane says, raising his eyebrow.

"See what I did there, little brother?" I say.

"Touché, big brother. That was a teaching moment, for sure."

I wink at him. "Watch and learn, son."

"Well, *Titanic* notwithstanding, Captain Ahab *not* catching Moby Dick is a shitty-ass, pointless ending, if you ask me."

"Peenie, Ahab *not* catching the whale is what makes it literature instead of *Fast and Furious* 7. The whole point is that Ahab becomes so obsessed with catching his great white whale, his obsession drives him to madness and, ultimately, hastens his demise."

"*Hastens?*"

4

"Hastens. Causes something to happen quicker than it otherwise would. Read a book on occasion, man."

Keane shrugs. "I'm too busy watching *Fast and Furious 7*." He flashes me his dimples. "Seriously, Ry, does your head hurt from being such a fancy-pants literary scholar?"

"It's not like I've got a PhD in American literature," I say. "I read *Moby Dick* in high school English, same as everybody else other than you, right along with *The Catcher in the Rye* and *The Great Gatsby*."

"Were the endings of those other books as shitty-ass as *Moby Dick*?" Keane asks. "As long as you're spoiling the classics for me, you might as well spoil 'em all."

"How the hell did you make it through high school without reading any of the classics?"

"Dude, I was too busy striking out batters and slaying it with the hot-chick brigade to waste my time reading about whales and rye-catchers and Gatsbys."

"But how the hell did you pass English Lit?" I ask.

"I had help from some tutors." Keane winks. "Some very *pretty* tutors."

I laugh. Classic Keane.

"So tell me the endings of those other books already, Master Yoda," Keane says, casting his line out into the lake again. "Were they as shitty-ass and pointless as *Moby Dick*?"

I take a long sip of my beer, gathering my thoughts. "Well, it's been over ten years since I read them, so don't hold me to it, but I think Holden Caulfield winds up in an insane asylum and The Great Gatsby dies without getting the girl."

"What the motherfuck?" Keane shouts, much too loudly for our serene environment. "*Nobody* gets the whale throughout *all* classic literature?"

"You want a happy ending, read a romance novel, son."

"Well, shit, maybe I will. Life is shitastic enough without reading books with depressing endings. If *I* ever write a book, it's gonna be whales and weed and wahoos for everyone!"

I laugh.

"Hand me another beer, would you, baby doll?" Keane says. "Literary analysis always makes me hella thirsty."

I hand my little brother a beer out of the cooler.

"Thanks, Captain. That's why I love you the most."

For several minutes, we sip our beers in silence and stare at the glassy lake.

"I think we should use a different kind of bait next time," Keane says after a while. "The fish are laughing at us. You hear 'em down there? They're like, 'Hahaha! What a couple of twatheads!'"

"A good workman never blames his tools."

"Okay, then I blame *you* for buying shitty bait."

"Hey, back to Olivia for a sec," I say. "What's the 'gigantic' red flag you see? I don't get it at all."

"Then you're blind. Dude, if she's not showing you anything but beauty-queen perfection for a solid month, then she's most definitely a closet psycho."

"Fucking Colby. When did you talk to him?"

Keane looks genuinely surprised. "I didn't. Colby said Olivia's a closet psycho?"

"Yeah, in those exact words. We were together when I met Olivia in a bar, and Colby was like, 'You dabble with the blonde one, there's gonna be a *Fatal Attraction*-style boiled bunny in your future, man. That one's a closet psycho, for sure.'"

Keane laughs heartily. "But you dabbled anyway?"

I shrug. "If you saw Olivia, you'd understand."

"There you go thinkin' with your dick again, Ry. Haven't you learned by now?"

"Oh my God. You're one giant dick, Peen. For fuck's sake, everyone calls you Peen."

"Yeah, but we're talking about you, not me." Keane shakes his head. "Rule number one for a handsome and happy life? Listen to Colby Morgan, every time. And rule number two? Listen to me, occasionally."

"Well, this isn't one of those 'occasional' times. You've never even met Olivia."

"I don't need to meet Olivia to know she makes my batshit-crazy radar go off like gangbusters."

"Based on what?"

"Based on the evidence. You said there's nothing wrong with her. That's enough right there. But, on top of that, you're the prettiest

Morgan brother of us all—which is saying a lot, considering how pretty we four are, especially me—and women are biologically programmed to want to mate with the prettiest males. Just look at peacocks. You think that tail is just for yucks?"

"Dude, I'm not even remotely thinking about 'mating' with Olivia. It's been a fucking month."

"Bullshit. You're *always* thinking about mating—I've never met a dude who wants babies more than you. It's not normal, Ry."

"I haven't said a word about that to Olivia. Of course not."

"Good. Don't talk about that shit with any woman for at least six months or you're gonna get yourself mixed up with a gold-digging baby-momma in record time."

I shake my head.

"It's true, brah. Open your eyes. You've got a fancy-pants career that's bringing in the duckets-by-the-buckets. Plus, along with that pretty face of yours, you've got those coolest-guy-in-the-room tattoos on your arms and a permanent I'm-gonna-fuck-you smolder. Women can't resist that shit. Add to all that your boner to change shitty diapers and any woman's gonna tell you whatever you wanna hear to lock you down."

I roll my eyes. "You haven't even met Olivia, Peen. She's not like that."

"Dude, stop being Forrest Gump about this girl. She's Katniss-Everdeening you with her crossbow and you're sitting there with a hard-on talkin' 'bout, 'Life is like a box of chocolates.' Well, you know what I say to that, Rum Cake?" Keane puts his palm to the side of his mouth and shouts his next words at the top of his lungs: "'Run, Rum Cake, Run!'"

I laugh. "Not so loud, Peenie. You'll scare the fish."

"There ain't no fish to scare, son." Keane leans back in the boat. "But, regardless, you've got bigger fish to fry than a few skittish fishes. I hate to break it to you, Captain, because I really do love you the most and respect you even more, but odds are two to one your new gal pal's a bunny-boiling loon. Based on the totality of the circumstances, this girl's nothin' but a huntress on safari and the big-game prey she's hunting is one Captain Ryan Ulysses Morgan."

"Okay, enough. I wish I'd never brought Olivia up in the first place. I never said I was in love with her or that she was The One or that I had any desire whatsoever to procreate with her. All I said was, 'So far, so good.' Now shut the fuck up and at least *try* to catch a fucking fish before I pummel those dimples right off your face."

We sit in silence, staring at our motionless fishing lines in the lake for a long while, the silence between us thick with my extreme annoyance. But when I notice Keane absentmindedly rubbing the bright pink surgery scar on his left elbow, my irritation with him instantly vanishes.

"How's the arm?" I ask.

Keane's eyes are trained on the surface of the water, his lips pressed firmly together.

"Keane?" I ask.

He looks at me.

"How's the arm?"

He exhales. "The team flew me out last week to check on my progress. It was *no bueno.*"

My stomach tightens. "What happened?"

"It was worst-case scenario, man. I got on the mound and couldn't get my fastball going and my curveball was for shit."

"But it hasn't even been a year since the surgery. You just need time."

"Most guys are back on the mound after seven or eight months, Ry. It's been nine. I'm out of time."

"Bah. A little bit longer and you'll be good as new, I'm sure of it."

Keane shakes his head. "They cut me."

"*What?*"

"Nine days ago."

"But... why didn't you say something?"

Keane shrugs.

"Have you told Mom and Dad?"

"I haven't told anyone but Zander—and that was only because he walked in on me one night when I was crying like a baby."

"Aw, Keaney." My heart physically hurts inside my chest. "You should have told us. We'd have circled the Morgan-wagons around you."

"I've just been processing it, I guess."

"Aw, Keane. I'm so sorry. I know how long you've dreamed about pitching in the major leagues."

"Yeah, well, a dream plus ten cents will get me two nickels, right?"

I grimace. "Don't say that. I know you're disappointed, but don't talk like you're giving up on dreaming altogether. You're only twenty-two, little bro. Keep your chin up. I tell you what: how about I pay your rent for a couple months—you know, just to give you a little breathing room while you figure out your next dream?"

"Thanks, but it's okay. I've got some money saved and Zander said he's good to cover rent for a couple months."

A loud cheer erupts from a nearby boat and we both look toward the noise, just in time to see a young boy pulling a ridiculously large trout out of the water.

"Ho-lee shit," Keane says. "Look at that thing."

"That's a huge fucking fish."

"What kind of bait was that kid using, I wonder? Should I row over there and ask him?"

"Nah." I hold up my beer can. "I'm good just sitting here, talking to you. Fuck the fish."

Keane flashes me a crooked smile that melts my heart. "Okay. Cool."

"Is that k-e-w-l?"

"Of course. Top honors, brah."

For several minutes, we sip our beers and watch as the kid in the other boat takes photos of himself with his monstrous fish, his whoops of laughter wafting to us on the breeze.

"Remember when Colby caught that huge fish that time?" Keane says.

"I'm surprised you remember that. You were only like five or six."

"I don't remember much except the look on Bee's face when he pulled that thing out of the water. Oh, and I remember Kum Shot puking on Dad's shoes that day in the boat. Ha! That was awesome."

"Poor Kat," I say, memories of our poor seasick sister flooding me. "Half my childhood memories of her involve her puking."

"Half my adult memories, too," Keane says, and we both laugh. "Man, I truly thought Colby was Superman that day."

"So did I." I take a sip of my beer. "Still do."

Keane looks at me. "Hey, Ry, seriously—I really think you

9

should respect Superman's intuition about this Olivia chick. Just, for all our sakes, do a serious gut-check before you fall fast and hard and start bringing her to family dinners."

"Who do you think I am? Zander Shaw? I never fall 'fast and hard' for anyone—you know that. And you know I'd never bring anyone to a family dinner unless I was one hundred-percent sure she was The One. Now shut the fuck up and catch yourself a fucking whale, Ahab. I got this."

"Oh, you got this, baby doll?"

"I got this, sweetheart."

"Then perhaps you won't mind putting your money where your mouth is?"

"What do you have in mind?"

"Twenty bucks says, within three months, So-Far-So-Good-Olivia turns into What-the-Fuck-Was-I-Thinking-Olivia—the worst fucking nightmare-shit-show-bunny-boiling-loon-catastrophe of your entire dating career."

I laugh. "You're on, fucker. But, just to be clear, the bet isn't whether Olivia and I break up within three months from sheer apathy, it's whether she's turned into an epic nightmare of staggering proportions."

"Precisely."

We shake on it.

"You know what?" I say. "Fuck it. Let's make it fifty bucks, just to make things interesting."

"Oh, Mr. Fancy-pants wants to up the ante, does he? Okay, High Roller. You got yourself a deal." He shakes my hand again and chuckles to himself. "Oh, man, I can't wait to profit off your misery, you cocky fuck. You committed the cardinal sin of disregarding Superman's advice, and now you're upping the ante on me? Ha!" He throws his head back and lets out a demonic laugh that reverberates across the quiet lake. "Let the bunny-boiling begin!"

Chapter 2
Tessa

"Hey, Tessa," my best friend, Charlotte, says, answering my call.

I'm sitting at a small desk in the corner of my brand-new bedroom in Seattle, surrounded by stacks of still-unpacked moving boxes, gripping my phone in one hand while massaging my forehead with the other. "Josh just called," I say into the phone. "He and Kat are back from their trip to South America and you'll never guess what's happened—not in a million years."

"Miss Perfect is having Josh's quintuplets?"

"Even more shocking than that. Josh just flat-out said to me, 'Theresa, I'm gonna ask that woman to marry me.'"

"*What?*" Charlotte blurts, sounding as flabbergasted as I feel. "Have aliens captured the real Josh Faraday?"

Charlotte's never met my boss, actually, or his perfect, pregnant girlfriend of mere months, Kat Morgan; but after listening to me babble and drool about Josh "The Playboy" Faraday for years, including listening to me throw major shade at the insufferable string of heiresses and supermodels he dated before finally falling in love with regular-girl-from-Seattle Kat, we've both just sort of gotten used to chatting about Josh like Charlotte knows him personally.

"Oh my God, Tessa," Charlotte sputters. "When's Josh gonna pop the question?"

"As soon as he can 'find a ring worthy of her.' He's going ring shopping on the down-low with Kat's mom tomorrow."

"I'm shocked."

"*You're* shocked? For the past six years, every time one of his friends has gotten engaged or married, Josh has sworn marriage isn't

11

in the cards for him. And now he's like, 'T-Rod, I'm gonna get Kat a rock so damned big, she's gonna need a crane to carry it around!'"

"Well, hang on. Just 'cause he's buying the girl a rock doesn't mean he's ready to commit to her for the rest of his damned life. Über-wealthy people get engaged all the time and never actually tie the knot. I've seen it a thousand times on *TMZ*. To a guy like Josh, buying The Hope Diamond for his girlfriend is the equivalent of a normal guy buying his girlfriend a twenty-dollar gift card to Claire's."

I burst out laughing. Thank God for Charlotte.

"Maybe he's just feeling pressure to give Kat a ring to keep her parents from hurling an axe into his back?" Charlotte suggests. "You know, for knocking up their precious baby girl?"

"No, he's not proposing to Kat because of the pregnancy—that's what trust funds and support agreements are for. And he's certainly had plenty of friends who've gone that route to show him how. Nope, The Playboy wants to ask The Party Girl to be his wife for no other reason than he's madly in love with her."

"Well, holy shit," Charlotte says. "I guess their little vacay down south went well, huh?"

"Apparently."

"Thanks to you," she says. "Did they love all the arrangements you made for them in Buenos Aires?"

"Of course. I know Josh—and I know my city."

Charlotte sighs. "I'm actually kind of sad about all this. What the heck will we talk about if not Josh's string of horrible women?"

"Oh, I'm sure we'll figure out a new topic of conversation."

"Why are you being so mature about this? You're allowed to be a little bit petty and immature—at least with me. Even though you like Kat and you're genuinely happy for Josh—blah, blah, blah—you can still be a tiny bit bummed that your previously slim chances at bagging your boss are now officially zero."

"Sweetie, I've never genuinely wanted to 'bag my boss.' I had a harmless crush on him for a while, that's all. That's what happens when a *very* sheltered twenty-one-year-old starts working for an outrageously hot guy straight out of college who's only a few years older than her. Six years later, I like to think I've matured and grown well beyond that stupid girl. At this point, I think of Josh more like a big brother than anything."

"Mmm hmm—a *smokin' hot* big brother."

"Okay, a stepbrother."

We both giggle.

"Regardless, I would have had to be delusional to think my boss would ever make a move on his personal assistant. He's *Josh Faraday*."

"Babe, this isn't an episode of *Downton Abbey*. Just because Josh never made a move on his personal assistant doesn't mean the *idea* of him doing it was ridiculous. Men lose their shit over you all the freaking time and you know it. You're the Argentinian Angelina Jolie."

I laugh. "That's a huge stretch, babe—but, thank you. And, no, I don't know men lose their shit over me 'all the freaking time.' Not at all."

"That's because you never go out these days, and, when you do, you've got your guard up. I mean, I get it—Stu really did a number on you and your confidence took a hit." She pauses. "You know what you should do? Go out and find yourself some hottie and have yourself some no-strings, toe-curling sex with a stranger for the first time in your life. That ought to give you a little spring in your step if you're feeling blue."

"I haven't had a lobotomy, Char—I'm not gonna have a one-night stand."

Charlotte sighs. "Okay, fine. Don't have sex with a stranger, just go out and flirt with one. Whenever I'm feeling kind of blue, you know what I do? I go to a bar in my uniform and flirt with hotties—and, lo and behold, my frown always turns upside-down. You'd be shocked how many men have whopping flight-attendant fantasies." Charlotte gasps. "Hey, I just had a great idea. Why don't you hop a flight down here to L.A. and come out with me and my work-friends tonight? I have an extra uniform you can wear. Hotties would swarm you."

"I can't believe I'm saying this, but I'm tempted. I've been missing you so much since the move, at this point, I'd probably agree to anything to see you. But, unfortunately, I've got a bunch of meetings tomorrow with vendors for Josh and Jonas' grand opening party next week, so I can't get away. Plus, thanks to Josh's phone call a few minutes ago, it seems I've now got an elaborate marriage proposal to arrange."

"Josh asked *you* to arrange his proposal?"

"Just the logistics. He came up with The Big Idea on his own."

"Lame."

"Why? Arranging logistics for Josh's big ideas is literally my job."

"Honey, 'executive personal assistant' or not, no woman should ever be expected to help the man she loves propose to another woman."

"Gah! Stop it, Char. I don't 'love' Josh—or, at least, not like that. Yes, I used to have a *crush* on him way back when, and, yes, this past year when I was so devastated about Stu, I *maybe* fantasized about Josh once or twice while using my battery-operated-boyfriend—but it's awfully hard for a girl to get too delusional about her chances with a boss who's never so much as ogled her in six years."

"Oh, please. Surely, Josh 'The Playboy' Faraday has ogled your double Ds at least a thousand times in six years."

"Nope. Not once. He's always been the consummate professional with me. But why are we even talking about this? Josh is marrying Kat and having a baby with her and they're gonna live happily ever after while I die miserable and alone and untouched by human hands for the rest of my freaking life. There's nothing to talk about."

Charlotte laughs. "Oh, Tessa."

"It's okay. I'm just having a pity-party today. I'll bounce back tomorrow. It's got nothing to do with Josh, *per se*. I just wish I could find a guy somewhat *like* him out there, you know? A good guy who's also hot as fuck—and also loyal and faithful and available. Does such a man exist?"

"Well, no offense, but how do you expect to find a guy like that if you never go out and flirt with anyone?"

"I don't know anyone in Seattle, Char. I'm not gonna go out all by myself to a bar and flirt with strangers."

Charlotte lets out a loud puff of air. "Okay, that settles it: I'm coming to Seattle."

"When?"

"Right now. I'm at LAX now—I just got off a shift. I'll hop the next flight to Seattle and be there in a couple hours. Easy peasy. I won't even have to miss a day of work—I'm sure I can swap shifts with a friend based in Seattle."

I let out an excited squeal. "Oh my God, Charlotte. Thank you! I've been missing you so much these past three weeks."

"But, listen up, girl: if I'm gonna fly a thousand miles to see you on a whim, then you're gonna do what I say tonight. You're gonna wear the damned uniform I bring you and flirt your hot little ass off, okay?"

"Okay, okay."

"Promise?"

"Promise."

Charlotte giggles. "Tonight, you're not gonna be Josh Faraday's logistics-arranging, numbers-crunching, spreadsheet-creating executive personal assistant. You're gonna be 'Samantha the Randy Flight Attendant.'"

"Oh my God, you nut job. Fair warning, though: I'm not gonna hop into some stranger's bed, just 'cause I'm wearing a flight-attendant uniform."

"How long has it been since you've slept with someone? Since Stu?"

"Yep. Nine months and three days, but who's counting?"

"Not even a make-out session?"

"Nothing. Not even a kiss."

"Ooph. My vagina just vicariously turned to dust. Okay, Theresa Rodriguez, I'm officially your fairy godmother tonight—your wise and slutty fairy godmother—and I'm making it my mission to get you kissed by a hottie tonight."

"The hottie would have to be pretty damned hot for me to even consider kissing him, but, okay, I'll keep an open mind. So, where are we gonna find this hottie-I'm-gonna-kiss, Slutty Fairy Godmother?"

"Wise and slutty. Don't forget the 'wise' part."

"So sorry, darling. So, where are we going?"

"I dunno. I'll ask my friend based in Seattle where we should go. Just the other day, she was telling me about a couple places she said were hottie-wonderlands. I think one of them was called The Pine Box?"

"Whatever, I'm in. Thanks for coming to see me."

"I'm not coming to see *you*—I'm coming to see, *Samantha.*" She giggles. "See you soon, girlie. I love you, Crazy Girl."

"I love you, too, Nut Job. Bye."

Chapter 3
Ryan

I enter the bar and survey the room. "If you're up for trying a new place, I recently went to a cool little place with Kat and my brother," Josh said when I called him this afternoon and suggested we grab drinks tonight. "It's called The Pine Box."

And, so, here I am.

I scan the faces in the room, looking for Josh; and when I don't see him, I stride to the bar, settle myself onto a stool, and order a drink.

Yeah, this is definitely a cool little place. As much as I like it, though, I'd make a few adjustments, if it were mine. The layout doesn't optimize the flow to the bar and the "specialty drinks" menu could use a little jolt of originality. Plus, that corner in the back—the one currently filled with crates and boxes? That's the perfect spot for a foosball table. That's a cryin' shame, I tell you—a tragic waste of space.

The bartender places my drink in front of me. "You wanna open a tab?" he asks.

I gotta assume everyone who grabs drinks with Josh Faraday expects him to pick up the tab—a natural assumption when a guy drives a Lamborghini, I suppose—so I'm thinking I'll give the poor rich guy's pockets a break tonight. "Thanks, Tim," I say, looking at the bartender's nametag. "Yeah, let's open a tab—I'm expecting a buddy. And, hey, whatever my buddy says about paying the bill when he gets here, drinks are on me tonight."

I've only met Josh once, actually, about three weeks ago at my parents' house, when my little sister, Kat, brought her new boyfriend home to meet our entire family. Everyone except Keane, that is, who was too busy shaking his ass for dollah billz as Seattle's newly christened "Peen Star" to make the dinner. But just one spaghetti dinner and four foosball games later, and I already knew Josh Faraday was a long-lost Morgan brother. In fact, as I recall, I texted Keane later that night to tell him Josh had just usurped his spot as "the one I love the most." I must say, Keane took the news remarkably well.

Of course, when Kat shocked us all by revealing she was carrying Josh's baby at that dinner three weeks ago, my whole family instantly realized we had no choice but to accept Kat's baby-daddy with open arms; but the truth is, we all liked Josh so much, we would have opened our arms to him, regardless of Kat's bun in the oven.

Which brings me to why I'm sitting here at The Pine Box right now. Despite what Kat said at dinner three weeks ago about marriage "not being in the cards" for her and Josh, it seems Josh has secretly asked my mom and dad for their blessing to propose. So, of course, I texted Josh right away and asked him to drinks, suddenly feeling the need to explain two things to my soon-to-be brother-in-law: one, when he marries my sister, he'll be getting a helluva lot more than a wife—he'll also be getting a family, including four brothers who'll always have his back, come what may; and, two, fuck number one— if Josh screws up and breaks our sister's heart, the Morgan Brothers will turn into the Morgan Mafia so fucking fast, Josh won't know what hit him.

My phone pings with an incoming text and I look down, expecting it to be from Josh—but, nope, it's my extremely hot but crazy-as-fuck girlfriend (or, as of about an hour ago, my ex-girlfriend?), Olivia.

"Sorry, babe," the text from Olivia begins.

I roll my eyes. That woman should get "sorry, babe" tattooed onto her forehead.

"I shouldn't have said all that stuff to you," Olivia's text continues.

No shit.

"But you shouldn't have stormed out like that and there was certainly no need to say you wanted to break up. We just had a fight, that's all. It happens. It doesn't mean we're 'fundamentally incompatible.' I was just pissed, that's all, and I had every right to be, not only about that bitch at the restaurant, but also about how women always throw themselves at you. I can only assume it means you don't tell them up front you're in an exclusive relationship. AND THAT PISSES ME THE FUCK OFF!!!!"

I clench my teeth. This is Olivia's idea of an apology? What a fucking loon. How the hell did I let myself get hooked up with a woman as jealous and possessive as Olivia? It's not my fault that blonde in the restaurant slipped me a note, totally unsolicited, when she thought Olivia had gone to the restroom. Emphasis on the word "thought" in that sentence. *I've been eavesdropping on you and your girlfriend,* the blonde's note said. *It sure sounds to me like your relationship is about to go bye-bye. When it does, feel free to call me for a little fun. Or, hell, call me tonight. I won't tell.*

Yeesh. The look on Olivia's face when she lurched at me out of nowhere and snatched that piece of paper out of my hand was so fucking scary, I almost screamed in terror. Of course, true to form, I laughed my ass off, instead—and, man, did that piss Olivia off even more.

I take a long sip of my drink.

For fuck's sake, I didn't solicit that note tonight—I hadn't even noticed that blonde sitting with her friends at the next table. And that's exactly what I told Olivia when she accused me of flashing the woman some sort of nonverbal "let's fuck behind my girlfriend's back!" signal throughout dinner. Ridiculous. I'd never do that to a girlfriend of mine, even if it turns out she's a fucking loon and not even close to the person she pretended to be for the first month of our relationship. Plus, not that it matters, but I wasn't even remotely attracted to that blonde at the next table and wouldn't have taken her up on her offer, even if I'd been single. Yeah, I know Olivia is a classic blonde, just like the woman with the note, so Olivia automatically thinks I'm all about banging blondes; but, honestly, my attraction to Olivia was kind of an aberration for me. Give me a dark-haired, dark-eyed beauty over a blonde any day of the week, man—I swear to God, it's like I'm genetically programmed to lose my shit over girls like that.

But, regardless, even if I were a sucker for girls who look just like Olivia, does she really think I'm the kind of douche who'd hit on one woman while out with another? Gimme some fucking credit.

18

And, hey, as long as I'm compiling my List of Reasons Olivia's Tirade was Complete Bullshit, the truth is, I'm not all that into one-night stands these days, either. Been there, done that. Nowadays, I strongly prefer getting to know every inch of a woman I'm attracted to, both inside and out, night after glorious night.

I take another long swig of my drink in an attempt to loosen my clenched jaw.

There's nothing I hate more than being accused of cheating. Like I've told Olivia over and over: I don't cheat. I'm a Morgan, after all, and Morgans don't cheat. Not on our women. Not in sports. Not in school or business or even in a stupid game of beer pong. Do I blurt, "I have a girlfriend!" like some pussy-whipped loser with girlfriend-inspired Tourette's syndrome every time a female so much as smiles at me or says, "Hey, don't I know you from the gym?" No, I don't. But does that mean I'm gonna fuck every attractive woman who flirts with me? *No.* Because, first off, at that rate, I'd be fucking twenty different women a day. I mean, come on, I'm a commercial real estate broker, after all, and that means I come in contact with a *lot* of different people on a daily basis, including women, some of them highly attractive. And, second off, regardless, I'm not sure if I've mentioned this, but... *I don't fucking cheat!*

I drain my drink and slam my empty glass down on the bar.

I can't take it anymore. Life's too short to be this miserable. I'm officially done. That's what I told Olivia when I stormed out of her place right before coming here, and, contrary to what she obviously believes, I meant every word I said.

I grab my phone off the bar and tap out a quick text to Olivia: "I meant what I said. We need to talk. Are you gonna be home later? I'll come over." I'm tempted to add, "Fuck off! I'm done with this nightmare of a cluster-fuck of a fucking relationship, you crazy fucking bitch!" But I refrain because my darling momma would kill me if she found out I'd cut the last, dangling cord with a girl over text—or, for that matter, told her to "fuck off" and called her a "crazy fucking bitch".

"Another one?" Tim the Bartender asks, motioning to my empty glass.

"Sure. Thanks."

I tap out a second text, this one to my soothsayer of a little brother. Not that he's gonna reply to me any time soon—Keane's the absolute worst about answering his texts. "Hey, Peenie," I write. "Remember two months ago when we were fishing at Green Lake and I said you were wrong about Miss Perfect? FML. I owe you 50 bucks. I broke up with her earlier tonight. Text Colby for me, would you? I'm too embarrassed to tell him myself. Make sure to tell him I'll never doubt my Master Yoda again."

I put my phone on the bar and scan the place again, looking for Josh. He's definitely more than fashionably late. I pick up my phone again. "Hey, Lambo," I write to Josh. "We still on to meet at The Pine Box? I'm sitting at the bar."

I make small talk with the bartender for several minutes until, finally, my phone rings with an incoming call from Josh.

"Hey, man," I say, answering the call. "What's up?"

"I'm sorry, Ryan. I was just about to leave my house to meet you when Kat started barfing like the Exorcist."

"Oh, man. Poor Kat. My mom said the whole 'morning sickness' thing has been rough on her. Tell Kat I hope she feels better soon."

"I'm sorry I didn't text you earlier. I got caught up helping Kat and didn't realize the time. I just don't feel good about leaving her tonight."

"Oh, yeah, definitely stay with her," I say. "I'm not at all surprised, by the way. Has Kat told you one of her many nicknames growing up was The Barf-o-matic?"

Josh laughs. "Hey, why don't you come over to our place, instead? I'm still down to hang out and I'm sure Kat would love to barf on you. I've got a pool table and a fully stocked bar."

"Sounds great," I reply. "Maybe we could make a drinking game out of Kat's misery? 'Everyone drinks *once* when Kat pukes and *twice* when she gets barf in her hair!'"

"Yeah, and then we all run for our lives when Kat starts beating the shit out of everyone playing our fun little drinking game."

"Excellent point. Ix-nay on the drinking game." I chuckle. "So it seems you've already discovered my sister's fully capable of murder, huh?"

"You call her The Barf-o-matic? I call her Madame Terrorist."

I laugh. "I'm gonna have to steal that."

"Hey, is it okay with you if I invite my brother and his new wife to our little impromptu soiree? Jonas keeps saying he wants to meet one of the fabled Morgan brothers I keep talking about."

"Of course. I'd love to meet him."

"I think you already know his new wife, Sarah, right?"

"Yeah, Sarah and I have partied together a few times over the years, mostly at Kat's birthday pub crawls. Sarah's a great girl."

And hot as fuck, I might add.

In fact, my sister's best friend since her freshman year in college is exactly the type of girl I'm attracted to the most: dark hair, olive skin, big, brown eyes, and curves for days. I love all types of women, don't get me wrong (thank you, God, for making females in all their glorious shapes and sizes), but I must admit the Sarah Cruzes of the world have always turned my head the most. Add Sarah's wit and intelligence and fantastic sense of humor on top of her boner-inducing packaging, and I'll be the first to admit I've always had a massive crush on her.

If I remember correctly, I started hitting on Sarah the first time I met her at one of Kat's birthday shindigs three or four years ago, but Kat put the kibosh on that shit right quick. "Leave my bestie alone, Bacardi," Kat warned me sharply. "No Morgan peen gets inside my best friend unless you're planning to marry her and make her my sister under God, which we both know ain't gonna happen any time soon when it comes to a slut like you. I'm not gonna let the biggest player of all my brothers break my best friend's heart and make it awkward for me to invite both of you to future birthdays." And, so, seeing as how I was a wee little lad of twenty-four or so at the time and Kat was absolutely right, not even remotely thinking about settling down with any one girl—even a girl as incredible as Sarah Cruz, I dutifully respected my sister's off-limits designation and left her smoking-hot bestie alone. I consoled myself for the next year, as I recall, with a string of Sarah look-alikes, none of whom could hold a candle to the original.

"So, I'll see you in a bit," Josh says. "I'll text you the address."

"Yeah, great," I reply. "I've got to take care of a small snafu first, but I'll head over there right afterward."

"Everything okay?"

"It will be soon. Just gotta cut the last dangling thread on something. No biggie."

"Take your time. We'll be here."

I shove my phone into my pocket, wave to the bartender for my bill, and pivot toward the front door, intending to hightail it to Olivia's to confirm we're absolutely through in no uncertain terms... but a jaw-dropping sight stops me dead in my tracks: two flight attendants, a curvy brunette and a petite redhead, are standing just inside the front entrance of the bar... and the brunette is, oh my fucking God, a jaw-dropper of epic proportions. Dark hair. Olive skin. Curves to make a man drop to his knees and thank the mighty lord for his beneficence.

For a long beat, I stand stock-still, staring at the brunette bombshell at the door, my dick subtly tingling, my chest tight, my head suddenly filled with rather graphic visions of myself fucking the living hell out of that woman from behind, one fist gripping her hair, the other cupping her breast... until finally, slowly, and without consciously commanding my body to do it, I take a step backward and lower my ass onto my stool.

Chapter 4
Ryan

The really hot one isn't scoping out the place at all, but her friend sure is. Oh, yeah, the petite redhead is definitely the scout in this duo. She's checking out the room and every man in it like a hungry lioness looking for her next meal. Her eyes are scanning, scanning, making calculations... hunting. And then... *boom*. The scout's eyes land on me at the bar and stop moving. She flashes me a full, beaming smile and I smirk ever so slightly in reply.

The redhead grasps her hot friend's forearm like she's cuffing a felon and leans urgently into her ear. The hot brunette whispers in reply to her friend, her head turned away from me. And now it's Red's turn to whisper something again.

Back and forth they go as I shift my ass on my stool. I know I'm somewhat of a vain motherfucker—I fully admit that—but I'd bet anything those two women are talking about me right now. At least, I sure as fuck hope they are.

Finally, they stop talking and Hot Brunette begins nonchalantly looking around the room at everything and everyone other than me. Because, of course, that framed picture on the wall of the Seattle skyline is endlessly fascinating. Okay, clearly, the girl's actively *not* looking over here—probably trying to come off like her eyes aren't being pulled like magnets on steel to me. Fine with me, sweetheart. Play your little game. I'll wait.

Okay, Hot Brunette's gaze is fiiiiiinally migrating, ever so slowly, toward me at the bar.

Here she comes.

Her gaze is drifting toward me.

Getting closer.

23

Hang on. Wait. What the fuck? Hot Brunette's eyes have already swept down the full length of the bar and right past me... too fast for me to hold her gaze or even flash her a quick smile. And now she's chatting with her red-haired friend again.

I glance to my left. There's a man and woman sitting immediately next to me with two open stools on their far side. "Hey, would you two mind shifting down a couple seats?" I ask the man. "I'm trying to free up two stools next to me." I motion toward the duo at the door by way of explanation and the dude smiles broadly.

"Sure thing," he says, getting up. "Good luck."

And that's all the invitation Redhead needs. Without hesitation, she grasps her friend's upper arm like she's wrangling a misbehaving toddler out of a candy store and literally drags her toward the two open stools.

Come to Papa, baby.

As Hot Brunette walks toward me, she keeps her head down and eyes averted, giving me a chance to ogle her undetected—hot damn!—but about twenty feet away, she unexpectedly lifts her head and looks straight at me... and then doesn't look away for a long beat—long enough for me to know I'm fucking toast.

Heat floods my entire body.

I smile at her, my pulse pounding in my ears.

Hot Brunette returns my smile and quickly looks down again, her cheeks blazing, but I've already seen my future in her eyes, as surely as if I've peered into a crystal ball: I'm about to become Captain Ahab and this beautiful woman my whale—and, clearly, there's not a damned thing I can do about it.

Chapter 5
Tessa

"...for all his tattooings he was on the whole a clean, comely looking cannibal."
—Herman Melville, *Moby Dick*

"Jackpot!" Charlotte blurts into my ear.

"What?" I turn my head toward whatever or whoever Charlotte's looking at with such unmistakable lust in her eyes, but she grabs my forearm and squeezes hard, snapping my attention to her vise-like grip. "Ow," I say, grimacing. "What the...?"

"Don't look!" Charlotte hisses, her eyes wide. "The hottest guy ever is sitting at the bar right now. Oh my effing God, *don't look*."

"Charlotte, you're kind of hurting my arm, honey."

"Sorry." She lets go. "I had to squeeze something so I wouldn't pass out from all the blood whooshing into my cooch, all at once."

"Well, squeeze your own damn arm next time the world's hottest guy gives you a lady-boner." I rub my forearm. "That hurt."

"Sorry." Charlotte gasps and squeezes me again. "Tessa, he's looking right at you."

"Or you. We're standing right next to each other, babe."

"No. He's definitely looking at *you*. Oh, wow, you should see the hungry look on that man's gorgeous face. Oh, God, he's mentally eating you out."

"Jesus, Char. Now we've both got lady-boners. I'm gonna look."

"No, no, not yet. Let him salivate a bit longer. Holy hell, he wants you. He's staring at you like a starving man at a butcher shop window."

"You're crazy."

25

"I'm not crazy—he's not even trying to be subtle about his attraction to you."

"One little look."

"*No.* Men are hunters—let the man hunt. You don't want him thinking you're a slam dunk."

"Well, I'm *not* a slam dunk. I'm not even an easy lay-up." I snicker. "Or a jump shot. Or a free throw." I snort. "Or even a fade-away."

"Okay. I get it. You're a whiz with basketball puns." Charlotte bites her lip, her eyes still trained over my shoulder like lasers. "Good God, he's making my mouth water."

"Okay, now you're just being a bitch, Charlotte McDougal. At least tell me what the guy looks like."

"Like a man with a very big dick."

I laugh. "How many martinis did you have at that last bar?"

"Just two. And a shot. Oh, and another shot." She snorts.

"Well, slow down High Speed. You get loose lips when you drink. Don't embarrass me."

"Never." She narrows her eyes at her target. "Gah. He's perfection."

"At least tell me what he looks like."

"He's white. Light brown hair. Cheekbones to die for. Tattoo-sleeves on both arms. Muscles in all the right places. Swagger, swagger, swagger. Gah. He's perfect. Seriously, though, what straight man needs cheekbones like that?"

"Maybe he's not straight."

"Honey, he's looking at you like he wants to mack down on your pussy. Clearly, he's not a man who's looking for a gal-pal."

"I'm gonna look."

"Okay. But just don't be too obvious about it. Glance around the room first."

"Got it."

I begin looking around the room, anywhere and everywhere but in the direction Charlotte's been staring for the last few minutes until finally letting my gaze drift toward the bar area and then sweep down the full length of the bar, straight past a muscled god with tattoos on his arms... *Holy motherfucking shit!* I look away, my heart raging in my chest, and lean into Charlotte's ear. "Holy fuck, he's hot."

"Like I said."

"I can't do this, Char. I've been out of practice for too long. The last really hot guy I flirted with was Stu, and look how that turned out."

"Tessa, you just now flirted with all those guys at the last bar and you did great."

"Because none of those guys even remotely interested me. But *this* guy... one glance and I don't have a few butterflies flapping around in my stomach, I've got an entire flock of bald eagles."

"It's mind over matter, babe. For all you know, this guy could be a total asshole underneath those cheekbones. You were just going on and on the other day about how society places far too much value on physical appearance, remember?"

"Yeah, but that was my *brain* talking. Now that I'm seeing this guy, my body's telling my brain to shut the fuck up."

"Don't worry. I'll get the conversation started while you get your bald eagles under control, okay? Just join in whenever you're comfortable."

I mumble something incoherent.

"You got this. You're Samantha the Randy Flight Attendant, not Tessa the Executive Personal Assistant—and Samantha's a shameless flirt."

I look down at the uniform I'm wearing and my stomach clenches. "Crap. I forgot I'm dressed like this. Maybe I should—"

Charlotte gasps and clutches my arm. "Oh my God!" she blurts, cutting me off. "Mr. Hottie just cleared two stools right next to him!" She grabs my upper arm and begins dragging me across the room. "Come on, *Samantha*. Let's get that lady-boner of yours flying at full mast for the first time in nine months."

Chapter 6
Ryan

"There she blows! There she blows! A hump like a snow-hill! It is Moby Dick!"

As the ladies settle onto their stools, Tim the Bartender comes over to take their drink orders, which I add to my tab. Introductions are quickly made: the cute redhead is Charlotte and the sexy brunette who, thankfully, took the stool right next to mine, is Samantha.

"She's 'Samantha the Randy Flight Attendant,'" the redhead chirps with a cartoon wink, leaning sideways across her gorgeous friend's ample chest to tap my forearm.

"Is that so?" I ask, laughing.

Samantha looks mortified. "Ignore my drunk friend, please."

"I'm not drunk," Charlotte says brightly. "Just highly buzzed. Although, admittedly, I can't feel my face or toes."

I raise my glass. "To not being able to feel our faces or toes."

The three of us clink glasses—and, as we do, I'm able to sneak some solid eye contact with Samantha before she looks down at her hands, her cheeks on fire.

"So how'd you two ladies wind up at The Pine Box?" I ask, directing my question to Samantha's downturned face. "It's nowhere near the airport."

"A friend of mine recommended it," Charlotte replies breezily. "She told me hot men always seem to hang out here and, by God, she was right." She blatantly looks me up and down like she's assessing a side of beef. "As my namesake spider in E.B. White's classic masterpiece would say, you're 'some pig!', Ryan."

When I shoot Samantha an amused look, she giggles and explains, "Drunk Charlotte likes to quote *Charlotte's Web*."

28

I laugh.

"So have you been here before, Ryan?" Charlotte asks.

I peel my eyes off Samantha. Good God, I feel magnetically pulled to this woman. "Uh, no. This place was picked by my buddy. He was supposed to meet me here, actually, but had to cancel last minute." My phone pings with an incoming text and I hastily reach into my pocket and turn it off. If Olivia's texting me right now, I don't wanna know about it. "So where are you girls from?" I ask.

Charlotte nudges her friend's arm. "Ryan wants to know where we're from, Samantha."

Samantha clears her throat. "L.A."

"Just here for a one-night layover," the redhead says. "The glamorous life of a flight attendant."

Samantha shifts in her seat. "Well, the glamorous life for Charlotte, anyway. She's the real flight attendant here—I'm just dressed like one."

I laugh, thrilled to see Samantha's loosening up enough to start cracking jokes.

"So, *Ryan*," the redhead says. "Wanna hear something jaw-dropping?" She leans across her friend's ample chest and puts her hand on mine, forcing me to peel my eyes off Samantha's stunning face. "Samantha here hasn't been so much as kissed in nine freaking months!"

"Charlotte!" Samantha blurts. "*No!*"

The redhead waves dismissively at her friend. "Honey, we don't have all night to get this show on the road." She looks at me. "My friend's been in a post-break-up slump for a while, so I'm wondering if you'd do me a huge favor and shamelessly flirt with her tonight—you know, maybe help her get her groove back? I'm trying to remind her it's actually fun to go out and meet new people on occasion."

Samantha covers her face with her hands. "*Charlotte.*"

"I'm one step ahead of you, Charlotte," I say smoothly. "I've been shamelessly flirting with Samantha since she walked through the door—and definitely *not* as a favor to you or anyone." I flash Samantha my most seductive smile. "So what do you say, Samantha? How about you let me buy you another drink and do my best to remind you it's fun to go out and meet new people on occasion?"

Samantha bites her lower lip.

"Oh, for the love of fuck," Charlotte barks. "Just say yes. The chemistry between you two is through the roof."

Samantha blushes. "*Yes*. Thank you. I'd love to have a drink and get to know you a bit, Ryan."

"*Fabulous*," Charlotte says, shooting up from her stool. "My work here is done. I'm gonna hang out with those two nice gentlemen in the corner who've been shooting me 'come hither' stares since we walked in." She grabs her martini off the bar. "Holler if you need me, girl, and I'll come running."

With that, Charlotte sashays across the room, drink in hand, leaving me to my own devices with the curvy flight attendant who's making my heart race and my skin buzz—the beautiful woman who's inexplicably making me wonder for the first time in my life if maybe, just maybe, that whole "love at first sight" thing might not be total and complete bullshit, after all.

Chapter 7
Ryan

"Charlotte's a force of nature," I say as we watch Samantha's petite friend strut across the bar like she owns the place.

"She hasn't always been this crazy," Samantha says. "Sorry. She's been going through this whole life-transformation, self-emancipation thing lately."

"No need to apologize for her. Charlotte's the best wing-woman ever." I take a deep breath, trying to control the unbelievable racing of my heart. *Holy fuck, I want to have sex with this woman.* "So tell me a little bit about yourself," I say.

"You first," Samantha says. "I'm feeling a little tongue-tied at the moment, to be honest."

I beam a reassuring smile at her. "What would you like to know?"

"I dunno," Samantha says. "Maybe just give me a brief overview about yourself?"

"A 'brief overview'?" I say. "Damn. The *one* time I didn't bring a Power Point presentation with me to a bar and the prettiest woman in the place asks me for a 'brief overview'?"

Samantha smiles sheepishly. "I sound like I'm conducting a job interview, don't I? Shoot. It's been a while since I've done this."

I touch her forearm. "I'm just teasing. It seems I've morphed into a fourth-grader with a crush around you. Next thing you know, I'm gonna be pulling your hair." She raises her eyebrows and I suddenly realize what I've just said. *Shit.* "I meant," I stammer, "you know, like a boy pulling a girl's pigtails on the playground, not..." I trail off. Fuck. Now the only thing I can think about is fisting this gorgeous woman's thick, dark hair while I'm fucking the hell out of her.

31

Samantha smiles. "I know what you meant. And, don't worry, I can handle a little teasing—I've got two brothers."

I take a deep, steadying breath. What is this crazy chemistry I'm feeling? "Ah, a woman with brothers," I say, scooting my stool a tad bit closer to hers, my body on fire. "Now that's a woman who's learned some serious survival skills. I've got three brothers and a sister, and, thanks to all the merciless teasing we've put my sister through, she's grown up to be the biggest badass of us all."

"Hey, that's a good item for your 'overview,'" she says. "You've got three brothers and a badass sister. Where do you fall in the birth order?"

"I'm the second oldest. My older brother's the heir and I'm the spare. The rest of my siblings were created solely for our entertainment."

Samantha laughs.

"And, as far as the rest of my Power Point goes: I'm twenty-eight. Born and raised in Seattle. I'm a Taurus—which I only know because my sister used to babble about astrology at the dinner table every night when I was growing up. Oh, and I can fold a fitted sheet better than any hotel maid. Seriously, it's my superpower."

"That's an impressive superpower. No matter how hard I try to fold a fitted sheet, it always winds up in a crumpled-up ball in a cabinet."

"There's a trick to it. I'd be happy to show you sometime. And while I'm at it, I could show you all my sheet-related tricks, some of them even more impressive, if you like."

"Wow, how generous of you. I'll be sure to add 'skilled with sheets' to your Power Point."

"Please do. Oh, and here's something kinda meta for my Power Point: I love Power Points."

She giggles. "So do I, actually."

"They're the best, right? They get you everything good in life. When I was eleven or twelve, I used a Power Point to convince my mom to let me get a dog from the local shelter."

"Power Points makin' dreams come true," she says.

"One manipulative kid at a time," I add.

We both laugh.

"I did the same thing when I was fifteen," she says. "I made a Power Point to convince my dad to let me go to a high school dance."

"You needed a Power Point to get to go to a dance?"

"I wasn't allowed to date 'til I turned sixteen."

"Oh my God. The humanity."

"It was okay—I went to an all-girls school so it's not like I had lots of opportunities to date, anyway. But when I'd just turned fifteen, this boy who lived down the street asked me to the local public school's dance, so I made this detailed Power Point and argued my case, and, finally, my dad relented and let me go as a 'one-time dispensation.'" She laughs. "It certainly helped that the boy had *zero* game—oh my God, I could have been in a phone booth with that poor boy and not realized he was standing there with me."

I laugh. "Did you at least have fun at the dance?"

"It definitely didn't live up to the hype."

"No first kiss?"

She shakes her head. "My first kiss was at age eighteen." She shrugs. "But, hey, this isn't *my* Power Point yet. We're still on yours."

"I've already told you everything, unless you have any questions for me."

"You mean, like, 'Ryan, where do you envision yourself in five years'?"

I laugh. "Whoa. This really *is* a job interview."

She giggles. "I was totally kidding. But now that I've asked it, I'd love to hear your answer."

I pause, considering how best to answer the question without sounding like I've got no game, and finally decide to just let it all hang out. "In five years, I envision myself married with children and the owner of my own bar."

Her cheeks flush. "Oh." She opens and closes her mouth like a fish on a line.

I suddenly feel the distinct need to change the subject. "Oh, I totally forgot the most important item for my Power Point: I make the best guacamole in the world."

She bites her lip seductively. "'*In the world*'?"

"In the world. It's another superpower."

"That's a really bold statement, sir."

"Bold, but true."

"Well, I definitely gotta taste this 'world's best' guacamole of yours. I *love* guacamole."

"One taste and you're gonna fall head over heels in love with me."

"Sorry, it's gonna take a bit more than some amazing guac to make me fall in love with you. I'm extremely left-brained, I should warn you. Just gimme the facts."

"Ah, give you the facts and leave the guacamole? Got it. Sounds like I'd better make a Power Point with a whole bunch of charts and graphs and statistics about what a great guy I am if I want to make you fall in love with me."

"No, no. Show me a Power Point with numbers and graphs *while* I'm tasting your guac." Her face suddenly turns bright red. "That is, I mean, *if* making me fall in love with you... is... your... goal." She literally palms her forehead and quickly takes a gigantic sip of her drink.

And just like that, the only thought in my head is: *I want to make this girl fall in love with me.*

The song playing in the bar switches from "Shape of You" by Ed Sheeran (great song) to a song I don't recognize—but, by the way Samantha reacts to it, there's no doubt she's already a fan.

"What is this?" I ask.

"'*Bailando*' by Enrique Iglesias. It's my absolute favorite."

She sings along for a moment—and even though I don't understand a word since the song's in Spanish, the sight of her singing along to a song she loves is taking my breath away.

"What's Enrique Iglesias singing about?" I ask.

"Oh, the usual," she replies, smiling. "Lust and love. He's saying he wants to be with her, live with her, dance with her, kiss her, have sex with her. He says she takes his breath away when he looks at her and that he's having a chemical reaction to her. That sort of thing."

My skin pricks.

"What's your favorite song?" she asks, picking up her drink.

My heart is racing. "Probably 'Sex on Fire' by Kings of Leon."

"Ah, a lusty love song for you, too."

"Definitely. Add that to my Power Point, please."

"Done. Anything else?"

I take a long sip of my drink and take a deep breath. Damn, this woman is making my head spin. "Nope," I say. "I think we're done with my overview. Your turn."

"Well, hang on. We should probably add you like pirate-themed tattoos." She motions to my forearms.

"Good point. Oh, and I'm a huge sports fan. Add that, too. You like sports, I hope and pray?"

"I *love* sports."

"What's your favorite?"

"Soccer."

"*Soccer*? Well, shit. That's the only sport I don't follow. But that's okay—it just means I'm a free agent. So what soccer team am I gonna start rooting for with you? The L.A. Galaxy?"

"Hell no. River Plate, baby. *Viva la Banda.*"

I look at her blankly.

"They're one of the two biggest teams in Buenos Aires. My dad was born there."

"Really? That's cool. I'd love to go to Argentina someday. My sister's been to Buenos Aires. She absolutely loved it."

"Yeah, that's my town. It's the best." She leans her elbow onto the bar and shoots me a sexy smile. "Holy hell, you're good at this, Ryan."

"At what?"

"This flirting thing. You're *almost* making me forget about the flock of bald eagles flapping around in my stomach."

I lean my elbow onto the bar in mimicry of her position. "Making you feel relaxed is all part of my master plan."

"Oh, you've got a master plan, do you?"

"Of course."

"What is it, if I may ask?"

I'm suddenly having crazy thoughts that simply can't be said out loud. "Well, getting you into my bed, of course," I say smoothly. It's a gross oversimplification of what I'm actually thinking, of course— but a true statement, nonetheless. "There's no particular time frame for execution of my master plan, by the way," I add. "As far as I'm concerned, this is a marathon, not a sprint, baby."

She assesses me for a long, heated moment, until, finally, she raises her glass and levels me with burning eyes. "A toast," she whispers, a sexy smile dancing on her lips. "*To master plans.*"

Chapter 8
Ryan

"Enough about me," I say to Samantha, putting my refilled drink back onto the bar. "Let's hear your 'brief overview' now."

Samantha takes a long sip of her new drink, puts it down on the bar, and exhales. "I'm twenty-seven. A Virgo, though I know nothing about astrology other than the fact that Virgos effing rock—well, if you think people who are 'kind, perfectionist, hard-working, dependable, and practical' effing rock."

"That's the list of Virgo traits?"

She nods. "We Virgos are real party animals, aren't we?"

"Bah. Party animals are overrated. Personally, I'm a big fan of 'kind, hard-working, and dependable' animals.

She smiles broadly at that.

"Do all the Virgo traits accurately describe you?" I ask.

"To a tee. I'm a total left-brainer, like I said. I'm organized. A perfectionist. I like to have all the facts and plenty of time to process before making major decisions. Virgo, Virgo, Virgo, right down the line."

"I'm a Taurus right down the line, too: stubborn, independent, materialistic, ambitious, reliable, and, most importantly, sensual—a real sex god."

"And, just like that, we're back to your master plan."

"And skills with sheets."

"Awfully clever of you to slip 'sensual sex god' in there. *Bravo.*"

"I'm not 'slipping' anything into anything. It's an astrological fact: male Tauruses make the best lovers. Look it up—it's written in the stars, baby."

36

"Okay, I will." She pulls out her phone and taps out a search. "Well, whaddaya know?" she says after a long beat, her eyes trained on her screen. "Taurus men are sex gods!"

"Like I said. It's cosmically pre-ordained."

Her eyes widen. "Does *all* this stuff accurately describe you?"

"I dunno. Lemme see." She hands me her phone and I read the blurb on her screen, which basically says: The male Taurus *reaaalllly* loves sex (true); he takes his sweet time in the bedroom because, to him, the journey is just as important as the destination (amen); he's got Olympic-level endurance in the sack (yup); and, most importantly, he's ultra-focused on pleasing his partner (fuck yeah!). "You'd think that blurb was written specifically about me," I say, handing Samantha's phone back to her.

Samantha raises an eyebrow but doesn't speak.

"What does that site say about female Virgos' sexuality?" I ask.

She taps out a search and reads something on her screen and, ten seconds later, her face contorts into an adorable expression I'd call "embarrassed pride."

"By the look on your face, I'm guessing whatever that says is dead-on-accurate?" I say.

She nods. "Amazingly so."

Samantha hands me her phone and I read the blurb out loud: "Female Virgos have strong, adventurous sex drives and are up for anything—*with the right partner*. But, due to their naturally cautious and perfectionist inclinations, female Virgos are highly selective about their sexual partners and usually not at all promiscuous. In fact, the typical Virgo woman would rather abstain from sex altogether, sometimes for long stretches of time, than leap into sex with a partner who, in her view, falls short of her incredibly high standards." I hand Samantha's phone back to her, my pulse quickening. "Sounds like getting the green light from a female Virgo is the brass ring. I ought to print out that blurb and tack it to a vision board. 'Hashtag: life goals.'"

Samantha chuckles. "I'm not quite as big a perfectionist as this makes me out to be." She flashes me a sexy smile. "But close."

Oh, man, my entire body's buzzing. So, my little Virgo's been waiting for a guy worthy of her for the past nine months, has she? And when she finally finds him, she'll be "up for anything"? "Give me more of your 'overview,'" I say, my dick tingling. "We got sidetracked by our cosmically pre-ordained sexual inclinations." I glance down at Samantha's incredible curves. "Or, at least, I did."

Her eyes devour me from head to toe for a long beat. "Oh, I'm equally distracted, I assure you."

Holy shit, I want this woman. "So tell me the rest of your Power Point. I'm dying to know everything there is to know about you."

"You now know everything. Other than, as previously mentioned, but it bears repeating: my heart shall always belong to my beloved River Plate. *Viva La Banda.*"

"Were you born in Argentina?"

"No. L.A. But, growing up, I spent summers in Argentina, visiting my dad's side of the family. Their winter, my summer."

"And your mom is from the U.S.?"

She nods. "From L.A. My dad came to L.A. to open a dance studio in Hollywood—he was a championship ballroom dancer in Argentina. And that's how my parents met—my mom and her fiancé came into my dad's studio to take lessons right before their wedding."

"Ooph. Sounds like your dad taught your mom's fiancé how to cha-cha right out the door."

"Exactly."

I laugh. "Holy shit. That's savage."

Her face turns bright red. "My dad always says the fiancé was nothing but a 'minor inconvenience' to him 'taking what he instantly knew was rightfully his.'"

I lean forward, suddenly feeling an overwhelming urge to kiss her. "Do you look like your dad?"

"I'm his twin."

"Then it's no wonder your mom dropped her fiancé like a bad habit when she met him. She's only human, after all." I touch my fingertips on Samantha's forearm, and the simple act of touching her sends goose bumps erupting all over my body.

Our eyes are locked for a long, heated beat.

She clears her throat and takes a sip of her drink—a move that prompts me to move my hand from her arm and place it on the bar.

Slow and steady, Ryan. She's telling you not to rush her.

"Are your parents still married?" I ask.

"Yup," she says. "Thirty-five years."

"Still in love?"

Her face turns red again. She nods. "My dad likes to say my mom 'hung the moon.'"

"Oh, I like that. I've never heard that expression."

"What about your parents? Still married?"

Why the fuck is my heart pounding like a steel drum all of a sudden? "Uh, yeah. And my dad definitely thinks my mom 'hung the moon,' too. My whole family does. She's an incredible woman." I swallow hard. *Oh, Jesus. I don't understand why my heart is suddenly racing.* I look down at her hand on the bar, suddenly overcome with the desire to not only touch it again, but to hold it in mine. But I stop myself, fairly certain she'd pull back. I'm definitely not getting a leaps-before-she-looks vibe from this girl.

"So, did I get the job, sir?" she asks playfully, picking up her drink again.

"Not quite yet," I reply. "There's still one bit of information we need." I lean my elbow onto the bar and flash her my most seductive smile. "Why the *fuck* haven't you been kissed in nine months? It's incomprehensible to me."

She rolls her eyes. "Oh my God, I'm gonna kill Charlotte."

"I gotta assume you get hit on every day, especially in your line of work. You got something against kissing?"

"Of course not. I love kissing. I've just had one of those lulls that tends to happen after a break-up when you're not a bar-hopping, Tinder-swiping kind of girl."

"In other words, a Virgo."

"Exactly."

"But why not so much as a kiss? Haven't you, you know, been on a date?"

She shakes her head.

"Wow. And you haven't missed human contact?"

"Of course, I have. *A lot.* But, you know, there are mechanical substitutes for boyfriends these days."

"Baby, there's no substitute for the real thing."

She blushes. "True."

I lean forward. "Please don't feel shy or embarrassed to talk to me. Revealing our vulnerabilities is the only way true intimacy can happen."

She looks absolutely floored. "'True intimacy'? Not words I'd expect a tattooed dude in a bar to use."

"Well, I don't *live* in the bar. Sometimes I walk the streets. Go to work. Go to the gym."

"You know what I meant."

"Yes, I did."

She places her palm on my forearm and my cock jolts at her unexpected touch. "Are you looking for 'true intimacy,' Ryan?"

"Absolutely," I say without hesitation. "I'm done with the bullshit. I'm just so over it." I look into her dark eyes. "To be perfectly honest, I'm looking for something real. I just haven't found it yet."

Her eyes blaze. "So am I."

We stare at each other for a long beat, the heat between us palpable, my dick hard. *I want this woman.*

"Please tell me what the fuck happened in your last relationship to make you check out from dating for so long," I say. "I want to understand so I don't do whatever the fuck that fucker did."

She shrugs. "It's kind of embarrassing."

"Hmm. Is it *highly* embarrassing or only *slightly* embarrassing?"

She purses her lips, considering. "Slightly."

"Okay, no biggie then. You can tell me that story now, and some other 'highly embarrassing' story when I take you out to dinner."

A glorious smile spreads across her face. "When are you taking me out to dinner?"

"As soon as humanly possible. Tomorrow night?"

"Great."

I'm smiling from ear-to-ear. "You like steak? Sushi? Italian? Indian?"

"Surprise me. I've never been out on a date in Seattle. I'm at your mercy."

"I'll take you to my all-time favorite place. And, after dinner, I'll take you on a little tour of my city—I'll show you all the cool spots— and, after that, I'll take you to this little bakery with the best cupcakes in the city. They'll blow your mind."

"Thank you. Wow. That sounds amazing."

There's a long beat as we stare at each other, smiles plastered on our faces, heat wafting between us, our chests visibly rising and falling. Shit, I feel like my heart's gonna explode. *I want this woman.* "I think we should do a shot, don't you?" I say. "I suddenly feel like this is a celebration."

"Abso-fucking-lutely," she replies, making me laugh. "What are we celebrating?"

The start of something real, I think. But, of course, that's not what I say. "How much fun it is to go out and meet new people, on occasion," I say.

She laughs. "Perfect."

I signal to the bartender. "Tim? Bring us some shots of tequila, sir. This gorgeous woman and I are celebrating."

Chapter 9
Ryan

Samantha puts down her empty shot glass, a devious smile on her face. "I tell you what," she says. "I'll tell you my 'slightly embarrassing' story if you tell me one of yours first, *plus* answer one question of mine with complete honesty."

"Why do you get a bonus question? It should be a tit-for-tat exchange."

"It's basic supply and demand. I've got a monopoly on the information you want, so I'm naming my premium price."

"That's price-fixing, Argentina—and, news flash, it's illegal."

"In the U.S., maybe, but I've got dual citizenship." She crosses her gorgeous legs and juts her spectacular chest at me. "You call it price-fixing, but where I come from, we call it 'Wednesday night.'"

Oh my God, she's the sexiest woman alive. "This is highway robbery," I say playfully, a huge smile plastered across my face.

Samantha shrugs. "Okay, then, I guess we'll just talk about the weather. Gosh, I hope it doesn't rain tomorrow night when you take me to dinner because I'm planning on wearing a dress with not a whole lot of fabric covering right *here*." She places her palm on her spectacular chest, right below the cute little flight-attendant scarf tied around her neck.

Oh my God, I want her. "And to think you started out tonight so demure and shy," I say, my voice turning husky. "What the fuck happened to you? It turns out you're an Argentinian shark underneath that pretty veneer. Good God, you're more of a shark than most lawyers I know."

"So make me a counter-offer, then."

"Nah, I don't need to make you a counter-offer, sweetheart—I agree to your terms. I would have agreed to anything. I was bluffing."

She giggles. "Good to know."

"But only because I'm so damned motivated to put *you*—I mean, excuse me, this *deal*—to bed."

She shoots me a look that could flash-melt an ice cube. "Yet again, it all comes back to your master plan."

"Always."

"So tell me your 'slightly embarrassing' story first," she says. "Show me how it's done."

I tell her the 'slightly embarrassing' story of the time my pants split down the front at prom, right after I'd been named prom king, as a matter of fact, as I attempted to perform a *Saturday-Night-Fever*-inspired splits-maneuver in celebration of my royal victory, and my dick popped out of my pants and dangled under the stage lights in front of the entire student body—and she laughs her beautiful ass off.

"Oh my God. How were you only *slightly* embarrassed?" she asks. "I would have been traumatized for life."

"Bah. No biggie. Thankfully, by then, I'd been in enough locker rooms to know my dong had absolutely nothing to be embarrassed about." I wink.

She rolls her eyes. "And now we're right back to you being a sex god."

"Always."

"How the heck did your dong pop out of your pants in the first place? You weren't wearing underwear?"

"Of course, not. A dude can't wear underwear with leather pants."

"Oh my God. This story just keeps getting better and better. You wore *leather* pants to prom?"

"I thought I looked like Lenny Kravitz—which is coincidental, seeing as how I had the exact same wardrobe malfunction Lenny did, just a decade before he did. I'm telling you, ten years later, Lenny totally stole my moves—in more ways than one, actually."

"Oh, yeah. I saw that photo of poor Lenny." She smirks. "He had nothing to be embarrassed about, either."

"See how that works? Dudes with confidence let our dongs fly. No shame in our game."

She giggles. "Will you pretty-please bring a prom photo with you tomorrow night? I'm dying to see your leather pants. But, please,

43

bring a shot from *before* the Big Dong Reveal—I have no desire to see your underage peen."

"It's okay—it wouldn't be kiddie porn. I'd just turned eighteen."

"No, thanks. I have no interest in teenage peen, whether it's legal or not."

"I'm just teasing. I don't actually have a dong-shot. Just a fully dressed prom photo which I'll happily bring *if* you'll promise to bring yours. I'll show you mine if you show me yours? And we'll also exchange prom photos."

"No-can-do. I went to an all-girl's school, remember? We didn't have a prom. In fact, I didn't go to a single school dance after that one I told you about."

"Why the hell not?"

"Because I didn't get asked. But neither did any of my best friends, including Charlotte, so I didn't feel like too big a loser."

"You went to school with Charlotte?"

"Since second grade."

"Wow, how cool." I look across the room at Charlotte to find her yucking it up at a boisterous table full of men and women.

Samantha follows my gaze. "Looking at Charlotte now, it's hard to believe she didn't forcibly drag some guy to his own school's dance." She chuckles. "But, actually, Charlotte was a bit of a goody-two-shoes in high school."

"Were you?"

"Oh, God, definitely. The worst."

"Was it a Catholic school?"

"Yup. Uniforms and nuns. The whole nine yards."

I lean my elbow on the bar and flash her a huge smile. "So, did you wear a cute little plaid skirt like some kind of Argentinian Britney Spears?"

"Yep. That was me. I danced down hallways in pigtails and plaid, singing 'Oops, I Did It Again' in Spanish. *'Oops, Lo Hice Otra Vez.'*"

I chuckle. "Oh, man, my teenage self would have been obsessed with you. Of course, my teenage self wouldn't have understood a damned word you were singing, but he wouldn't have cared in the least."

"You don't speak any Spanish?"

"Not at all. Two years of high school Spanish and to this day I don't know anything except black is *negro,* white is *blanco,* beer is *cerveza,* and bathroom is *baño.*"

"Two *years* of Spanish and you're that useless? For shame."

"It wasn't my fault—I couldn't focus. The Spanish teacher was ridiculously hot." I laugh. "I just needed a tutor, that's all. Oh my God, if you'd been at my high school... How do you say 'rice' in Spanish?"

"*Arroz.*"

"If you'd gone to my school, I'd have been all over you to be my Spanish tutor like *blanco* on *arroz.*"

"Charm me all you like, Romeo, but I'm not buying it. You were Mr. Prom-King-Big-Man-on-Campus. If our paths had crossed, you'd have been way too distracted by all the cheerleaders and Extroverted Barbies throwing themselves at you to notice the quiet girl sitting in a corner with a book."

"Bullshit. Put you in a room with a million Extroverted Barbies and cheerleaders and anyone else, back in high school or today, and I'd go straight for you like *blanco* on *arroz* every time."

She shoots me an adorable smile that sets my soul on fire. *Oh my God, I'm having a chemical reaction to this woman. I want to drag her out of here and rip off her clothes and kiss and lick and suck every square inch of her and then fuck her 'til she's speaking in tongues.*

Samantha clears her throat. "Okay, so it's time for you to answer my question. You said you'd answer one question of mine, remember?"

I lean back on my stool. "Sure. Hit me."

"You promised total honesty."

I grab her hand. I can't resist touching her anymore. "Baby, I know of no other way."

Chapter 10
Ryan

Samantha looks up at the ceiling, apparently gathering her thoughts. "Okay, my question—and remember, you promised to answer it honestly—is: what are you thinking right now?"

I raise my eyebrows.

"Not what you were expecting?"

"No."

She shrugs.

"Oh boy." I take a long sip of my drink and clear my throat. "See, the thing is, this is gonna be a hard question to answer because I'm thinking so many things, all at once."

"Okay, then tell me all the things."

"But, see, some of the stuff I'm thinking—a lot of it, actually—is extremely..."

"What?"

"Sexual."

She smirks. "Why do you think I asked the question, Sherlock?"

My cock jolts. *Whoa.*

"It's okay, honey," she says, her eyes burning like hot coals. "I'm a big girl. As long as you're being completely honest, I wanna hear it. I don't think you realize all the facial expressions you've been making. I'm dying to know what's going on in your head."

Holy shit. This woman is rocking my fucking world. "Okay. Well, uh, to start with, I'm thinking, 'Holy shit, this woman is rocking my fucking world.'"

She smiles.

"And I'm thinking, 'She's gorgeous and sexy and that body of hers is *insanity*.'" I pause, gauging her reaction. So far, so good. "I'm

46

also thinking, if I'm being honest, 'I'd give anything to see that smokin' hot body of hers naked.'" I pause again. She still seems receptive. "And that thought immediately leads me to *imagine* you naked." I pause again, assessing her reaction. Again, she looks highly receptive. "You seriously want me to keep going?"

She nods. "Please."

My heart is racing. "And now that my brain's got you buck naked, I'm thinking in great detail about what I'd like to do to you in that state."

She bites her lip but remains silent.

The song overhead changes to "Use Somebody" by Kings of Leon. Not the song I mentioned to her before, but close enough to make me feel like the universe wants me to keep going. I scoot forward a bit more, until our legs are touching, and whisper, "I'm thinking I want to touch and lick and suck every inch of your naked skin—literally, every inch of it, without holding back, without inhibitions..." I pause to gauge her reaction again... and, yep, she's giving me an enthusiastic green light. I interlace my fingers in hers, my heart racing. "God, I wanna know what you taste like. Baby, I wanna slurp you up. Suck on your tip. Have you sit on my face and penetrate you with my tongue as deep as it'll go."

Her eyes widen in shock, but I don't care. She asked me the question, and now I'm answering it.

"Sweetheart, I wanna lick you right on that delicious bull's-eye of yours, that one little spot that'll make you growl like a fucking animal, until you're writhing and screaming and wetter than you've ever been and making sounds you've never made before and literally screaming my name—and then, when you can't stand it anymore—when I'm so hard I feel like I'm gonna die if I don't get inside you—I wanna push myself inside you and send us both to fucking heaven."

She lets out a barely audible yelp.

I stroke her fingers in mine. "But most of all, baby, I'm thinking, 'Holy fuck, I've never felt this kind of intense, soul-stirring, boner-inducing connection with someone in my entire life.'"

She lets out a shaky breath.

"And not just 'cause of your physical appearance, but because you're smart and witty and funny. Because I feel like I've known you my whole life."

There's a very long beat.

Our eyes are locked.

Her unbelievable chest is rising and falling sharply.

My dick is rock hard.

"And that's pretty much everything I'm thinking," I say. "For now. Oh, and I'm wondering why you haven't been kissed in nine months. But I already told you that."

"Holy shit," she says after a long beat.

"Did any of that offend you?" I ask softly, my stomach clenching.

She shakes her head.

"You sure?"

Samantha runs her fingertips across the sword tattoo on my forearm. "Whatever the female equivalent is of every damned word you just said, that's what I'm thinking, too."

I let out a shaky breath. "*Excellent.*"

Her fingertips float up my arm, this time tracing the pirate design there. "*However*," she says, and my body instinctively tenses. "As unbelievably sexy as all that was to me—and please believe me, it was—I feel the need to make a few things crystal clear, just so I don't mislead you."

I nod, my dick rock hard, my chest tight.

"First, I have zero hang-ups when it comes to sex—I absolutely love it."

"Glad to hear it. I'm a big fan of it myself."

"I gleaned that." She smiles. "And I think that's fantastic. Nothing wrong with that. But you need to know I don't do no-strings sex. For me, sex is something special reserved for an exclusive relationship. I'm not talking about a ring, don't worry, I'm just saying I need to know we're both committed to there being nobody else." She trains her blazing eyes on mine. "The good news for you, however, is that when I finally feel ready to say yes, you can be certain I'll give myself to you completely, no holding back."

My cock jolts. I can barely breathe. As crazy as it sounds, I'd promise this girl exclusivity right now and mean it, if it meant I could take her to my bed and fuck her tonight. In fact, fuck it, I'm tempted to tell her exactly that.

Oh, wait.

No.

I can't do that.

Fuck my life.

Olivia.

Shit. Thanks to the bunny boiler, I can't take Samantha to my bed tonight—I can't even kiss her tonight, not when I woke up this morning in Olivia's bed. Not when I still have Olivia's kisses from earlier today on my lips and my break-up with her is mere hours old (and, arguably, maybe not even completely finalized?).

"I like to take things slow," Samantha continues. "I'm sorry, it's just how I'm wired. I'm a cautious person by nature."

I clear my throat. "That's fine with me."

Samantha scrutinizes my face. "You're sure I haven't scared you off?"

"Not at all. Whenever the timing's right, I have no doubt we're gonna be the eighth wonder of the world."

She chuckles.

"The slow boat to China, it is, sweetheart. But, um, just as a point of clarification: when you say you like to 'take things slow,' what's the general timeframe you're thinking about? Something along the lines of nine months or some fraction of that?"

She laughs. "A fraction of that. Maybe one-ninth, at most?" She arches an eyebrow. "Would that be doable for you?"

"Very," I say, even though, admittedly, a month is probably the longest I've ever gone without sex in my adult life. But, hey, given what I feared Samantha might say about her timeline, a month sounds like falling off a log. "Just do me one favor, please," I say. "For the love of God, tell me the 'slightly embarrassing' story of why the *fuck* you've gone nine months without so much as a kiss. Honestly, I'm dying to know."

"Oh, yeah. *That.*" She sighs and signals to the bartender. "Another round, Tim!" She shoots me a snarky look. "If I'm gonna tell you this stupid story with the kind of breathtaking honesty you just showed me, then I'm gonna need to be quite a bit drunker than this."

Chapter 11
Ryan

Samantha and I slam our empty shot glasses down onto the bar at the same time.

"Smooth," she says.

"You feeling good, Argentina? 'Cause I'm feeling damned good."

"Lemme see, Romeo." She pinches her cheeks. "Cheeks numb. Inhibitions long gone. Body on fire. Judgment critically impaired." She winks and flashes me an enthusiastic thumbs-up. "Yup. I'm feeling good."

I laugh. "Good. Now, please, for the love of God, tell me your 'slightly embarrassing' story already."

She sighs. "It's not really fair to make me follow your exciting 'King Dong of the Prom' story with a boring story about nine months of unintentional sexual hermitude. Talk about a boner-killer."

"Come on, dude," I say. "You're filibustering."

"Okay, okay," she says. She lets out a long exhale. "It's just so stupid."

"I love stupid. Wait 'til you meet my younger brother."

She pauses, apparently gathering her thoughts. "Nine months ago, I broke up with my boyfriend—this guy named Stu—after finding out he'd cheated on me ten gazillion times during our two-year relationship."

"Ooph. What a dick."

"Total dick."

"Did you love him?"

"I did. I was absolutely decimated when I discovered his extracurricular activities. I'd had no idea. I'd trusted him completely.

So, of course, I felt completely blindsided and betrayed, but I think the worst part was feeling like I had a defective 'picker,' you know? Like, I couldn't trust my own feelings anymore. I couldn't understand how the hell I didn't see his true colors in all that time?"

My chest tightens sharply. Shit. When Samantha finds out about my quick turnaround with Olivia, is she gonna think I'm hiding my true colors from her? Shit. All of a sudden, I'm thinking maybe I should tell Samantha all about Olivia tonight, just to avoid possible misunderstandings later?

Samantha continues, "I think I was just razzle-dazzled by Stu's good looks and charm and the whole 'quasi-celebrity thing' and I just blindly trusted."

"Hold up. Stu was a quasi-celebrity?"

"He's an athlete. It doesn't matter. So, anyway, that whole experience really shook me to my core and made me really skeptical about love and my own judgment, and then, on top of all that, a mere three months later, I..." She trails off.

I wait.

"And, um, three months later, my heart still hadn't mended, so I decided to take a break from dating and work on myself for a while. So, now, *voila*, here I am."

I narrow my eyes. She's totally bullshitting me, obviously. She was clearly about to say something different about the three-months-later thing, but I decide to leave it for now. "So what's the 'slightly embarrassing' part of that story?" I ask. "Your lying-ass prick of an athlete-boyfriend cheated on you and so you took a break for a while—a long while, granted, but, still, there's nothing embarrassing about that."

"It's embarrassing that he cheated on me."

"Why? Him cheating on you reflects poorly on *him*, not you. Seriously. To think otherwise is completely fucked up."

She exhales with relief.

"Is that seriously why you didn't want to tell me?"

"Yeah. I mean, he cheated on me for *two* years and I had no idea. Not a shining moment for me. Plus, I don't want you thinking I'm, you know, asexual or something because I've gone so long without sex. Trust me, I'm most definitely not asexual, I assure you."

"Well, yeah, obviously. I've got no doubt your motor runs hot. It's wafting off you."

51

She blushes.

"I'm guessing you're actually a little vixen when you get going." I scoot closer. "So has it been really hard for you to, you know, go without for nine months?"

"Excruciating. But, you know, I'm a Virgo. I've got high standards. Plus, like I said before, I've got a battery-operated-boyfriend who's been very faithful to me—he loves me and no one else."

"But this whole time you haven't been tempted to have sex with some guy not up to your standards? Just for the fuck of it?"

She shakes her head. "I'm just not wired that way."

"Wow. There hasn't been a single human guy you've been attracted to in nine months?"

"That's not what I said."

"Oh. Interesting. So there was someone you were attracted to? And he didn't make a move? Is he gay?"

"No, he's not *gay*—he's my boss."

Whoa, whoa, whoa. I lean back, floored.

She continues, "Don't get the wrong idea—he's totally unavailable. He's never so much as flirted with me. And now he's getting married, so that's a done deal. But, yeah, if I'm being completely honest, as I promised to be, when Stu and I broke up, I kinda thought, 'Hey, now that my boss and I are both single at the same time for the first time in six years, I wonder if he'll maybe make a move on me?'" She chuckles. "It was just a little crush, that's all. And, like I said, now he's getting married so, that's that. But, hey, at least now you know I'm not made of ice, right?"

My heart is pounding ferociously in my ears. "But are you still hoping to start something with this guy? Like, if his marriage doesn't work out or if he makes a move on you behind his wife's back, are you gonna ditch whatever relationship you might have going to leap at the chance?"

"What? *No.* Oh my God. I shouldn't have brought him up. Thank you, tequila." She shakes her head. "How the hell did we get on that topic in the first place? Ryan, listen to me, my little crush on my boss wasn't even about him, *per se*—it was more that he's the gold standard of the *kind* of guy I'd like to find for myself, that's all."

Her words are doing nothing to assuage me. I feel flooded with jealousy. Has she been off the market for nine fucking months because she's been jonezing for this boss of hers the whole time—some pilot or maybe the CEO of the entire fucking airline? Shit. I can't stop myself from going full-on caveman here. It's ridiculous, I know—but, as far as I'm concerned, this woman is already mine. *Mine.* And I'm not gonna sit here and let some douchebag-pilot steal my future girl—

"Ryan?" Samantha says, cutting off my rambling thoughts.

I look at her, my jaw tight.

She's looking at me like I'm certifiable. "Are you okay? You look upset."

I try my damnedest to loosen my jaw and smile at her, but I can't do it. If I'm acting like a bunny-boiling loon right now, so be it. I've never felt this kind of connection with anyone in my life and I'm sure as fuck not gonna let some asshole-pilot cock-block me before I've taken her out to fucking dinner. "Sorry," I grit out. "I know I have no right to feel this way, but I'm honestly feeling ridiculously jealous of your boss—I'm worried you're maybe really hung up on him and I'm walking into a no-win situation here."

"Oh, sweet Jesus," she mutters. "God, I never should have said a thing about him. Haven't you ever had a little crush on someone you knew was unavailable? A professor? Your best friend's girlfriend?"

"Sure," I reply, instantly thinking of Sarah.

"Well, having a crush on an unavailable person doesn't mean you think the person's the great love of your life, does it? It just means that person is attractive to you, and you think to yourself, 'Oh, that's the kind of person I'd like to find.'" Samantha beams a sexy smile at me that stops my heart and hardens my dick. "If it assures you at all, I can honestly say, for the first time in nine months—maybe even the first time *ever*—I think maybe I've found a guy who might very well be setting a new gold standard for the kind of guy I'm looking for."

And, just like that, she somehow managed to calm me the fuck down. Fuck the boss, whoever he is. I'm being a loon. "I feel the exact same way," I say. "I've never felt this kind of connection before. I don't even know how to react to feeling this way."

"I get it," she whispers. She leans into me and kisses my cheek, sending goose bumps radiating all over my body. I grasp her hand

and lean into her face to kiss her, but, at the last minute, remember I can't do that. *Not tonight.* My first kiss with this woman who might very well become the great love of my life can't occur when I've still got the faint taste of Olivia on my lips.

But, oh, shit, I can't resist stealing a tiny little taste of her skin. Just a little nibble—something completely harmless. I turn my head and lay a soft kiss on Samantha's cheek, inhaling her scent, my dick throbbing with desire.

"Ryan," she whispers. She lays a return-kiss on my cheek, her hand grazing through my hair.

"I want you," I whisper into Samantha's ear. "I want to kiss you. I want a taste."

She lets out a shaky breath and whispers into my ear: *"Quiero besarte y lamerte, por todo el cuerpo."*

"Whatever you just said, it was hot as hell," I whisper, my body shuddering with arousal.

Her warm, wet tongue flickers briefly against my ear, making my entire body convulse like she's zapped me with a Taser gun.

She lays a soft kiss on my cheek, and then another, a move that turns my hard-on to steel. *"Quiero follarte, una y otra vez,"* she whispers into my ear, her voice low and sexy.

I nuzzle my nose into her hair and breathe in her scent, my fingertips caressing the smooth nape of her neck. *Oh my God, I want this woman.*

"Quiero sentir tu lengua entre las piernas."

My brain might not know what she's saying to me, but my body sure does. I kiss her cheek, nuzzle my nose into her hair again, kiss the soft flesh next to her ear—and she quivers with arousal. "Whenever you're ready for me," I coo into her ear, "I'm gonna make you feel so fucking good, baby. The pleasure I'm gonna give you is gonna change your life."

A little groan escapes her throat.

I lay a soft kiss right next to her ear again—and then a soft peck onto her cheek, and another on her neck, this one with tongue, and she responds by moaning and clutching my forearm. Okay, I can't resist: I bite her neck and she gasps.

"Kiss me, Ryan," Samantha whispers into my ear. She skims her lips across my stubble. *"Bésame."*

"Tomorrow night," I whisper back, my heart racing. "On our date. Something to look forward to, baby."

She sighs, obviously disappointed.

Fuck. I gotta come clean. If this woman's gonna be who I think she is, I've got to make sure there's no room for future misunderstandings. I disengage from her. "There's something I need to tell you," I say, shifting on my stool, trying to rearrange my hard-on. "It's not a big deal, okay? I just want to be sure you know you can trust me going forward, Samantha."

Out of nowhere, her face drains of color. Her hand absently shoots up to the cute little scarf around her neck. "Crap. Ryan, there's something I need to tell you, too—something I should have told you—"

A shrieking voice behind my shoulder screams my name, cutting Samantha off mid-sentence.

"I knew it!" the voice shouts. "You motherfucking cheater!"

I close my eyes.

Fuck my life.

Olivia.

Chapter 12
Ryan

"Ahab and anguish lay stretched together in one hammock."

I'm at Josh's jaw-dropping house (or, as Kat dubbed it when I arrived, "the cozy little mud hut" she now calls home), playing pool with Jonas, Josh, and Sarah (the current game being Josh versus Jonas) while my poor, beleaguered sister sits crumpled on a chaise in the corner, a blanket wrapped around her slumped shoulders, her face the color of Kermit the Frog.

"Anybody need a refill?" Josh asks from behind a fully stocked bar. "What about you, Captain Morgan, can I interest you in a little Captain Morgan?" He holds up a bottle. "I'll make you a spiced mojito that will change your life."

"Thanks, Lambo," I reply, handing him my empty glass. "Forget drinking 'til I can't feel my face or toes—tonight, I'm drinking 'til I can't feel my soul-searing pain."

"That's precisely what Uber's for," Josh says.

"So, finish your story, Ryan," Sarah says from a stool at the bar. "The whole thing's like a car crash I can't look away from."

"There's not much more to tell. Olivia blasted into the bar and started spewing all kinds of crazy bullshit, Samantha bolted, and that was that: the heaven I thought I'd found with the flight attendant of my wet dreams turned into the soul-searing hell of my worst nightmare."

"Tragic," Josh says, and everyone joins him in expressing sympathy.

"Meh," I say, doing my best impression of a dude *not* on the verge of a nervous breakdown. "That's life. Sometimes it sucks ass. I just gotta wipe off my knees and move on, right? Nothing I can do about it now."

56

I'm totally full of shit, by the way: I don't feel the slightest bit ready to "wipe off my knees and move on" at the moment—but there's no way in hell I'm gonna admit that to this crowd. I've known Josh a matter of weeks and I'm just now meeting Jonas, and neither of them seems like the kind of dude who'd be able to relate to a guy feeling this wrecked over a woman this fast. And so, rather than whine and wail in front of my soon-to-be brothers-in-law, I clamp my lips together, grab the spiced-mojito-that's-gonna-change-my-life from Josh, and drag my weary ass to an armchair next to my green-faced little sister.

"Hey, Kum Cake," I say. I pat her head like she's a little doggie—something I've been doing since Mom brought her home from the hospital when I was three-and-a-half—and settle into my chair.

"Hey, Rum Cake," she replies. "Thanks for not telling everyone it was me who told Olivia where to find you."

I take a long sip of my drink and remain mute.

"You hate my guts right now, don't you?" Kat says.

"No."

"Yes, you do. If you didn't hate my guts, you'd be teasing me about it. Teasing is how we Morgans show our love; silence is how we show our barely contained impulse to commit murder."

I take another long, slow sip of my drink, resisting the urge to lay into Kat for ruining my fucking life. "Your face is the color of Kermit the Frog," I say evenly. "And I'm not the kind of man who kicks a frog when she's down—especially not a pregnant one."

Kat pulls her blanket up around her shoulders and exhales. "I'm so sorry, Ry. I replied to Olivia's text without thinking. I wasn't trying to torpedo your life, I swear."

I sigh. "I know, but it's basic Morgan Bro Code, dude: if a woman has to ask where your brother is, odds are high it's because your brother *intentionally* failed to mention his whereabouts to her. Duh-motherfucking-duh, Kum Shot."

"I know. I just... Gah." She touches her tiny baby bump. "It's hard to think clearly when the human you're crock-potting is poisoning you from the inside out."

"Hence, the reason I didn't bring it up while telling everyone what happened tonight."

Kat exhales in exasperation. "How the hell was I supposed to know Olivia had turned into a bunny-boiling loon? It's your own damn fault for keeping Peen in the loop and not me. Who does that?"

"When did you talk to him?"

"About thirty minutes after I'd already replied to Olivia's text, unfortunately. Sure would have been nice if I'd talked to that knucklehead *before* Olivia's fateful text." She sighs. "I'm really sorry, Ryan."

"It's okay, Jizzy Pop."

Kat snorts. "I must say Peen's got some rather highfalutin plans for your fifty bucks. You'd think the guy won the Powerball lottery the way he was gloating about his 'windfall.'"

"Fucking Peen."

"See, normally, the phrase 'fucking Peen' works in any fucked-up situation. But this one time, you can't blame Magic Mike for your misery, son. Keane *and* Colby warned you about the loon and you ignored them both? Inexcusable."

"I fucked up."

"I mean, come on. I understand going against Peen's advice, but *Colby's*? Felony stupid, dude."

"I just said I fucked up. And you can drop the holier-than-thou attitude, by the way. I seem to recall you ignoring Colby's sage advice when you brought that senator's-son-douche home from college that time."

"How does that help your argument? When *I* ignored Colby's sage advice, I wasn't a twenty-eight-year-old grown-ass man who'd already witnessed how ignoring Colby's sage advice had worked out for his stupid-ass little sister. As you might recall, I promptly got obliterated by that douche after ignoring Colby's advice. Certainly, a more intelligent man would have learned from his sister's horrendously stupid mistake."

I take her hand and squeeze it. "Shit. Sorry, Jizz. I shouldn't have brought that guy up. Colby told me you were really wrecked over that fucker." I let out a long, dejected exhale. "I'm just a grenade tonight. Save yourself and stay far, far away from the shrapnel."

"You really liked this flight attendant, huh?"

I nod.

"I had no idea you had a flight attendant fetish."

"I don't. Well, I mean, yeah, when she first walked into the bar in her sexy little uniform, I'd be lying if I didn't instantly imagine a little role-play."

Kat laughs. "God, we share a brain."

"But two minutes after I started talking to her, I forgot all about my teenage fantasies and I was just totally into her. The chemistry between us was just through the roof."

"Like, on a scale of one to ten?"

"Eighty-thousand-and-seventy-three."

"Holy shitballs."

"I've never felt anything like it—not even close. It felt like..." I trail off and shake my head.

"Like what?"

"Never mind."

"What?"

"I'm gonna sound like Dax."

"Well, this I gotta hear."

I pause.

"Come on, Bacardi," she says. "You know I love Daxy the most. I won't judge."

I close my eyes for a long moment, gearing up to say the most pussy-whipped thing I've ever said about a woman in my entire life. "I felt like I was *reuniting* with Samantha rather than meeting her for the first time. I felt like she was my long-lost love from another life."

Kat's face morphs into an expression of pure compassion. "Wow." She pauses. "That *does* sound like something Dax would say." She hastily pulls out her phone. "In fact, I'm gonna text that little gem to Daxy right now. Fifty bucks says it goes straight into his next song."

"I'm not taking that bet. I'm done betting on anything ever again."

Kat begins tapping out her text.

"Make sure to tell him to thank me when he wins the Grammy for Best Song."

"Goes without saying."

Jonas' voice wafts through the air, drawing my attention to the game being played across the room. "Eight ball off the rail, ricochet off the two and into the side pocket."

"This, I gotta see," I murmur. I stand to watch Jonas take his complicated shot, just in time to see him sink it. It's a feat that prompts Jonas' new wife to throw her arms around his victorious neck and pepper his entire face with kisses.

"I hate playing against you, Jonas," Josh grumbles, followed by a long string of expletives.

"Then stop playing against me," Jonas shoots back.

"So, hey, Ryan," Kat says.

I look down at her in her lounge chair.

"Am I forgiven or are paybacks gonna be a bitch?"

I pat her head. "There's nothing to forgive, Jizz Master Flash," I say. "Like I said, I'm the one who fucked up tonight. I have no one to blame for the fiasco of tonight but myself."

"Hey, Ryan, you want next game?" Josh asks from across the room. "Hopefully, you'll have more luck beating Jonas than I just had."

"Nah," I say. "I'll just watch the slaughter from here." I sit back down in my chair. "I'm too busy wallowing in self-pity to concentrate on pool."

"So tell us the rest of the story, Ryan," Sarah says. "You never told us what happened after Samantha bolted."

"Nothing. That's what's causing my soul-searing pain. Samantha bolted when Olivia started calling me a 'cheater' and Samantha a 'cunt,' and by the time I made it outside after ever-so-politely telling Olivia to please fuck off, Samantha and her friend were already gone." I swig my drink. "And you wanna hear the cherry on top of the shit-show-sundae? I never got Samantha's phone number or last name, which means this incredible woman is out there somewhere, this woman I could totally imagine being the mother of my future babies, and she's thinking I'm a lying, cheating scumbag-asshole, and there's absolutely nothing I can do about it."

Everyone expresses some variation of sympathy for my situation.

"Hmm," Sarah says, her brow furrowed. But she doesn't continue.

"Oh, Sarah Cruz," Josh says. "I know that 'hmm.' Are you thinking smart-girl thoughts over there?"

"Maybe," Sarah replies. She addresses me. "Did Samantha pay for her own drinks tonight, by any chance?"

I look at her quizzically. "No, I paid."

"Dang it. Well, I mean, I'm glad you're a chivalrous guy and all, but in this one instance, it would have been helpful if you were a cheap bastard. I was just thinking if Samantha had used her credit card to pay for a drink, maybe you could go down to The Pine Box and sweet-talk the bartender into telling you her last name from her credit card receipt."

"Boom," Josh says. "And that's why we call her Sarah *Fucking* Cruz."

"First time in my life I'm bummed not to be a cheap bastard," I mutter.

"I like the way you're thinking, though," Jonas says to Sarah. "Maybe you're onto something."

"Probably not," Sarah says, waving at the air dismissively. "Odds are high the bartender wouldn't have given Ryan her last name, anyway—in this day and age, there's too big a risk Ryan might turn out to be some kind of stalker-creeper."

"Yeah, but let's keep going with this line of thinking," Jonas says. "Let's help Ryan find her." He looks pointedly at his brother. "Josh, why not bring in the big guns to help a brother out?"

At that, Sarah and Kat erupt with enthusiasm for Jonas' idea, whatever it is.

"It's a long shot," Josh cautions. "Henn's a fucking genius, but he can't turn water into wine."

"Henn?" I ask.

Josh proceeds to tell me he's got a hacker-buddy from college named Peter Hennessy who's apparently "freakishly talented at tracking people down," oftentimes based on "the tiniest shards of information." "Just ask Jonas," Josh explains. "Henn found Sarah for him when Jonas had nothing to go on but her first name and an anonymous email."

I look at Jonas and Sarah, expecting them to elaborate on that intriguing bit of information, but they don't say a peep. "Why'd Jonas have only Sarah's first name and an anonymous email?" I ask, my curiosity too great to resist. "Did you two meet on hot-girls-dot-com or what?"

I meant the latter question as a stupid joke, of course. Sarah's a law student, for cryin' out loud, and Jonas is a highly respected businessman in Seattle. But the minute I see the look of absolute mortification on Sarah's face, I know I've hit a nerve somehow.

I press my lips together, not quite sure how to backtrack from the awkward moment.

"Sarah and I met through a high-end online dating service," Jonas says smoothly, sliding his arm protectively around his wife's waist. "Sarah worked at the service processing applications, and I applied—and when she read my application and the plethora of arrogant statements I'd made therein, she took it upon herself to send me an anonymous email that set me straight about a few important things." He squeezes Sarah and kisses her temple.

Sarah grins. "And the reason I sent Jonas my email anonymously was that it was against the company's rules for intake agents to contact clients. And then Jonas called me out of the blue and asked me out to dinner—even though I'd told him only my first name and used a dummy G-mail account."

"And that's all thanks to Henn getting her phone number for me," Jonas adds. He looks at Sarah, a huge smile on his face, his eyes blazing. "I'd read Sarah's email and felt like my very life depended on finding her. It was crazy to track her down based on nothing but her email, but I felt like I had no choice in the matter."

Goose bumps erupt all over my arms and back of my neck. Holy shit. Jonas just perfectly articulated exactly how I'm feeling right now—like I have no choice but to find Samantha and explain that everything Olivia said about me, including what she said about me soliciting that note from the blonde in the restaurant earlier tonight, was complete and total bullshit.

"I'd never felt anything like the madness that overtook me," Jonas continues. "It felt dangerously close to obsession." He chuckles. "Okay, that was bullshit—I'm trying to make myself sound semi-normal. It was obsession. Total and complete."

Everyone laughs.

"I felt this indescribable connection to Sarah, just that fast," Jonas adds. "It was like nothing I'd felt before—and yet, I didn't even know Sarah's last name, where she lived, what she looked like, or anything whatsoever about her, other than the few clues she'd unwittingly provided me in her email. So that's when I called Josh and asked for his help."

"Because I'm wise and powerful," Josh interjects.

"Because he's wise and powerful," Jonas dryly echoes. "And he 'wisely and powerfully' called his college buddy Henn, thank God— and the rest, as they say"—Jonas holds up his hand, displaying the wedding band on his finger—"is history."

Holy fuck, I feel like my heart's gonna explode. It seems I've met two soulmates tonight: Samantha and Jonas Faraday. "Thanks for telling me all that, Jonas," I say. "You seriously just gave me chills."

"Me, too," Sarah says, flashing an adoring smile at her husband.

"I can't believe you were that determined to find Sarah based on nothing but an email," I say.

Jonas smirks. "It was one hell of an email."

Sarah laughs.

I can't help but laugh with Sarah. *Damn.* All these years, I always suspected buttoned-up Sarah Cruz was a little vixen behind closed doors—I could just sense it. And now, Jonas' story all but confirms it. Ha! "But weren't you at least a little skittish about tracking Sarah down when you hadn't even laid eyes on her?" I ask Jonas.

"Nope," Jonas says. "Like I said, I was instantly obsessed. I knew my reaction was totally irrational, but I didn't care. I hadn't seen Sarah with my physical eyes, but I'd seen her with my soul, which I personally consider to be a much more reliable information-gathering mechanism than my physical senses."

Whoa. I glance at Josh for his reaction to that statement, and Josh flashes me a smile that plainly says, "Meet Jonas Faraday."

Jonas continues, "And before you think I'm some kind of saint who doesn't care about physical attraction, I did wind up seeing a photo of Sarah before our first date—a photo Henn retrieved for me from her student file." Jonas looks at Sarah and smiles. "And my physical eyes were beyond thrilled with what they were seeing, right along with my soul."

Sarah slides her hand into Jonas' and rests her cheek on his shoulder.

I bite the inside of my cheek, letting everything Jonas just said sink in.

"So, Ryan," Josh says, drawing my attention to him. "I think what Jonas is trying to say in his very unique way—and, please, bro, correct me if I'm wrong here—is that he gets where you're coming from."

Everyone laughs.

"That is correct, sir," Jonas says.

"So if you wanna give Henn a call and see if maybe he can help you out," Josh continues, "we'll hook you up."

"I'd love it," I say, my heart lurching into my throat. "Although I don't see how your friend could possibly track Samantha down. Unlike Jonas, I don't have an email or any other kind of online activity for Henn to trace."

"I don't think he'd necessarily need that," Sarah says. "Right, Josh? Henny tracked down Oksana the Pimpstress for me without an email address, remember?"

"Yeah, but only because you'd figured out all those great leads for him to follow, thanks to your friend at the post office," Josh says.

Whoa. I'm totally confused. What the fuck are these people talking about?

"Good point," Sarah says. "Well, then, I guess we'll just have to figure out some leads for Henn to follow here, too. A little brainstorming and we'll probably have a whole list of leads." She looks at me. "You game to try a little brainstorming to find your flight attendant, Ryan?"

"Of course," I say, even though I'm not quite sure what the hell good it will do. "Thanks."

The four of us drag chairs around poor, pathetic Kat and ready ourselves to "brainstorm."

"Okay, first things first," Sarah says, her tone all business. "Did Samantha mention her age?"

My pulse quickens slightly. "Twenty-seven."

Sarah beams a full smile at me. "Now see? Two seconds of brainstorming and we've already drastically narrowed the field of flight attendants named Samantha."

"Well, assuming that's Samantha's actual age," Jonas chimes in. "Common wisdom is that men lie about their height and women lie about their age."

"Samantha wasn't lying about her age," I say confidently. "Or anything else, for that matter. That's what I liked about her the most: she doesn't have a bullshit-bone in her body."

"My kind of girl," Jonas says. He winks at Sarah.

"Yeah, mine, too," Josh says dryly, barely able to keep himself from cracking up. "Gotta love a woman who doesn't have a bullshit-bone in her body."

"Consider yourself punched," Kat says weakly, her head lolling to the side.

Josh grabs Kat's limp hand. "Aw, babe, I adore your bullshit-bone along with every other gorgeous bone in your body. You know that. I'm all-in, PG."

Kat smiles weakly, apparently satisfied with that explanation. "Yeah, I know, PB."

Inexplicably, my heart has begun clanging with excitement. Could this really work? "I don't know if it helps at all," I say, "but Samantha also said she's a Virgo."

"Fabulous," Sarah says. "Now we've got a thirty-day window for Samantha's date of birth. You never know what information Henn might find useful when he's poking around."

"But poking around *where*?" Josh says. "That's the question. It's not like there's some centralized database cataloging all humans by first name, age, and occupation."

Sarah's face lights up. "Her employer, then."

"Precisely," Jonas says.

Sarah looks at me. "Ryan, did Samantha say which airline she works for?"

My shoulders slump. "No. We didn't talk about our jobs at all. It was refreshing, actually."

Josh's phone buzzes and he looks at it. "It's Henn, replying to my text. He says for us to call him in thirty minutes. He's gotta finish something and then he says he'll be happy to talk to us."

"Great," Sarah says, clearly energized. "Hmm. I gotta think, even if Samantha didn't identify her airline, she probably said something from which we could *deduce* it."

"Like what?" I ask.

"Like, I dunno, maybe she mentioned her regular route? Or what time her usual flight departs or arrives? I'm grasping at straws here, I know, but I think figuring out Samantha's employer is our best shot at tracking her down."

"I agree," Josh says. "Henn's got to have somewhere specific to target or it'll be like shooting a flare gun into outer space."

I think for a moment. "Well, she mentioned she flies out of

L.A.," I say tentatively. But there's something else, something much more important, niggling at my brain. But I can't... *Boom.* All of a sudden, my brain clicks into place. "She was wearing a scarf around her neck as part of her uniform," I blurt, excitement flooding me. "And it had a pattern on it." I close my eyes, trying to visualize it. "Little red triangles—I think it was a logo."

"Brilliant." Sarah pulls out her phone and searches for a moment, scrunching her nose adorably as she does. "Were the triangles like this?" she asks, shoving her phone under my nose.

"Maybe. I don't know."

"Hang on." Sarah swipes at something on her phone. "How about this?"

"Yes!" I say, adrenaline flooding me in a torrent. "That's it!"

"Holy crappola!" Sarah exclaims. "Oh my God. *Look.*" She holds up her arm to show me that her tiny hairs are standing on end. "*Goose bumps!*"

Kat chuckles. "You're such a little badass, Sarah."

"Great work, baby," Jonas adds.

"Sarah Fucking Cruz," Josh says.

Sarah's eyes are on fire. "Kerzoinks, guys, I think this is gonna work." She lets out an excited breath. "Okay, so here's what we know so far: Samantha is a twenty-seven-year-old Virgo flight attendant who works for Delta Airlines out of L.A. That's a shit-ton of breadcrumbs for Henn to follow, wouldn't you say?"

"Enough breadcrumbs to lead him straight to Ryan's doorstep, I'd imagine," Jonas says.

"You'll forever be my George Clooney, Sarah Cruz," Josh says adoringly.

Kat begins to mumble something about us going "*Ocean's Eleven*" on Samantha's ass, but mid-sentence, she abruptly stops talking, clamps her hand over her mouth, leaps up from her chair, and careens out of the room.

Josh stands slowly, rubbing his face. "That's my cue, guys. Poor Kat. I'm sure she's gonna be down for the count tonight. Jonas, do me a favor and set the alarm on your way out, okay, bro?"

"Sure thing."

"You've got Henn's number?" Josh asks.

"Yup. We'll call him in fifteen. Go tend to Kat."

"Yeah, I gotta lie down with her. When Kat's feeling really shitty like this, she likes me to rub her back and sing James Bay to her 'til she falls asleep." He looks at me. "Will I see you at the grand opening party for Climb & Conquer next week?"

"Wouldn't miss it," I say, bro-hugging him. "Thanks for taking such good care of my little sister." I lower my voice to a whisper. "And, hey, have fun ring-shopping with my mom tomorrow."

"Oh, Momma Lou told you about that, did she?"

"She hasn't stopped talking about it. She's a wee bit excited."

"So am I. God willing, Kat will say yes."

We all reassure Josh that Kat will most definitely say yes—"duh" is how Sarah puts it—and Josh leaves to help Kat.

"Back to brainstorming," Sarah says, settling back into her chair. "Did Samantha mention her ethnic background?"

"She said she was born and raised in L.A., but that her dad's from Argentina."

"Oooh," Sarah says. "I bet Samantha's really beautiful, then. Every single Argentinian woman I've ever met has been stunningly beautiful."

"Yeah, that's exactly the word for Samantha," I say. "*Stunning.* She took my breath away the minute I saw her."

Sarah nudges Jonas on the shoulder. "Hey, isn't Theresa's family from Argentina?"

"Yeah, she's the one who recommended Josh take Kat to Buenos Aires, remember?"

"Well, there you go," Sarah says. "Like I said, Argentinian women are all stunning."

"Who's Theresa?" I ask.

"Josh's personal assistant," Sarah says. "Theresa Rodriguez."

"Also known as T-Rod," Jonas adds. "She runs Josh's life."

"And T-Rod's stunningly beautiful," Sarah adds. "Hey, love, do you have a photo of T-Rod on your phone?"

"Why would I have a photo of T-Rod on my phone?"

"I thought maybe from the wedding? Maybe she's in one of the group shots?"

"I don't have any of those shots on my phone—just a few select favorites of you and me."

"It's okay," I interject. "I'm sure T-Rod's stunning, but I've got another Argentinian I'm currently a bit obsessed with."

"Baby, stay focused," Jonas says playfully. "The poor guy's losing his mind."

"Sorry," Sarah says, looking sheepish. "I didn't mean to get us off track. I was just trying to prove my point about Argentinians being beautiful."

"No problem," I say to Sarah, smiling at her. "I'm sure I'll meet T-Rod at some point and instantly realize you were completely right."

Sarah giggles. "Okay, anyway, back to the Argentinian woman you actually care about: do you know if Samantha speaks Spanish?"

Memories of Samantha's whispered voice in my ear flood me, sending blood straight into my dick. "Yeah, she speaks Spanish," I reply, trying to keep my voice sounding neutral.

"That might be helpful to Henn," Sarah says. "You never know. Maybe there's some sort of annotation about bilingual employees in Delta's employee files."

My heart lurches into my throat. "Delta's employee files?"

Jonas and Sarah look at each other like I've just screamed, "Someone, please, cut off my dick!"

"Where'd you think Henn would look?" Jonas asks slowly.

I run my hand through my hair, my stomach suddenly doing somersaults. "Facebook? Some census bureau database? I guess I didn't think it through. I've never worked with a hacker before."

"So... you're comfortable with the idea of Henn hacking into the Census Bureau but not an airline's employee files?" Jonas asks.

"I guess it just seems *particularly* illegal to hack into a company's private employee files. I mean, I can't even pretend that shit is legal."

Jonas shrugs like that's an obvious statement. "What Henn does is definitely illegal. But no harm will come of it, I can personally assure you. Henn will go into the database, look around, get the information, and leave without a trace. That's what he does."

"But..." I begin. I run my fingers through my hair, collecting myself. "You don't think it's crazy for a dude to hack into an airline to find a girl with whom he chatted in a bar? I feel like if I do this, I'm crossing some line I'll never be able to un-cross."

"And what line would that be?" Jonas asks calmly.

"The line between sanity and insanity?"

Jonas laughs. "Sanity is highly overrated, my friend." He looks at Sarah. "In fact, it's my experience a little infusion of madness is a very good thing."

Sarah smiles.

Jonas addresses me. "But, hey, given I'm a dude who hacked into the University of Washington to find a woman I'd never laid eyes on, take my opinion with a grain of salt. But either way, we gotta call Henn and let him know what you wanna do because he's a busy guy." He pauses. "So what's it gonna be, Ryan? Are you gonna listen to your brain or your soul?"

I twist my mouth, considering the situation, and quickly realize I've got no choice. "I'm gonna listen to my soul," I say.

"Atta boy," Jonas says, a huge smile spreading across his face. "No regrets that way."

I nod definitively. "If I don't do this, I'm gonna go to my grave wondering 'what if.'"

"Worst two words in the English language, as far as I'm concerned," Jonas says. He begins scrolling through his contacts on his phone, presumably looking for Henn's number. "My two cents? If your soul is shouting at you about Samantha half as loudly as mine did at me about Sarah, then, in my opinion, you have no choice but to listen the fuck up."

Chapter 13
Tessa

"...and that's why the Climb & Conquer brand embodies adventure, fitness, and, most of all, the pursuit of excellence," Josh's brother, Jonas, says into his microphone, and everyone packed into the massive gym applauds enthusiastically.

I'm at the grand opening for Josh and Jonas' chain of new rock-climbing gyms, observing the festivities from a spot at the far back of their flagship Seattle location. At the moment, the Faraday twins are standing on a stage in front of an idle band, the two of them kicking off the party by telling everyone about their shared passion for climbing and their company's inspiring mission to make the world a better place—and, honestly, after what happened last week at The Pine Box, being here among these excited, happy people on this joyous occasion feels like a balm for my downtrodden soul.

As busy as I've been this past week pulling this event together, I haven't been able to stop thinking about Ryan from The Pine Box—about how charismatic and honest and *emotionally intelligent* he seemed to be—about how truly certain I was I'd finally met the man of my dreams—and about how totally *wrong, wrong, wrong* I turned out to be about him (surprise!). Talk about a girl with a defective picker! Every freaking word Ryan said, every smile he flashed me, every touch of his fingertips—and, in those last few, delicious moments, every soft kiss of his delectable lips on my cheek and ear and neck—every swirl of his tongue on the sensitive flesh under my ear—and, oh God, that *bite* on my neck—made me absolutely dizzy with desire for him. No matter what I babbled to Ryan about wanting to "take things slow," I'm certain if we'd wound up going out on our dinner-date as planned, I would have wound up naked and spread-eagle in that man's bed for dessert, the city-tour he'd promised me be damned.

"...a part of each person's individual but universal quest to find the ideal version of himself..." Jonas says to the rapt crowd, eliciting enthusiastic applause.

I rub my forehead. Crap. I've got to stop thinking about Ryan. What's the freaking point? As I so jarringly found out last week at The Pine Box, he has a *girlfriend*—a very blonde and "Extroverted Barbie" girlfriend (!) who's my physical opposite in every way. Plus, as his charming girlfriend so eloquently informed me when she stormed into the bar, it seems Prince Charming hit on a blonde during a dinner date with her earlier that same night, the very second his raving bitch of a girlfriend got up to use the bathroom. Oh, but that con-artist-player didn't stop there. Oh, no. He then proceeded to head out to a meat-market-bar later that same night *all by himself* (yeah, *sure,* he was waiting for a friend who never showed up!) to hunt for yet *another* blonde to fuck behind his girlfriend's back (and then, when no blonde presented herself, apparently decided instead to settle for hitting on the dark-haired idiot in a flight-attendant uniform).

Good God, why do men like Ryan and my ex-boyfriend, Stu, even bother having girlfriends if they're simply going to compulsively cheat on them? I don't get it. Do they have raging Madonna-whore complexes—they love having a good girl at home on standby while they fuck their hidden fantasies on the down-low every chance they get? Although, I must admit, Ryan's girlfriend didn't strike me as anything close to the Madonna by any stretch of the imagination, so maybe scratch that particular psychoanalysis.

Well, whatever the motivation for Ryan and men of his ilk, the bottom line is they're all scumbags. It makes me physically ill remembering how Ryan so expertly wooed me that night at the bar, the same way he surely wooed the blonde in the restaurant earlier that same night. I could scream when I think about Ryan flashing that panty-melting smile at me and coaxing me to reveal more and more of myself to him (in the name of fostering "true intimacy," of course!), not to mention the way Ryan snowed me with complete bullshit-lines like, "I'm looking for something real" and "Put you in a room with a million Extroverted Barbies and I'd go straight for you like *blanco* on *arroz* every time." *Asshole.*

"And that's why Climb & Conquer is all about reaching higher than you ever thought you could reach, literally and metaphorically," Jonas says from the stage, his face aglow. "It's about becoming better than you ever thought you could be."

The crowd erupts into enthusiastic applause and I join them, partly because I'm hoping the physical act of clapping my palms together will somehow miraculously trigger my brain to stop thinking about Ryan from The Pine Box; and, also, even more so, because I'm genuinely inspired by Jonas' obvious passion for what he's saying.

After watching Jonas for a moment longer, my gaze drifts from him to his gloriously handsome brother and then grazes across the backs of all the heads in the large crowd. Oh, hey, I think the back of that one guy's head in the middle of the pack belongs to Josh's longtime hacker-friend, Henn.

Hey.

An idea pings my brain.

Maybe I should ask Josh if it's okay to ask Henn to help me track down Ryan? I know it's stupid for me to want to contact Ryan, seeing as how, one, he's a lying cheater-player-douche, and, two, I'm the one who fled the bar without a backward glance when his girlfriend showed up and started reading him the riot act and calling me a "cunt." But, for some reason, I haven't been able to stop fantasizing about contacting Ryan and, at least, getting the chance to give him a piece of my mind... and also, maybe, hearing him out?

The truth is, now that I've had a week to process everything (I always do my best thinking after having a bit of time to process), I deeply regret not sticking around for at least a couple minutes outside the bar that night, just in case Ryan maybe came outside and wanted to talk to me. I mean, obviously, there's nothing Ryan could have said in that moment to Febreze-away the stench of his two-timing-assholery, but, still, I can't help wondering what he *might* have said if I'd stuck around long enough to hear it. I mean, crap, at the very least, I should have given myself the opportunity to tell the guy he's a complete asshole, right? Maybe then I wouldn't feel this almost desperate need to talk to Ryan again.

So, okay, that's what I'll do, then: I'll ask Josh if it's okay for me to pull Henn aside during this party and... Wait. *No.* Am I stupid? I can't ask Josh for Henn's help to find Ryan! How the heck would that conversation go? *Well, Josh and Henn, there's this guy named Ryan I met last week at The Pine Box and I'm desperate to find him and ask him if every single word out of his mouth was a lie, or only some of them. Why do I need your help to find Ryan, you ask? Oh, because Ryan never told me his phone number or last name because his girlfriend burst into the bar and started calling him a "fucking cheater" and me a "cunt" before we'd exchanged our contact info. Isn't that awesome? Believe me, it was super-duper awesome!*

Yeah, obviously, I can't breathe a word about my encounter with Ryan to Josh and Henn.

Ah, who am I kidding? Even if I could enlist Henn's assistance, he wouldn't be able to find Ryan, anyway, not based on what little I know of him. What hacker, no matter how talented, could possibly find a guy named "Ryan" knowing only that he's twenty-eight, a Taurus, has three brothers and a sister; was born and raised in Seattle, makes amazing guacamole, and can fold a fitted sheet?

"And as part of our genuine commitment to extraordinary aspiration," Jonas continues from the stage at the front of the gym, "Climb & Conquer has identified certain designated charities we'll be supporting with a portion of our proceeds."

My eyes continue skimming the backs of heads in the packed crowd. The place seems to be filled with lots of twenty-something-year-old fitness types as I would have expected, but there also seems to be a surprisingly large number of families and older—

Oh my fucking God. My brain freezes mid-thought. My heart stops mid-beat.

I put my palm over my mouth.

The back of that guy's head way over there in the middle-front of the packed audience looks like it belongs to Ryan from The Pine Box!

I clutch my chest.

Could it be?

I crane my neck, trying to get a better look—but, damn it, the crowd is too packed for me to make out the guy's build or see if his arms are covered in tattoos.

Oh my freaking God.

It's not a crazy thought, is it? I'm not hurtling into some sort of psychosis? I mean, it's perfectly reasonable to think the one man on earth I'm thinking about at this very moment, the man I haven't been able to stop thinking about this entire week, might be one of the four hundred or so people in a city of three-and-a-half million who *happens* to be standing in this room right now?

I close my eyes and take a deep breath.

Motherfucker.

I'm doing it again.

I'm glimpsing yet another "Ryan" in yet another crowd, the same way I've done at least ten times this past week. On Monday morning alone, I spotted Ryan three different times—once at the gym, another time at Starbucks, and a third time sitting in the adjacent lane in traffic; and, of course, none of those "Ryans" turned out to be Ryan from The Pine Box. At Starbucks, for instance, "Ryan" turned out to be an attractive man of about forty, holding a toddler. And on Tuesday, when my pathetic brain spotted "Ryan" walking into a bank, that guy turned out to be a black man. A highly attractive one, I might add, but most definitely not the man I'm currently obsessed with. And so it went all week long—Ryans, Ryans, everywhere, and not a drop to drink or kiss or suck or lick. And, on top of all that, don't get me started on how many times I suddenly heard "Sex on Fire" playing in banks and grocery stores. Gah!

"Miss Rodriguez?" a female voice says, drawing me out of my rambling thoughts. "Clarissa Taylor, Channel Seven News."

"Yes, of course," I say, shaking the woman's hand. "I'm so glad you could make it."

"My pleasure. The mission statement of Climb & Conquer is inspiring." The reporter smirks. "Plus, the Faraday brothers are what we in the industry like to call 'easy on the eyes.'" She glances appreciatively at Josh and Jonas onstage. "They're definitely gonna make for good TV."

I follow the reporter's gaze to the guys onstage. "They look like superheroes up there, don't they?" I say. "Superman and Thor."

The reporter chuckles. "I like that. I think I'll make that the theme of my piece: 'Seattle's own Superman and Thor, climbing indoor mountains in a leap and a bound.'"

"Oh, that's great. The guys will love it. Do you have everything you need for your story?"

"Almost. We've got footage of the gym and the crowd and the guys' speeches, but I'd love to get an up-close-and-personal interview with both brothers—something where we can clearly see their pearly whites and baby blues."

"Sounds good. Let's wrangle them as they come offstage. Follow me."

I lead the reporter and her cameraman toward the stage at the front of the gym, working my way along the left periphery of the crowd, weaving in and out of protruding rock-climbing walls and packed people, until we arrive at the side of the stage.

Finally, after Jonas and Josh have given their concluding remarks, posed for a flurry of photographs, and stolen a few private moments with their beloved women, all while the band plays a rousing rendition of "Shout!", I usher the guys toward the reporter. Phew. I think my work here is done. Time to hunt down the latest "Ryan" (only to discover he's actually an eighty-year-old man with a walker, I'm sure), and then head home to crash with a bottle of wine, a smutty book, and my battery-operated-boyfriend—the only boyfriend in the past three years who hasn't been a real dick to me.

But, what the fuck, no! My ever-unpredictable boss isn't following me toward the waiting reporter. To the contrary, with a cocky smile and wave to Jonas and a mischievous wink at me, Josh takes a hard left and strides with great purpose into the crowd.

Okay, now I'm pissed. I've worked tirelessly to get top-notch media to cover this event for Josh (and Jonas), and now, when the most popular TV reporter in Seattle wants to conduct a double interview for her Thor-and-Superman-themed story, Josh can't be bothered? "Josh!" I yell, trying to get my rogue boss's attention. But it's no use. He's gone.

Motherfucker.

For several minutes, I hang around watching Jonas gracefully answer the reporter's questions, and when it's obvious the reporter is putty in Jonas' hand, I turn to leave, eager to do a quick lap of the gym in search of Ryan Number Eleven and then head out for the day.

But I've no sooner taken two steps away from Jonas than he politely calls my name. I turn to look at him, eyebrows raised.

"Could you please find my brother and ask him to join the interview?" Jonas asks. His tone is calm and in control, but his eyes are burning with intensity. "Make sure you tell him I said *please*?"

"Sure thing, Jonas," I reply, my stomach knotting up. Poor Jonas. I don't know him nearly as well as I know Josh, but it's no secret to me the guy would rather gouge his eyes out than give any kind of speech or interview. "I'm on it."

I spot Josh in an alcove behind one of the more challenging rock-walls, talking to a fifty-something blonde I instantly recognize as Kat's beautiful mother. I met Mrs. Morgan at Jonas and Sarah's wedding last month and fell in love with her after we'd struck up a conversation while waiting in line for the bathroom and then continued chatting for another twenty minutes after using the facilities. I don't remember everything about my conversation with Mrs. Morgan that night. As I recall, we were both pretty buzzed on champagne and the band was cranking. But I most certainly remember two things about our encounter: one, I couldn't stop giggling with Mrs. Morgan as she told me the secrets to her own happy marriage ("laughter, forgiveness, and *lots* of hanky-panky"); and, two, I walked away from Mrs. Morgan thinking, "That woman is the human equivalent of chicken noodle soup."

I stride toward Josh and Mrs. Morgan, determined to physically drag my wayward boss to his camera-shy brother if need be, but I stop short when I realize the pair seems to be enjoying an intimate moment. Specifically, it appears Josh is peeking into a ring box while Mrs. Morgan looks on excitedly.

I wait and watch as Josh slides the ring box into his pocket and kisses Mrs. Morgan on the cheek. Mrs. Morgan hugs him. Josh looks anxious. She's obviously assuring him.

Okay, I gotta go in now—I've got a job to do.

I tap my boss on his broad shoulder. "Josh."

Josh turns around, his face aglow.

"Jonas asked me to come get you," I say, doing my best to communicate the urgency of Jonas' request with my body language. "He wants you to join the interview. He says *please*." I motion across the room to where Jonas is still talking to the reporter and scowl at Josh ever so slightly to let him know he'd better get his playboy-ass over there, *pronto*.

Josh chuckles. "Okay, Josh to the rescue."

Josh says goodbye to his soon-to-be-mother-in-law with an exuberant hug and a kiss—a display of affection so earnest and effusive, it makes my heart melt—and, after a quick fist-bump and cocky wink at me (Jesus, that man's a cocky bastard!), Josh lopes away like the superhero he is to save the day, leaving me standing alone with Kat's mom.

"Hi, Mrs. Morgan," I say, putting out my hand. "Remember me? Theresa Rodriguez? We met at Jonas and Sarah's wedding."

"Of course, I remember you, Theresa," Mrs. Morgan says, ignoring my hand and going in for a warm hug. "I loved chatting with you that night—it was one of the highlights of the wedding for me."

"For me, too."

"Plus, there'd be no forgetting who you are, what with Josh talking about you so affectionately when he and I went ring-shopping together last week. He couldn't stop talking about how indispensable you are to him—and how trustworthy and kind."

"Really? He said that? Wow. Thank you for telling me that, Mrs. Morgan. That means a lot to me."

"Please, call me Louise. Or Lou—that's what my friends and family call me. Actually, if you really wanna make my day, call me Momma Lou." She giggles. "Josh started calling me that the other day and it tickles me pink. I'm hoping maybe he and Kitty will teach the baby to call me Gramma Lou."

"Momma Lou it is. But only if you'll agree to call me the name my friends and family have always called me: Tessa."

"Oh, that's pretty."

"Thank you. I'm named after my Grandmother Teresa, so my family has always called me Tessa to avoid confusion. Actually, nobody outside of work has ever called me Theresa—I've always been Tessa."

"Tessa suits you. It's elegant and down-to-earth, all at once, just like you."

I blush. "Thank you. I could say the same about you, Momma Lou."

We talk for a bit about the success of the party, and then Mrs. Morgan looks at me sideways, a sparkle in her eyes.

"So, *Tessa*," she begins, "I know this is maybe an incredibly forward thing to ask, but are you single, by any chance? I meant to ask at the wedding but chickened out."

I open my mouth and close it again.

"The reason I ask is I've got this son who just broke up with his girlfriend last week—thank God—apparently, she was a real piece of work. And I really think you two would hit it off. I thought about setting you two up the minute I met you at Jonas and Sarah's wedding, actually—I know my son's taste in women and I'm positive he'd *really* like you—but, like I said, he still had a girlfriend a month ago so I decided not to meddle. But now that he's single—thank God—I feel like it's fate you're both here today." She leans forward. "I've actually got quite a gift for matchmaking. Ask anyone."

Okay, I'm having several simultaneous thoughts here:

First, Kat has a brother? Who knew? I must say, if he looks anything like his jaw-dropping sister, he's one dude I wouldn't kick out of bed for eating crackers.

Second, oh my God, Louise Morgan is adorable. Would I want my own mother to meddle in my love life the way she's trying to do for her son? Hell no. But, hey, Mrs. Morgan's not my mother so I'm actually finding her meddling irresistibly charming.

Third, no offense to Louise intended, but whatever type of woman she thinks her son wants to screw, I can almost guarantee he secretly wants the polar opposite. In my experience, mommies really don't know their grown sons as well as they think they do.

And, finally, fourth, but not least, there's no way in freaking hell I'd hook up with Mrs. Morgan's son, no matter how handsome he surely is, even if she's right and I'm somehow his idea of the perfect woman. Why? Because he's Kat's freaking brother! I mean, come on, what if this guy and I were to hit it off and miraculously fall in love and get married and have three gorgeous babies (which, at the end of the day, is the point of dating in the first place), am I truly gonna feel comfortable having Josh and Kat as my brother- and sister-in-law? Ha! *No.* The idea gives me hives. Plus, besides all that, I honestly don't care about meeting Mrs. Morgan's son right now, however gorgeous and wonderful he might be, because I'm currently way too obsessed with the idea of finding Ryan Number Eleven to think about any other man.

"Wow, thank you, Mrs. Morgan—*Momma Lou*," I say. "I'm honored you'd even think of setting me up with your son. The thing is, while I'm technically single at the moment, it's because I want to be. I've had a string of bad luck in the romance department lately. My last boyfriend was a real doozy, and then, just last week, this guy I really liked asked me out on a date and then turned out to have a girlfriend."

"Oh no."

I laugh. "Yeah, that guy last week really took the wind out of my sails. So I'm taking a bit of a break from the 'search for love,' as it were, just for a while." Reflexively, my gaze drifts across the gym to confirm that Josh made it to the interview with Jonas. He did. "So, um, I mean no disrespect, Mrs. Morgan, but I think I'm just gonna lay low for a little while longer, at least until I figure out why I seem to be attracted to cheating scumbags."

"Well, if you don't mind me saying, it sounds to me like you've got it backwards, honey," Mrs. Morgan says. "If you've been meeting nothing but scumbags lately, that's all the more reason for you to meet my son. He's one of the good ones, honey—and, like I said, he's for sure single. He and his girlfriend broke up last week. Thank God."

I grin at her. Damn, she looks so earnest and hopeful—but if her son and his girlfriend broke up only last week, then that's even more reason for me to avoid him like the plague: being some guy's rebound relationship isn't high on my List of Things to Do. "Thank you, Mrs. Morgan. *Momma Lou.* You're so sweet. But I'm just not up for getting my feet wet in the man-pool quite yet. Let's give your son a bit of time to play the field after his break-up and me some time to restore my faith in mankind again, and then we'll revisit the idea at some later date?"

Mrs. Morgan smiles. "All right, honey. A rain check it is. It sounds like we're gonna be seeing each other again at a certain wedding, so perhaps I'll introduce you to my wonderful son then."

"Sounds like a plan."

We say our goodbyes as the band launches into an energetic cover of my all-time favorite song *"Bailando"* by Enrique Iglesias (one of the perks to being the girl who organized the party is approving the band's song list). And then, for a long moment, I watch Louise dance her way across the gym to join her husband... who's standing next to a human slab of godly perfection leaning on crutches. Oh my effing God! Is *that* guy Mrs. Morgan's "wonderful" son? I feel like screaming, "Wait, Momma Lou! I take it all back! Introduce me now!" I laugh to myself. I think I'm a wee bit horny these days. And, holy hell, that guy on crutches is gorgeous! Actually, now that I'm getting a good look at Mr. Handsome on Crutches, I'm realizing he totally reminds me of Ryan from The Pine Box.

Ah, jeez. There I go again. Hello, Ryan Number *Twelve*!

I've got to get a grip.

It's not like Ryan and I had some sort of soul connection, even though it felt that way at the time. I have to remember Ryan had a girlfriend when he was saying all that amazing stuff to me, even the part about him "looking for something real." And that means Ryan from The Pine Box is a liar and a scumbag and a player and I shouldn't believe a word he said. Which is why I'm going to wipe the guy from my mind forever and never think of him again... right after I find Ryan Number Eleven.

As the partygoers around me rock out to the last, energetic chorus of *"Bailando,"* I scour every inch of the gym in search of Ryan Number Eleven, but, dammit, he's nowhere to be found. Shoot. He must have left the party already. Well, I guess it's a sign from the universe: it simply wasn't meant to be.

Time for me to make like Ryan Number Eleven and get the hell out of Dodge, too. I pull out my phone and tap out a quick message to Josh and Jonas: "Congrats on an amazing grand opening, guys! I'm heading out now. The stage, tables, chairs, etc. will be hauled away at 6:00 and the cleaning crew will come shortly thereafter. I'm so proud of you both and excited to watch you climb and conquer the world! XO T-Rod."

Chapter 14
Ryan

"It's not down on any map; true places never are."

"Those are the employee-identification cards of all fifty-seven Samanthas currently employed by Delta as flight attendants," Henn says. "When I couldn't find a perfect match across the board—name, age, Virgo, hair color, eye color, Spanish-speaking, residence in L.A.—I decided to grab screen shots of every Samantha on their roster, just to be on the safe side."

I'm standing with Henn and Kat in a small office at the back of Climb & Conquer's gym, swiping through headshot after headshot of unrecognizable women on Henn's phone, the muted sounds of Josh and Jonas' grand opening party wafting through the closed office door. The band's current song is *"Bailando,"* just in case I want to be tormented by yet another reminder of Samantha.

"Thanks for trying, Henn," I say, swiping past the very last photo, my shoulders slumping. I hand Henn's phone back to him with a long sigh. "Just as you suspected, Samantha's not here."

"Yeah, I figured. Sorry, man," Henn says.

"I'm the one who's sorry," I say. "I sent you on a wild goose chase. And I was so sure there were little red triangles on Samantha's scarf—I would have sworn on a stack of bibles I got that detail right."

"Meh," Henn says. "Memory can be a slippery motherfucker. It's no big deal. Now that we know for sure Samantha's not with Delta, we'll just have to expand our search, that's all."

"But expand our search to what?" Kat pipes in, taking the words right out of my mouth. "Aren't there, like, hundreds of airlines in the world?"

"Five thousand, actually," Henn says. "But only *nine* of them, including Delta, had flights from L.A. to Seattle on the day in question."

"Ooooh," Kat says. "Brilliant, Henn."

"I'm confused," I stammer. "Even if you're able to narrow the field of potential airlines to eight, how do you know which of those eight to hack?"

"I don't," Henn says matter-of-factly. "Which is why I'm gonna hack all eight of 'em, beginning with the biggest and working my way down the list."

My heart leaps with a sudden jolt of hope. "You'd be willing to do that for me?"

"Of course."

"But won't that be a lot of work for you?"

Henn waves at the air. "It's all good, Captain Morgan. Kat's been going on and on about what an awesome brother you are and how bad she feels about texting your ex-girlfriend that night; plus, I'm happy to report my life's the most fucking awesome it's ever been, thanks to Kat setting me up with my girlfriend, so I'm definitely in the mood to pay it forward by helping Kat's big brother." He winks at my sister and she coos like a cockatiel at him.

"Thanks, Henny," Kat says. "I hate seeing Ryan looking so sad and knowing it's all my fault."

"I told you not to worry about it, Kat," I say. "And I'm not 'sad'—I'm obsessed and tortured and hurtling into a dark abyss of madness from whence no man could crawl. But I swear I'm not sad."

We all laugh.

"Unfortunately, I'm not kidding," I mutter.

"Well, then, dude, it sure sounds like I'd better find this amazing girl for you," Henn says. "There shall be no 'hurtling into an abyss of madness' on my watch, dude."

"Thanks, Henn. At least let me pay you for your time."

"Your money's no good to me, Captain," Henn replies. "Kat's family to me—which means you're family, too."

"But hacking into *eight* airlines?" I say. "Come on, man. That's too much work to do for free."

"Bah. The odds are low I'll need to hack all eight of 'em to find your girl—I might even get lucky and find Samantha at the first airline. Plus, like I said, I owe Kat big. I could hack a thousand airlines for you and still not repay my debt to Kat."

Kat smiles proudly. "See, Ryan? Unlike you, Henn appreciates my gift for matchmaking."

I roll my eyes. "Kitty, no offense, but you're batting zero as far as I'm concerned. The *one* time I begged you to set me up with a certain someone, you refused and said it wasn't a match."

Kat scoffs. "*Because you were a slut.*"

"Whatever." I roll my eyes. "The point is, Henn, you gotta let me pay you, man. Please. I'll feel like a douche otherwise."

Henn shakes his head. "Would it make you feel any better to learn I recently got paid a mint for a job I did for Josh and Jonas in Vegas? I can afford to do this *pro bono.*"

"Henny's a *mill-ion-aire* now," Kat says proudly.

"Holy shit," I say, flabbergasted. "Josh and Jonas paid you a *million* bucks for a job?"

Henn shrugs. "It was a big job."

"What was it?"

"Saving the world," Henn replies.

"From the evil empire," Kat chirps, and the two of them chuckle.

I can't tell if they're yanking my chain or what the fuck they could possibly be talking about if they're serious, but all of a sudden, I'm too excited to care. "All right, then, cool. Thanks so much. You really think you can find her?"

"I don't see why not," Henn says. "If she's a flight attendant who flew from L.A. to Seattle on the day in question, then it's only a matter of time before I find her."

"Well, she's either a flight attendant or she's got some seriously fucked up fashion sense," I say.

We all laugh.

"Don't worry, I'll find her," Henn says. "Fair warning, though, it might take me a while to get going on your job—I've got a bunch of other projects already in the pipeline."

"Oh, I totally understand."

Kat looks down at her watch and her eyes pop out of her head. "Holy-I-Totally-Lost-Track-of-Time, Batman!" she blurts. She lurches over to the office door and swings it open violently, blasting the small room with the last bars of "*Bailando.*" "Consider this meeting officially adjourned, fellas. Josh is gonna be here any minute for a private grand-opening-celebration, and you two cock-blockers most definitely can't be here when he arrives."

Chapter 15
Ryan

"I'll put your food order in and be right back with your drinks," the waitress says.

"Thanks," I say. I turn to say something to the highly attractive woman sitting across from me—a mortgage broker in a little black dress whom I met earlier tonight at a real-estate-industry mixer in the bar downstairs—but for the life of me I can't think of anything to say to her. *Why the hell did I agree to grab a bite with this woman, again?* After only ten minutes of sitting here in this restaurant with her, I'm already wishing I'd accepted Keane's invitation to get stoned with him and Zander and play Call of Duty, instead.

"I love your tattoos, Ryan," my date coos from across the table.

Shit. I can't for the life of me remember if this woman's name is Kylie or Kayla or Kiera and, at this point, it'd be too awkward to ask her a fourth time. "Thanks," I say, and then (because my mother would cut off my balls if I didn't reply to a woman's compliment with one of my own), I hastily add, "I, uh, like your dress."

Kayla-Kylie-Kiera glances down at her little black dress. "Thank you. I just got it yesterday." She looks back up at me and twirls a strand of her dark hair around her finger. "Did I mention I've always had a thing for tattoos?"

I nod. Actually, she's mentioned it, like, seven times in the space of an hour. "Do you have any?" I ask, simply because it's too weird for me not to say *something* to hold up my end of the conversation, as vapid and uninteresting as it is.

"No, but I'm thinking I might get one soon. Maybe an angel with a tear running down its cheek? I just have to figure out where to put it. Do you have tattoos on your torso, or just on your arms?"

Why am I not feeling this at all? She's objectively gorgeous—so what's my problem? "Um. I've got some on my chest and one on my left ribcage, too."

She motions to the tattoo on my left forearm. "Are all of them pirate-themed?"

"Not all of them. But, yeah, a lot of them. I've got a big bottle of rum on my rib-cage."

"Yo, ho, ho and a bottle of rum?" she asks.

"Something like that." Of course, if I were even remotely interested in this woman, I'd tell her the backstory of the whole pirates-and-rum theme decorating my body, but I don't care nearly enough to bother.

"So freaking sexy," my date says. She bites her lip. "I'd definitely like to see your bottle of rum." She bites her lip. "And touch it." She reaches across the table and brushes her fingertips across my hand. "Any time."

Well, that wasn't subtle. If there were a class on "How to Tell a Man You Want to Fuck Him Tonight Without Saying the Words 'I Want to Fuck You Tonight,'" this woman could teach that class.

There's a long beat.

Apparently, she's waiting for me to say something, but I'm not in the mood to say a damned thing.

"So, you're a fan of pirates, huh?" she finally asks, filling the awkward silence.

"Yup," I say blandly.

"Cool," she replies, like I've just said something eminently interesting.

I smirk to myself. This would be funny if it weren't so fucking painful.

I open my mouth and close it again, unable to muster the energy for small talk.

She smiles at me. "Are you shy, Ryan?"

I smile at her. I've never been called shy a day in my life. But shyness would be the kindest excuse for our blatant lack of chemistry, so I decide to throw the poor woman a bone. "Yes, I'm very shy."

"Well, don't worry—I happen to love shy men." She winks. "And, by the way, you're doing great."

Thank God, the waitress appears with our drinks, camouflaging the awkwardness of the moment, and I quickly take a long gulp of my liquid painkiller.

After a moment, What's-Her-Name puts down her margarita and flashes me her most seductive smile. "I'm sure everyone tells you this all the time," she says, "but you have the most beautiful eyes."

Oh my God. It's all I can do not to roll my "beautiful" eyes and run out of the restaurant screaming. This isn't a conversation, it's a prolonged Instagram post. "Thanks," I say. I take a deep breath. "You, uh, have really beautiful hair."

Kaylie-Kyla-Katie pets her dark hair from root to end like it's a cat on top of her head. "Thanks. I use this conditioner from Brazil infused with tree nut oil—it really fortifies the shaft." She tugs on a thick chunk of her hair, apparently demonstrating the efficacy of her Brazilian conditioner. Either that, or she's demonstrating how she'd yank my shaft if given half the chance.

I shift in my seat. "So, hey, why don't you tell me a little bit about yourself... please?" Yeah, that "please" got tacked onto the end there because I suddenly realized the name I was about to call her— "Kendra"—probably wasn't right.

Thankfully, my uninteresting date takes the bait and launches into what's sure to be a lengthy and painfully uninteresting monologue, thereby giving me some much-needed time to gather my thoughts.

Okay, so yeah, my fixation on Samantha these past six weeks hasn't been rational—what kind of loon doesn't feel attraction for a single woman for six fucking weeks because he can't stop comparing every goddamned woman he meets to some flight attendant he chatted with in a bar? In my defense, though, I think my complete withdrawal from womankind these past six weeks hasn't been so much about Samantha, *per se*, as my need to regroup after the whole Olivia fiasco. I mean, Jesus, getting involved with that woman was felony stupid—a lapse in judgment I'll never understand—which means taking time off to figure my shit out is a smart and mature thing to do. Yeah, that's it—I'm just being smart and mature.

Honestly, as I'm putting some real thought into this, I'd be willing to bet my super-charged attraction to Samantha that night six weeks ago had less to do with Samantha herself and more to do with my fractured state of mind that particular night. I bet if I met

Samantha for the first time tonight—maybe downstairs at that real-estate mixer—there'd be no more chemistry with her than I'm feeling right now with Kiera-Kylie-Kendra.

What's-Her-Name giggles loudly, drawing my attention to her monologue: "And so, I finally decided to get into mortgage banking because, obviously, my childhood dreams of becoming a ballerina weren't gonna pan out, especially not with boobs like these!"

I glance at her boobs, note the objective beauty of them, and tune out again.

You know what? I'm acting crazy. What the fuck am I hoping to achieve by imitating a monk these days? Yeah, sure, I *prefer* sex with a partner I want to see again and again, but it's not a necessity. I used to be a total manwhore back in the day. What the fuck happened to that guy? As I well know, sometimes, sex can be about nothing more than sex and there's nothing wrong with that. I certainly don't need to sit around for another six weeks (or, God forbid, *months*), saving myself for a woman Henn might never find.

Yeah, fuck it.

Time to get back on the horse and stop acting like a fucking lunatic-monk.

I tune back into whatever my date is saying, poised to suggest we take our food "to go" and maybe eat it at my place... but the minute I hear what she's saying ("... and that's why I prefer Chihuahuas to huskies!"), my dick shakes its little head, flips me the bird, and says, "Fuck naw, motherfucker—fuck naw."

"Excuse me, Kendra," I blurt, bolting upright.

Her face falls. "*Kelsey.*"

I cringe. God, I'm such a dick. "Sorry. I just remembered I have an important call to make. I'll be right back." Without waiting for a reply, I stride toward the front of the restaurant, swiping through my contacts list for Henn's phone number as I go, just as the song overhead in the restaurant flips to a new song: "*Bailando*" by Enrique Iglesias.

Chapter 16
Ryan

"Ahab is forever Ahab, man. This whole act's immutably decreed."

"Why, hello there, Captain Morgan," Henn says, answering my phone call. "How's it going, sir?"

"Hey, Henn Star. Great. Good. Couldn't be better. How are you?"

"Well, let's just say if I were a superhero in a comic strip, my name would be 'Captain I'm-So-Fucking-Awesome!'"

I chuckle. "That's great, Henn."

"So, I take it you're calling because you're losing your fucking mind about Samantha?"

"How'd you know?"

"Well, first off, you sound like the Energizer Bunny on crack right now. And, second off—wait, you're not on crack, are you?"

"No. I'm currently high on Enrique Iglesias and nothing else."

"Oh, good choice. Love that guy. And, second off, when I met you at the Climb & Conquer party, you looked like a man on the verge of a nervous breakdown back then, so I can only imagine how perilously close to the edge of the cliff of insanity you're teetering a full four weeks later."

"Actually, it's been *six* weeks since the grand opening party, not four. But who's counting? And I'm not teetering 'perilously close' to the edge of the cliff of insanity, I'm dangling over it, holding onto a root in the ground by my little pinky."

"Holy shit, it's been *six* weeks since the party? Wow, time flies. I'm sorry, man, I got super busy with a bunch of big projects for the feds. Plus, right after the party, I stopped everything to help Josh with his proposal to Kat."

"You helped Josh with his proposal? Kat didn't tell me that. All she said was the proposal was 'an amazing porno-fairytale.'"

Henn laughs. "I wasn't there—I worked my magic behind the scenes. Plus, besides all that, Hannah finally moved to L.A., so I've been having fun with her. Fun fact: when your amazing girlfriend finally lives in the same city with you, working twenty hours a day doesn't seem nearly as exciting as it used to."

"Amen to that. I'm happy for you, brother."

"Yeah, thanks, but your happiness for me isn't keeping you from going batshit crazy, is it?"

"Not at all."

"You're completely obsessed, aren't you?"

"I prefer to call it 'hyper-focused.'"

"Yeah, that's what all madmen call it."

We both laugh.

"How bad is it?" Henn asks.

"Well, let's see if this story encapsulates my current state of mind for you: I'm currently on a dinner date with a smokin' hot woman in a little black dress with perfect breasts who, not five minutes ago, told me she wants to touch a tattoo currently covered by my shirt—and then added she wants to touch it 'any time'; and, right after she said all that, I bolted from the table to call you because I can't stand the thought of touching any woman other than Samantha."

"Wow. Your pecker's holding out for Samantha."

"Stubborn little prick," I say.

"*Idealistic* little prick."

"Dude, I don't want anyone but her. It's torture."

"That's so cool," Henn says.

"*Cool*? I just said it's torture."

"We should all be so lucky to be tortured like that."

"But I met her once in a fucking bar. This reaction is beyond over-the-top. It's crazy."

"I think it's cool. When in doubt, always listen to your prick—it's all-knowing."

"Um, pretty sure that's the exact *opposite* advice my father gave me as a teenager."

Henn laughs.

"Seriously, man, I think I've lost my mind," I say. "I've been going full-on Captain Ahab over this woman for six fucking weeks—a woman I've never even kissed. It makes no sense, but I can't stop thinking about her. *Yearning* for her."

"Well, duh. She left her glass slipper behind on the palace steps and you found it. Who could resist that? Those fairytales are classics for a reason, man—they tap into our collective id."

"Henn Star, you're a man after my own heart."

"Thanks, Captain Ahab," Henn says warmly. "Look, all I'm saying is, if you're the lucky guy who found Cinderella's glass slipper on the palace steps, then, by God, it's your duty to turn the kingdom upside-down looking for her."

Whoa. This nerd's given me more clarity in one phone call than I've had for the past six fucking weeks. "You're a genius, Henn," I say. "Thanks."

"Hey, it's not brain surgery: the heart wants what the heart wants. Or, I guess, the pecker. Some things are immutably decreed."

"'Immutably decreed'?"

"Indubitably."

I laugh.

"Anything like this ever happen to you before?" Henn asks.

"Fuck no. I swear to God I'm normally the sanest Morgan brother of them all. Well, actually, the second sanest—it's awfully hard to out-sane Colby Morgan." I sigh. "You still think you're gonna find her?"

"Dude, I'll find her. There are only so many airlines and so many Samanthas. Just tell your pecker to do a crossword puzzle or something and wait it out. I got this. I promise I'll get cracking on the Search for Samantha in the next week or two—three at the outside. Regardless, I'll get back to you before we leave for Josh and Kat's wedding in a month. I certainly wouldn't want your pecker feeling peaked in paradise."

"Thanks, Henn. I appreciate it. God help me if I'm still obsessing about this shit in Hawaii."

"Looks like it's gonna be an amazing week," Henn says. "But that's Josh Faraday for you—he doesn't do parties half-assed."

"My sister told me Josh's assistant—what's her name again?"

"T-Rod."

"That's right. My sister told me Josh put T-Rod in charge of planning the week and she's lined up a whole bunch of stuff for us, like luaus and helicopter rides and—"

Henn cuts me off. "Hey, Ryan? Sorry to cut you off, but didn't you say you left some poor woman with perfect breasts sitting at a table when you called me?"

Every hair on my body stands on end, all at once. "Oh, shit," I blurt. "God, I'm such an asshole. Talk to you later, man. Thanks again."

Henn laughs. "Any time, Captain Ahab. Oh, and, dude? Let the poor girl down easy. I don't think you realize just how studly you are. You're kind of the shit, man, hate to break it to you. Try to be kind about letting her down."

"Will do. Thanks."

I hang up and stride back to Kayla-Kylie-Katrina at our table.

When I approach, she looks up from her phone and smiles. "Everything okay?"

"No, actually." I signal to the waitress for the check. "I'm sorry, Kendra, but—"

"Kelsey," she corrects, cutting me off.

"*Kelsey*. Sorry. You're incredibly beautiful and a great conversationalist and this has nothing to do with you whatsoever—but I've got to call it a night."

Chapter 17
Ryan

"[T]hen all collapsed and the great shroud of the sea rolled on..."

"Fuck," I say softly, holding my phone against my ear with white knuckles. I'm lying in bed, naked and alone. It's a state of being that's become par for the course for me these past two months. Henn's crushing words are sounding in my ear.

Right before answering this call from Henn, I'd just finished jerking myself off while watching the music video for the Spanish-language version of "*Bailando*" (because, holy shit, the lead actress-dancer in the red dress *totally* reminds me of Samantha!)—and I was about to drift into a happy, blissful sleep, content in the knowledge that a genius-hacker was out in the world doing God's work for me, when Henn called. And now, not thirty seconds into this phone call, I'm wide awake and feeling like I've been punched in the gut.

"I'm really sorry, Ryan," Henn says. "I was so sure." He sighs. "At this point, the only thing I can think is her legal name's gotta be something different than Samantha. It's not all that uncommon, actually. Did you know Miley Cyrus' given name is Destiny Hope? But do you think Miley has ever introduced herself to a guy in a bar as 'Destiny Hope'? I think not."

I rub my forehead with my free hand. "Yeah, it's gotta be something like that. A nickname different from her given name. Shit."

"Ironic, huh? I scoured nine airlines' databases and it turns out you were probably right about Delta all along—we just didn't have the right name to search."

I sigh. "Well, can we run another search in Delta, then? Like, I dunno, maybe look at the files of all twenty-seven-year-old female flight attendants?"

"The database isn't set up to search that way. I'm sure I could limit my search to flight attendants only, but without a name or employee-number, that's about all I could do—and that'd be a helluva lot of files to look through."

"Hey, I'm totally willing to review them myself. I'll fly down to L.A. some weekend, whenever you're free, and sift through them."

"Ha! You think you'd need a *weekend* to get through all those files? Ryan, Delta's got, like, eighty thousand employees. Even if I could narrow things down to flight attendants for you, it'd still probably take you a month to sift through everything, and that's if you do it without a day off."

"Oh."

"I'm sorry, man. I know how badly you wanted this."

"It's okay. I should have known: Captain Ahab doesn't catch the whale."

"Yeah, well, I was really hoping this time he would. The name thing just turned out to be an unexpected snafu."

"Yeah, I know. It's okay. It's karma for me being cheesy enough to tell a girl I'd be all over her 'like *blanco* on *arroz.*'"

Henn laughs. "You said that to her?"

"Yup. That's how bad I had it for her." I close my eyes and take a deep breath. "But, okay. No more whining allowed. I've got no choice but to turn the page and try to look at the silver lining here. I mean, hey, here's an upside: I get to have sex again, right? With someone not nearly as great, but, hey."

"That's something."

"And not a moment too soon, man. Is it possible for a guy to die from lack of sex? Because, if so, you'd better read me my last rites."

"No, I'm quite certain lack of sex can't be fatal; otherwise, I'd be dead. Not these days, of course, thanks to Hannah, but I've had some dry spells in my time that would have been terminal, if that were a thing. Oh, hey, heads up, if manwhoring is gonna be your thing again, you'd better tell Kat. At the Climb & Conquer party, she told me if the search for Samantha went bust, she was dying to play matchmaker with you and T-Rod."

I roll my eyes. "Great. Just what I need."

"Hey, I wouldn't be so quick to say 'no, thanks.' T-Rod's gorgeous."

"Yeah? Actually, I think Sarah said something about that, come to think of it."

"You know Reed Rivers—the guy Josh and I went to UCLA with?"

"Yeah. I mean, no, I haven't met him yet, but my little brother Dax is hoping to get his band signed by Reed's record label. Why?"

"Well, just to give you an idea of T-Rod's allure, Reed Rivers can get any woman he wants—literally—he even dated Isabel Randolph for a while—and he's *always* had a thing for T-Rod."

"Then why the fuck is my dumbshit of a sister scheming to set *me* up with her?" I shout. "I'm not gonna horn in on fucking Reed Rivers."

"No, no. I meant Reed *wants* to hook up with The Mighty T-Rod—not that he's ever gonna get to do it." Henn laughs. "T-Rod's like a sister to Josh. No manwhores allowed, especially not the biggest manwhore we know. Reed's a great guy—the absolute best—but when it comes to women, trust me, he's a menace."

"How old is T-Rod?"

"A few years younger than Josh, I think. Twenty-six or twenty-seven, maybe? She started with him right out of college. She's a real straight arrow, which is why she's the perfect person to keep Josh in line. But that's why he's always felt really protective of her. You should have seen Josh after T-Rod's last boyfriend played her. Josh pretty much wanted to hire a hitman to kill the guy."

"Interesting," I say. "I'll keep an eye out for her in Hawaii. But, obviously, no matter what Kat thinks, I shouldn't touch T-Rod with a ten-foot pole. No sense pissing Josh off, right?"

"Yeah, probably for the best—unless you're planning to marry her."

"Nope. I'm done looking for true love, son. Next week in paradise, it's gonna be mai tais and no-strings fuckery with cocktail waitresses for me. I give up."

"Don't give up. Now you're making me sad."

"Sorry. I give up."

"If you say so. But, hey, if you happen to get some newfangled idea about how to find your Cinderella between now and then, don't hesitate to give me a call and I'll jump on it for ya, okay, Captain Ahab?"

"Thanks, Henn Star. But, nope. I'm officially done with the Search for Samantha. I'm officially done with love. It's all pointless."

"Shit, man. I'm so sorry."

"Hey, there are worse things than a guy deciding to have a whole bunch of meaningless sex."

"I wouldn't know."

I laugh. "I'll see you in a week, Henn Star. I'll buy you a drink in Maui."

"Josh isn't letting anyone pay for a single thing all week long."

"I know. That's why I said it."

Henn laughs. "I'll see you soon, Captain. Aloha."

I hang up the phone, lie back onto my bed, and stare blankly at the ceiling, wracking my brain for something, *anything*, I might be missing—some search I could possibly ask Henn to run as a last-ditch effort to find Samantha. When my mind draws a complete blank, I sigh, turn to my laptop, and press the "replay video" button on that fucking Enrique Iglesias song, swearing to myself this will be the very last time.

Chapter 18
Tessa

I kick the bottom of my (super cute) wedge sandal against the door of Josh and Kat's bungalow, my arms otherwise engaged with a large cardboard box. I look at my watch. Two o'clock on the button. Damn, I'm good.

A warm, plumeria-scented breeze wafts over me, rustling my sundress. I close my eyes and take a long sniff of the fragrant air, allowing myself the small luxury of reveling in paradise for a blissful half-second.

I open my eyes.

Break over.

Ain't nobody got time for that.

Exactly two months ago, I received a text from Josh, informing me that Kat had said yes to his marriage proposal (no surprise there) and instructing me to "pull together" a "weeklong-destination-wedding-shindig" in Hawaii (the particular Hawaiian island and resort to be determined by me, based on logistical concerns) for two hundred of Josh's and Kat's closest friends and family.

Of course, nothing in Josh's text would have elevated my heart rate in the slightest were it not for the kicker at the end: Josh wanted all this wonderfulness to occur in exactly two months.

And, now, here I stand, two months after receiving that crazy-ass text from Josh, and, it seems, I've managed to pull off the impossible, exactly as requested. But that doesn't mean I've retained a shred of my sanity during the process.

Oh my gosh, when this week's over and Mr. and Mrs. Joshua William Faraday have ridden off into the sunset, this lifelong good girl is gonna finally go rogue. Yep, the minute my work obligations are done, I've decided I'm gonna do something I've never done before: namely, I'm gonna scour the resort grounds for that yummy tattooed bartender I flirted with for an hour late last night after arriving here—a hottie who made it abundantly clear he'd be more than willing to screw me during my stay. And I'm gonna have myself some no-strings vacation-sex with a complete stranger. Oh my gawd, I can hardly wait. It'll be my first sexual contact with an actual human in about a year, and, man, oh, man, I'm beyond aching for it.

But I'm getting ahead of myself. Sex with a hot stranger is what's on tap a week from now. Right now, I've still got a thousand and one things to do to ensure this week goes off without a hitch. And do them, I shall.

I grab my phone and tap out a quick text: "Aloha, boss. I'm standing at the door to your bungalow. Remember our 2:00 meeting, Mr. Faraday? I've got a bunch of stuff to tell you and Kat before the Morgan group arrives in an hour."

Thirty seconds later, I receive a reply from my darling and ever distractible boss: "Sorry, Miss Rodriguez. The almost-Mrs. and I got sidetracked." Winking emoji. "We're hopping into the shower now. Come on in and grab some rum punch from the bar and we'll be out in a Hawaiian minute. JWF."

Chapter 19
Ryan

"The path to my fixed purpose is laid with iron rails, whereon my soul is grooved to run."

"You wanna watch a movie?" Colby asks. He holds up his iPad. "I've got *The Drop* loaded up. Tom Hardy."

"Oh, yeah, Dax said that was really good," I say. "Lemme just hit the bathroom first." I unbuckle my seatbelt and move up the aisle, high-fiving and fist-bumping every passenger along my route. My glad-handing isn't nearly as creepy as it sounds, by the way, since I'm flying on a private jet filled exclusively with my immediate and extended family and their plus-ones. But when I get to the bathroom, it's occupied, so I stand and chat with my cousin Julie and her brand-new husband and stepdaughter, Coco.

"How old are you again, Coco?" I ask.

"Eight."

"That's right. I liked being eight—I slayed life when I was eight." I notice the book on Coco's lap: *Charlotte's Web*. "You like that book?"

"It's my favorite. I've already read it three times."

"What's your favorite part?"

"When Charlotte writes stuff like 'humble' and 'terrific' in her web to save Wilbur's life."

"Yeah, that's cool. I liked that part, too." I look at the bathroom door. It's still occupied. "So, hey, Coco, can I ask you a huge favor? Will you be my partner for chicken in the pool this week? My brother Keane said he and his best friend, Zander, are gonna 'beat my butt' in chicken, no matter what partner I choose, so I wanna get a really good one to make sure I beat the crud out of them." I lean forward. "I don't know if you've had a chance to talk to Keane much yet, but let's just say if he were Wilbur, Charlotte wouldn't be writing 'humble' in her web about him."

Coco shoots me a gap-toothed smile. "I know. When Keane was standing here waiting for the bathroom a minute ago, he said he was gonna 'beat my butt' in hula dancing." She rolls her eyes.

"And what'd you say to that?"

"I said, 'There's no such thing as beating someone's butt in hula dancing, *Keane*,' and he goes, 'Yeah, keep telling yourself that, small fry—that's what losers in hula dancing always say.'"

I laugh my ass off. "Dang, Keane's full of himself. All the more reason for us to team up and beat his butt, right?"

She nods.

"Okay, then, it's settled: you and me, Coco Puff, we're gonna take that clown and his best friend down like they're the Cleveland Browns wearing sparkly crowns in Chinatown."

Coco giggles and we shake on it.

Just then, the bathroom door swings open in front of us, and, speak of the arrogant devil himself, Keane-the-Peen-Morgan appears in all his dimpled glory, his muscles bulging under his tight T-shirt, his eyes sparkling. "Yo, Captain," he says, patting my cheek. "Hey, Coconut." He fist-bumps her. "You getting yourself mentally prepared for when I'm gonna beat your tiny booty in hula-dancing?"

Coco giggles uproariously. "There's no such thing, Keane. Hula dancing's just for fun."

"If that's what you think, then you'd better fasten your hula skirt, baby doll, because you're about to get whooped."

"Hey now, I wouldn't rile the 'baby doll' up," I say. "Coco Puff's just agreed to be my partner in chicken and we're gonna take you and Zander down."

Keane clutches his heart. "Say it ain't so, Coco Chanel Number Five. I wanted you to be *my* partner in chicken. I was just smack-talking you as reverse psychology so you'd join *my* team."

"Nope," Coco says, jutting her chin. "Ryan and I are gonna take you and Zander down like, um, Charlie Brown riding a merry-go-round at the dog pound."

Keane throws his head back and belly laughs at that. "Look at that! She's already smack-talking like a true Morgan. Awesome!"

My cousin Julie turns to her new husband, Travis. "Sorry, babe, I warned you."

"Bah, don't worry, Jules," Keane says, waving dismissively. "We'll only teach the little brahita here G-rated stuff, I swear." He swats at Coco's tiny thigh. "Scooch over, Hot Coco. I'm gonna teach you everything you need to know to be able to rumble in the Morgan jungle like a pro."

Coco giddily unbuckles her seatbelt and moves onto her dad's lap, allowing Keane to assume her seat and commence his utterly ridiculous tutelage of her.

I watch my brother-the-professor and his enraptured student for several minutes, thoroughly entertained, but when the conversation moves from the highly entertaining topic of "The Art of Nicknaming" to the book on Coco's lap, my bladder reminds me why I got up from my seat in the first place and I hightail it toward the restroom.

"What's your favorite part?" I hear Keane ask Coco behind my back.

"When Charlotte writes stuff about Wilbur in her web."

"What's your favorite thing Charlotte writes?"

"'Some pig.'"

Keane laughs. "Funny, that's exactly what my last girlfriend wrote about *me* in *her* web!"

I slip inside the bathroom, chuckling to myself—fucking Peen— and then I lock the door behind me, unzip my fly, and... promptly freeze with my dick in my hand.

Oh my fucking God.

With lightning speed, I finish my business, barrel out of the bathroom, and flag down a flight attendant. "Excuse me," I say, my heart racing. "Is there Wi-Fi on this flight?"

"Of course, sir." She tells me how to access it and I career back to my seat, a bat out of hell.

"Everything okay?" Colby asks as I settle into my seat next to him.

"Everything's fantastic," I reply, grabbing my laptop. "I just gotta send out a quick email and then all my dreams will magically come true."

"Wow, if only everything in life were that easy."

My chest tight, I bang out an email to Henn: "Henn Star!

Samantha had a friend at the bar! A redhead named Charlotte. She was wearing the exact same uniform as Samantha, right down to the Delta logo on her scarf. She's gotta be 27 or so because Samantha said they've been friends since second grade. OMFG! I don't know if you're already on your flight, but if you happen to get this message before you head out to the airport and can somehow get me Charlotte's phone number ASAP, I'll name my firstborn after you, boy or girl, I swear. Thank you!" I press send on the email and look at Colby, my skin on fire. "*Captain Ahab's back, motherfucker.*"

"What's going on? You look like a madman."

"The specifics don't matter, Bee. All that matters is that I'm on the hunt for my Argentinian whale again and I just figured out how to harpoon her."

"Who is she?"

"The sexiest woman alive."

"Aw, come on. You gotta give me more than that. What's going on?"

I tell Colby everything, no detail left out, no matter how embarrassing, and when I'm done talking, Colby says, "Holy shit, Ry, you've gone completely insane."

"I know. But maybe not quite as insane as it appears. I've also been working my ass off these past few months on the biggest deal of my life, so that's kept me busy." I quickly tell Colby a bit about the deal (the sale of a large industrial complex), and about how my big, fat commission has brought me that much closer to my lifelong dream of opening my own bar, and Colby congratulates me. "Plus," I continue, "I'm sure these past three months of being a monk have at least in part been about licking my wounds from Olivia. I gotta be honest, I'm pretty skittish these days, brother. God help me if I get myself mixed up with another sociopath."

Colby shakes his head. "See what happens when you don't listen to me?"

"I'll never disregard your advice again, Master Yoda."

Colby looks thoughtful for a moment. "Seriously, though, this quest you've been on seems pretty fucking crazy. You know that, right?"

"Yeah, I know. But it can't be helped. 'The path to my fixed purpose is laid with iron rails, whereon my soul is grooved to run.'"

Colby looks at me funny.

"*Moby Dick,*" I say, answering his unspoken question.

"Why the fuck are you quoting *Moby Dick?*"

"I've been reading it again lately."

"Oh, that's not a sign of insanity or anything."

I shrug.

"Dude. Listen to me, okay?" Colby says. "Whenever you find this girl, as you surely will because you're the most relentless motherfucker of all of us, I strongly recommend you *don't* tell her right off the bat about this crazy-as-shit 'Captain Ahab' quest you've been on for her. I mean, anyone who knows you would know this crazy search is a once in a lifetime thing, but she doesn't know you. More than likely, if she finds out you hacked a bunch of airlines to find her, she's gonna think you're a total nut job. So, please, just take my advice this time, and, when you finally find your whale, just play your cards close to your vest at first, at least 'til she gets to know you a bit."

"How can I do that? When I finally contact her, out of the blue after three months, she's gonna ask me how the hell I tracked her down. And what can I say to that? At that point, I won't have any choice but to tell her the whole truth."

Colby considers that. "Yeah, shit. You're right. Bummer. I guess there's no way around it. Oh well. Hopefully, she won't run away screaming when you tell her you're a fucking loon."

"I can't worry about that now. First things first, I gotta find the whale—second things second, I'll do whatever's necessary to harpoon her." I swat Colby's thigh. "Now start the movie, Old Wise One. Distract 'Captain Ahab' from his fucking 'iron rails.'"

Chapter 20
Tessa

Whew. I've just finished walking Josh and Kat through my detailed itinerary for the coming week—a jaw-dropping smorgasbord of water sports, tours, luaus, booze cruises, and more, all of it cooked up by my amazing activities director and me—and, thank God, both Josh and Kat have expressed unadulterated elation about all of it.

"Fantastic," I say, exhaling with relief. "Now let's move on to the menus I've preliminarily approved with the head chef."

"I'm sure the food's gonna be great," Josh says breezily. "'In T-Rod we trust.' What I really wanna know is what's inside that box?" He motions to the large cardboard box I left sitting by the front door when I came in.

Kat squeals. "Oh my God, is that the jerseys, Tessa?"

I put down my iPad. I should have known these two happy-campers would rubber-stamp all my decisions, from top to bottom, seeing as how that's what they've done every step of the way over the past two months. "Yup," I reply. "The box arrived in the nick of time. There was a last-minute glitch, but don't worry—I handled it."

At Kat's direction, Josh retrieves the box and opens it, revealing two hundred brightly colored sports jerseys, each of them two-color-reversible with SPF protection and emblazoned with "Team Josh and Kat" across their fronts.

"I figured they'd be a cute party favor for guests," Kat says proudly. "And they're functional, too. We can switch up team colors during volleyball and cornhole and stuff." Josh begins to express his enthusiastic approval, but Kat cuts him off. "But, wait, there's more!" she exclaims. "Nicknames!" Kat turns the two jerseys in her hands over to reveal they're stamped across their backs with Josh and Kat's respective pet names for each other: "Playboy" and "Party Girl."

"I love it!" Josh says. He leaps up, peels off his white linen shirt and pulls his brand-new jersey over his head. It's a maneuver that reveals Josh's mouth-watering torso and tattoos for a brief moment and, admittedly, makes my clit jolt as surely as if he'd just pressed a vibrator between my legs.

Hey, maybe I'll track down that hot bartender later tonight, right after the opening party, instead of waiting until the end of the week.

"It's perfect!" Kat exclaims, beaming at Josh in his bright blue jersey. She leaps up from the couch, her baby bump leading the way, and throws her arms around her fiancé's neck. Of course, Josh proceeds to kiss the hell out of Kat and for the next minute or so, the two of them get completely lost in each other.

Ho hum. My boss and his fiancée are practically dry-humping each other in front of me. La, la.

After watching Josh and Kat kiss for a long beat (it's kind of hot, actually), I finally force myself to look away, my face on fire and my clit pounding like a jackhammer. *Damn.* That's some sexy kissing going on over there. (And, man, do I wanna do that very thing with a hot guy—*any* freaking hot guy at this point.)

Finally, when I hear Josh say, "Show me all the jerseys, babe," I look at them again. They're seated together on the couch, side by side, their limbs intertwined.

I clear my throat. "Yeah, Kat, let's see the jerseys," I say brightly, even though I don't have any desire to see them. I mean, I'm sure the nicknames are cute and all, but I've got a mountain of stuff to check up on before the Morgans arrive in thirty minutes, and, as a practical matter, I won't recognize any of the nicknames. I've never met ninety percent of the people invited here by Josh and Kat, after all, and I've never scrutinized their guest list, either, since all travel for this week was arranged by the travel agent and wedding stuff by the wedding coordinator. But, of course, since my disinterest in the names is immaterial (and understandably so), the Parade of Nicknames dutifully begins.

"Suzy B, Issy, Coco Puff, Soph-a-Loph, Perv, Hockey-Makeup, Dripper, Cha-Cha, Lala!" Kat exclaims as she pulls each jersey out of the box and tosses it onto a nearby chair. "Brooklyn Bridge, Silverback, Selina-Bellina, Rocky, Trishy-Wishy, KC, Ketchup, Jacky-V!"

Gah. I was right—I don't recognize any of these nicknames. I covertly check the time on my phone and quietly have a heart attack. The Morgans should be here in about twenty minutes. But Kat's still going strong with the jerseys.

"Baby Cuz, Cheese, Rock Star, Peen, Captain..."

Okay, I can't resist asking about that second-to-last one. "*Peen?*" I blurt. "Who's that?"

Kat giggles. "My brother, Keane."

"Is Keane gonna be pissed you're making him wear 'Peen' on his back all week?"

"Not at all—everyone calls him 'Peen.' As a matter of fact, when Keane used to play baseball—he was a star pitcher in the Cubs' minor league system—his fans would hold up signs whenever he struck out a batter that said 'We love Peen!'"

"Really?" Josh says. "I didn't know Peen had actual fans."

"Are you kidding?" Kat says. "Keane was a star. Not only was he a lefty with a ninety-three-mile-per-hour fastball and a nasty slider, he knew how to play to the crowd better than anyone." She addresses me. "Keane was about to get called up to the Cubs when he got injured. It was a crushing blow."

My mind races back to the Climb & Conquer party three months ago, when I spotted that gorgeous hunk of man-meat on crutches standing next to Mr. Morgan. Wowzers. So that hunky guy was about to get called up to pitch for the Cubs? Yeah, he definitely looked like an athlete. "I saw Keane at the grand opening party," I say. "He was standing next to your dad on crutches. Does it look likely he'll be rehabbed and ready to pitch by the start of next season?"

"Oh, no, no, that guy on crutches wasn't *Keane*—that was my oldest brother, Colby. He's a firefighter. Colby had a terrible accident on the job earlier this year. He's lucky to be alive."

"Oh. Wow. How scary. I'm so sorry."

"And, no, to answer your question, Keane unfortunately won't be going back to baseball. He injured his pitching elbow and surgery didn't go as planned."

"Oh no," I say. "I'm so sorry. Was Keane at the grand opening party? I don't think I saw him there."

"No, he said he'd come, but the loser didn't show up. Typical. I'm sure he was too exhausted from shaking his ass for dollah billz the prior night to drag his sorry ass out of bed."

I look at Kat quizzically, not sure I'm drawing the correct conclusion here.

"Keane's a stripper," Kat confirms, reading my mind. "Seattle's answer to Magic Mike. And guess what his stage name is?"

"*Peen*?" I venture.

Kat giggles. "'Peen Star'!"

"No, not anymore, babe," Josh pipes in. "Peenie changed his stripper-name a few weeks ago. He's 'Ball Peen Hammer' now."

"*What*?" Kat says, laughing uproariously. "No."

"Yup."

"Why the hell did Keane do that to himself? That's a ridiculous name."

"He needed a new one. It seems your knuckleheaded brother had to go into the stripper equivalent of the Witness Protection Program." Josh explains that Keane ran into "a bit of trouble" on the stripper circuit—something having to do with Keane "banging too many clients," and my stomach revolts. What is it with hot men and meaningless sex? I truly don't understand it. Isn't there a hot guy on this planet who prefers to commit wholeheartedly to one woman at a time—and then, shockingly, remain irrevocably faithful to her through good times and bad? Is that too much to freaking ask these days, for the love of God—that there be *one* available man like that?

Josh continues: "But don't say anything to Peen about his stripper woes, okay? I know you Morgans are ruthless when it comes to razzing each other, but, apparently, Keane's *really* embarrassed about the whole situation and doesn't want anyone to know."

Kat pouts. "Why the hell do you know all this juicy family gossip and I don't? You're not even an official member of my family yet, and everyone's already confiding in you more than me? I'm thoroughly offended."

Josh laughs. "I only know about Peen's troubles because when the shit hit the fan, he called Rum Cake for help and Rum Cake called me. So, of course, we got Henn involved and he saved the day."

"Well, this I gotta hear."

"Later, babe." He motions vaguely to me. "T-Rod's probably jumping out of her skin about the thousand-and-one things she *thinks* she should be doing right now."

I shoot Josh a snarky look that tells him he's read my mind and he winks.

"And, like I say," Josh continues, "Keane doesn't want anyone knowing about his little stripper-Armageddon, so we'll spare T-Rod the gory details."

"I'm sure that's for the best," I say. "So, Kat, just a hunch, but I'm thinking your family kinda likes nicknames?"

Kat giggles. "Oh, you noticed?"

I laugh with her. "Which brother is 'Rum Cake'? The older one on crutches or the younger one whose band is gonna play for everyone tomorrow night?"

"Neither. The second-oldest. I've got four brothers."

"You've got *four* brothers?" I say. "Wow. Well, I'm definitely looking forward to meeting all of them—and your entire extended family, too." I look down at the time. "Which I'll be doing in approximately twelve minutes when the Morgan bus arrives." I shove my iPad into my bag and stand. "Shall we head to the lobby to greet the Morgans? If it's okay with you, after you say some welcoming words, I'd like to tell everyone about the itinerary and make sure they download the app—"

"Actually, Tessa," Kat says, cutting me off. She motions for me to sit back down. "There's something Josh and I want to talk to you about before we head over to greet everyone."

The hair on the back of my neck stands up. "Sure." I lower myself back down onto my chair. *Crap.* This is it—I know it is—the moment I've been dreading for the past two months: Kat's about to tell me my services will no longer be required after the wedding. Yeah, yeah, I realize she's been incredibly sweet to me these past two months, and, yes, I'm aware she's taken to calling me Tessa—a habit she adopted when she heard her mom calling me that during a shopping excursion for Kat's wedding dress with her mom, Sarah, and me—which she insisted I join because, she said, I know Josh's taste better than she does. But, come on. I'm not a fool. A piece of me has always known Kat's only been luring me into a false sense of security with all her crazy kindness, all in the name of cutting me off at the knees when she becomes Mrs. Faraday. And I can't say I blame her. What sane woman would want another woman managing every aspect of her husband's life the way I do for Josh? Surely, Kat is going to want to do everything for her new husband all by herself, as she should.

"Oh my gosh, Tessa," Kat says sympathetically. "Don't look so worried, honey. I just want to show you the last jersey in the box, that's all." Without further ado, she pulls the final jersey out and holds it up, revealing the nickname on its back: *T-Rod.*

Relief floods every cell in my body, all at once. "Wow. Thank you," I say, taking the jersey from Kat. "That was so sweet of you to order this for me." I try to smile broadly but my cheeks feel tight. "How'd you slip that sucker into the order? That was sneaky of you, Kat."

Kat looks at Josh and smiles. "She doesn't get it."

"Well, then I guess you'd better explain it to her."

Kat looks at me. "You don't get it, do you?"

I stare at Kat blankly. "Get what?"

"Honey, this jersey isn't a party favor, it's an *invitation.*"

I'm utterly confused and I'm sure my face shows it.

Josh chuckles. "Theresa, Kat and I want you to be our guest this week."

"Huh?" I say stupidly.

Kat lays her cheek on Josh's shoulder and her palm on his chest. "You've worked so incredibly hard for us to make this party amazing and now we want you to kick back and enjoy the fruits of your labor." She points her index finger at me menacingly. "We want you to be our guest and we won't take no for an answer, Tessa."

"But..." I sputter. "There's too much work to do."

Josh scoffs. "If there's still shit to do, hand it off to the dream team you hired. You do have a dream team, right? Because, otherwise, you're fired for embezzling from me."

I roll my eyes. "I'm not embezzling from you, Josh."

Josh laughs. "Yeah, come to think of it, you don't seem to spend the truckloads of money I already pay you, so I don't know why you'd steal even more." He beams a huge smile at me. "What the hell do you do with all the money I pay you, by the way? I've been meaning to ask you."

"I buy shoes," I say. "Lots and lots of shoes."

Josh chuckles.

"I love those sandals, by the way," Kat says. "Adorbsicles."

"What's your size? I'll order you a pair. Do you prefer this color or—"

"Nice deflection, T-Rod," Josh says. "But I'm on to you."

I sigh. "Look, guys. I really appreciate you thinking of me—it means more to me than I could ever express—but I can't be a guest like everyone else. How could I possibly do that when there's so much to oversee?"

Josh shrugs. "Easy. You just say 'YOLO,' knock back a few shots, have faith in the team you hired, and have the time of your life. Pretty simple, if you ask me."

I argue the point for a bit, but it's futile. Josh and Kat's minds are clearly made up.

"You're family, T-Rod," Josh says, shocking the hell out of me—Josh has never said anything like that to me before. "It'd be weird to have you working all week—not to mention embarrassing to me. You want people thinking I'm a world-class douche for making you work this week? Come on, dude. Don't make me look bad."

"Tessa, we insist," Kat says, and I'll be damned, she looks completely sincere.

My chest is tight. This is a bit overwhelming, actually. Josh considers me family? And his bride is insisting I attend their weeklong celebration at this swanky resort as a *guest*? I swallow hard. "Thank you," I say softly. "I accept your invitation. Once your guests have all arrived safely at the resort, I promise I'll hand everything off to the activities director and her team and make myself available for emergencies only."

"Perfect," Josh says. "Beginning with the opening party tonight, I better see you drinking and letting loose. You got that, Miss Rodriguez?"

I sigh. "Yes, Mr. Faraday."

"I'll give you a bonus if you get shit-faced tonight, by the way."

"I never get shitfaced. And I don't need a bonus from you, but thank you."

"Hey, there's a first time for everything."

"I make no promises."

"Get three sheets to the wind for me," Josh says. "Please?"

"I'll get *one* sheet to the wind," I say.

"Make it two, as a wedding gift to me."

"Fine. Two it is. But you know I hardly ever drink."

"That's why I want you to do it for me. Kick off the week with a bang."

"Yes, sir. So is that it? I'm ordered to stop working and get drunk as soon as everyone has arrived at the resort?"

Josh looks at Kat. "Is that it, Almost-Mrs.-Faraday?"

Kat smiles. "That's it, Almost-Husband. Thank you again, T-Rod. You've been a lifesaver and a great friend throughout this whole process. Now I see why Josh adores you so much."

My cheeks flush. "It's been my pleasure. I couldn't be happier for you two."

It's the truth.

Of course, I would have preferred to hate Kat's guts the same way I've hated the ones who've come before her, especially his horrific ex-girlfriend, but, dammit, Kat's so damned Charlotte-like in every way, it's been impossible for me not to feel anything but fierce, undying love for her. (Bitch.)

"Well, should we head down to the lobby to Meet the Morgans?" Josh asks.

I look down at my watch. "Absolutely. In fact, we'd better bust a move, y'all."

Kat squeals and leaps up from the couch, her adorable baby bump leading the way. "Let Josh and Kat's Weeklong Wedding Shindig begin!"

Chapter 21
Ryan

"He offered a prayer so deeply devout that he seemed kneeling and praying at the bottom of the sea."

A moment ago, the entire Morgan group including me stepped off the chartered bus that collected us from Kahului Airport, and now we're walking behind a beautiful woman in a Hawaiian-print dress, headed toward the grand entrance of the sprawling beachside resort that's about to become our home away from home for the coming week.

About twenty yards from the threshold of the lobby, my phone pings with an incoming text from Henn that stops me dead in my tracks: *"Charlotte McDougal,"* the text reads, followed by a phone number and the following note: *"Please name your firstborn Hennessy, rather than Peter. Thanks."*

I stop walking and let the herd stream past me on both sides, my heart exploding in my chest.

"Everything okay, honey?" my mother asks, coming to a stop next to me.

"Yeah, I just need to make a quick call." Without waiting for my mom's reply, I sprint away, shouting over my shoulder. "Will you get my room key for me, Mom? Thanks! That's why I love you the most, woman!"

I find a little bench next to a koi pond about fifty yards away from the hotel entrance and sit down, my chest heaving, and then, with shaking fingers, dial the number supplied by Henn.

"Hello?" a female voice says.

My heart stops. "Charlotte?"

"Yes?"

"Charlotte the flight attendant with red hair?"

"Yes? Who's this?"

I clear my throat. "Hi, Charlotte." I swallow hard. Shit. My throat is dry. "This might sound crazy, but this is Ryan Morgan, the guy you and your friend Samantha met about three months ago at The Pine Box?"

There's dead silence on the other end of the line.

"In Seattle?" I add.

More silence.

Shit. Did Henn get the wrong redheaded Charlotte the Flight Attendant for Delta? I clear my throat again. "I bought you and Samantha drinks at the bar and then you went to sit with some guys at a table in the corner and—"

Charlotte cuts me off. "Yeah, I remember you, Ryan. I'm just shocked to hear from you after all this time."

"But you remember me?"

"Of course. You've got pirate-tattoos all over your arms. Blue eyes. Chiseled jaw. Ridiculous muscles. Cocky grin. Swagger, swagger, swagger."

I exhale with relief. "Yeah, that's me. Well, I don't know about the *swagger* part, but, yeah, I've got—"

She cuts me off: "You wanna know why I remember you so well, Ryan?"

Uh oh. I don't like the tone of her voice.

"Because it's not every day my best friend says yes to a date with a guy—in fact, other than you, it's now been a full year since she's said that magic word to a single guy—and, believe me, she gets hit on *a lot*."

I know I should feel bad about Charlotte's revelation, but I feel nothing but elated. "Wow, that's—" I start to say, but Charlotte interrupts me.

"Let me cut to the chase here, Ryan," Charlotte snaps. "To be honest, my friend thinks you're a complete asshole and so do I. You—"

"But that's why I'm calling," I blurt, cutting her off. "If you'd just let me explain—"

Charlotte cuts me off again. "No, *asshole*. You're gonna let me talk, or else I'm hanging up."

I take a deep breath. "Okay."

"Like I said, my friend thinks you're a complete asshole and so do I. You shamelessly pretended to be Prince Charming to get into my friend's born-again-virgin pants and then let her get blindsided by your blonde pterodactyl-girlfriend! You think my friend's forgotten what your girlfriend told her about you? About how you hit on some woman at dinner earlier that same night, the minute your girlfriend got up to use the bathroom? About how you lied to your girlfriend and told her you were meeting your sister's boyfriend that night? And let's not forget the lovely things your shrieking blonde pterodactyl of a girlfriend screamed at my friend, too! Nice language. What a classy girl you've got there, Ryan. It was no wonder my friend ran out of there, crying."

"Samantha *cried*?"

"Fuck, yes, she cried. Here she thought she was making this amazing connection with the perfect guy who was looking for something 'real,' and the next thing she knows his girlfriend shows up and starts calling her a 'cunt' in front of the entire freaking bar? And then she finds out you're actually the kind of guy who trades phone numbers with women when you're out on a date with—"

I cut her off. I can't help it. "No, no. That was bullshit. I didn't 'trade phone numbers' with anyone. Please, listen to me—"

But Charlotte doesn't listen to me. Instead, she talks right over me, obviously enraged. "So if you think you can call me after all this time and just expect—" She abruptly pauses. "*Hey.* How the hell are you calling me after all this time? I didn't give you my number."

Shit. Why didn't I anticipate this question from Charlotte? "Um..." I begin.

"How'd you get my number, Ryan?"

Oh, shit. I'm fucked.

Should I tell Charlotte I have a buddy that works for Delta? Or that Samantha gave me Charlotte's number or that... *Shit.* My thoughts are racing. What lie can I tell and get away with it? I gaze down at the koi pond in front of me for a long beat. If I tell Charlotte the truth, she's gonna think I'm a stalker and not let me near her friend. Will she hang up and maybe even call the police? But if I don't tell her the truth, how the hell will I convince her to trust me enough to give me Samantha's phone number?

I exhale a deep, long sigh. I know it in my bones: if I'm gonna have any shot at getting this woman to lead me to Samantha, then I've got to take a leap of faith and lay myself bare to her. And so, that's exactly what I do.

I tell Charlotte the entire story of the past three months, omitting Henn's name and how I hooked up with him in the first place, beginning with the true story of what happened in that restaurant with the blonde and ending with my sudden idea to seek out Charlotte's phone number today.

When I'm finished talking, I wait for Charlotte's reaction, my heart clanging fiercely in my chest, praying from the depths of my soul Charlotte won't freak out and hang up on me.

But there's nothing but silence on the line.

"Hello?" I say, my breathing shallow. "You still there?"

"Yeah," Charlotte replies (thank God). "Sorry. I'm just... Wow. Who is this hacker guy? How'd you find him?"

"He's a friend of a friend. I can't say more than that."

"And you've been looking for my friend all this time—and... holding out for her?"

"Yeah, but it's not quite as crazy as it sounds. I think I've felt the need to take a hiatus from the dating scene, anyway, to lick my wounds from the Bunny Boiler."

"The 'Bunny Boiler'?"

"My ex. The pterodactyl. You know, like in *Fatal Attraction*?"

"I've never seen it."

"Oh. Well, Michael Douglas cheats on his beautiful wife with a closet-psycho who then breaks into his house and boils his daughter's pet bunny."

"Whoa."

"Charlotte, please believe me: I've never done anything this crazy in my life." I run my hand through my hair with one hand and press the phone against my ear with the other. "Honestly, I'm not completely sure why I've been so fixated on this one particular woman when I've got plenty of other options. All I know is I don't want anyone else. I can't stop thinking maybe she's The One." I pause, gathering my thoughts, my heart clanging. "Okay, maybe she's not gonna end up being the woman for me—I'm not so far gone that I don't still realize that's a definite possibility here—but I feel like I owe it to myself to find out, once and for all, so that, either way, I can just move the fuck on. At the very least, I wanna clear my name with Samantha so she knows the stuff I said to her that night wasn't bullshit and that the horrible shit Olivia said about me wasn't true. I'm not a lying, cheating douche. I swear to God, Charlotte. I'm not perfect, but I'm a good guy."

"Why the hell didn't you just tell her all that yourself that night? You should have chased her down. Now, after all this time, it might freak her out to hear from you, to be honest."

"I *did* chase her down that night! Jesus Christ! I was stuck in the bar talking to the pterodactyl for no more than ninety seconds and then I sprinted outside to find you guys, but you were already long gone."

"Oh, crap. That's right. I forgot we took off so fast."

"It was like you vanished into thin air."

"Yeah, an Uber had just pulled up to the bar to let someone out as we were running outside, so we hopped into the backseat."

"Great. The entire universe, including Uber, was conspiring against me that night."

"Or working in my friend's favor. She was crying pretty hard that night, Ryan—and not just over you. Her prior boyfriend did a number on her so I think the whole situation just made her feel really hopeless about men. She kept saying her 'picker' was 'completely defective' and that she was 'gonna become a nun.'"

"Charlotte, I swear to God, I've never felt so excited about a woman as I felt that night. Never. I haven't stopped searching for her ever since."

There's a long beat of silence.

"Charlotte. Please. I'm wrecked. She's Cinderella and I'm holding a glass slipper."

Charlotte lets out an audible exhale. "I wanna help you," she says tentatively. "But the thing is I don't know if Cinderella would want to hear from you again. The one-two punch of Mr.-Soccer-Star-Douche and Ryan-from-the-Pine-Box-Douche hit her pretty freaking hard."

"Mr. *Soccer-Star?*"

"Yeah. Her ex plays for The L.A. Galaxy."

My heart seizes. Holy shit. I already figured Samantha could get any guy she wants, but this revelation has turned my vague conjecture into hard, inescapable truth. "Charlotte, please," I blurt. "You gotta help me. I know you said she hasn't dated in a year, but what if some pro-athlete, alpha-male, rich dude is sitting in first class on whatever flight she's working right now, and he's asking her out to dinner and saying all the right things, and she's finally saying yes to someone besides me for the first time in a year?"

Charlotte snorts. "I guarantee you that's not what's happening at this particular moment."

"You never know. She's not gonna keep saying no to guys forever. God help me if today's the day she meets some smooth-talking tech CEO on one of her flights. Come on, Charlotte. *Please*."

Charlotte sighs. "Okay, I tell you what, Pirate Boy. I won't give you my friend's number—trust me, that would be a cluster fuck of epic proportions for all involved—but I'll give her yours."

"No, no, no. *Please*," I choke out. "I've been sitting around with my thumb up my ass, waiting for a phone call from my hacker-friend for what seems like my whole life. I physically *need* to take control of this situation now."

"Sorry, that's the best I can offer you. I'm still not completely convinced you're not deranged."

"Neither am I," I mumble, and Charlotte laughs. "Well, will you at least tell her the whole story? You know, try to convince her my intentions are sincere?"

"Hell no. That's your crazy-ass story to tell, not mine. I'll give her your number and tell her to call you and then I'm out."

"But she won't call me if you don't butter her up for me, Charlotte."

"Nope. Sorry. I've got no butter for ya, sweetie. I'll give her your number and tell her you're dying for her to call you. And that's it."

I grunt in frustration. "Do you want me to beg you? Because I will. I've never begged a woman in my life, but I'm begging you now, Charlotte McDougal." Even though Charlotte can't see me do it, I sink to my knees on the soft grass in front of the koi pond and tilt my face up to the glorious blue sky. "Please, Charlotte McDougal. *I beg you.* I just got down on my knees for you at the edge of a koi pond. I'm *pleading* with you, Charlotte. *Praying* to the fish gods you'll help me. Oh, look, the koi are praying with me, putting their little fins together."

She laughs. "You're very strange, Ryan. I'm not sure you're helping your cause right now, unless convincing me you're a nut job is part of your strategy?"

"I'm kneeling at the edge of a koi pond."

"Okay, well, that's totally normal. Look, you can pray with your fish-friends all you want, dude, but I'm not giving you my best friend's phone number and I'm not gonna try to convince her of anything, either. She thinks you're a total and complete dick and, hey, for all I know, she's right. So, whatever she decides to do with your phone number, that's up to her."

"And if she doesn't call me? What then?"

"Then I guess you'll just have to gather all your crazy-marbles off the floor, stuff 'em back into your head or feed 'em to the fishies, and move the fuck on."

Chapter 22
Ryan

"... and the great floodgates of the wonder-world swung open."

I barrel into the lobby, my mind reeling from my call with Charlotte. Samantha *might* call me... and she might not? Three months of waiting and searching and obsessing has led to *that*? Fuck my life. And fuck Charlotte.

A smiling woman in a Hawaiian dress places a flower lei over my head while a dude offers a tray of mai tais. I grab two drinks, pound the first one, and scan the spacious lobby of the hotel while sipping the second.

About half our group is still standing in line for check-in while the other half is scattered around, chatting and drinking happy juice. I spot my mom and dad nearby, talking to my uncle, and shuffle my sorry ass toward them, glancing around the breathtaking lobby as I go. Wow, this place is really—

Holy shit.

I choke on my mai tai. There's a woman at the far end of the lobby with her back to me... who... even from this distance... and even from behind... looks *exactly* like... *Samantha.* Well, at least as far as I can remember Samantha after all this time. But, still, holy fucking shit, I'd swear it's her!

For a long beat, I can't move. Have I had a psychotic break? I'd swear on my life that's Samantha's ass. And hair. And skin. And something in the way she's tilting her head as she talks... Could it really be her? She's talking to another woman with a clipboard, and by the way she's gesticulating as she talks... It seems fucking crazy, I know, but there's suddenly no doubt in my mind: *that's Samantha.*

Without consciously intending to do it, I begin loping toward the mystery woman, my heart thudding painfully in my chest. Every cell in my body is vibrating. My skin is electrified. I'm feeling exactly the way I did when I first laid eyes on Samantha at The Pine Box—like my soul is on fire. Shit, even if this woman isn't Samantha, then fuck it, I'm gonna seduce her tonight, regardless, because, glory be, this is the first woman in three fucking months who's managed to make my dick sit up and take notice.

I'm mere yards away from the woman now—close enough to hear her voice.

Oh my God, that voice! "Samantha," I choke out, but she doesn't react. "Samantha?" I shout, this time from two feet behind her. But, still, she doesn't turn around. I lurch around to the front of her... and promptly have a fucking heart attack.

The entire world is buckling and warping around me.

Oh my fucking God.

She's even more beautiful than I remembered her.

I was a fool to think these past three months of monkish-ness have been about anything or anyone other than her. She's the woman of my dreams. *I want her.*

"Samantha!"

Chapter 23
Ryan

"Ryan?" Samantha gasps, looking as shocked as I feel. "How...?"

"I can't believe it," I say, my heart leaping. "How the hell are you here?" I glance down and notice the clipboard in Samantha's hand—and suddenly, the fruitlessness of the past three months makes perfect sense to me. "You *work* here? Oh my God, you quit Delta and now you work at this resort?"

Samantha looks absolutely stricken. Panicked, I'd even say. She turns to the woman standing next to her. "Could you excuse us for a moment, Marnie?"

The woman nods and leaves.

Samantha trains her panicked gaze on me. "I don't understand how you're here."

I can't wipe the smile off my face. "It's fate. My sister's getting married here. I'll be at this hotel all week for her—"

"Ryan!" my mother's voice sings out behind my shoulder.

I glance to my right to find my mother gliding toward me, a key-card in her hand and a huge smile on her lovely face. "I got your room key, Rummy-o," Mom says gaily. "Your dad's over there talking to Uncle Mikey about golf so I—" Her eyes land on Samantha and she squeals with glee and throws her arms around her—and, for the second time in thirty seconds, the world is warping and buckling around me.

My mother knows Samantha?

"It's so good to see you, honey!" Mom says, squeezing Samantha tightly.

I've never been so confused in my entire life. How the fuck does my mom know Samantha?

"Hello, Mrs. Morgan," Samantha says, returning Mom's hug as I stand aside, my mouth agape and my mind completely blown.

"Momma Lou, remember?" Mom says, wagging her finger playfully at Samantha. "We had a deal, remember?"

Samantha's eyes flicker to me briefly and then back to my mother. "Yes, of course," she says, looking remarkably like a caged animal. "Momma Lou."

Mom slides her arm around my waist, nuzzles into my side, and gives me a squeeze. "I'm so glad you've finally met my wonderful son I was telling you about."

Samantha's eyes flicker nervously between me and my mother. "No, not yet. He just now walked over to introduce himself."

Mom's eyes light up. "You mean to tell me Ryan saw you across this crowded lobby and headed straight for you? Ha! Do I know my son or what?" She giggles. "This is the son I told you about at the party—the one I was sure would want to meet you." Mom looks at me and beams a massive smile at me. "So you saw this beautiful woman and headed straight for her, huh?"

Samantha's cheeks flush.

"Well, for goodness sakes, let me introduce you," Mom says. She turns to Samantha, smiling. "Tessa, this my son, Ryan."

Tessa? Did my mom just call Samantha "Tessa"?

Mom continues, "Ryan's a very successful commercial real estate broker in Seattle and, like I told you at the party, he's a truly wonderful person—and I'm not just saying that because he's my son. He's one of those people everyone always falls in love with." She graces me with a lovely smile. "And, Ryan, sweetheart, this is my lovely friend, Tessa. She's—"

Loud applause and raucous cheers erupt in the crowd behind us, and all three of us turn toward the source of the hoopla to find Josh standing on a bench, commanding the crowd's attention with a drink in his hand. "Aloooha, Morgans!" he booms, holding up his drink with a huge smile on his face.

"Aloha!" everyone shouts in reply, raising their drinks.

Josh says a whole bunch of stuff I can barely process, most of it expressing his elation to be joining "the coolest family in the world," and then he says with great flourish: "So, without further ado, let's get The Mighty T-Rod up here to give you a brief overview of the week so we can get this party started!"

I glance around the room, curious to finally lay eyes on this purportedly "gorgeous" personal assistant I keep hearing about, and much to my complete and utter shock, none other than Samantha begins gliding across the room toward Josh.

Holy fuck. My jaw just clanked onto the floor. Samantha is... *T-Rod?*

Samantha steps up onto the bench next to Josh and flashes the crowd an incredibly fake smile. "Hi, everyone," she says, her voice tight. She waves and raises a drink, but her eyes are blazing with obvious distress.

"Hi, T-Rod!" everyone booms back to her. Well, everyone except me, of course. I can't speak. Or move. Or breathe. Or pick my jaw up off the floor. In fact, I can't even muster enough brain-power to blink my eyes.

Samantha or T-Rod or *Tessa...* or whatever the fuck her name is... proceeds to babble about I-have-no-fucking-idea-what. I think she's talking about the itinerary for the coming week? But... I'm... not... sure. *Mind. Fuck. Mind. Fuck. Mind. Fuck.* Samantha is T-Rod? Josh's personal assistant? Henn hacked into *nine* motherfucking airline databases to find a woman who's Josh's fucking personal assistant? *Mind. Fuck. Mind. Fuck. Mind. Fuck.* Why the fuck was she wearing a flight attendant uniform that night? Is she a sociopath? Did she think she was Leonardo Fucking DiCaprio in *Catch Me If You Can*?

I clench my jaw.

No wonder Charlotte wouldn't give me Samantha's phone number. She had to call her sociopathic friend in advance and make sure she got her story straight before contacting me.

Rage floods me. My blood flash-boils. How many other guys has this woman played the same trick on? Is this how she keeps herself amused while sitting around waiting for her "hot boss" to finally make his move?

Oh my God.

My head snaps up and my eyes lock onto Josh's smiling face.

Josh... is... Samantha's... boss.

Holy fuck.

What the fuck did Samantha say about her boss? *I've always had a little crush on him,* she said. *I kept hoping he'd make a move on me, but he never did.* Heat flashes throughout my body like an electric current.

Samantha wants to fuck Josh—my sister's soon-to-be husband.

I look at Josh again, my blood thumping in my ears. And then at Samantha. And then at my sister. And, suddenly, it's taking every shred of self-control in my body not to lurch over to that bench, grab Samantha by the arm, and physically drag her away from my poor, oblivious, pregnant sister.

Kat.

My sister's standing adjacent to the bench, right next to the man she loves and his ever-devoted personal assistant, looking up at both of them adoringly, her palms resting on her baby bump, a huge, clueless smile on her face. Has my sister unwittingly opened her heart to a woman who might be some sort of sociopath who's gunning for Josh?

My eyes train on Josh again for a long beat. I scrutinize him with eagle eyes. There's no doubt in my mind he's currently head over heels in love with my sister. But what's gonna happen the first time Josh and Kat get into a knock-down-drag-out fight (which, let's face it, is inevitable at some point when it comes to my mercurial sister)? Is Josh gonna turn to his loyal personal assistant for some much-needed comfort after Kat's lost her mind and said God-knows-what in the heat of the moment? Yeah, I know Josh seems like a great guy, the best guy in the world, actually—and, man, he sure seems to have endless patience with my crazy-ass sister—but great and patient men stumble all the time, don't they, when the right opportunity presents itself? Especially when that "right opportunity" is a sexy-as-fuck Argentinian-sociopath who's bided her time for years, waiting for the perfect moment to strike.

My eyes flicker to Samantha and an overwhelming cocktail of adrenaline and rage and rejection courses through me. Who the fuck is this woman? I thought she was the real deal. "She doesn't have a bullshit-bone in her body" is what I said about her to the Faraday brothers, and now I discover she lied to me about something as simple as her fucking name and occupation? What the hell else did she lie about?

"So you'll definitely want to download the app we created..." Samantha is saying to the crowd, holding up her iPad by way of demonstration. "That way, you can check into whatever tour or activity we've got set up and—"

"Excuse me?" I bellow across the lobby, my arm shooting up rigidly over my head.

Everyone in the crowd turns to look at me.

"Sorry, to interrupt," I say, trying to keep my voice from sounding like a hitman's. "But I don't think I caught your name?"

Samantha's cheeks flush. She smashes her lips together.

"She's the Mighty T-Rod!" Josh shouts, and everyone laughs.

Samantha's blazing eyes are fixed on mine. "Theresa," she replies softly.

"I'm sorry, what was that?" I ask, putting my palm to my ear. "Did you say—"

"*Theresa*," she barks, cutting me off. She grits her teeth. "But feel free to call me T-Rod."

"Ah, *Theresa*," I say, my eyes trained on hers, every muscle in my body tensed. "Thanks for repeating that for me. I thought you said something else entirely. My bad." I smirk. "I certainly wouldn't wanna call you by the wrong name all week, would I?"

Samantha shoots me a smile that doesn't reach her eyes and turns her attention back to the crowd. "So, like I was saying, if you have any trouble downloading the app—"

"And what's your last name, *Theresa*?" I bellow.

"*Ryan*," Kat snaps at me. "What the heck?"

Samantha ignores my sister's chastisement. "Rodriguez," she says, her voice steely, her eyes flickering with homicidal rage. "My name is Theresa Rodriguez. *T-Rod*. And you're Ryan Morgan, right?"

"Yep. That's what they call me. I've never introduced myself by any other name in my life, so, yep, that must be my name."

She's glaring at me, her nostrils flaring... and, strangely, I must admit, something in the way she's looking at me is making my cock tingle like a motherfucker.

"Hey," I say. "I just got the *T-Rod* thing. It's like A-Rod, huh? Cool."

"Alex Rodriguez *wishes* he were half the MVP Theresa Rodriguez is," Josh says, and everyone chuckles.

"But isn't there yet *another* name you go by, Theresa-T-Rod?" I ask innocently. "I'm sure I've heard you introduced by yet *another* name at some point. You're the girl with infinite names."

"Tessa," my sister shouts. "But you've gotta earn the right to call her that, Rum Cake." She smiles at Samantha. "Has my brother earned the right to call you Tessa yet, honey?"

"Nope," Samantha says quickly, and everyone laughs.

Kat smiles at me. "Patience, Rum Cake." She winks. "Charm her and you never know what might happen."

Everyone laughs again.

Samantha's eye twitches. "Any more questions, Ryan?"

"Yeah, one more, actually." Everyone turns to look at me, huge smiles on their faces. Obviously, everyone's enjoying this unexpected game of tennis. "What exactly is your occupation, *T-Rod*? Sorry, I didn't catch that. I could have sworn you said you were a—"

"Oh, for the love of God!" Kat bellows. "Come on, Captain! Yes, we can all see T-Rod's gorgeous, but you're just gonna have to wait 'til the opening party later tonight to hit on her."

Everyone laughs raucously and shouts all sorts of stupid things about poor T-Rod needing a bodyguard and me being the biggest ladies' man in the entire family and she'd better watch out and blah, blah, blah. (If ever there was a moment when I'd strongly prefer to belong to a normal family, now would be it.) And the whole time, I can't take my eyes off Samantha. It makes no sense, since she's a fucking sociopath and a liar and a mind-fucker of epic proportions, but, hot fucking damn, the more I stare at her across the lobby, at the way she's blushing and fidgeting and basically looking like a woman walking the plank on a pirate ship, I can't stop wanting to wrap her in my arms and tell her it's gonna be all right. And then strangle her. And then fuck her 'til she screams for mercy.

Fuck!

Samantha's been looking down at her toes for a long beat, and when she finally looks back up, her eyes are hard and decidedly unfriendly... and my cock lurches at the sight of her.

"No, it's fine, everyone," T-Rod says evenly, her dark eyes locked with mine. "I don't think I've explicitly told you all what I do yet." She smiles, but her eyes are filled with nothing but murderous rage. "I'm Josh's personal assistant. I've worked for him for six years—I started with him straight out of college and he's like a brother to me—so I couldn't be more thrilled for him to marry someone as wonderful as Kat."

The entire crowd cheers and raises their drinks—and, all the while, Samantha's flashing me barely disguised daggers of hate. "Does that answer your question, *Ryan*?"

I nod slowly and flash her a snarling smile. "Why, yes, it does. Thanks so much."

Samantha takes a huge breath, looks at the crowd, and flashes yet another fake smile. "*Great.* So, unless anyone else has any further questions, I'll just direct you to my phone number at the top of the itinerary."

I roll my eyes to myself. *Now* Samantha's giving me her phone number? Fuck my life.

Samantha-T-Rod-Tessa continues. "So if there's *anything* you need this week, please find me or call me and—"

"Aw, hell no," Josh bellows, cutting her off. "Starting tonight, T-Rod's a guest this week, just like everyone else. If you guys need anything, you should call... T-Rod, who should they call?"

"Marnie or Laila." She points out two women in the crowd, and both of them wave and confirm they're here to fulfill our every wish, need, and desire all week long and that T-Rod is most definitely one of the guests.

"Okay, everyone, you got that?" Josh says. He puts his arm around Samantha's shoulders. "T-Rod's promised Kat and me she's gonna let loose and have fun and drink far too many mai tais tonight, so I hope I can count on all of you Morgans to help me hold T-Rod's feet to the fire on all her promises."

There are enthusiastic shouts from Morgans far and wide, most of them male, all of them pledging to personally shove T-Rod down a greased chute toward debauchery, but no one in the crowd is more enthusiastic in his pledge to ruin T-Rod's good name (whatever the fuck it is) than my little-brother-the-manwhoring-stripper. I can't hear every word Keane's raucously shouting across the lobby toward the obvious object of his dick's desire, but I can most certainly make out the word "*pleasure*" and the wolfish grin on his Captain-America face.

Motherfucker.

Samantha or T-Rod or Tessa (or whatever the fuck her name is) gets down from the bench and is immediately swarmed by Kat and my mom and several other enthusiastic Morgans, so I march straight across the room to my horny-as-fuck little brother, and, without warning, grip his neck from behind, yank him forcibly back, and whisper hoarsely into his ear through clenched teeth: "Don't even think about it, Peen Star—she's off-limits, motherfucker. *She's mine.*"

Chapter 24
Ryan

Keane wrestles free from my grasp and stumbles forward, rubbing the back of his neck where I gripped it like a vise. "Jesus, Dr. Spock. Take a chill pill, brah." He scowls and rubs his neck. "*Ow.*"

In reply, I whack Keane across the top of his head five or six times in rapid succession like a rogue ceiling fan, and he takes cover under his muscled forearms, laughing his ass off. "Jesus, Rum Jungle. Did you take a crazy-pill today? Calm the fuck down, Fuck-i-nator."

But I'm not done. I grab a fistful of Keane's T-shirt and lean into his face, the vein in my neck bulging, my teeth bared. "I saw the way you were looking at her, fuckwit. Stuff your eyes back into your head and your pecker into your pants and back the fuck off, *Ball Peen Hammer.*"

"I was just appreciating the girl's bountiful assets, which any man can plainly observe, thanks to that lovely sundress she's wearing. You don't have to—"

Without warning, I grab a fistful of Keane's dirty blonde hair and forcefully yank his ear to my lips. "She's off-limits, fuckface. This is your last warning."

Keane slaps my arm and pushes my chest and breaks free of my grasp, his face bright red and contorted in shock. "Jesus, Ry. Chill the fuck out. *Seriously.*" He pulls down his T-shirt and smooths his tousled hair. "I got it, Captain. The girl's off-limits. *No problemo, señor.*"

I nod definitively.

Keane flashes a dimpled smile. "But, hey, *just out of curiosity,* what's the reason for the off-limits designation? Is it just 'cause she's Josh's assistant? 'Cause if that's the snag, that certainly doesn't—"

127

I violently rip the flower lei off Keane's neck, open my hand in front of his nose, and let the flower petals in my grasp float slowly to the ground. "It's quite simple, Peeno Noir," I say. "The girl's off-limits 'cause I said so."

Keane laughs. "Jeez, so much for Rum Cake's 'aloha spirit,' huh?"

"I'm not joking, Peen. She's mine. No room for debate. Roger?"

"Okay, okay. Rabbit." He pokes my shoulder. "But just tell me this: have you already dabbled with this one or did you just now see her across a crowded room and get struck by some kind of Zander-Shaw-style lightning bolt?"

I glance across the lobby at her, my jaw muscles pulsing. She's chatting with my cousin Julie and Julie's new husband (and, holy fuck, does Samantha look un-fucking-believable in that sundress). "I haven't dabbled yet," I reply, and decide to leave it at that.

Keane shrugs. "Well, gosh, Captain, if that's the case, then there's really no need for an off-limits designation. Sure, we've never shared an igloo yet, but that doesn't—"

I whack Keane across the top of his head again, this time much harder than before, barely suppressing my urge to punch him in his pretty teeth, and he covers his head and yelps.

"I'm joking!" Keane shouts, laughing. "Dude, get a sense of humor. It was a *joke*."

"I have no sense of humor about this one, Keane."

"Obviously. *Jeez*." Keane rubs the side of his head. "Damn, that actually hurt that last time." He sighs. "Look, gimme some credit, okay? First off, you know I don't do igloos." He shudders. "*Gross*. And, second off, I'm dumb but not stupid. You've obviously been struck by some kind of lightning bolt here, and I'd never in a million years try to get in the middle of that. I'm a dick, not an asshole."

I take a deep breath and try to loosen my fists. "Thanks. Sorry I hit you so hard."

"No problem. Just lay off the hair next time, would you?" He shakes his head like he's in a shampoo commercial. "It's my crowning glory."

I violently muss his hair and slap his cheek and he leaps away from me, laughing.

"Stop it! Jesus. What's gotten into you? I've never seen you so violent in all my twenty-two years, and I'm including the time you came at me with a chainsaw."

"I didn't come at you with a chainsaw, dumbfuck—it was a *Flowbee*."

"Well, whatever. It was a loud, terrifying appliance aimed at my head. Traumatic, by any measure."

I laugh, despite myself. Fucking Peen. "Just stay away from her, little brother, or I'll come at you with a chainsaw for real."

"I already said I'd lay off, fucker. Seriously, take a Valium or something. Your crazy's hanging out, brah." He winks, flips me off, and strides toward Zander, who's currently standing twenty yards away talking to Dax and Dax's two best friends and bandmates, Colin and Fish. "Come on, boys!" Keane hollers, hoisting the remnants of his broken flower lei into the air. "I gotta get myself lei'd again!"

I spot Samantha in a corner, chatting with that same woman with the clipboard, and stride across the room toward her, my heart racing and my dick tingling.

When I reach her, I wordlessly grip her forearm and lean into her ear, making sure not to let my hard-on graze her hip. "Hey, Argentina," I whisper hoarsely into her ear, my nose nuzzling into her hair. I inhale her scent and my hard-on turns to steel. "My room in ten, you little sociopath—and don't be fucking late."

Chapter 25
Tessa

"Asshole!" I breathe to myself as I walk. I'm marching along a lovely winding pathway lined with hibiscus and plumeria trees, heading toward Ryan's room on the far side of the resort, homicidal rage coursing through my veins. "Bastard!"

My phone buzzes with an incoming text and I look at it. It's Marnie, my right-hand woman for this week, texting with an update on some guests' arrivals.

I tap out a quick reply: "Something's come up. Please handle the next few arrivals for me. Thanks."

I'm about to shove my phone into my bag when I notice a text from Charlotte from about a half-hour ago: "Hi, Crazy Girl. I know you're super busy today, but call me when you can. You won't believe who just called me out of the blue! OMFG!"

I smile to myself. Charlotte's love life is never dull, that's for sure. I shove my phone into my bag. I'm sure Charlotte's got a fabulous story to tell me, as usual, but I don't have time to hear it at the moment. Right now, I've got to convince an asshole-player-douche not to torpedo my entire life by telling Josh and Kat the stupid thing I admitted to him three months ago at The Pine Box. *Motherfucker*!

And, by the way, why the hell is Ryan so enraged about the "Samantha" thing? Okay, okay, I told him a fake name and occupation, but it was a victimless crime, dude! It's not like I went on and on about my "glamorous career" throughout our conversation. To the contrary, I didn't talk about my supposed profession even once! It's not like I promised him some sort of friends-and-family-discount on flights! So, what's his freaking deal? Jeez, the way Ryan looked at

130

me in the lobby, I swear he wanted to strangle me with his bare hands. Or screw me. Or, heck, maybe I was just projecting my own impulses onto him, because, hot damn, that's exactly what I wanted to do: rip his clothes off and screw him like an animal and then strangle him with my bare hands. Not normal.

Okay, get a grip, Tessa. Focus on the task at hand. Ignore the fact that your crotch is currently swollen and throbbing. Your only tasks right now are twofold: one, to immediately stop wanting to fuck a lying scumbag (because that's not normal!), and, two, to convince said lying scumbag to keep his big mouth shut about the stupid little crush you admitted to him.

I reach Ryan's door.

I'll just remain calm and explain things to him, that's all. I'll stay cool and calm and convince him there's no reason whatsoever to tell Kat or Josh or anyone else a word of what I said. In fact, I know! I'll threaten him that if he outs me, I'll tell every single member of his family he's a lying, cheating scumbag who collects phone numbers and asks women on dinner-dates behind his girlfriend's back.

Yes. So that's the plan, then: Remain calm, cool, and rational; and, as necessary, fight fire with fire.

I take a deep breath, shift my weight in a vain attempt to relieve the incessant pulsing in my crotch, and rap twice on the sexy bastard's door.

Chapter 26
Tessa

The door to Ryan's room opens and there he is, the lying bastard himself, a panty-melting vision of blazing blue eyes, taut muscles, and ink.

Ryan leans forward slightly in the doorframe and the smell of his cologne fills the air between us. "Hello, *T-Rod*," he says caustically.

I inhale deeply, titillated by his delicious scent. "Hello, Kat's brother," I say, matching his caustic tone. Holy hot damn, I've never in my life experienced this bizarre cocktail of hatred and arousal, all at once.

Ryan's gaze fixes onto my heaving chest for a long beat and then scorches a path slowly up to my face. "Gosh, *T-Rod*," he says, his eyes blazing. "Thanks for coming to my room for a little chat." He smiles like an executioner unsheathing his sword. "I know you must be incredibly busy these days, planning... and plotting... to *fuck... your... boss.*"

My heart stops. *Oh, no he didn't.*

Ryan continues breezily: "So have you figured out your plan of attack for fucking my sister's fiancé yet? Are you maybe gonna wait 'til Josh is shitfaced drunk this week and offer him a little quickie in the final hours before he says 'I do'?"

I clench my fists.

"Or maybe you're gonna swoop in right after my sister's given birth to Josh's baby girl and—"

I can't listen to another disgusting word. In a fit of rage, I lunge at him, my fists raised, my heart racing, my only intention to make him shut the hell up through any means necessary, but he's much too strong and quick on his feet to let an inexperienced ass-kicker like me

132

get the best of him. In a flash of heat and blazing blue eyes and clenched teeth, the bastard's got both my wrists firmly in his grasp and he's pulling my screeching body into his room and kicking the door closed behind us.

"Asshole!" I yell, struggling to free myself from his iron clutches.

"Sociopath," he spits back.

In one fluid motion, he shoves my back against a nearby wall, pins my arms above my head, and presses himself against me, and when I feel the unmistakable sensation of his steely hard-on jutting against my crotch (right against my clit, as a matter of fact), I lose all resolve to resist him. I grind myself into the hard bulge in his pants and strain my face up to kiss him—and the second my lips make the barest of contact with his, he groans loudly, releases my arms, grabs my face, and presses his lips against mine like a man possessed.

When Ryan's tongue slides into my mouth, my entire body jolts like I've just stuck my finger into a light socket. I throw my arms around his neck and press my body against his and let his tongue and lips lead mine in what's truly the most electrifying kiss of my entire life. Or, hell, maybe it's just been so damned long since I've felt this particular sensation, I'm easily impressed. But, either way, oh my God, in this moment, I'd swear on a stack of bibles this is the most passionate kiss of my life! If I didn't know any better, I'd swear this man was being reunited with his long-lost love—either that or he's just escaped from a ten-year prison stint and I'm his first glorious taste of freedom.

"Samantha," Ryan breathes against my lips, and every cell in my body explodes with arousal at the sheer perversity of him calling me by that name. Damn, that's hot. And liberating as hell. He's kissing Samantha the Randy Flight Attendant and not Tessa Rodriguez? Fine by me. Because guess what, fuckwad? I'm not kissing you, either—I'm kissing the distant memory of my perfect Prince Charming—the sexy, articulate, *honest* guy I initially *thought* I'd met at The Pine Box.

Unexpectedly, Ryan pulls out of our kiss and grabs ahold of my face, his features intense. "Leave now if you still need to 'take things slow,'" he says, his eyes wild. "I know I said I could do that, but I can't—not anymore. One more taste of you and—"

I press myself forcefully into his hard-on, shutting him up. "Do you have protection?" I grit out.

He nods furiously.

"Then, let's use it."

"Thank you, lord."

In a matter of seconds, he's got us both stripped down to our underwear and I'm ogling his jaw-dropping muscles and tattoos and—oh my God!—his two pierced nipples! Holy hell, I think I'm about to faint from sheer arousal at the mere sight of him! But my stunned ogling is short-lived because, in seconds, we're absolutely mauling each other against the wall, our breathing hot and urgent, his murmurs of "Oh my God" and "You're so fucking gorgeous" and "I've waited so fucking long" reverberating in my ear.

He removes my bra with dire urgency and the instant my breasts tumble out of their bondage, he leans down and sucks greedily on my left nipple, whispering about how my breasts are "perfect" and how he's "waited his entire life" for this moment.

I run my fingers furiously through his hair and claw at his broad shoulders and, finally, when I can't contain my fervor any longer, I grip his hair and pull his face off my nipple and lean down and return the favor, swirling one of his unbelievably hot nipple piercings in my mouth. Oh, God, this is heaven on earth. Why the hell did I think I had to be in a committed relationship to do this with a man? I was a freaking fool.

Ryan slams me against the wall again and yanks my undies to the floor, and the next thing I know, he's kneeling before me, his large hands gripping my ass like it's a life preserver thrown to a drowning man, his warm, wet mouth voraciously consuming my throbbing clit.

Sweet Mary and Joseph. I'm rapidly coming undone.

A weird sound escapes my throat—good lord, I'm cooing like a mutant dove possessed by the devil.

Ryan moans from between my legs. "Come for me, *mind-fucker*," he whispers. "Come on, baby."

He slides his fingers deep inside me while his tongue continues its glorious assault on my clit, and my body clenches sharply, just once, around his fingers.

"That's it, mind-fucker," he says. "Come on, baby. Oh, God, I'm so fucking turned on." He increases the intensity of his fingers' and tongue's movement, and, suddenly, it's like he's turned up the flames on my gas grill.

I grip Ryan's hair violently and smash my crotch into his hungry mouth, all manner of crazy-ass sounds and exclamations and expletives spewing from my mouth.

"That's it, sociopath," he murmurs. "Oh, God, you taste good."

My skin pricks.

My toes curl.

Heat floods my crotch.

My abdomen burns.

And that's it.

A tsunami of pleasure rips through me, a torrent of deliciousness that makes every freaking muscle enveloping Ryan's hand wrench and twist and clench.

I throw my head back into the wall, completely enraptured—oh, thank you, Jesus! After a full year without this exquisite sensation, I'm suddenly certain I can't go another day without it, ever again.

In a flash, Ryan's lips are on mine and we're groping and gasping and kissing like our lives depend on it. I reach into his briefs, desperate to stroke him, and when I grip his massive erection, much to my shock, my fingers meet with an unexpected sensation: *a tiny loop of metal at the base of his dick.*

My hand freezes.

"I'm pierced," he whispers hoarsely. He peels off his briefs and tosses them onto the floor and I'm treated to the vision of Ryan Morgan in all his naked glory: insane muscles, sexy tattoos, pierced nipples (oh my God!), and an exceptionally large dick that's... yup... *pierced at the spot where his penis meets his torso.*

I stare at Ryan's pierced hard-on for a very long beat, my heart and clit pounding with equal force. *Wow.* His piercing is a thin metal ring about the size of a quarter with a small metal ball at its center arc. Fascinating. I've never seen a dick piercing before, actually, and have never had any particular curiosity to do so. But, now that I'm seeing Ryan's, I must admit, it's hella sexy. He's a work of art, from head to toe—and from arms and chest to nipple to dick. I let out a shaky breath, blood flooding my crotch. "Did that hurt?" I ask.

Ryan's practically gasping for air. "When I got it? No, not too bad. And any pain was well worth it."

"Because it heightens your pleasure?"

He smiles like a shark. "No, sweetheart. Because it's gonna heighten yours." With that, he grabs his pants off the floor, fishes into his pocket, and pulls out a foil packet—and, ten seconds later, he's looking up from his condom-covered erection, a look of white-hot desire on his face. "I've waited so long to get inside you."

I make a face like he's full of shit. "Yeah, I'm sure the ten minutes it took for me to walk from the lobby to your room was excruciating for you."

His eyes darken. "You have no idea what you're talking about." Without warning, he turns me around, presses me into the wall, and grips my hair, his body hulking over my backside.

I gasp, utterly shocked at my unexpectedly vulnerable position—and how much I like it.

He leans into my ear and whispers, "You're a mind-fucker. You know that?"

Maybe I should be scared right now at his flash of rage toward me, but I'm not at all: the only thing I'm feeling right now is excitement... and a sudden desire to twist the knife. "Little white lies," I grit out, straining against his grip on my hair. "It was a victimless crime, asshole. At least I'm not a lying, cheating sack of shit like you."

He grips my ass and leans into my ear and I feel his erection poking my ass. "You have no fucking idea what you're talking about, you fucking sociopath." He slides his hand between my legs and begins caressing me and my body seizes with pleasure. "Were you even gonna show up for dinner the next night?" he whispers. "Or was standing me up part of the fun?"

I open my mouth to reply, but a groan comes out instead. Oh, man, I don't know what he's doing down there between my legs—nobody's ever touched me quite like this before—but, damn, it feels amazing. "Fuck you," I whisper. "If anyone's a sociopath, it's you, fuckboy." Oh, God, his hand between my legs is magical. And I must admit I'm digging this hatred-thing we've got going on right now. It's sick as fuck—but damn near the sexiest thing I've ever experienced in my life.

"Did you like mind-fucking me, baby?" he whispers into my ear.

His hand between my legs is absolutely owning me while his other hand grips my hair firmly and his dick presses ferociously into my ass.

"I loved it," I reply.

Without warning, he growls like a grizzly bear and spanks my ass— and, much to my shock, my clit and everything attached to it spasms violently in response. I groan loudly, my arousal spiking like crazy.

"Oh, you like being spanked, mind-fucker? Shocker," he growls, just before spanking me again.

I open my mouth to chastise him—to tell him he's got no right to smack my ass like that and that it's demeaning and kinda hurts, but the words are halted when, much to my utter shock and relief and pleasure and absolute gratitude, I'm suddenly (and quite involuntarily) making that demon-possessed-pigeon sound again, only, this time, ten times louder than before. One more spank and my body releases with the best orgasm of my life, by far, not even a contest. My insides are warping, wrenching, buckling from a place so deep inside me, I didn't even know it existed before this moment.

In a frenzy of heat, he enters me from behind, still yanking my hair mercilessly, and begins riding me 'til I'm moaning and growling and begging him not to stop.

"Say my name, sociopath," he commands, and I do. Oh, God, yes, I do. In this moment, I'd do anything this man demanded of me—literally, anything—if only he'd promise to never, ever stop fucking me like this.

I come. Again. It's impossible, but true.

My knees are wobbling.

I'm gasping for air.

But he's not done with me yet.

He spins me around to face him, shoves my sweaty back roughly against the wall, and, thank the lord, enters me again, all the effing way.

"Samantha," he chokes out as his hard-on nails me against the wall. "I've waited so long."

I throw my arms around his neck and my thighs around his waist and, in response, he grabs my ass and picks me up and bangs me into the wall, kissing me voraciously as he fucks me, impaling me ferociously like he's trying to pin me to the wall like a grocery list on a bulletin board.

"What the fuck are you doing to me?" he breathes, his thrusts beastly.

I cry out, his piercing driving me absolutely wild in this new position. Oh, for the love of all things holy, that little metal ball banging against my clit feels so effing good, it should be illegal. Oh, Jesus, I've never felt anything quite like this. It's absolutely tormenting me. I feel like a wild animal, completely out of control. Why the hell have I spent my entire life thinking the pinnacle of sexual satisfaction can only happen between soulmates? Ha! Clearly, that's not the case.

"You like that, baby?" Ryan growls into my ear.

I babble something completely incoherent in reply (something that involves calling him a "fuckwad," I think) and he smashes his lips into mine and grabs my hair, his shaft pumping deliciously in and out of me, that little metal ball sending me into pure ecstasy. Oh my effing God. I'm nonverbal. Utterly, savagely, completely enraptured. I swear, if this asshole asked me to marry him right now, I'd say "hell yes," if only he'd promise to fuck me exactly like this twice a day, every day, for the rest of my life.

"New position," he whispers. "You need a new position to get you there again."

I beg to differ, but my opinion apparently doesn't matter at the moment.

Ryan quickly guides my slack body onto the floor, his eyes burning and his brow beaded with sweat, hikes my thighs up around his shoulders, and furiously mounts me. And, glory be, the minute he starts grinding his hips in a way that makes that little metal ball hit my clit with deadly precision, I come underneath him, convulsing and growling like a grizzly bear possessed.

"Samantha," he whispers into my ear again, the passion and intensity in his voice heart-stopping. Good lord, when he says my fake name, why does it sound like he's saying a sacred prayer? "*Samantha.* Oh, God, baby, I'm gonna come. Oh, fuck. *Samantha.*"

He jerks and shudders and groans loudly, clearly experiencing one hell of a release, and I wrap my thighs around him and grab his ass and kiss his mouth and, basically, feel like I'm being infused with a very illegal drug.

When Ryan's body finally stops bucking and quaking, he kisses my cheek and rolls off me onto his back, and for a long moment, we lie silently on the floor like two sweaty sardines in a can, our chests heaving violently with our effort.

"Holy fuck," Ryan finally murmurs after a long moment. "Samantha the Randy Flight Attendant is hot as fuck."

I can't help but laugh. "And Kat's brother is a fucking sex god."

Ryan's breathing is ragged. "You ever come that hard before, mind-fucker?"

"No, asshole, I haven't, as a matter of fact. Not even close."

Ryan exhales a long breath. "Yeah, me, either. Not by a long shot. Holy shit, that was epic. I actually thought I was gonna die."

I can't believe my ears. Ryan's never come that hard before? Not 'by a long shot'? How is that possible? I'd have thought this manwhore would have made a career out of coming exactly that hard with all his many conquests. I mean, come on, this is the guy who traded numbers with some woman in a restaurant the minute his girlfriend got up to use the restroom, and then went to a bar that same night to do it again, so I can only imagine how many partners this fucker has in any given week. Plus, come on, the guy's got a piercing at the base of his dick designed for nothing but giving women orgasms. Clearly, Ryan Morgan's a fuck machine.

Ryan pulls the condom off his dick, ties a knot at its top, and lets out a long, satisfied sigh. "And that's what's known as 'fulfilling my master plan,' baby."

Chapter 27
Ryan

"God, you're an asshole," Samantha (or T-Rod or Tessa or whatever-the-fuck-her-name-is) says through clenched teeth, abruptly sitting up.

I laugh. "It was a *joke*."

She glares at me.

"You sincerely think fucking you *here,* in Hawaii, in the hotel where my sister's getting married—*after* finding out you Leonardo-DiCaprio'd me—was all precisely according to the 'master plan' I brilliantly hatched three months ago at The Pine Box?"

She can't keep from smiling.

"Sweetheart," I say, "if this crazy-as-fuck shit show is how I *intended* to execute my 'master plan' to bone the fuck outta ya, then I really should be using my incredible powers at commanding the universe for something a bit more high-minded than getting laid. You know, like brokering world peace or manipulating the stock market?"

Samantha-T-Rod-Tessa makes an adorable face. "Actually, you didn't execute your master plan," she sniffs. "Not as stated, anyway."

"Excuse me? Are you experiencing pleasure-induced amnesia? I just made you come, like, four times."

She smirks. "Yes, but you said your master plan was to 'get me into your bed.'" She motions to the neatly made, fluffy white bed across the room. "If you're gonna be so cocky as to call your shot, you'd better sink your damned shot, as called."

We both laugh.

Damn. For the past three months, I've been so busy watching that damned Enrique Iglesias video and thinking about how sexy Samantha is, I'd forgotten how funny she is, too. "Fair enough," I say. "I'll be sure to sink my shot exactly as called next time, Argentina."

"There won't be a next time, Romeo," she says. "This was a one-time lapse in judgment that, as of this moment, never happened."

I pick up the semen-filled condom-balloon next to me and hold it up. "Pretty sure it happened."

She shrugs. "I have no memory of how that sperm got inside that condom. In fact, who are you? Have we met? And why is my crotch throbbing?"

"Why bother with post-coitus bullshit? We both know what we just did rocked both our worlds and we can't wait to do it again. Why waste valuable time denying that when we should be talking about where round two's gonna happen—my room or yours?"

"Sorry, Colby. I have no idea what you're talking about. Oh, wait. I'm sorry. You're *Keane*. Damn you Morgan brothers, you all look the same to me."

"Could we please skip the bullshit? Thanks."

"Oh, you wanna skip the bullshit *now*? Well, guess what? I would have liked to skip the bullshit three months ago when your girlfriend blasted into the bar and called me a 'cunt.'"

"Here we go. Olivia wasn't my girlfriend by then. I'd already broken up with her earlier that day. And if we're gonna talk about that night in the bar, then let's back up a wee bit and start the discussion with, 'What the fuck were you doing wearing a fucking flight attendant uniform, Leonardo DiCaprio?'"

"It was a victimless crime, you big cry-baby," she says, but before I can reply, her phone pings loudly in her bag a few feet away on the floor and she grabs it. "Shit," she blurts, looking at her phone. She hurriedly stands and grabs her underpants and bra off the floor. "Fuck!"

"What's wrong?"

"You mean besides the fact that I just slept with a cheating, lying manwhore without an ounce of integrity in his entire, tattooed, pierced, perfect body?"

"Yeah, besides that."

"You mean besides the fact that I'm trapped on an island for a full week with said manwhore *and* will likely see him at least once a year for the rest of my life at birthday parties for Gracie Louise?"

"Yeah, besides that stuff, too."

She finishes clasping her bra and bends down to gather her sundress off the floor. "The travel agent just texted me. There's some sort of glitch with the airport transportation for Josh's fraternity brothers and their plus-ones, all of whom will be touching down at the airport any minute now." She pulls her dress over her head. "Not to mention, the activities director texted to tell me Josh's Uncle William and the Faraday group is currently *en route* from the airport—a group I've got to personally greet because, based on past experience, William Faraday is inevitably gonna have a thousand unexpected issues with his bungalow, no matter how objectively perfect it is, and I'm the only one who always knows how to smooth things over with that finicky fucker. So, if I don't get my ass to that lobby right now, we're most likely gonna be playing Musical Bungalows with Uncle William for at least an hour 'til he's fully satisfied." She turns her back to me, implicitly asking me to zip up her dress, which I do. "God, I never should have done this," she mutters.

I stride to my suitcase to grab a pair of swim trunks and slip them on. "Aw, come on. You can't possibly regret having the best sex of your life."

She rolls her eyes. "I don't. But why'd I have to do it *today*? If I wanted to live dangerously for the first time in my life, I should have picked another time, not to mention another guy, but that's a whole other story."

"I notice you didn't deny you just had the best sex of your life. And, sweetheart, trust me, you didn't come like that because you were living dangerously for the first time—you came like that because you were fucking *me*. I'm the secret sauce. No one else could have done that to you."

She sits on a chair and begins strapping on her heels. "Well, when I have meaningless sex with the next guy, I'll let you know if you're right about that."

My entire body revolts at the thought of her fucking anyone but me, but I clench my teeth and force myself not to wig out. I grab a T-shirt from my suitcase and pull it over my head, taking deep breaths to steady myself. "You didn't answer my question. Why were you wearing the uniform?"

"Oh, please. You're trying to make *me* the villain of this story? Ha! I told one little white lie in a bar—you're the one without an ounce of integrity in your stupid, perfect body."

"I'm losing patience with you, my darling sociopath. I politely request you please tell me the truth about the uniform-bullshit right now, because, if it turns out you're literally a sociopath, then I'm not gonna be all that thrilled about you working alongside my sister's husband, especially when I know you'd give your left tit to fuck his brains out at your first opportunity."

She snarls at me. "You're disgusting."

"You're not answering my question."

She exhales and crosses her arms over her gorgeous chest. "I find it ironic you're demanding proof of my integrity when you're the guy who asked me out when you had a phone number in your pocket from earlier that night and a girlfriend sitting at home."

"That's total bullshit. But we're not talking about me yet—we're talking about you. Why were you wearing the uniform? And were you planning to meet me the next night or was that just part of the whole shtick—going to bars, giving a guy epic blue-balls, making a date, and laughing about it later?"

She rolls her eyes and shakes her head. "I gave you a fake name and occupation in a bar, Ryan—I didn't inject you with Ebola. It was a one-time silly lark during a night out with my extremely crazy friend, not a crime against humanity. Certainly, the same thing happens in bars all over the world every night of the week."

My temper flares. My heart rate spikes. "Bullshit. People don't have the kind of connection we did in bars every night of the week. Maybe women in bars give fake names and occupations to stupid meatheads they don't see any potential with, but, unless it's Halloween, they most certainly don't wear official flight-attendant uniforms and, unless they're pretty damned heartless, they don't stick with their fake stories when the dude they've been mind-fucking all night has made it abundantly clear he's feeling something once-in-a-lifetime—something he's literally never felt before." Oh my fuck, my voice is breaking. I can't even pretend my heart isn't bursting wide open as I speak. "If you thought I was just gaming you," I say, the vein in my neck throbbing, "if you thought I was just saying whatever the fuck I had to say in order to get you into bed, then that settles it: you truly are a fucking sociopath."

She looks pained. "Ryan, no. I..." She swallows hard. "I swear, it truly was a one-time thing. A silly lark. That's all."

My chest is tight. I feel like I can't breathe. "But why didn't you tell me the truth? Couldn't you see I was losing my mind over you?"

She closes her eyes briefly and takes a deep breath. "I can't do this right now. Uncle William and the Faradays will be here any minute and I've got a job to do. Honestly, I don't see how you're making this about my stupid uniform when you were lying through your teeth the whole time. *You weren't single, Ryan.* You acted like you were falling in love with me on the spot and yet you had a fucking girlfriend the whole time. I told you my boyfriend had cheated on me and how much it hurt me and yet you had no qualms about using me to cheat on your girlfriend? How could you do that to me? Fuck you if you think me wearing a uniform came even close to any of that."

"We're gonna talk about all of that. But first I need to understand how you didn't feel the impulse to tell me the truth."

She looks utterly exasperated. "Oh my God. You're insane. Fine. Not that I owe you any explanation, but here's the whole, stupid story, you big cry-baby: I'd just moved up to Seattle and was missing Charlotte, so when she—"

"Wait. *You live in Seattle?*"

"Yeah, I'd relocated from L.A. a few weeks prior. Josh moved back to Seattle for Climb & Conquer."

My mind is racing. "But you told me you live in L.A."

"No, I told you I'm *from* L.A., which is true. Born and raised."

"But you said you flew in from L.A. and came straight from the airport."

"No. *Charlotte* said *she* flew in from L.A. and you just assumed she meant both of us. I never said that. In fact, right off the bat, I explicitly told you *Charlotte* was the flight attendant, not me, and that I was merely dressed like one."

I feel like my head's exploding. Holy shit, she *did* say that, didn't she? How could I have not remembered that detail when I was sending Henn on his wild goose chase?

She continues: "Ever since my break-up, Charlotte had been begging me to come out with her and wear one of her uniforms, so I finally said 'Fuck it, I'll do it.' And then, just my luck, the first time I did it, I met you—the most gorgeous man I've ever laid eyes on. The minute I saw you, I regretted wearing that stupid thing, which is why I blurted the truth, right off the bat. I knew you thought I was joking, but, still, it made me feel better to say it out loud. And, then, when we started talking, I got so absorbed in our conversation, I forgot I was wearing the damned uniform—a state of mind helped along by all those martinis and shots you kept feeding me, I'm sure." She looks wistful. "And then, when we were just about to kiss... when your lips were on my cheek and you were whispering into my ear..." She closes her eyes for a moment, apparently lost in a memory. "You called me 'Samantha,' and, all of a sudden, I knew I had to tell you. So I told you I had something I needed to tell you—and that's precisely when your *girlfriend* came in and called you a 'cheater' and me a 'cunt' and screamed about the blonde at dinner and I got the hell out of Dodge."

"Oh my God," I say softly, completely bowled over. Everything she's just told me rings completely true. Holy fuck, I've been such an idiot. "Samantha. I mean, T-Rod. Listen to me. I can explain everything."

"Oh, I'm sure you can. You're awfully good at 'explaining everything,' aren't you?" Her features harden to steel. "So, fine, be outraged at my purportedly sociopathic tendencies. But I'd look in the mirror before I started slinging 'sociopath' around, if I were you. It wasn't me who was gathering phone numbers and dinner dates and fuck buddies behind my girlfriend's back."

"Theresa, you've got me all wrong," I say. "Listen to me, okay? I'd already broken up with my girlfriend earlier that night, way before I got to the bar—and all that shit she said about me was completely untrue."

Theresa scoffs. "Oh, you'd already broken up with Psycho Barbie? Well, that's funny because she obviously hadn't gotten the memo. You do realize you have to say the magic words 'I want to break up with you' *out loud* and not just think 'em in order to break-up with someone?"

"I didn't *telepathically* break up with her," I say. "I told her out loud. If she didn't understand, that wasn't my fault."

Anger floods Theresa's features. "That's got to be the dickiest thing I've ever heard a man say in my entire life. *If she didn't understand you were breaking up with her, that was her fault?"* She laughs maniacally. "Okay, Ryan, you're right. My bad. I've totally misjudged you, the same way I misjudged my scumbag ex-boyfriend, I guess. You've explained everything and you're a fucking saint."

"I didn't say I'm a saint. I just said—"

"Never mind," she says. "It doesn't matter. Either way, whether you're a saint or a sinner or something in between, this thing between us is a total nonstarter, anyway, as I'm sure you'll agree."

"Fuck no, I don't agree—I couldn't disagree more."

"Are you high? Even if you were Mr. Wonderful, which you're so obviously *not*, you're Kat's brother."

"I don't see the dilemma."

She scoffs. "If I'm gonna have meaningless sex with a fuck buddy, I'd strongly prefer not to have to see him repeatedly at kiddie birthday parties and gym grand openings for the rest of my life."

"What if we're not gonna have meaningless sex? What if I want something more than a fuck buddy?"

She laughs. "Okay, fine. Let's play make-believe for a moment. Let's pretend Psycho Barbie never happened and you're actually some kind of Prince Charming with actual morals and ethics. What are we gonna do, go out on a double date to the movies with Josh and Kat and whenever Josh wants popcorn, I'm gonna reflexively pop up to fetch it for him? I've never 'hung out' with Josh socially in my life. I'm his *employee. I work for him.*"

I laugh. "You're his assistant, not his butler. If I can hang out with him, you can. It's not like I'm some multi-millionaire, either."

"You're missing my point."

"No, I'm not. You just have to get over your weird employee-thing and just be yourself. Using your example, if we were out at a movie and Josh wanted popcorn, then I'd get it when I got up to get ours, or, if Josh was being a dick about it, we'd tell him to go fuck himself and get his own fucking popcorn. It's not rocket science, Theresa. You'd treat him like anyone else."

"And then what? Get fired? Or feel weird about it? After six years, I'm supposed to tell my boss to get his own fucking popcorn?" She shakes her head. "This is ridiculous. I'm not gonna argue about Josh's popcorn. It was a freaking *metaphor.* What I'm saying is you're a nonstarter, okay? This was fun and what you did to me just now felt freaking amazing—I'm not gonna lie—it truly was the best sex of my life, hands down, so thank you for that—but it was just sex, Ryan. I'm not suddenly falling all over you because you're handy with your fingers and dick and tongue."

"Jesus."

"Sorry. It is what it is. From here on out, the only rational thing to do, for all the reasons I've stated, is for both of us to say, 'Gosh that rocked!' and then pretend it never happened. I swear, the next guy I fuck will be someone I never have to see again."

I clench my jaw. "I'd very much appreciate it if you'd refrain from talking about fucking anyone else when my dick was inside you literally minutes ago."

"I'll talk about whatever I want. You have no say in what I do."

"I sure as hell do."

A shadow crosses over her face. "Is that a threat? Are you threatening to tell Josh and Kat what I said in the bar?"

"What? No," I say. "That's not what I meant."

She looks panicked all of a sudden. "Tell me now: are you gonna tell Josh and Kat that stupid thing I told you?"

I shrug. "I don't know, to be honest. I have no desire or inclination to tell them jack shit about that—but I don't know if I can trust my gut yet. I gotta feel things out. If it turns out you're planning to swoop in and steal my sister's man at some point, then I'd hate to look back and think, 'Shit, I shoulda warned my sister to watch you like a hawk.'"

Her features harden. "You truly are an asshole, you know that? I swear to God on my life I don't want Josh. I swear it on the lives of my brothers and parents and niece. Yes, I had a little crush on my boss a while back, during a time when I was feeling like I'd been eaten by a wolf and shit into a ditch, and, yes, this year has been hard for me so having a little fantasy-crush felt a whole lot safer than venturing into the cruel world; but, like I told you that night, my feelings for Josh weren't specifically about him, but more about the kind of guy he represents." She juts her chin. "Plus, I've come to adore Kat and would never do anything to hurt her. That's the God's truth. And, hey, as long as I'm telling you the God's truth, I admit that, yes, I *do* love Josh. Fuck it. I love him. Just not in the way you mean. He's like a very hot brother or cousin. I can appreciate his hotness and still realize he's off-limits because we'd make three-headed babies, okay?"

I laugh, despite myself. God, she's funny.

She continues, "You're telling me you can't objectively appreciate the hotness of any of your cousins? Or of Kat?"

I cringe. "Please don't."

"But you know your sister's objectively hot, right?"

"Just, please, don't."

"My point is that loving Josh the way I do means I genuinely want him to be happy—which means I want him to be with Kat. *Of course.* Any moron can see Josh and Kat have the kind of epic love story anyone, including me, would kill to have." She quickly glances at her watch. "Shit. I've gotta go. I never should have done this."

In a sudden torrent, every feeling I had for this woman three months ago in that bar crashes into me again, only with more intensity than ever. "Theresa, listen to me," I breathe. "We need to talk. I need to explain everything to you."

"Fuck you and your 'explanations,' Ryan. I'm done with men full of excuses and fucking explanations. If you want to tell Josh and Kat what I told you at the bar and ruin my entire life, simply because it makes you feel like some sort of superhero-protector to your sister, then let the chips fall where they may. That says more about you and your poor judgment and massive ego and lack of empathy and lack of faith in love than it could ever say about me and some stupid, illusory crush I might have had months ago on my boss whom I've never even once hung out with outside of work, by the way. But right now, whatever you're gonna do or not do, I've got a job to do and, by God, I'm gonna do it to the best of my ability because I'm proud of how good I am at my job—really fucking proud!" Her eyes suddenly fill with tears. "The only thing I ask, out of basic decency, is two things: please don't tell anyone we had sex, please, because it would be very embarrassing to me and I especially don't want it getting back to Josh and Kat and making things awkward and strange for them at their wedding and future events; and, two, this entire week, please be polite and conversational toward me so as not to raise suspicion, but, otherwise, leave me the fuck alone!"

Oh my God. She's out of control. She hates me. She absolutely hates me and it's killing me. "Theresa. Hang on. You're acting like a fucking loon. You gotta let me—"

Without another word, she flips me off, juts her chin, opens the door, and marches out of the room.

I stand stock-still for a minute, my heart racing. I can't follow her—she's heading to the lobby to meet the Faraday group. Should I... what the fuck should I do? I don't fucking know. All I know—literally the only two things I know at this moment are: one, I want her, now more than ever, and, two, before this week is over, no matter what the fuck I have to do, I'm gonna make that woman mine.

Chapter 28
Tessa

As I walk along the winding pathway toward the main lobby, I can't stop chastising myself. What the hell is wrong with me? *I fucked Ryan Morgan*? And then I flew off the handle and lost my mind and screamed at him afterwards? Talk about poking the snake. Shit! Why didn't I let the man talk? Strength comes from silence more than anything else, not shrieking and crying. Damn! He obviously wanted to say something, so why didn't I let him do it? Maybe, whatever it was, I could have used it to convince him to keep his stupid mouth shut this week.

Crap! I never should have gone to his room. I had important work to do, and yet I chose to spend an hour, smack in the middle of guests' arrivals, to play Hide the Pierced Salami (and Magical Fingers and Talented Tongue) with Kat's freaking manwhore of a brother? Inexcusable! By definition, a girl's not supposed to see her one-night stand (or, in this case, her one-afternoon stand), ever again, and here I've dipped my toe into the casual-sex pool for the first time with a man I'm going to see all week long here in Hawaii and also at least once a year for the rest of my life in Seattle? Gah!

My phone buzzes with an incoming text and I pull it out as I continue walking toward the lobby. The driver for Uncle William, Jonas, Sarah, and Sarah's mother is moments away from arriving. I reply to say I'll meet them in the lobby and then continue scrolling through additional texts. There's a text from Marnie letting me know the Morgan group has hit the private beach for some fun in the sun. More scrolling and I see an inquiry from Reed Rivers about the wedding reception—something about a surprise musical guest he wants to arrange as a gift to Josh and Kat. I reply to Reed saying no problem, we'll talk about it when he gets here.

As I cross the threshold into the spacious lobby, I shove my phone into my bag and scan the place. Phew. There's no sign of the Faraday party yet.

My phone pings with a text and I pull it out again. "Hey, Crazy Girl!" Charlotte writes. "Can u talk now? I've got 30 minutes before hopping my flight. If not now, talk tomorrow?"

I tap out a quick reply: "Hey, Nut Job, can't talk now. Sorry. Tomorrow good. Lots to tell you!" I press send and bite my lip. God, I'm dying to tell Charlotte about the whole Ryan situation. She's gonna lose her freaking mind when I tell her. Shoot. I can't resist dropping a little hint. "This Crazy Girl's got a crazy story to tell you when we talk!" I write. "I HAD SEX! (Cue the fireworks, champagne bottle uncorking, and a choir singing!) And, guuuuuurl, it was gooooood. Best sex of my life! I'm not gonna tell you who it was who made me see God (four times!!!) until we talk (because I want to HEAR your shrieking reaction!!!), but let me just say this: the guy's a blast from my past and a complete asshole and I had no idea he'd be here but he is! I shouldn't have done it, but I threw caution to the wind and fucked him on a complete whim, for no other reason than I wanted to get laid! Yeehaw! I think you might be on to something with the whole meaningless sex thing. Woooheeeeee! Good stuff! Talk to you tomorrow. XO T."

Chapter 29
Ryan

I scan the private beach. White sand. Turquoise water. Palm trees swaying in a gentle breeze. And all of it bathed in glorious, Hawaiian sunshine. There's a crowd of Morgan-related folks snorkeling just beyond the shore break, and a whole bunch more, including Josh and Kat and Dax and his two buddies, frolicking in the waves. It looks like Coco and Keane are burying Zander in the sand up to his neck, and Mom and Dad and a whole mess of Morgans are hanging out in a cabana. *Paradise.*

If ever there was the perfect place to try to pull myself together and calm myself down, this would be it. Jesus. The last couple hours have been an emotional and physical roller coaster like nothing I've experienced before. How the hell did Samantha turn out to be T-Rod? And how the motherfuck did things with T-Rod veer in a matter of minutes from her banging me like a mad monkey to her screaming at me with tears in her eyes that she wanted me to leave her the fuck alone?

Fuck! My head is spinning. What I need is an impromptu session with my lifelong therapist to figure my shit out. I search the beach and quickly find him, all by his lonesome, reclined on a lounge chair in bright blue swim trunks, a bucket of beers next to him and a book in his hand.

"Hey, Bee," I say as I take the lounge chair next to my big brother.

Colby looks up from his book. "What took you so long? Mom said she texted you to come to the beach over an hour ago."

"I took a nap." I indicate the bucket of beers next to him. "Hand me one of those, would you? Whatcha reading?"

152

Colby shows me the cover of his book: *Hillbilly Elegy*.

"Dad was reading that on the plane. Is it good?"

"So far, yeah. Interesting."

The unmistakable sound of our sister squealing with glee wafts through the air, and we both look toward the sound in time to catch Josh bounding into the ocean with a bikini-clad Kat in his arms.

"Looks like Kat's feeling a whole lot better these days," I say. "For a while there, I thought the poor girl was gonna barf up a baby."

"Look at her belly in her bathing suit," Colby says. "So damned cute."

"Yup, she's a cutie patootie, you might even say," I reply, doing my best Keane impression, and we both chuckle. "You gonna go in?" I ask, motioning toward the aquamarine ocean.

"Nah." Colby indicates his left leg and I glance at it, taking note of the long, angry scars running down his thigh and shin—and, just that fast, my mind flashes back to the horrible night mere months ago when my big brother lay unconscious in a hospital bed with my family huddled around him, all of us praying he'd make it through the night.

"I thought swimming was supposed to be good for the leg?" I say.

"In a swimming pool. My physical therapist said she doesn't want me battling waves and the uneven ocean floor just yet."

"Ah." I stare out at the ocean for a moment. I didn't come over here to make small talk with Colby, but I can't seem to figure out how to go about telling Colby about the life-changing series of events that happened to me today. I'm not even sure I understand them myself.

"Okay, let's hear it," Colby says, pulling me out of my thoughts.

I look at him.

"You look like a madman again, Ry. I assume you got some news about your Argentinian whale?"

I laugh. Fucking Colby. "Yeah." I exhale. "You're not gonna believe this, but she's here."

"In Maui?"

"No, *here*—literally—at this resort."

Colby makes a truly comedic face. "But Josh rented out the whole... She *works* here?"

I bite my lip, forcing myself not to smile. "She's T-Rod."

Colby makes another hilarious face. *"What?"*

"The Whale is T-Rod."

"What the fuck are you talking about?"

I laugh. "It seems 'Samantha' gave me a fake name and occupation at the bar. I found out when I walked into the lobby."

"But what about the flight attendant uniform?"

"Her friend's a flight attendant. I guess it was a 'girl's night out' kind of thing."

Colby pauses briefly, apparently processing everything I've just said, and then he throws his head back and bursts into booming, hysterical laughter—a ten out of ten on the Colby-Morgan-laughter scale—and, even in my state of complete mind-fuckedness, I can't help smiling at the sound of his uproarious laughter.

"So that's why you were such a dick to T-Rod when we first got here?" Colby asks, wiping his eyes.

"I was pissed," I say. "She sent me on a wild goose chase, man."

"Bullshit. T-Rod didn't send you on a wild goose chase—*you* sent you on a wild goose chase. All that girl did was yank your chain in a bar, the same way girls have been yanking guys' chains since bars were invented."

"That's exactly what she said."

"Oh, so you've talked to her about it? Did she know about you being Kat's brother before you got here or was it a mutual mind-fuck when you walked into the lobby?"

"A total and complete mutual mind-fuck. And, yeah, we talked, but only briefly. I was too shocked and pissed at her to say any of the bleeding-heart shit I'd planned to say to 'Samantha,' so I basically grilled her about the uniform-thing and then she had to go."

"So you didn't tell her about your crazy quest?"

I shake my head.

"Thank God. What'd she say about the uniform—just that she was having fun?"

"Yeah."

I tell Colby everything T-Rod told me about why she wore a uniform that night, opting not to mention that said conversation happened in my hotel room right after we'd fucked each other's brains out, and when I'm finished talking, Colby says, "Women are hilarious. Remember how Kat used to go to bars and say she was 'Matilda Blackburn from Australia'?"

"I forgot about that," I say. "I sure wish I'd remembered that little nugget before I let Henn loose on the entire airline industry."

Colby chuckles. "How any guy ever believed Kat was Australian with that ridiculous Crocodile-Dundee accent of hers, I'll never know."

"Nobody ever *believed* Kat," I say. "Guys just played along, hoping to get laid by the hot girl with the fake Australian accent."

Colby laughs. "Probably."

"So you're not thinking T-Rod's a closet psycho for wearing the uniform?" I ask.

"Naw," Colby says. "She said it was a one-time thing, right? Kat must have done that kind of thing fifty times and she's moderately sane. Sounds to me like T-Rod's got a party-girl-friend like Kat, that's all. Plus, T-Rod's worked for Josh for years, right? And he obviously trusts her with his life."

"Good point."

"I mean, I only saw the woman for fifteen minutes in the lobby, so I could be wrong, but my initial impression of her was thumbs-up. If I get a closet-psycho vibe from her as the week goes on, I'll let you know, but I doubt it."

"Thanks, man."

"And, in the meantime, just do yourself a favor and take things slow," Colby cautions. "You got lucky as hell you didn't need to tell T-Rod the whole crazy story of your Search for Samantha. Now you've got the luxury of taking your time." He pauses, thinking for a beat. "I do recommend you tell her about Olivia being batshit crazy, though—and definitely clear up what really happened in the restaurant with that other woman. You certainly don't want Theresa thinking you're a complete douche. Oh, and one more thing: you'd better make damned sure she's not off-limits as far as Josh is concerned before you dabble with this one. She might very well be 'honorary little sister' territory for Josh, and you certainly don't wanna... What?"

I cringe, my stomach clenching.

"Why do you look like that, Ryan?" Colby asks.

"Like what?" I ask.

"Guilty as hell."

"Because... I already fucked her."

"*What?*" He pauses, his mouth hanging open. "When? Ryan, we've been here for an hour and a half!"

"I fucked her ten minutes after we got here. I lied, sorry: I wasn't taking a nap when our dear mother texted about the beach—I was boning the fuck outta T-Rod."

Colby bursts out laughing again, and he keeps right on laughing for what seems like several minutes. Finally, when his laughter has subsided enough for him to speak coherently, he sighs happily, rubs his eyes, and says, "Captain Morgan, you're my fucking hero."

Chapter 30
Ryan

"How the hell did you pull that off?" Colby asks, sitting up in his lounge chair.

"It was very easy to do, strangely enough," I say. "When T-Rod was done giving her speech about the itinerary, I walked over to her and whispered in her ear, 'My room in ten.'"

"And...?"

"And she showed up ten minutes later and I fucked her."

We both laugh.

I look out at the ocean for a beat, shaking my head. "I wasn't even trying to be James Bond. I was pissed about the uniform thing and wanted to read her the riot act in private. So, she knocked on my door, obviously pissed as hell about the whole Olivia thing, and I opened my door and said something really dicky to her, and she took a swing at me. Sort of. Clearly, the girl's never thrown a punch in her life. And then we *immediately* started fucking the hell out of each other." I snap my fingers. "Just like that. Craziest damned thing that's ever happened to me." A wide smile spreads across my face. "And the best."

Colby raises an eyebrow. "So did the reality of harpooning your Argentinian whale live up to the fantasy?"

"Smashed it to smithereens, brother."

Colby smiles. "*Awesome.*"

"Best I ever had," I say. "For her, too. She didn't even try to deny it. Damn, Bee, I thought I knew what good sex was—I've had some good sex, as you know—but I had no idea it could be *that* fucking amazing."

"Holy shit, Ry. Enough. I haven't gotten laid in months. I'm happy for you and all, but don't wave a juicy hamburger in front of a starving man."

"Sorry, I can't help it: I've had crazier; I've had kinkier; but I've never, ever had better. Not even close."

Colby chuckles. "You wanna hear something funny? When I saw you drooling over T-Rod in the lobby, I was kind of pissed at you."

"Why?"

"I was like, 'Jesus, dude, for three months you've been going full-on Ahab over this Argentinian whale of yours, and then you take one look at this T-Rod woman and the whale's instantly a distant memory?'"

I laugh my ass off. "Oh my God. That's so Colby of you to defend the whale's honor. You're so *you,* no matter the situation."

Colby shrugs and sips his beer.

"Funny thing is, if the whale *had* been someone other than T-Rod, I would have kicked her to the curb in two seconds flat, exactly the way you thought I did at first sight of T-Rod. Jesus God, did you see T-Rod in that dress today? I'm only human."

"She's smokin' hot, I must say," Colby agrees. "But like I said, I'd prefer we not dwell on your good fortune."

We both laugh. Colby's full of shit, of course: this is what we do—what we've always done. We talk about girls, no holding back, whether it's feast or famine for the other guy.

"As hot as she is, though," I continue, "my attraction to her isn't about that. I mean, it doesn't hurt she looks like a wet dream, not gonna lie, but my pull toward her is based on something way beyond that. It's something... I dunno... *reflexive?*"

"Yeah, it's called a boner."

"No, no, I meant 'reflexive' in a spiritual way. A pre-ordained kind of way. She's triggered some reflex for my *soul.*"

"Oh, Jesus. She's turned you into Dax."

"I know—pummel me for it later."

"Explain it to me."

I consider for a minute. "You know when the doctor bangs on your knee with the little hammer and your leg kicks?"

Colby nods.

"When you were a kid, did you ever try *not* to kick your leg, just to see if you could do it?"

Colby laughs. "Every time."

"Me, too. But I'll be damned, I *always* kicked." I shrug. "Well, best way I can describe it, that woman is a hammer to my knee, only my 'knee' is my mind, body, and soul. She looks at me and, I'll be damned..." I kick my leg. "*Kick.*"

Colby laughs. "How do you fool everyone into thinking you're so normal all the time?"

"It's quite easy, actually. I just think, 'What would Colby do?' And that's what I do."

Colby grins at me. "I'm not quite as normal as you think."

"Oh, yes you are. The sanest of the bunch. Hey, can I tell you something crazy?"

"You mean everything you just told me isn't already 'something crazy'?"

I ignore his jab. "The minute I met Samantha—or T-Rod or Tessa, whatever the fuck her name is—I felt like she and I used to be passionately in love in some past life—you know, like completely obsessed with each other. And then we died and our souls got recycled, or whatever happens to souls, and we popped out as two totally new people without any memories of our past life together... and then, we stumbled upon each other in that bar, and our souls instantly remembered everything, even though our brains didn't; and now that we've kissed and touched and fucked, my soul's like, 'Fuck you, motherfucker, if you think I'm *ever* gonna be separated from that woman again.'" I press my lips together, shocked at what just spewed from my mouth. "God, that was some crazy-ass shit, huh?"

But Colby looks unfazed. He's sipping his beer quietly, looking out at the ocean, nodding like what I've said makes perfect sense.

I wait, but he doesn't say anything. "Go ahead. Tell me I'm a loon," I say.

Colby smiles at me, his blue eyes full of warmth. "Why would I call you a loon? You know for a fact I'm feeling the exact same way in my life. I couldn't have said it better myself. To tell you the truth, Ry, that little speech is exactly why I love you the most."

I can't help blushing. "Thanks, Bee."

"Plus, that's the kind of stuff Dad always says about Mom."

"Dad says stuff like that? He's never said it to me."

"Go fishing with him alone some time and he'll surprise you. He doesn't express things quite the way you just did—but, yeah, in his own way, Dad says exactly the same stuff about Mom. He often says he was 'born to love her.' Pretty cool, huh?"

I suddenly feel overcome with an intense urge to find T-Rod and drop to my knees and make her understand I'm not some manwhore looking to get laid—that I've moved mountains to find her because I've known from the first moment I saw her that she was meant to be mine. But I can't do it. I know I can't. She won't believe me. And, in fact, she'll probably tell me to fuck off. "So what should I do about this girl, Bee? I want her, man—in a way I've never wanted anyone before—and, for once in my life, I'm not sure how to get what I want."

"Well, shit, man, it sounds like you've already got her," Colby says. "You said, 'My room in ten,' and she came running."

"No, you don't understand. She made it clear what we did was 'meaningless' to her—which is understandable, given that, thanks to the whole Olivia situation, she absolutely hates my guts."

"Yeah, I'm kinda confused about that. She screwed you, even though she *hates* you?"

"Correct. She fucked me, thinking I'm a lying, cheating scumbag. I tried to clear up the Olivia stuff, but she didn't believe me, so I dropped it. Plus, I was way too focused on the uniform thing to care too much about anything else."

Colby looks incredulous. "But..." He shakes his head like I've mind-fucked him. "This is crazy."

"I know. This is the very thing I wanted to talk to you about. This girl is a total mind-fucker, I swear to God. Back at The Pine Box three months ago, when she thought I could potentially be her Prince Charming, she made a big thing about needing to 'take it slow,' and, I swear to God, she wasn't gaming me. And now that she thinks I'm a total douche-player, she's jumping my bones within ten minutes."

Colby sips his beer and looks thoughtful.

"What are you thinking, Dr. Colby? I can see your wheels turning."

"You think she's got major trust issues, this one?"

"Definitely." I tell Colby everything I know about T-Rod's break-up with Mr. Soccer Douche.

"Okay, so here's what I think," Colby says. "Fucking a *known* scumbag isn't a risky activity for her. She's fully aware of your douchebaggery. Or so she thinks. And, therefore, she thinks she can't get blindsided by it. So she figures she can have some meaningless fun with you without any chance of getting hurt. It's not true, of course—people like her don't know how to separate sex and emotion, but she doesn't know that because she's never tried it before. I mean, she might be able to keep herself from feeling something for you after one sesh, but, I guarantee you, if you have sex with her all week long, she'll fall for you, whether she wants to or not. My advice? Fuck her like a rock star by night and hang out with her by day and be your awesome self and let things happen organically. If thinking you're an asshole is what got her into your bed in the first place, let her keep thinking it until it seems like she's open and receptive and trusting enough to really hear you out."

"So your gut says I shouldn't tell her about the Search for Samantha right away?"

"Hell no. Of course, she deserves to know about all that, just not right off the bat. At first, just give her what she *thinks* she wants—no-strings sex. Tell her this week is about fun and feeling good, no attachments, and that no one will ever know, blah, blah, blah. Make sure she feels safe with you and that you'll never, ever tell anyone about—oh, wait, no, even better: beg *her* not to tell anyone. Ha! Tell her you don't want Josh to find out and get pissed at you for dabbling with his honorary little sister. If she thinks she's in a position of power, she'll feel extra safe with you and trust will easily follow."

"Brilliant."

"At some point, she'll realize she's not capable of no-strings sex and that's when you'll tell her about the quest and all the other crazy-ass 'souls reuniting' shit you just told me and she'll be thrilled to find out you're not the manwhoring-cheater she thought you were."

"Damn, Bee. You're a fucking genius."

"Just keep your cards close to your vest this whole week and tell her—"

"Oh, shit, Colby!" I blurt, cutting him off. "Her friend! I called T-Rod's flight-attendant friend and told her the whole story and begged her to tell 'Samantha' everything!"

"Well, shit, son, you better get on the horn right quick and tell that friend not to say a damned word. If anyone's gonna tell T-Rod what a loon you are, it'd better be you—and only when you're good and fucking ready."

Chapter 31
Ryan

"Oh, for crying out loud!" Charlotte shouts, picking up my call. "Am I gonna need to get a restraining order against you, Ryan from The Pine Box? I haven't had a chance to talk to my friend yet, okay? It's only been three hours since we spoke. Cool your freaking jets, Skippy."

I open my mouth to reply, but Charlotte forges right ahead before I can say a damned word.

"Actually, it's probably a good thing you called, come to think of it. I wouldn't have called you about this, but as long as I've got you on the line, I should tell you: there's been a startling development since we last spoke—and, now, I don't think you should get your hopes up about my friend calling you."

Colby's blue eyes are locked with mine as I press the phone against my ear. He gestures like he's dying to know what's happening on the call and I hold my index finger up, telling him to be patient.

Charlotte continues, "I got a text from my friend and, well, I'm sorry to be the bearer of bad news, Ryan, but it seems the exact thing you were worried about happening has happened."

"What thing?" I ask.

"Remember, you said you were worried that, after a year of saying no to guys, my friend might finally say yes, out of the blue, before you'd had a chance to talk with her? Well, I guess you've got ESP or something because it seems that's exactly what's happened."

"What did she say?"

"Well, her text was a bit vague, but I know her really well, and I'm ninety-nine percent sure she's planning to get back together with her ex-boyfriend."

162

My heart lurches into my throat. "*What*? You mean the soccer player?"

"Yeah. Stu."

I'm suddenly panicked. "Why do you think that? Did she tell you that?"

Colby's eyes widen as he watches me.

"No, but it's the only thing that makes sense. She said she hooked up with a 'blast from her past' who's an 'asshole.' She just flew to Hawaii last night for a wedding and the only blast-from-her-past-asshole who could *possibly* be at that particular wedding would be her ex-boyfriend. And if she had sex with her ex-boyfriend, which is the only logical asshole-blast-from-her-past it could have been, then that can only mean they're getting back together because my friend would *never* in a million years have casual sex, *ever*." She makes a sound I'd characterize as an audible shrug. "Hence, I truly think she's getting back together with Stu."

It's taking every bit of my self-restraint not to burst out laughing. "Why would Stu be at the wedding in Hawaii?" I ask.

Colby looks at me quizzically, like he's dying for a hint of what's happening on this call, but I simply wink at him, telling him everything's fine.

"He used to be friends with the groom—this guy named Josh," Charlotte says. "To be honest, I wouldn't have thought Josh would have invited Stu to his wedding after the way Stu treated my friend— I thought Josh had cut him off completely. But there's no one else in her life who could possibly fit the description of being a 'blast from her past' and an 'asshole.'"

"Well, *I* fit that description," I say, a smirk dancing on my lips.

I can hear Charlotte's eye-roll across the phone line. "I meant there's no one else who fits that description *and* who could be in attendance at Josh's wedding."

Okay, I've had my fun. "Charlotte, it's me. I'm the blast-from-her-past-asshole. I'm here in Hawaii with your bestie. Oh, and when I say 'your bestie,' let me be clear I'm not talking about a flight attendant named Samantha; I'm talking about *Theresa Rodriguez*, the personal assistant to my future brother-in-law, Joshua William Faraday."

There's dead silence on the line.

"I'm Kat Morgan's brother," I say, chuckling. "Ryan *Morgan*. And, surprise! I had sex with Theresa, oh, about three hours ago—right after I'd arrived here and walked into the hotel to find 'Samantha' standing in the lobby."

"Oh my God."

"Crazy, right?" I ask.

"*Insane*. How the hell did you get Tessa to have sex with you so damned fast? You told her about your crazy Search for Samantha and self-imposed celibacy?"

"No. Strangely enough, I haven't told her anything about the past three months. That's exactly why I'm calling you: to tell you I'm not gonna tell her that stuff yet, and I'd very much appreciate you not telling her, either."

I tell Charlotte everything about my thought process and, when I'm done, Charlotte makes a noncommittal sound.

"You can't keep all that from her," she says. "She deserves to know."

"Of course, she does. And I promise I'll tell her everything before we leave Maui. But do I need to tell her all of it *today*? Cut me some slack. I've been searching for a flight attendant named Samantha for three months. Let me get my bearings before I have to bare my soul like that to some woman I just found out is named Theresa."

Charlotte doesn't reply.

"Charlotte, everything I felt when I met 'Samantha' in that bar, I'm feeling it again with Tessa, only even more so—and she's obviously feeling it, too, or she wouldn't have said yes. Just let us get to know each other this week without all the insanity getting in the way."

"You'll do it this week, before you leave Maui?"

"I promise."

Charlotte exhales. "Okay, I won't say a word this week. I don't know why I trust you, but I do."

"Thanks, Charlotte." I give a thumbs-up sign to Colby and he fist-bumps me.

"But I have three conditions to my silence," Charlotte says, "and you have to swear on a stack of bibles you'll honor them."

"Anything."

"Swear."

"I swear."

"First, you gotta tell her this week."

"Done."

"Second, when you tell her, keep my name out of it. She never needs to know I agreed to keep my mouth shut. If she were to find out, she'd be pissed as hell at me."

"I won't utter your name. I swear. Thank you."

"It's really important, Ryan. Don't throw me under the bus. I've known this girl since second grade and I've never lied to her. This past year, she's felt utterly betrayed—beyond devastated. She's always been a huge believer in honesty and integrity, but these days, she's ultra-sensitive about it."

"I understand. I promise. Your name won't pass my lips. What's your third condition?"

"At the end of all this, don't you dare break my girl's heart. *Don't you fucking dare*. If anyone's gonna get a broken heart here, or even so much as a splinter in a fingertip, you'd better make double-damn sure it's *you*."

Chapter 32
Ryan

Charlotte and I hang up our call and Colby immediately pounces on me, wanting to know everything she said, but before I can say much of anything, Josh approaches our lounge chairs and we both clamp our mouths shut.

"Hey, hey, it's the man of the hour," I say to Josh. "What's up, brother?"

"Hey, guys." Josh looks at me. "Kat asked me to drag you out to sea, Ryan. We're gonna snorkel with your parents and a bunch of Morgans before we gotta head in for dinner."

"Cool. You good, Cheese?"

Colby holds up his book and beer. "Have fun, Jacques Cousteau."

Josh and I amble across the sand toward a thatched hut filled with snorkeling equipment, chatting as we walk about the week's upcoming activities.

"T-Rod pulled the whole week together for us," Josh says. "That girl never lets me down. She's not just my right-hand, she's my right arm and leg, too."

I smile and nod, but my stomach is suddenly clenching. "She seems extremely organized," I say lamely.

Josh continues, "I had a chance to chat with Henn earlier today, right before he boarded his flight."

"Oh, yeah? How's he doing?"

"Good. He said you two are still hot on the trail of that flight attendant you met at The Pine Box?"

My stomach seizes. *Shit.* "Yeah, I, uh, had one last Hail-Mary-idea earlier today. It's kind of a last-ditch effort type thing."

"Henn also said something about her being Argentinian? I didn't

166

know that. I must have been with Kat when that detail came up." Josh cocks his head. "You got a thing for Argentinians, Captain?"

My stomach flips over. "Nope. Not really. Can't say that I do."

"'Cause I noticed you scoping out T-Rod in the lobby when you first got here. Did you know she's Argentinian?"

"She is? Oh, cool." Okay, this is getting really uncomfortable. "I wasn't scoping her out, in particular, I was just being a smart-ass. Sorry if I offended her. Or you."

"Not at all. No worries. Hey, I think you should put some sunscreen on your face, Rum Cake. You're getting a little red." He smirks.

"Thanks. Fucking Seattle, right? I'm gonna burn to a crisp out here this week."

We reach the hut with the snorkeling gear and Josh exchanges "alohas" with the guy behind the counter. "My almost-brother here needs some gear, please."

"Sure thing, Mr. Faraday. And you, sir?"

"I've already got mine from earlier," Josh replies.

The guy turns to gather whatever equipment is needed for me and Josh leans his elbow on the counter, his eyes locked with mine. "T-Rod's like a sister to me, Ryan. Been with me six years. I can't help but look out for her, especially ever since this dude I was sort of friendly with broke her heart this past year."

I open my mouth and close it again. *Shit.*

"Here you go, sir," the guy behind the counter says, handing me a mask and snorkel and fins. "You know how to use all that?"

I peel my eyes off Josh's intense face and smile at the guy. "Yep. I'm good. Thanks."

Josh grabs his gear from a nearby chair and we begin walking toward the water where every member of my family (other than Colby) is standing in the shallow waves, putting on masks.

Josh continues, "T-Rod met that douche 'cause of me, so her broken heart was indirectly my fault. I'd asked T-Rod to gather some signed sports memorabilia for this children's charity I support—you know, signed jerseys, balls, that kind of thing. So, she goes to pick up everything from various teams around L.A. and the next thing I know this one soccer guy I sort of knew is texting me, 'You've been holding out on me, Faraday!' So I asked T-Rod what that was about because she never says a damned word to me about her personal life, and it turns out she's got a dinner date with the guy that very night. Fast-forward however many months and they've moved in together and they're talking about marriage and how many kids they want. Fast-forward a year after that and it turns out he'd been fucking around on her the entire time, pretty much from day one, in every city he'd played in, the whole time he was telling her he wanted her to have his babies."

My heart squeezes painfully. No wonder T-Rod doesn't trust me as far as she can throw me.

We reach the waterline and Josh stops to put on his fins, so I do the same, my heart pounding ferociously in my chest, my mind reeling.

His fins on, Josh stands upright and crosses he muscled arms over his chest, his forearms covering the "grace" tattoo inked across his pecs. "Needless to say, I'm not friends with that piece of shit anymore."

My stomach turns over. "Understandably."

For a long beat, Josh looks at me like I've got a condom in my pocket with "Suck this, T-Rod!" written in Sharpie on it, and then he smiles and says, "You ready?"

I nod.

We begin trudging into the ocean toward the small group already snorkeling beyond the shore break. "You ever been snorkeling before?" Josh asks breezily, like the last five minutes never happened.

"Uh, yeah, a couple times in Mexico."

"Kat keeps joking her belly's gonna pull her down to the bottom like an anchor. I keep saying it's gonna make her float like a buoy. God, I hope I'm right." He chuckles.

I smile, but I'm too mind-fucked right now to return his breeziness.

"Spit on the glass to keep it from fogging up," he says, motioning to my mask. "It's an old trick." By way of demonstration, he spits on the glass and proceeds to smear his saliva around and then dunks his mask in the ocean—and I do the same. "Oh, hey," Josh says casually, still working on his mask. "I've been meaning to ask you: what were you planning to tell me the night we were supposed to meet for drinks at The Pine Box? Anything in particular?"

I suppress a smirk. *Bravo.* This is a master class right here in a dude gently laying down the law. Pretty impressive, I gotta say. "Nothing too intense," I reply. "I just wanted to welcome you into the Morgan family and tell you if you ever need anything, big or small, you're acquiring four brothers who'll always have your back." One side of my mouth hitches up. "And, of course, I'd planned to make it abundantly clear to you, and still do, frankly, that if you do a damned thing to hurt my sister, the Morgan Brothers will turn into the Morgan Mafia so fucking fast, you won't know what hit you."

A huge, beaming smile spreads across Josh's face to match mine. "Well, I can certainly understand you feeling that way, Ryan. In fact, I'd expect nothing less from a dude who cares deeply about his little sister."

I nod. "I'd expect nothing less, too."

"Good. Glad we're on the same page." He swats me on the shoulder and motions to my mask. "Now put your mask on, bro. Your momma's been asking about her beloved Rum Cake for the past hour and, God knows, we don't wanna disappoint our sweet Momma Lou."

Chapter 33
Tessa

Okay, let's start with the good news: Uncle William has had some sort of brain transplant, in a good way. I greeted him and his longtime companion, Katya, in the lobby, along with Jonas and Sarah and Sarah's mom, and offered to personally show the Faraday family's patriarch to his bungalow (so I could nip any and all inevitable issues in the bud); but, much to my shock and utter delight, Uncle William put one arm around Katya's shoulders and the other around his new niece Sarah's, beamed a genuine smile at me, and said, "I'll be thrilled with whatever accommodations you've arranged for us, Theresa."

I swear it took all my restraint not to do a happy dance, right then and there—I'd just gained a full hour in my day! "Great," I said, and I just was about to add, "So I'll see you all at the opening party, then?" when Uncle William said he was hoping to say a quick hello to Josh and Kat and Kat's "wonderful parents" (whom he'd met at Jonas and Sarah's wedding), wherever they might be on the resort grounds, even before getting situated in his bungalow. "Of course!" I chirped. "Follow me!"

And now, fuck my life, I'm leading Uncle William, Katya, Jonas, Sarah, and Sarah's mother to the private beach where, I'm quite certain, we'll find not only Josh and Kat and Kat's "wonderful parents," but Ryan Fucking Douchebag Morgan, too.

Which brings me to the bad news. The very, very bad news. I'm about to come face to face *again* with Ryan, the one asshole on the planet I currently wish to avoid as much as humanly possible.

Our group of six reaches the entry area for the private beach and, as everyone oohs and aahs about the breathtaking scenery, I scan the area, looking for Josh and Kat... and The Asshole.

"Josh and Kat must be in the water," I suggest.

"Oh, I see Mr. and Mrs. Morgan," Sarah says, pointing toward the shoreline. And, sure enough, Louise and Thomas Morgan are emerging from the water, hand in hand.

So, of course, off we go—our merry band of six heads toward the water.

Gah. Why am I feeling like that poor, unsuspecting girl at the beginning of *Jaws*—the one who wandered into the ocean for a drunken midnight swim and unexpectedly became a human McNugget?

We reach Mr. and Mrs. Morgan. Enthusiastic conversation ensues, which quickly attracts a whole bunch more Morgans to our party, including Josh and Kat. And through it all, though I'm pretending to be sane and relaxed and focused on the people and conversations around me, I'm actually losing my freaking mind with anticipation.

Oh, God, there he is at the other end of the beach. He's walking out of the ocean with Dax and Keane and some guys I don't know, all of them carrying snorkeling gear.

Whoa. I must say Ryan looks damned delicious dripping wet. *Holy moly.* I'm not normally an ogler—I'm usually pretty good at keeping my eyes firmly in my head, no matter how attractive the male specimen; but, dude, I'm quite certain my eyes just popped out of my head and plopped onto the sand.

I force myself to look away from Ryan as he walks toward the group, resolving never to look at him again as long as I live, but, two seconds later, when it's clear no one's watching me, I can't resist looking at him again, just for a quick second.

Oh good lord, that man's body is a work of art. Literally. It's funny, when Ryan and I were playing Hide the Pierced Salami earlier, everything happened so quickly and passionately, I wasn't able to get a good long look at him. But now that I've got some time to scrutinize him properly as he strides toward the group, I'm noticing all sorts of details about him that escaped me before. For instance, earlier, I didn't get a good look at that large booze-bottle-tattoo he's got inked on his left ribcage. And those "V" cuts peeking out of the top of his swim trunks? Divine. I'd like to kiss my way—

"... is that right, Theresa?" Josh asks.

Gah. I immediately stop ogling Ryan and look at my boss. "*Yes*," I say confidently, as if I've been listening all along. I smile at Josh like a flight attendant who's just been asked by a passenger, "Excuse me, miss, why have all the gas masks suddenly dropped down in the main cabin?"

"That's what I thought." Josh turns his attention back to Jonas. "T's got the entire itinerary in her head—the woman's a human spreadsheet, just like you, bro. So, anyway, yeah, like I was saying, tomorrow we bike down the volcano and the next day we'll..."

I stop listening.

My crotch is throbbing.

My chest is tight.

Ryan's closing in on the group and I've gotta pull myself together and act naturally. But what's acting naturally around Ryan Morgan? If we hadn't had sex earlier, and I'd only met him today, would I stare at Ryan lasciviously or look away every time he approached? Would I talk to him breezily or stammer, or would I simply run away, screaming, utterly bowled over by the sheer spectacle of his gorgeousness? I genuinely don't know what the hell "acting naturally" would be around someone as glorious as Ryan Asshole Morgan.

Oh, God. Ryan and his little group have reached my group and they're now greeting everyone with hugs and kisses... and, dammit, despite my brain screaming at me to look away, away, away, far away, from that hot-as-hell lying, cheating scumbag, I just can't seem to do it. He's just so... damned... *hot*.

Greetings and introductions completed, Ryan's smoldering eyes meet mine—and, the minute they do, I feel like I've been struck by a lightning bolt. *I want him.* I try to look away. But I can't. *I want him.* He's got me under some sort of spell. *I want him.*

Ryan slowly works his way around the outer edge of the group toward me, until, finally, he's standing right next to me, shoulder to shoulder, not looking at me, pretending to listen to one of the many simultaneous conversations occurring in the group.

"Oh, hey, T-Rod," Ryan finally says, as if he's only just now noticed me.

"Oh, hey, Colby," I say, staring at his mother as she talks to Uncle William.

Ryan turns to face me, lays his palm on his beautiful chest, and beams a huge smile at me. "I'm *Ryan*." He motions up the beach to his brother. "That's Colby over there." He points at his other two brothers on the far side of the crowd. "That's Keane in the bright orange trunks and Dax standing next to him."

"So sorry," I say sweetly. "It's impossible to keep you all straight. I've always been terrible with names."

Ryan leans toward me, a cocky smile on his lips, and whispers, "Yeah, no shit, *Samantha*."

I narrow my eyes and stare into the crowd. "Victimless crime, fucker," I whisper.

"Hey, T-Rod!" Josh says.

I raise my eyebrows and look at my boss.

"How many people per helicopter?"

"Six," I answer smoothly. "We've chartered a fleet of five to run tours staggered throughout the day on Wednesday."

"So exciting!" Kat squeals, and then she and Sarah hug excitedly, apparently out of pure joy.

I glance at Ryan to find him still staring at me, his blue eyes smoldering.

I stare back, entranced. I've never seen a more exquisitely beautiful face in my entire life. Too bad it's attached to such an asshole.

Ryan licks his lips and brazenly looks me up and down, his eyes settling on my chest for a beat. Which I can't say surprises me—I bought this sundress precisely because it flatters my curves. Oh, man, there's no doubt about it: Ryan's ripping my dress off with his eyes right now, and I must admit, that's exactly what I want him to do... which means I'd better get the hell out of here before I let myself get chomped like a human McNugget. I make a big show of looking down at my phone. "Whoa, look at the time. Gotta go. I'll see everyone at the party tonight."

Nobody reacts. Nobody cares. They're too absorbed in their conversations with the people they love the most in this world to pay any mind to Josh's personal assistant. And that's just fine with me. Peace out.

Without another word or so much as a glance at Ryan, I turn on my heel and lope away from the group. *Oh my God*, get me the hell away from that gorgeous great white shark before I give in to my primal instincts and fuck the living hell out of him. (Again.)

"Hang on," I hear Ryan's voice call out behind me. "Hold up, Theresa."

I stop. Crap. I turn around and smile at him like a cheerleader for the losing team. "Yes?" I ask primly. "What can I do for you, Dax?"

Ryan chuckles and puts his palm on his gloriously inked chest. "I'm *Ryan*. Dax is the guy with the band—*Ryan's* the guy who fucked you earlier."

I gasp and quickly look behind him to make sure nobody's heard him. "*Ryan*," I say urgently. "Someone might overhear you."

He flashes me a cocky grin.

"Walk with me, Romeo. Holy hell."

We begin walking along the sand toward the hotel. "Are you planning to torture me like this all week?" I whisper. "Because if so, please don't. I'm not here for your sick amusement—I've got a job to do."

"We both know it's not your job you're thinking about 'doing' right now, Argentina." He snickers. "So when you wanna have round two?"

"Not gonna happen," I say. "It was a one-time thing, like I said."

"Then why have you been looking at me for the past ten minutes the way a kid looks at a melting ice cream cone—like you're dying to lick up all the drips?"

I stop walking and stare at him. *Oh, God, yes. I wanna lick up all the drips.* "I assure you, the only way I've been looking at you for the past ten minutes is the way a dog-walker looks at a steaming turd in the grass: *ew*."

Ryan bursts out laughing. "God, I love it when a beautiful woman is funny. That's the whole package right there. *Damn*."

I exhale with frustration, even as my eyes drift to his pierced nipples. "I don't want to play this game," I sniff. "I've got work to do and I don't want everyone seeing us talking and start to think we've got something going on. If I want another round of meaningless sex, I'll screw the tattooed bartender I met last night, not Kat's brother."

"Okay, that's it. Don't say that shit again to me. You understand? Never again." He grits his teeth. "If you're gonna have sex this week, meaningless or otherwise, it's gonna be with me and only me."

My clit is practically vibrating, I'm so turned on. "Look, Ryan, I'm not doing this with you. Just tell me what you want so I can smile and nod and not actually listen to you and then walk away without any intention of doing whatever it was you asked."

Ryan crosses his muscled arms over his beautiful chest and assesses me for a long beat. "You really hate me, don't you?"

I'm instantly taken aback by the earnest expression on his face. "Yes," I say, but even as the word comes out of my mouth, I'm not sure it's the sum total of how I feel about him. "And deservedly so," I add. "You're a lying, cheating scumbag-asshole-douche. Now just, please, tell me what you want."

Ryan sighs and runs his hand through his hair. "Okay, all kidding and flirting and bantering aside, I sincerely want your assurance you'll keep quiet about everything that's happened between us."

I'm shocked as hell and I'm sure my face shows it. "Of course," I say. "I'm surprised you're... Oh, I get it: you don't want me cramping your style with the cocktail waitresses out by the pool?"

He rolls his eyes. "Could you stop hurling missiles at me for two seconds? I'm being sincere. I don't want Josh to find out about us. He's obviously protective of you and if he finds out I've already helped myself to a heaping portion of your very delicious pussy, he's gonna be pissed."

I must admit, he's throwing me for a loop. I thought for sure I was gonna have to beg and plead and, quite possibly, threaten to keep Ryan from blabbing about our little tryst. "It goes without saying I'm not gonna tell anyone," I say. "I don't want Josh or Kat or anyone else to know, same as you. Probably more than you."

"Good," Ryan says. He sighs like I've just lifted the weight of the world off his shoulders. "Josh made a big point of telling me he views you like a little sister earlier, and I don't want him thinking I've got no respect for The Bro Code."

"Josh said I'm like a sister to him?"

"Yep. And that means you don't have to worry about me telling my sister or Josh about your little crush. I was already inclined to keep quiet about that, like I said, but if Josh thinks of you like a sister, then there's obviously no risk of anything ever happening between you two. So, don't worry, I'm turning the page on all that. It's done. I swear on a stack of bibles."

Oh my God, I'm so freaking relieved, I could pass out. "Thank you," I breathe.

"Likewise, this fling of ours is nobody's business, either," he adds. "What happens in Maui, stays in Maui."

I can't believe how much stress Ryan's just lifted off me. "Well, thanks, but I keep telling you, there's no 'fling' here, just a one-time, meaningless walk on the wild side for me that will never happen again. With you, anyway."

"I told you to stop doing that." He glares at me. "What the fuck? You fucked me mere hours ago. You don't think I have feelings?"

I'm flabbergasted. This guy's an epic manwhore who hits on women when his girlfriend gets up to use the bathroom and me talking about some other, *hypothetical* man I *might* screw one day "hurts his feelings"? Ridiculous. "So is that all you wanted from me, Ryan?" I say, my tone snippy. "You stopped me to ask me not to tell anyone about our little tryst?"

He takes a step forward and my body instantly reacts to his sheer physicality. "No, that's not even close to all I want from you, but, yes, that's what I wanted to talk to you about at the moment."

"Great. I promise I won't tell anyone." I put out my hand and he shakes it—and, when our skin touches, I feel an electric current jolt through me. I quickly pull my hand away, my heart racing. "So, if that's it for now, I gotta go work."

Ryan motions like he's allowing me to leave. "Off you go, Theresa Rodriguez. Go forth and be the personal assistant you are, as opposed to the flight attendant you pretended to be."

I roll my eyes and turn to go, muttering, "Victimless crime, dude," under my breath.

"Oh, wait, one more thing, Samantha-T-Rod-Theresa-Tessa," Ryan says politely.

I exhale with exasperation. "What, Colby-Dax-Keane-Ryan?"

"Have I earned the right to call you Tessa yet? 'Cause you just don't seem like a 'Theresa' to me."

"Sure," I say. "Call me whatever you want."

"Cool. Thanks. Tessa it is."

"Honestly, I don't go by Theresa, other than at work. Everyone in my real life has always called me Tessa."

"Then why do you go by Theresa at work?"

"I really gotta go, Ryan."

"Just answer the question."

I sigh. "Because when I drafted my résumé for this temp agency right out of college, I thought it seemed more 'professional' to put my formal name on it. So, naturally, when the temp agency sent me to Josh, he called me 'Theresa,' and I just went with it. I was only working for him for ten hours a week at first, running stupid errands, so I was like, 'Meh, who cares what he calls me.' And then I just got used to it and never corrected him. If I were applying for a job today, I'd obviously not be an idiot and just put Tessa on my damned résumé. Live and learn. Anything else? Because I really gotta go."

Ryan grins but doesn't speak.

"Can I go?" I ask in a huff.

"Sure."

"Thank you. Have a great day." I turn to leave.

"Oh, wait. Yeah, there's one more thing, Tessa."

I turn around. "*What?*"

"You wanna fuck in my room or yours after the party tonight? Your choice."

I scowl at him. "I'm sorry. Have we met? Are you Keane or Colby or Dax? You Morgan boys look so much alike."

Ryan takes a step toward me, his eyes blazing, his body heat wafting off him, and my chest tightens with desire. "My name is Ryan Ulysses Morgan, sweetheart," he says, his voice low and intense. "*Captain Morgan.* And trust me, baby, you're not only gonna know my name before the night is through, you'll be screaming it at the top of your lungs." Without waiting for my reply, he winks, flashes me a panty-melting smile, and jogs toward his family and friends on the other side of the beach, leaving me with my jaw hanging open and my crotch pulsing mercilessly.

Chapter 34
Tessa

The opening party is underway on a large patio overlooking the moonlit beach. By now, every guest has arrived except for Henn and his girlfriend, Hannah (who should be here soon), and Reed Rivers (who changed his flight due to a work commitment and will now be arriving late tonight).

Everyone, including me, is drinking rum punch like it's water, chatting, and swaying happily to the pleasant Hawaiian tunes being cranked out by a five-piece band. It's all quite lovely, actually—the perfect environment for me to at least try to let loose, as I promised Josh and Kat I'd do.

I've pointedly not talked to Ryan yet tonight, and, in fact, I've somehow managed to not even glance at him, but I don't know how much longer I can resist staring at his beautiful lying face. In fact, the jig is up right now—I gotta look.

I scan the party and locate him talking to a few of Josh's fraternity brothers—and not three seconds after I've glanced his way, Ryan's eyes meet mine and his entire face lights up. With a tilt of his head, Ryan beams a cocky smile at me, winks, and touches the face of his watch, as if to say, "It's only a matter of time, baby."

I look away. *Cocky bastard.*

Thankfully, Mrs. Morgan approaches and introduces me to some of her family members and I'm drawn into pleasant conversation with some lovely people. Of course, I don't actually care about these lovely people right now—I only care about peeking over at Ryan Fuckface Lying Asshole Cheating Scumbag Morgan to see what he's doing now. God, I hate myself for giving a crap what he's doing. No, actually, I hate *him*. What the hell is wrong with me? How can I want to screw a man I don't even like? A man I don't *respect*? Is that how fucked up I've become—I'm willing to screw a hot guy just because he's hot?

Damn straight, I am.

I close my eyes and revel in my sexy memories for a moment. Honestly, I think Ryan's turned me into some kind of sex fiend after just one time with him. I've never felt this horny in my entire life. Wasn't finally having sex after a year supposed to quench my sexual thirst, not make it worse?

"That's where you're from, right, Tessa?" Mrs. Morgan asks me.

I open my eyes and look at her and nod, not knowing what she just said.

"What part?" Mrs. Morgan's sister asks.

"Of...?" I ask.

"Los Angeles."

Phew. I got lucky that time, but I've absolutely gotta stop tuning out of conversations to daydream about Ryan and his pierced dick.

I answer the questions and we talk about Los Angeles for a bit, and then, thankfully, Mrs. Morgan tells a story that allows me to tune out and think about the look of pure rapture on Ryan's face when he was moving inside me—the way he gripped my hair and moved his hips so confidently—so *passionately*—and, oh, the primal, ragged, near-desperate sound of his voice when he whispered, "Samantha" into my ear. True, it was kinda kinky when he called me that name—*but I loved it*.

"Hey, Momma," Ryan says, out of nowhere, accompanied by Colby. He kisses Mrs. Morgan on the cheek. "You look pretty tonight."

Mrs. Morgan hugs Ryan and Colby while I watch and focus every ounce of my energy on not maniacally shrieking, "I hate you, Ryan! Let's go fuck!"

"Hi, Tessa," Ryan says casually. He half-hugs me like he barely knows me (good boy!) and kisses me on the cheek chastely. "You look pretty tonight, too."

Oh, God, the smell of Ryan's cologne is filling my nostrils. *I want him.* I clear my throat. "Hi, Keane," I say. "Thank you so much. You look nice, too."

Colby laughs.

Ryan puts his palm on his chest. "*Ryan*. Keane's over there in the blue shirt." He motions to his brother across the party. "And that's Dax standing next to him in the black shirt. And this is Colby."

"Oh, gosh, I'm so sorry," I say innocently. "So many Morgans. Forgive me."

Colby flashes me a huge smile. "You're not alone in getting us mixed up. Our own mother used to call us by wrong names at least fifty times a day when we were growing up."

"It's true," Louise says, laughing. "I'd say, 'Ry-Ke-Da-Col-*Kitty*... whoever you are, get your butt over here and clean up your mess!'"

Everyone in the group laughs.

"Yeah, don't stress about names," Ryan says, his eyes locked with mine. "Names are irrelevant, if you think about it. 'A rose by any other name would smell just as sweet.'" He winks.

Whoa. Did Ryan just tell me he's done being mad about the whole 'Samantha' thing? By George, I think he did. And did he quote from *Romeo and Juliet* by pure coincidence, or as a little nod to the fact that I keep calling him Romeo?

"By the way," Colby says, extending his hand to me. "We haven't been formally introduced. I'm Colby."

I shake Colby's hand. "It's great to meet you. I've heard wonderful things about you."

"All of it true," Ryan says.

"You're a firefighter?" I ask.

Colby confirms he is and we talk for several minutes about his deep passion for his job, which, he explains, he's temporarily on medical leave from because of "an accident" he had on the job earlier this year. I'm curious to find out more about that, but something in Colby's tone of voice tells me not to ask him for details, so I refrain.

After a bit, Colby excuses himself to use the restroom and, the minute he slips away, I realize everyone else but Ryan has wandered away, too.

Ryan leans into my ear and whispers, "Man, I can't stop thinking about what I'm gonna do to you tonight."

I'm tingling all over at Ryan's words, but I adopt an expression of complete disinterest. "Like I keep telling you, there's not gonna be a Round Two, Romeo."

"I bet you're already soaking wet for me," Ryan whispers. "I wish I could slip my hand up your dress and inside your panties to find out."

Whoosh. Just like that, blood is flooding my crotch. "I need a drink," I say, and, without another word, I beeline to the bar.

Without missing a beat, Ryan walks alongside me.

"I wasn't inviting you to join me," I whisper. "I was giving you the brush-off."

"Can I be perfectly honest with you?"

"I don't know, Ryan, can you?"

"I feel addicted to you. I can't stop thinking about how much I wanna taste you again." He licks his lips.

"That's so weird because I'm not thinking about you at all."

"You look especially beautiful tonight."

"You look especially like a liar tonight."

"What does a liar look like?"

"Hell if I know. And that right there's my biggest problem in life."

We reach the bar and place our orders.

Ryan leans forward and whispers in my ear. "I can't stop thinking about how sweet you tasted. And how incredible you felt when I was inside you. It's like you were made for me. And when you came around my cock? Oh my God, I thought I was gonna pass out from sheer pleasure. So hot."

"Glad I could make your day. Now leave me alone."

He's absolutely unfazed. "Now that I've learned a bit about your cues and sounds, I'm gonna go for six next time."

I look at him quizzically. "Six?"

"Orgasms. For you. At least six. Maybe seven. Depends if I can hold on long enough. A guy's gotta have aspirations, right?"

I feel my cheeks flush. I'd never tell Ryan this, of course, but the fact that he brought me to climax more than once was a first for me— a truly mind-blowing first. I've heard about other women climaxing repeatedly during a single sexual encounter, of course, but, prior to Ryan, it's never happened to me, even when I've been really turned on and into a guy—and I've certainly never had an orgasm during intercourse itself. But, man, oh man, did Ryan flip some crazy switch inside me. And it wasn't just that I came multiple times that's got me so freaking sexed-up right now, it's how hard I came. Good lord, it was like nothing I've experienced before—like my prior sexual partners have been little leaguers and I finally got to The Show. "Six would be impossible," I say.

"Challenge accepted," Ryan says smoothly.

"I've never come close to that number," I say.

"Only because you haven't been with me," he says.

I open and close my mouth. Shit. Could he be right about that? Is he literally the only guy in the world who knows how to flip my switch? If so, God help me and any future guy I might sleep with because I don't think I'll be able to settle for anything less for the rest of my life.

"What's your record during one session?" he asks.

I take a gulp of my drink.

"One, right?" he asks. "I'm guessing you've always thought you were a one-and-done kind of girl."

I nod, my cheeks burning.

"You're not alone," Ryan says breezily. "You don't even know what you're missing so you don't know to shoot for more. And most guys feel like rock stars if they get their girl to come *once,* so it's a vicious cycle. Fucking pathetic."

I drain my drink and try not to look like I'm lapping up every word.

Ryan takes a long sip of his drink. "To be honest, I'm kind of obsessed with the female orgasm. I get off on it so fucking hard." He smiles. "The more I learn you, the more I figure out what your body likes best, the more I figure out your body's cues and sounds, the harder and more easily you're gonna come for me—and that's gonna make me a very happy boy." He licks his lips again. "I can't wait to see how far I can take you, baby."

I shift my weight, trying to relieve the unbelievable pulsing in my panties.

"You know what I'm dying to do to you right now?" he says, his eyes slowly migrating from my face to my breasts. "I wanna kiss and lick and suck those incredible breasts of yours, so hard you're gonna come from that alone."

"Ryan!" Kat's voice says, and my throbbing crotch freezes like a thief caught red-handed in the night. "Look who's finally here! *Henny!*"

Chapter 35
Tessa

Kat's accompanied not only by Henn and his girlfriend, a cute brunette with glasses Kat introduces as "Hannah Banana Montana Milliken," but also by Josh, Jonas, and Sarah. The group hugs Ryan and me and Josh asks if I've been keeping my promise to "let loose." When I assure my darling boss that, yes, I've been drinking rum punch all night long, Mr. Faraday seems unimpressed and demands we all throw back a shot of tequila, which we do. And, fifteen minutes later, as everyone's telling funny stories and laughing around me, I suddenly realize I've forgotten to feel self-conscious that I'm partying with my rich and powerful boss and his glamorous circle. In fact, dare I say it, I kind of feel like I'm hanging out with my own good friends. *And it feels awesome.*

I'm especially enjoying watching Ryan interact with the group. He's funny as hell and charming beyond words. Actually, if I'm being honest, watching Ryan tonight is making me feel about him the exact same way I did at The Pine Box. *Sigh.* Wait. No. What the hell is wrong with me? *Ryan's a liar. A cheater. An asshole.* I can't let myself fall under his spell again, just because he's physically perfect and utterly charming. Am I insane?

"Um, excuse me," I blurt, smack in the middle of Sarah telling a story. I quickly bolt away, determined to head straight to my room, tuck myself into bed, and hide for the rest of the week (my promise to Josh and Kat be damned!).

"The Mighty T-Rod!" Keane bellows as I stride past him. "Come here for a sec."

Crap. So much for my quick getaway. I stop and smile at Keane. He's standing with his best friend, Zander, his brother, Dax, and

183

Dax's two friends, Fish and Colin (the other two-thirds of Dax's band, 22 Goats).

I tell Dax and his bandmates I've watched a bunch of their videos on YouTube and loved them. It's true. After Kat informed me she wanted to have her younger brother's band play a concert for everyone, I watched some 22 Goats performances, just to see what kind of shit show we were in for, and I was shocked to discover the band is actually great. I ask the boys of 22 Goats how they got started, and they tell me they were best friends in high school. And, finally, I ask the boys why in the heck they're named "22 Goats."

"It's a really stupid story," Dax replies, but when I assure him I'm genuinely interested, he proceeds to tell me the whole, hilarious story, complete with showing me a Buzzfeed article about smiling goats he calls up on his phone.

As Dax talks, I laugh and laugh and feel more and more charmed by him. What a cutie. "I'm excited to hear you guys play tomorrow night," I say. "Kat had very few 'must-haves' for this week's itinerary, but a concert by 22 Goats was at the top of her list."

Dax chuckles. "Something tells me my big sister had an ulterior motive for requesting a 22 Goats concert this week."

"Oh, you mean Reed Rivers?" I ask.

Dax nods. "Josh sent him our demo a few months back, but he's never seen us play live."

"Has Reed listened to the demo?"

"Yeah. He said he loved it, but that he wanted to check out a performance before making a decision—but then I guess he got busy or distracted or whatever, and he still hasn't made it up to Seattle."

"So your clever sister brought the show to him," I say.

"That's the Jizz-i-nator for ya," Keane pipes in. "There's no stopping that girl when she sets her mind to something."

"The 'Jizz-i-nator'?" I ask.

Dax laughs. "It's a riff on Jizz, her lifelong nickname."

"You call Kat *Jizz*?"

"We call our sister any variation of splooge we can think of," Keane says. "Jizz, Kum Shot, Baby Gravy, Cream of Sum Yung Guy."

I make a face. "Sounds highly traumatizing."

"Our mother would agree with you," Dax says.

"Why on earth do you do that to poor Kat? Just to be cruel?"

"Hell no," Keane says, feigning offense. "Morgan boys are never *cruel*—just extremely mean."

"We're cruel to be kind," Dax adds. "It's not as bad as it sounds. Kat's initials are K-U-M. Under the circumstances, if we *didn't* call her Kum Shot and Jizz and all the rest, we wouldn't be doing our brotherly duty."

Keane interjects, "It's our parents' fault. If only they'd named Kat '*Rachel* Ulla Morgan,' she'd have a bunch of *rum*-related nicknames, just like Ryan. But did my clueless parents think of that? Nope."

"*Oh*," I say, an epiphany slamming me. "Ryan *Ulysses* Morgan. R-U-M. That's why everyone keeps calling Ryan 'Rum Cake'?"

"Yup," Dax says. "Rum Cake, Captain Morgan, Bacardi, Rum Jungle..."

"So *that's* what that bottle-tattoo on Ryan's ribcage is?" I ask. "A bottle of *rum*?" My cheeks flush. "I, uh, saw it on the beach."

"Yeah," Dax replies. "My dad says Ryan heard, 'Yo, ho, ho and a bottle of rum' as a toddler and has been obsessed with pirate-stuff ever since."

My head is swimming. I glance over at Ryan across the party, to find him still talking to the same Faraday-Henn group as before. *Captain Morgan.* Warmth spreads throughout my body. *Captain, My Captain.*

After a moment, Keane's voice draws me out of my hormone-induced reverie. "Don't stress it, little brother," Keane is saying to Dax. "Halfway through your first song tomorrow night, Reed will be begging 22 Goats to sign on the dotted line. And when he does, send him my way to negotiate the contract, son. I'll get you top dollar."

"Yeah, all of it in crumpled singles that smell like your balls," Fish says, and everyone laughs.

"Hey, nothing wrong with singles that smell like my balls," Keane says. "They've been paying my rent just fine."

"Hey, you know I love you the most, Peenie—and that's not a figure of speech," Dax says. "But you're the last person in the world I'd ask to negotiate a contract for me."

Keane laughs. "Probably a wise choice. Better ask Ryan." When my eyes involuntarily shift to Ryan across the room for the umpteenth time, Keane follows my gaze and nudges my arm. "That man right there is the greatest guy you'll ever meet, T-Rod. Any woman would be lucky to snag that dude." He lowers his voice. "And, fun fact? I've heard from a reliable source Rum Cake *really* knows his way around a cockpit, if you know what I mean, so I'd definitely hop aboard that jet plane and ride it all the way to the horizon if you get the opportunity." He winks.

I'm absolutely floored. *What the fuck did Keane just say to me?* And more importantly, *why* the *fuck* did he feel compelled say it? Ryan must have said something to Keane about us! Oh my God, I'm gonna rip that loose-lipped bastard limb from motherfucking limb!

"Yee-boy!" Keane says loudly, high-fiving Zander, pulling me out of my murderous thoughts. "You hear that, Z? Daxy loves me the most."

"Of course, he does, baby doll," Zander says. "We all do."

"It's cause I'm a giver, honey nuggets—it's a blessing and a curse."

"*Honey nuggets?*" I interject, my head spinning. "Baby doll?"

"Oh, that's nothing between those two," Dax says. "They also call each other 'Wifey' and a million other bizarre things two dudes in a straight bromance normally wouldn't call each other. You get used to it when you hang around them long enough."

"Ain't no shame in my game," Zander says. "Love is love. I'll say it loud and proud: *I love Peen.*"

We all laugh.

And, just like that, I'm having too much fun to focus on plotting Ryan's murder anymore, though I'll surely resume my plotting later. "So how'd this beautiful bromance between the two of you start?" I ask Keane and Zander. "Do you two work together?"

"Oh, hell no," Zander says. "I'm a personal trainer, not a professional ass-shaker. Actually, Peen and I met—"

"Hold up, Choco Nana," Keane says, holding up his hand. "Let me tell T-Rod the story of how we met."

"Oh, you wanna tell T-Rod the story of how we met, do ya?" Zander asks, a twinkle in his eye. "Sure, Peenie Weenie, be my guest."

Chapter 36
Tessa

Keane flashes his outrageous dimples and clears his throat. "Well, Tessa—may I call you Tessa?"

"Of course."

"Zander and I met at the gym about a year ago. I'd just finished my workout and had walked into the locker room to shower when, lo and behold, what did I see but a big, muscular black man standing buck naked in front of the locker next to mine."

Zander chuckles.

Keane continues, "So I go to my locker and strip down to my glorious birthday suit—the sight of which, by the way, has made many a woman spontaneously orgasm, I should mention; but, just before I head for the showers, I happen to glance at Zander's flaccid dong. And guess what I noticed about it?"

I cringe. "Um... I really don't... feel comfortable guessing, actually."

"*Zander and I had the exact same dick-tattoo!*" Keane blurts.

Everyone bursts out laughing, including me.

"Oh my God, Peenie," Zander says, laughing and shaking his head.

Keane continues, his eyes full of mischief: "Now, mind you, at the time, both our dicks were playing *Crouching Tiger, Hidden Dragon*, so our tattoos at that particular moment read 'W-D-Y.'" He leans forward like he's telling me a secret. "When I'm at full mast, my dick-tattoo says 'Wendy.'"

"Wendy?" I ask, giggling.

Keane nods. "My high school sweetheart and first love—the woman who so deftly stole my heart along with my virginity, the very beautiful and surprisingly flexible, Wendy *Johnson*."

187

Everyone laughs uproariously.

I don't know where Keane's ridiculous story is leading, but I must say I'm feeling highly entertained along the way. "Wow, Keane," I say. "What a romantic gesture. The guy who took my virginity gave me a bag of pretzels and a Coke." Everyone guffaws at that, and I feel elated to be able to make this particularly funny crowd laugh out loud. "I wish I were joking," I add dryly, and everyone laughs again.

"Gosh, Peen," Dax says. "I sure hope Wendy Johnson appreciated your tribute to her."

"As a matter of fact, no, Wendy Johnson, did *not* appreciate the heartfelt sentiment of my penis art," Keane says, looking appropriately forlorn. "A week after I got my pecker inked for her, Wendy dumped me to go to prom with another dude."

"Oh no," I say, but, of course, I'm smiling when I say it. "You must have been devastated."

"I was. Although I had to tip my cap to her prom date. You know what *that* guy's dick tattoo said?"

I shake my head, already giggling in anticipation of whatever he's going to say.

Keane pauses for comedic effect before saying, "'Prom?'"

Everyone laughs uproariously.

"So, anyhoozles," Keane says when the laughter has died down a bit. "Back to Zander and me and the inception of our bromance. So ZZ Top and I are standing naked next to each other in that locker room, pretty much crossing swords, and I look down at his flaccid dong with 'W-D-Y' inked on it, and I'm like, 'Twinsies!'"

Oh, man, it's quite possible Keane Morgan is the goofiest human I've ever met. How the hell is his ridiculous personality packaged inside a body that looks like Captain America?

Keane continues, "So I go, 'Hey, dude, I think we should be best friends.' And Zander goes, 'Let's get an apartment!' So the next day, we get an apartment and I'm thinking, 'Life can't get any better than this. When sex isn't involved, of course.'"

"And, just to be clear, all this bonding was inspired by nothing but matching dick-tattoos?" I ask.

"Correct. So, Z and I become besties and we're handsome and happy lads all the livelong day, both of us raking in the duckets by the buckets and making chicks our bailiwicks, until one tragic night when everything went to hell in a handbasket on us."

"Uh oh," I say. "What could possibly have gone wrong?"

"Thanks for asking," Keane replies. He leans toward me, an adorable expression on his face. "This works best when I have an interactive audience."

I laugh.

"So here's what happened," Keane says. "Z and I were lying on our couch, talking about girls, smoking weed, and I go, 'Hey, Z, I just realized I've never asked you about your 'Wendy' tattoo. And Zander goes, 'Wendy?' So I say, 'You know, whatever Wendy inspired the 'Wendy' tattoo on your dick.' And Zander replies, 'My dick doesn't say *Wendy*.' And I'm like, 'But your tattoo says W-D-Y, just like mine!'" Keane pauses and smiles, his eyes sparkling. "And you wanna know what Z said then?"

"No, Peen," Dax says dryly. "We've made it this far into your stupid fucking story and we don't wanna know what Zander's dick tattoo said."

Keane's smile widens and his dimples pop out of his face. "Z said, 'My 'W-D-Y' tattoo doesn't say 'WENDY,' baby doll. It says '*W*ELCOME TO SEATTLE. MY NAME IS ZANDER SHAW. HAVE A GREAT... *DAY*!'"

I burst into hysterical laughter along with everyone else.

Finally, when the group's laughter has died down enough for conversation to resume, Keane flashes me his irresistible dimples, pats me on the head like a puppy and says, "Z and I met in math class in eighth grade. I said, 'Yo, smart guy, will you help me with this shit?' And we've been best friends ever since."

Chapter 37
Ryan

Fuck my life.

I'm standing here talking to Josh, Kat, Jonas, Sarah, Henn and Henn's girlfriend, Hannah (whom Kat keeps calling "Hannah Banana Montana Milliken"), and, much to my horror, Henn's in the midst of telling everyone about the email I sent him earlier today. And as he does, maybe I'm paranoid, but it truly seems like Kat's face keeps lighting up with recognition, specifically when Henn says "Charlotte McDougal" and "redhead" and "Delta."

"So did you call Charlotte?" Henn asks me.

"Yeah, I left a voicemail for her, but she hasn't called me back yet," I reply, lying through my teeth. (What choice do I have?)

"Keep us posted," Henn says. "Hopefully, Charlotte McDougal will finally lead you to your Argentinian whale, Captain Ahab."

"Hey, will you all excuse me for a second?" Kat says. "I see Tessa over there talking to Dax and I want to make sure we're all set for tomorrow night's big concert." Without waiting for anyone's reply, Kat beelines across the party, straight to Dax and Tessa—a move that makes the hairs on the back of my neck stand up. *What the fuck is my diabolical sister up to?*

"So you're still totally into the flight attendant," Josh says, his eyes narrowed.

I look at Josh and my stomach clenches at the hard-ass way he's looking at me. Obviously, he's not thrilled to think I'm still obsessed with Samantha while simultaneously sniffing around his honorary little sister.

"I'm not still into the flight attendant," I reply lamely. "I just want to find her so I can clear my name with her, that's all. She thinks

I'm some sort of player-douche, and that's the furthest thing from the truth."

"What the fuck!" Henn blurts, drawing my attention away from Josh's hard stare. "You want to find Samantha to 'clear your name,' and not because she's your Cinderella? Jesus, that's hardly a reason to hack into nine airlines."

Fuck.

Henn looks at Jonas. "Back me up on this, Big Guy: Ryan said he had a big-time 'soul connection' with the flight attendant. It was never about clearing his name."

"Yup," Jonas says. "That's what he said. His soul was screaming at him to find her."

Aw, Jesus. Now Jonas is looking at me like I'm a complete asshole.

"No. Yeah. I *did* say that," I choke out. *Fuck*! "And I meant every word. It was all true. It's just that it's been so long at this point, I've had to start managing my expectations, you know, to protect my sanity. So, I've decided if this Charlotte McDougal doesn't call me back within the next forty-eight hours, then I'm just gonna have to force myself to move on and not think about Samantha anymore—just because it's not sane to do otherwise."

Now Jonas is looking at me like I'm not just an asshole, I'm a traitorous motherfucker, too. "Well, kudos to you if moving on is that simple for you, man," Jonas says. "Whether it's the sane thing to do or not, I certainly wouldn't have been able to turn the page on my search for Sarah the way you're saying, not if I'd invested the kind of time and effort you have and was as close as you are now." Jonas glances at his brother and they share a loaded look, and then Jonas returns his attention to me and smiles. "But, hey, I guess I'm just a much crazier fuck than you."

Chapter 38
Tessa

"Z and I met in math class in eighth grade," Keane says. "I said, 'Yo, smart guy, will you help me with this shit?' And we've been best friends ever since."

I giggle. "Oh my gosh, Keane. Did you come up with that ri-*dick*-ulous story on the fly, or is that your go-to answer whenever someone asks how you and Zander met?"

"On the fly," Keane says. "Bullshitting is kinda my superpower."

Zander chuckles. "If bullshitting could pay the bills, Peenie and I would be living in the penthouse suite."

"Bullshitting *can* pay the bills these days," I say. "It's called reality TV. Actually, in all seriousness, I bet if a casting agent—"

I feel an arm slide around my shoulders and I stop talking—and when I turn my head, I see Kat's gorgeous, smiling face a few inches from mine.

"Hey, Miss Rodriguez," Kat coos. "Are you having fun, as promised?"

I hold up my near-empty glass. "Yes, Mrs.-Faraday-To-Be. The rum punch is flowing and Keane just finished telling me the highly entertaining story of how he and Zander fell in platonic love thanks to identical dick-tattoos."

Kat laughs. "That's a new one. I thought Peenie and Z became besties after being trapped together in an elevator with a porn star." She shoots Keane a snarky look and he belly-laughs. "Fucking Peen," she mutters, but she's smiling. "So, Tessa, I came over here to make sure everything's all set for tomorrow night's concert?"

"Yep. I've got everything handled, my dear. The sound company will be here at three to start setting up; sound-check for the boys will

192

be at five, right before the luau; and, when the luau's over, we'll make an announcement telling everyone to head over to the nightclub for the show. And, don't worry, I'll personally escort Reed Rivers to the nightclub."

"Ah, you've figured out my dastardly plan, have you?" Kat says. I wink.

"Please do make sure Reed gets his ass over there," Kat says. "My worst nightmare would be for Reed to suddenly decide to take a stroll on the beach with a hula dancer after the luau."

"I'll get him there, by hook or crook," I say. "I promise."

"You're amazing, Tessa. Hey, come with me to the bar, would you, honey? I need another club soda and it looks like your glass is empty."

"Sure thing." I put my arm out and she links her elbow in mine and we stroll toward the bar like she's a duchess and I'm her merry maid, giggling the entire way.

"Have I ever told you how much you remind me of Sarah?" Kat says.

"Yup, you told me that while we were shopping for your wedding dress, remember?"

"That's right. And what did you say in response?"

"I said that was funny because you remind *me* so much of *my* best friend, too."

"Oh, yeah," Kat says. "And what'd you say to me then? I remember it was so cute."

"I said my best friend Charlotte is you to a tee, if only Charlotte had blonde hair instead of red and an additional five inches added to her legs."

Kat giggles. "I just love that my spiritual doppelgänger is a cute little redhead. What's Charlotte's last name again? I remember it was an adorable little leprechaun name."

"Wow, you have a great memory. Charlotte McDougal."

Kat lets out a loud squeal. "*Charlotte McDougal.* That's right. Oh, how I love that adorable name."

"Charlotte's name fits her. She's a sassy little leprechaun."

"To sassy leprechauns!" Kat says, raising her cup.

"Hear, hear!" I say.

"Let's go over there, honey," Kat says, pointing to a quiet area overlooking the moonlit beach. "I want you all to myself for a minute."

We walk a few paces to a secluded little spot, and I must admit, I'm feeling awfully special Kat wants to talk with me one-on-one for a bit, even if it's just for a few minutes, especially when she's got an entire party full of people who've flown thousands of miles to be with her.

"So pretty," Kat says, looking at the ocean. "It's truly paradise, isn't it?"

"It sure is," I agree. "Thank you for letting me enjoy it as a guest. I thought it'd be hard for me to take my employee-hat off, but I've found it shockingly easy." I take another long guzzle of my drink and giggle to myself about how buzzed I feel.

"You feeling okay, honey?" Kat says. "You seem a little wobbly."

"I'm great. *Fantastic*. But, yeah, a teeny bit wobbly."

"Hold onto my belly, sweetie—it's like a life raft."

I place both of my palms on Kat's hard baby bump. "Ah. Much better. Thanks."

"You don't get crazy-wild very often, do you?"

I shake my head. "I'm a Virgo."

"A *Virgo*? Do you know I love astrology?"

"No, I had no idea."

"I do. I've read a million books on it. I'm a whiz." She assesses me for a long beat. "Virgos are the careful ones—tender and sensitive but very cautious."

I nod. "That's me. Sensitive and cautious."

"They pay great attention to detail. They're precise. They're loyal as hell, love to help people, and absolutely hate feeling out of control."

"You've got me pegged, sister."

"Sucks to be you, then, huh?"

I laugh. "Sometimes."

"I can't imagine wanting to be in control all the time," Kat says. "In fact, losing complete control of myself is one of my favorite pastimes."

"Charlotte's the same way," I say. "And I must say, I'm beginning to think you crazy-girls might know something the rest of us don't. I've recently discovered losing complete control of myself—at appropriate times—has its advantages." I snicker to myself.

"God, it's amusing to be the only sober person at a party."

"Huh?"

"Nothing. Tessa sweetie, I was just thinking. Wouldn't it be fun if we got Charlotte and Sarah together to see if they'd fall as deeply in love as we have?"

My heart leaps. Kat Morgan and I have fallen "deeply in love"? I didn't realize that. I mean, I knew *I* had a major girl-crush on *Kat*, of course. Who wouldn't? But I had no idea the feeling was mutual. All of a sudden, I feel so much love for Kat, I want to grab her and kiss her. So, that's what I do. I put my arms around her and press my body into her baby bump and lay a big, fat kiss on her soft cheek. "You're sweet, Kat Morgan," I whisper. "Sweet as can be."

Kat giggles. "And you're drunk, Tessa Rodriguez."

"A little bit."

"But also really, really sweet," Kat adds.

"Thank you. So are you."

"You said that already."

"Oh, yeah. Well, you are."

Kat and I disengage from our embrace and she strokes my long hair for a minute, her hand around my waist. "I really think you should invite Charlotte to come here for the week," she says. "You're a guest, right? Well, every guest gets a plus-one. I'm sorry I didn't think of it before."

"You're so sweet, Kitty," I say, putting my cheek on her shoulder. "Sweet, sweet, sweet. I didn't know a woman who looks like a supermodel could be so sweet."

Kat laughs. "*You* look like a supermodel."

"No."

"*Yes.*"

"Sweet."

"So will you ask Charlotte to come to Maui? I'm dying to meet her."

"Okay. I'm supposed to talk with Charlotte tomorrow about this asshole I slept with, so I'll ask her then."

"Perfect. Wait, what are you gonna talk to Charlotte about tomorrow?"

"About an asshole I slept with today." Gah! This is exactly why I shouldn't drink on the job. "I mean, um, the other day. I shouldn't have slept with him—it was very bad of me—but I did it and I'm not at all sorry."

Kat's face is absolutely glowing. "Who is he?"

"Oh, just this guy," I say. "This hot guy who's probably gonna wind up breaking my heart and there's nothing I can do about it."

"Why do you think he's gonna break your heart?" Kat asks. "Maybe he's not an asshole, after all."

"Nope. He's an asshole. A lying, cheating scumbag-asshole. But for some reason, my body doesn't seem to care."

Kat strokes my hair again. "I like Drunk Tessa. She's a blabbermouth."

"Thank you."

"I vote you give the asshole a chance," Kat says. "Maybe he's got a perfectly good explanation for his purported assholery."

"Or maybe he's just an asshole."

We stare at the moonlight, cuddled up for a long beat.

"Hey, I was just wondering," Kat says. "Does Charlotte happen to work in PR, just like me? That'd be a crazy coincidence, wouldn't it?"

"Nope. No PR for Charlotte—she's a flight attendant."

Kat lets out a strangely demonic noise. "God, I love my life."

"I love your life, too, Kitty. I want your life."

"What airline does Charlotte work for?" Kat asks.

"Delta."

Kat lets out a little evil-laugh and then smiles at me sweetly. "Does Charlotte like being a flight attendant for Delta?"

"Oh, she loves it. It's her dream job. Wooh! I'm feeling *really* wobbly." I grip Kat's baby bump even more tightly.

"You okay?" Kat asks.

I nod.

Kat squeezes my arm. "I have a friend who's a flight attendant and she loves it, too. She especially loves the attention she gets from men whenever she wears her uniform, especially to bars—she says she feels like the sexiest girl in the world."

"Oh my gosh! That's exactly what Charlotte says!"

"No."

"*Yes*," I insist.

"Tell me more," Kat says.

"Charlotte says when she's in uniform, especially in bars, she attracts hotties like taking candy from horny babies—and believe me, Charlotte McDougal has no qualms about taking man-candy from horny babies in very large fistfuls." I snort.

"Wow," Kat marvels, "Charlotte really *is* my sister-from-another-mister. Too bad I never tried wearing one of my friend's flight-attendant uniforms to a bar—it sure sounds like it would have been a blast."

"Honey, if you'd worn a flight-attendant uniform into a bar, the place would have burst into flames if anyone so much as lit a cigarette."

We both laugh.

"I used to do stuff like that all the time, actually," Kat says. "Not anymore, of course." She holds up the massive rock on her finger. "Nowadays, I do all my role-play with Josh."

I blush.

Kat continues, "But back in the day, one of my favorite things to do was go to a bar with my friends to see what outlandish persona I could get some hot guy to believe."

"Like what kinds of outlandish personas?"

"Oh, all sorts. My favorite was Matilda Blackburn from Perth who worked at a crocodile farm. That one always slayed."

"Let me hear your Aussie accent," I say.

Kat gathers herself for a beat, shakes out her hair, and then says, "G'day, mate. Whaddaya say we ride our emus to Chris Hemsworth's house and have ourselves some brekkie?"

I giggle. "Is that your impression of an Australian or a pirate at Disneyland?"

Kat guffaws at that. "I do it much better when I'm shitfaced."

"Of course, you do. What were some of your other personas? This is fascinating."

"Sometimes, I said I was a pro tennis player named Olga Slovinskaya from the Czech Republic. That one was fun until this one guy happened to be fluent in Czech. Oh, and when I was feeling extra sassy, I'd sometimes say I'd just escaped from a cult and it was my first time out in a bar."

I laugh uproariously. "Well, jeez, honey, after all those crazy scenarios, wearing a flight-attendant uniform to a bar would have been anti-climactic. Believe me, it's not nearly as thrilling as it sounds."

Kat's face lights up. "Oooh, you've done it?"

My heart leaps into my throat. Shit. Did I just admit that to Kat? "Um."

"Aw, come on, sweetie pie, you can tell me," Kat purrs. "Have you worn Charlotte McDougal's flight-attendant uniform to a bar?"

Aw, fuck it. "Yeah. Once."

Kat squeals.

"Charlotte made me do it."

Kat lets out an evil laugh and then mutters under her breath, "Note to self: Call Agent Eric and tell him he's a piker."

"Huh?"

"Oh, nothing, honey. Now tell me the juicy details about that *one* crazy time you wore Charlotte's uniform to a bar. Did you meet any hotties?"

"Just one—the asshole I told you about earlier. But I don't want to talk about him." I throw back the rest of my drink. "In fact, I think I'm gonna go to bed now. We've got an exciting day tomorrow and I need to sleep off the rum—and you need to get back to your party." I give her a quick little squeeze. "Nighty night, Almost-Mrs.-Faraday. Thank you for always being so sweet to me, right from Day One. I truly adore you. You're my hero." I turn to leave, intending to sprint away before Kat corners me and asks me any more questions about the asshole I slept with, but she intertwines her arm in mine, keeping me anchored to her side.

"Hang on, love," Kat says. "If you're feeling wobbly, you shouldn't walk to your room alone. We wouldn't want you tripping and falling into a koi pond and passing out. I'll walk you to your room, just to be sure you get there safely."

"No, no. I'm just a little wobbly, not shitfaced. And you can't walk me to my room—this is your party, honey. You're the reason for the season."

"Good point. Then I'll get Colby to walk you. He won't mind. The firefighter motto is 'service before self.' Oh, wait. Shoot. I keep forgetting about Colby's leg. Darn it. Well, hmm." She turns around and scans the party like she's making an incredibly important decision. She taps the little cleft in her chin. "Well, I certainly can't ask Keaney to take you—he might hit on you, the horny bastard."

I laugh. "No, he won't. We already feel like brother and sister."

"Good. Because he's the most egregious manwhore who ever lived. Stay the fuck away from that one."

"Is Keane more of a manwhore than... your other brothers?" I ask. But, of course, the only brother I'm actually asking about is Ryan.

"My other brothers aren't manwhores. Not like Keane, anyway."

"Not even Ryan? He seems like a manwhore."

Kat smirks. "No, honey. Ryan's not a manwhore. He used to be, don't get me wrong—there was a time when I wouldn't let him touch any of my friends with a ten-foot pole. But not anymore. Nowadays, he's very much a one-woman kind of guy, by choice."

I tilt my head and look at her funny. "*Ryan?*"

Kat nods. "And Daxy's a whole other kettle of fish. He hates the whole groupie thing—he's actually always looking for a genuine 'soul connection.'" Kat shrugs. "So I guess it'll have to be Ryan or Daxy escorting you, then." She smiles sweetly. "Any preference between Ryan or Dax?" She arches one of her bold eyebrows—and suddenly, I get the distinct feeling this is a test of some sort.

"Um, nope, no preference whatsoever," I say, trying to sound sincere, although, I must admit, I'm praying Kat saves me from myself and picks Dax.

"Ryan, then," Kat says decisively. "I'm sure Dax will want to be at the party when Reed arrives later." She slides her hand into mine. "Come on, honey. Let's go ask Ryan to get you safely to your room."

"It's really not necessary," I say, the hairs on my arms standing up. *Kat's gonna ask Ryan to escort me to my room?* Oh, God, help me.

"No, honey," Kat says. "I don't want you walking alone when you're wobbly. Don't worry, Ryan is completely trustworthy and reliable. He's a real sweetheart, that one—a real knight in shining armor. Honestly, if I were gonna set you up with any of my brothers—or with any guy in the world, actually—Ryan would be the one." Kat smiles broadly. "Come on, sweetie. Let me take you to Ryan now. I'm sure he'll be thrilled to do it."

Chapter 39
Ryan

"What the fuck!" Tessa screams at me the second we're out of earshot from the party. "Have you told your entire fucking family about us?"

"Of course not. Why do you say that?" I ask.

I'm walking alongside her on a winding pathway that I'm assuming leads to her room, amused as hell at the furious way she's stomping her feet and swinging her arms as she marches two paces ahead of me.

"Because Kat just made a big point of telling me you're a 'knight in shining armor' and that you're the brother she'd set me up with, if that were her intention, and, right before that, Keane went out of his way to tell me you're the 'greatest guy in the world' and that 'any woman would be lucky to snag you' and that he'd *heard* you're some kind of sex god! What the fuckity-motherfuck did you tell them, Ryan Asshole Fucking Morgan?"

I chuckle. "My brother and sister said all that cool stuff about me? Wow. It's amazing how far a hundred bucks stretches these days."

"It's not funny, Ryan the Asshole! What the fuck did you tell them? One of them singing your praises like that *might* be sheer coincidence—but *both* of them on the same night—right after we *happened* to have fucked each other's brains out? I'm not a moron, Ryan!"

"Okay, tamp down the crazy a bit, sweetheart," I say, laughing. "You're being paranoid. I've said absolutely nothing to Kat. I swear to God. Not a word. For whatever reason, she's been wanting to fix us up ever since she went wedding-dress shopping with you and my mom—the same way my mom wants to set us up, for whatever reason. But that's based on some shit you did, not me. 'Fess up, Argentina, what the hell did you say to my mom and sister that made them fall head over heels in love with you and think we're a perfect match?"

"Fuck if I know!" she shrieks. "I've done nothing! I've said nothing! I've been my usual, boring, potted-plant self around them at all times. I have no freaking idea why they're both utterly convinced I'm some kind of beacon of wonderfulness who's destined to incubate your babies!"

I laugh. God, she's adorable.

"Now stop deflecting," she commands. "If you didn't say something to Kat, then you definitely said something to Keane. The guy couldn't stop staring at my tits all night long and yet he's pimping *you* out? It makes no sense unless you've said something to him."

"You've got Keane all wrong. He's a manwhore but he's got a heart of gold."

"Stop deflecting! I don't care about Keane's heart of gold. I care about whatever the fuck you told him to make him say all that nice stuff about you. You told him you've got dibs on me, didn't you?"

"God, you're smart. I really like that about you."

"Stop deflecting!"

"Okay, okay, yes, I told Keane to leave you the fuck alone because I've got dibs. But I didn't tell him we've already fucked, I swear. Actually, when I spoke to him about you, we hadn't yet fucked and I haven't said a word since."

"We hadn't fucked yet? But we had sex within two seconds of you getting here."

"I told him right before you came to my room."

"What *exactly* did you tell him?"

"I told him to stay away from you because you're mine."

"I'm *yours*?" she shrieks. "Ha! You think because you put your dick inside me..." She gasps and looks around, making sure no one's around to overhear—and then she starts over in a whisper. "You think because you put your dick inside me *once* you own me? Because you most certainly do *not* own me, sir. Not. At. All."

"Yes, I do—but not because I had sex with you once. I said you were mine before we had sex, remember? No, baby, I own you because the minute I saw you, I knew I was gonna fuck you better than anyone ever has or will—because our connection is unlike anything either of us has ever experienced before."

She hoots. "That doesn't mean you *own* me. It just means you... I dunno... somehow knew exactly how to turn me into some kind of sex-addict."

"You realize you didn't dispute any of my underlying assumptions?"

"Oh. Well. Let me dispute them now. Did you fuck me better than anyone ever has?" She pauses. "Actually, yes. Okay, I gotta give you that one. *But ever will*? I have no freaking idea. How can I know that without any basis for comparison?"

"You're saying I was your first sexual experience?"

"No, of course not—I'm saying you were my first *no-strings* sexual experience. Maybe the secret ingredient to our amazing chemistry wasn't *you,* per se, but the lack of connection I felt between my body and heart. Maybe *all* meaningless sex is that amazing when I genuinely despise my partner? How will I know until I try it again with someone else I equally abhor?"

My blood flash-boils. I grab her arm and stop her from walking, my eyes blazing. "Enough with that shit, Tessa. You can't say that shit to me. Never again. It's totally fucked up that you say that shit to me."

She smiles wickedly. "Oh, dear. You look a bit... riled up, Ryan." She wriggles free of my grasp and continues walking and I follow behind her, my chest heaving and my dick throbbing.

"Don't say that shit to me," I say evenly.

"Fine."

"Ever again."

"Fine."

We reach her door.

"Gimme your key," I say, putting out my hand.

She smacks her key into my palm in a huff. "How did I find you so attractive three months ago? I can't even remember what I saw in you. You're so utterly... annoying."

I wordlessly swipe her card-key while she continues talking behind me.

"Plus, you're cocky," she says. "And possessive. And full of yourself. You've obviously fooled your parents and siblings into thinking you're the greatest thing since sliced bread, but I've seen a side of you they haven't, obviously, and I'm not fooled."

I open the door and motion for her to step inside, which she does, her arms crossed over her chest, her eyes blazing.

I close the door behind me with a soft click and turn around.

And then, without further ado, we lurch toward each other and maul the living fuck out of each other.

Chapter 40
Ryan

"What he ate did not so much relieve his hunger, as keep it immortal in him."

We're a frenzied blur of hungry lips, groping hands, and voracious tongues. She's got my shirt off. My pants on the floor. I've got her dress off. Her bra unclasped.

"Oh, fuck, baby, you're my crack," I murmur into her mouth.

She makes a sound of arousal that makes every cell in my body strain for her.

I yank her undies down, off her hips, and she pulls sharply on my briefs, panting and gasping for air. I help her get my briefs off, and a second later, they're flying through the air and landing on a nearby lampshade.

She grasps my rock-hard dick as I bury my face in her incredible breasts and suck and grope and lick and bite and revel in them. *In her.*

I kiss and lick my way up from her breasts to her neck, and then devour her lips, and she strokes my shaft and balls and taint, making me lose my fucking mind. I slide my fingers between her legs and stroke her swollen, wet pussy 'til my fingers are slick with her juices and she's moaning like crazy.

I somehow manage to grab a couple condoms out of my pants on the floor, scoop her naked body into my arms, and carry her to the bed, kissing her voraciously as I go.

"I'm gonna make you come so hard, baby," I say, laying her onto her bed, the tip of my cock already beaded with pre-cum. "I'm gonna make you feel so good."

Her eyes blaze.

I lie alongside her and press my wet dick into her hip and take her nipple into my mouth and slide my fingers inside her, deep inside her. I begin massaging that particular spot at her farthest reaches—and with each stroke of my fingers inside her, and each word whispered into her ear about how hot she is and how much she turns me on and how hard I am for her, she keeps ramping up and up and up, until she's arching her back and writhing and groaning like she's being gutted.

"That's it, baby," I whisper. "Get it."

She makes a primal sound.

"Come for me," I grit out.

Whatever shards of inhibitions might have remained when we fucked the first time around have been obliterated now—she's clearly not holding a damned thing back. *And it's the sexiest thing I've ever seen in my life.* She's a wild animal, absolutely inhuman—which makes me feel like a wild animal, too.

"Say my name when you come," I whisper. "Say it for me."

She comes, my name barreling out of her mouth—and it's so fucking glorious, I almost come myself.

When she's done climaxing, I kiss her and stroke her again, this time working her G-spot. I ramp her up and up, stroking her, massaging, coaxing, until she jerks and shudders and comes for me again. I do it again and again to her, and each time, she heaves and screams and shudders and whimpers more and more forcefully, until, finally, it's like I'm dragging her body through the pits of hell and she's got tears streaming down her cheeks and sweat beading between her breasts and I'm on the cusp of coming myself, just from the pleasure of watching her lose herself so completely.

Without warning, she grabs my dick and bites my nipple so hard, I feel like I'm gonna black out from the glorious pain. "Fuck. Me. *Asshole*," she grits out.

Oh, God, my new three favorite words.

In a heartbeat, I've got my hard-on covered and I'm on top of her with her legs thrown straight up in the air. I slide into her warm, tight, wetness, and, at my entry, we both let out loud groans of relief and pleasure. She's perfect. Supernatural. Sex has never felt this good—she's a whole new species of woman.

I kiss her and fuck her, touching her beautiful face as I move in and out of her, grinding my pelvis at just the right angle to make that little metal ball at the base of my cock send her to heaven.

We shift positions. She wraps her arms and legs tightly around me, giving herself to me completely. Oh, God, the way this woman turns me on isn't normal. Every movement of our bodies, every beat of our hearts, feels preordained.

"I hate you so much," she whispers, but she's growling with ecstasy as she says it.

"Say you're mine," I grit out.

"Fuck you," she whispers, her breathing ragged.

"Nobody can make you feel this good but me," I whisper. "Admit it."

"Fuck you. Oh, God." Without warning, she arches her back violently, and lets out a sound that tells me she's a hair's breath away from total and complete rapture. "*I hate you.*"

"Fucking a guy you hate feels damned good, huh?"

She whimpers. "*Yes.*"

"Best you ever had."

She moans.

"Tell me you hate me again."

"I hate you."

I clasp my fingers in hers as I move in and out of her, slamming against her clit with my piercing over and over. "You like that?"

"Yes. Oh, God, yes. So good. So fucking good. I hate you so much."

Holy shit, my body's on the bitter edge. What kind of crazy fuck am I to be turned on by this woman telling me she hates me? But, oh my God, I am. Fuck, yes, I am. "Come for me, baby," I whisper. "Say my name for me."

She cries out, saying my name, as commanded, and my cock is squeezed and massaged as her muscles ripple with pleasure.

I increase the intensity of my thrusts, my body on the verge of a massive orgasm. At my fervor, she frantically cups my cheeks and kisses my lips and twists my nipples and claws at my back—all while I grip her hair and grind my body in and out of hers, barreling like a motherfucker toward my own release. When it finally comes, when my body finally lets go, the sensation is so intense, I feel physically disoriented by the pleasure, like I'm tumbling out an airplane at thirty thousand feet without a parachute.

Finally, when my body's quieted down, all I can do is lie on top of her, trying to catch my breath, my lips pressed against her sweaty cheek.

"Holy shit."

I roll off her and onto my back, drenched in sweat, peel my condom off, and look at her for a long moment. She's obviously in some sort of pleasure-induced daze. Her nipples are still hard as little pebbles. Her cheeks are flushed. Man, she looks ripe as a peach.

I touch her hard nipple and stroke the curve of her breast. "Holy shit, you're not even close to finished," I whisper. "Come sit on my face 'til I can fuck you again, baby. Come on."

I don't need to ask her twice. Her eyes blazing, she climbs over my face and lowers herself onto my lips and, thank you, God, I'm met with the unparalleled pleasure of warm, sweet slickness against my lips, and soft, smooth flesh against my cheeks, and the delicious taste of her pussy against my tongue. I slide my palms over her rocking hips and gently guide her movement over my face as I lap at her, coaxing her pelvis into movement in synchronicity with my hungry mouth.

After only a few minutes, she makes a truly crazy sound, so I double down on what I'm doing to her—and seconds later, she unfurls into my mouth.

I feel insatiable. I can't get enough. The more I taste, the more I crave. It's like she's burrowing herself under my skin and into my very soul.

I guide her off me and onto her back and begin kissing and licking every inch of her, my cock slowly springing to life again as I do, and before I know it, I'm hard as a rock and ready to go. I roll a condom on and guide her on top of me and, quickly, our bodies are gyrating passionately in perfect harmony.

Oh, yeah. Fuck yeah. Her incredible breasts are bouncing with the greedy movement of her body. Her dark hair is falling around her shoulders. Her skin is smooth and glistening with sweat. But the best part of all? The enraptured expression on her beautiful face. Truly, if there's something more beautiful than the expression on this woman's face in this moment, then it exists only in heaven.

"You're so beautiful, baby," I groan out. "Fuck anything else I used to think was beautiful. You're the only thing."

"Ryan," she chokes out. "What are you doing to me?"

"You're my drug," I grit out, my body on the bitter edge of release. "Oh, God. You're my drug."

She stiffens. And gasps. And then, God bless America, her muscles tighten and release and squeeze around my cock so forcefully, I come right along with her, a strangled cry erupting from me as I do.

When we're finished, she collapses on top of me, stretches her body on top of mine, and seemingly passes out cold.

After a few minutes, I'm so certain she's fallen dead-asleep on top of me, I begin rolling her unconscious body off me onto the mattress, but she surprises me by lifting her head and looking me square in the eyes.

"Oh, hello," I say.

"You're my boy toy," she says flatly.

I laugh. "What?"

"I have a freaking boy toy."

I chuckle. "Oh. Well, happy to oblige. I thought you were dead-asleep."

"I was just deep in thought. My mind is blown. I've fucked a man I don't respect or like—a man I actually kinda hate. *Twice*."

I laugh and kiss the side of her head. "Three times, technically. And you don't hate me. In fact, you're completely obsessed with me."

"Yeah, I'm obsessed with you. I don't deny that. But that doesn't mean I don't *hate* you."

I stroke her back and inhale her scent and feel my heart beating against hers. "Okay. Whatever floats your boat."

"It's not okay," she insists. "I honestly hate you, Ryan. When I think of you, my feelings of rage and anger aren't normal or healthy. *And* I'm completely obsessed with you because I love, love, love fucking you. Oh my God, I love fucking you so much."

I laugh. "Good. I love fucking you, too."

"But what does that say about me?"

"It says nothing about you. If anything, it says you should stop overthinking things and just enjoy yourself."

She rolls off me and sits next to me, clearly energized by something. "Ryan, listen to me. I just realized I'm a truly horrible person. I don't respect you at all, not even a little bit—which means I'm using you for nothing but sex. If our genders were reversed, I'd disgust myself."

"I'm perfectly fine with the situation." I pull her back down to lie with me, and wrap my arms around her. I kiss her cheek, pressing my body into hers. I inhale her scent and kiss her again. "Sweetheart," I whisper, stroking her back. "If thinking you're using me is what's getting you off so fucking hard, I'm all too glad to be of service."

Chapter 41
Ryan

"How it is I know not; but there is no place like a bed for confidential disclosures between friends."

"Let's order some room service," I say when it's clear Tessa's not even close to falling asleep. I roll toward the nightstand, looking for a menu.

"We can't *eat*," Tessa says. "This is, you know, a purely sexual thing we're doing here. A *fling*."

"Dude, let me explain how flings work in real life—it's not the way it seems in movies. You can't just fuck a guy and immediately make him do the walk of shame—first, you gotta feed him and *then* you can kick him out."

Tessa giggles. "*Fine*. But don't get any ideas about sleeping here. We've got a big day tomorrow and we need to get some solid sleep."

"Cool. Tonight's all about fucking, food, and flapping our gums; next time, we add forty winks to the itinerary."

"You sound like Keane."

"God help me." I grin at her. "Okay, well, I'm glad we're agreed: we'll do a sleep-over next time."

"We're not agreed about a damned thing. There won't even *be* a next time."

"How long are you gonna keep doing that?"

"Doing what?" she asks.

"Pretending this thing between us isn't inevitable?"

"It's not."

I sigh. She's wrong, of course—we're as inevitable as the sun rising and falling. But there's no reason to try to convince her of that

210

now. That's the thing about the sun, after all: it does its thing whether you like it or not.

We find a room service menu, place our order, and put on some music—a playlist I made specifically for her before heading out to the opening party earlier tonight. The first song that comes up is "Shape of You" by Ed Sheeran, an upbeat, vaguely Latin-reggae-sounding groove that prompts me to pull her up from the bed and ask her to show me some basic ballroom dancing steps... and, before I know it, we're doing a naked cha-cha (sort of) around the room.

When the Ed Sheeran song ends, we stretch out on the bed together as the next song—"Sex on Fire"—begins. I stare at her for a long beat, grinning, my head propped up by my elbow.

"What?" she asks.

"I could sit and stare at you like this forever and never get tired of the view."

"Honey, there's no need to butter me up," she says. "I already slept with you, remember? Seduction complete."

I wink. "I'm working on you for next time."

"Don't waste your time. We're one and done."

"You mean three and done?"

"Two and a half. But, whatever, we're done."

"We both know you're full of shit." I pat the bed. "Come closer and listen to my favorite song with me." She complies, scooching her body closer to mine until her beautiful face is mere inches from mine.

"You promise you didn't tell Keane about us?"

"I swear."

"And you haven't told Kat?"

"Not a word."

"And you haven't said anything to anyone else about me?"

My stomach clenches. "Just Colby."

Her body tenses. "What'd you tell him?"

I exhale. "Everything."

Tessa sits up, instantly enraged. "Fucker! You're the one who begged me not to tell anyone!"

"No, I begged you not to tell *Josh*, and, don't worry, Colby won't tell him or anyone else. Colby's been a locked vault since I was five, when he aided and abetted my very first felony."

She stares at me for a long beat, her anger visibly melting.

Finally, she rolls her eyes and lies back down next to me. "God, you're an asshole. How do you do that?"

"Do what?"

"Know exactly what to say to make me forget I'm mad at you. Now all I can think about is, 'Gosh, I wonder how Colby aided and abetted Ryan's first felony when he was five.'"

"Well, gosh, thanks for asking. Cuddle close again and I'll tell you the whole story." I pull her into my naked body and nuzzle my nose into her hair. "Now isn't this better than being mad?"

"This changes nothing," she whispers. "I'm still mad as hell you told Colby. It's just that my curiosity is stronger than my anger at the moment."

"Sex on Fire" ends and the next song on my playlist—"Beneath Your Beautiful" by Labrinth—begins. I hold her close and listen to the poignant lyrics of the song for a moment.

"Your very first felony?" she prompts, apparently not as swept away by the song as I am.

I kiss her head. "Okay. This is a Morgan-family classic: 'The Story of Ryan's Shitty Towel.'"

She giggles. "Oh my God."

"Once upon a time, five-year-old Ryan took a gigantic crap in the toilet in our house and was then dismayed to discover the toilet paper roll empty. But, of course, because I've always been a can-do kind of guy, I solved my dilemma by wiping my ass with the nearest useful implement—which happened to be my mother's precious Christmas hand towel hanging on a nearby rack."

"Oh, Ryan."

"It had little golden angels playing horns on it. Very pretty. Anyway, the minute I used Mom's pretty angel-towel to wipe my little ass, I remembered she'd told Colby and me very clearly we weren't allowed to touch her towels. And so, in an attempt to cover my tracks—pun intended—I re-hung the shit-streaked towel on the rack, exactly the way I'd found it and sneaked out of the bathroom."

Tessa laughs. "Welcome to the criminal mind of a five-year old."

"I was a criminal mastermind. So, seven-year-old Colby uses the bathroom a little while later and discovers the shitty towel hanging neatly on the rack, and he easily surmises the shit-wiper had to have been his stupid little brother, since Kat was a toddler in diapers, Keane was an avocado in our mom's belly, and Dax didn't exist yet. And you know what Colby did? If you think he ratted me out, you'd be wrong. Little Colby Morgan did the thing that laid the foundation of our brotherhood from that moment forward: he grabbed that shitty towel, sneaked outside with it under his jacket, and chucked it over our backyard fence into our neighbor's yard."

"Brilliant!"

"We were both geniuses."

"And did you two get away with it?"

"We sure did. For about twenty minutes."

Tessa giggles.

"That's how long it took for Mrs. Wheeler from next door to come knocking on our front door, the shitty towel in her hand."

"Fucking Mrs. Wheeler," Tessa says.

"Fucking Mrs. Wheeler," I agree.

"What'd your mom do to you?"

"She made us apologize to Mrs. Wheeler and to her, of course, and then she made us rake leaves off Mrs. Wheeler's lawn and our own until we'd 'worked off' the price of a replacement towel."

"God, I love your mom."

"She's the best. When I have kids, if my wife is half the mother my mom is, my kids will be lucky as hell."

Tessa's face flushes. "You want kids?"

"Hell yeah. You?"

She nods.

"How many?" I ask, my heart racing all of a sudden.

"Two or three, probably," she says. "You?"

"Four or five, in a perfect world."

Her eyes widen.

"But everything's subject to negotiation," I add quickly. "The most important thing is to find their momma first—the woman I wanna spend the rest of my life with. Everything else will follow naturally from there, I figure."

There's a long beat.

Oh my God, I'm falling head over heels in love with this woman.

"Tessa, I'm not the lying, cheating scumbag you think I am," I say softly, stroking her arm. "Will you hear me out for a minute?"

213

She nods, thank God, and, finally, for the first time, I'm able to tell her chapter and verse about the night we met, beginning with what actually happened at the restaurant with Olivia and the blonde with the note, and moving on to explaining exactly why I truly believed my relationship with Olivia had ended before I met her (though, I concede, I knew having one final, confirming conversation with Olivia was certainly in order).

When I'm done talking, Tessa looks at me thoughtfully. "I remember, right before Psycho Barbie came in, you said you had something to tell me."

I exhale the longest exhale of my life. "I was gonna tell you about Olivia, just to make sure we got off on the right foot."

She bites the inside of her cheek.

"What are you thinking?" I ask.

"That your explanation makes perfect sense and sounds incredibly sincere."

I exhale with relief.

"And also that, in my past relationship, my boyfriend had quite the knack for telling me explanations that made perfect sense and sounded incredibly sincere."

I rub my face. "Oh for the love of fuck, you're exhausting. At some point, you're gonna have to trust somebody again, Tessa—you do realize that, right?"

Tessa opens her mouth to reply, but before she says a word, there's a loud knock on the door. "Room service!"

Chapter 42
Ryan

"Ooooh, try this mango," she says, feeding me a piece.

"Amazing," I say. "I didn't even think I liked mango. Did you try some of this pineapple?"

She nods. "Amazing."

We're sitting at a table on the little patio just outside her room, overlooking the moonlit ocean, the warm night breeze wafting over us.

"I've got a proposition for you, Argentina," I say. "What do you say we fuck each other's brains out every night this week, totally on the sly—nobody ever has to know—and after this week, once we get back to Seattle, if one or both of us doesn't want to keep going, then, no problem, we'll both agree to move on, no hard feelings, and pretend this week never happened."

She takes a bite of food and chews it slowly, considering the idea.

Shit. My heart is clanging wildly. I'm going all-in right now and I know it. "What do you have to lose?" I ask.

"So it would be like a one-week vacation-fling?" she asks.

I nod vigorously. "Exactly. 'What happens in Maui stays in Maui.'"

She bites her lip.

"No commitment. No pressure. One week. The only thing you'd need to commit to—and this is non-negotiable—is exclusivity while we're here."

She takes a sip of water. "Definitely something to think about."

My stomach tightens. "What do you mean? It's a no-brainer."

She shrugs. "I've been drinking tonight. I'm not gonna make any decisions about anything 'til I'm completely sober."

215

"It's hardly a major life decision. There's no downside."

"I've never done anything like what you're suggesting. I just wanna think about it and not make a snap decision."

I open my mouth and close it again. What the fuck is wrong with this woman?

"Can I ask you something?" she asks.

"Anything."

"Do you have some sort of raging flight attendant fetish?"

"What? *No.* Why do you ask?"

"Because you were so damned furious with me when you found out I wasn't a flight attendant, and now that I'm getting to know you, that seems so contrary to your personality. All I can figure is maybe I'd dashed some raging flight-attendant fantasy you had."

"I don't have a particular boner for flight attendants. I was just pissed as hell you'd sent me on a wild goose chase."

She looks at me quizzically. "How did I send you on a wild goose chase?"

Shit. How the fuck did I let that slip out? I pause, considering my reply. Should I say fuck it and tell her everything, right here and now? My gut tells me not yet. "Bad choice of words," I say. "I just meant I was pissed I felt so connected to you and it turned out you'd lied. But Colby reminded me Kat always used to pull that kind of shit, too, which made me realize you're no more or less of a sociopath than her—although Kat's definitely on the sociopath-spectrum, so don't get too excited."

Tessa giggles. "Kat was telling me about some of her 'personas' from back in the day. That girl's got quite the imagination."

"You have no idea." I laugh. "Actually, all us Morgans have pretty active imaginations."

Tessa cocks her head flirtatiously. "You ever thought about maybe doing some kind of..." Her cheeks flash with color. "Role-play? Like, I dunno, maybe *pretending* you're screwing a flight attendant?"

My cock jolts. "Let's do it!" I blurt.

She giggles. "Well, I'm not *offering*. Just gathering information."

I flash her a wicked smile. *Sure, she is.* But, okay, I won't push it—I'll let my little Virgo warm up to the idea slowly and get her freak on when she's good and ready.

216

Tessa stretches her arms over her head and lets out a huge yawn, and her eyes flutter closed. She tries to open them, but it's clearly difficult. She looks like she's about to fall headfirst into her plate of fruit.

I stand. "Let's get you to bed, beautiful." I pull her up and walk her back into her room. I wait for her to brush her teeth and wash her face and then I tuck her into bed, kissing her gently on her soft lips. "Good night, Argentina. See you tomorrow. Thanks for feeding me before kicking me out. I feel so much less trampy now."

"You're still a tramp," she says sleepily, her eyes closed. "Don't kid yourself."

I touch her cheek. I'm physically aching to slip into bed right next to her and hold her close all night long. "Don't overthink my proposition, okay?" I whisper, stroking her hair. "I won't hurt you—I promise. I'll never hurt you, Tessa."

Tessa surprises me by grabbing my hand from her cheek and softly kissing it. "Thanks for an amazing night, Ryan," she whispers, looking at me dreamily. She opens her mouth and closes it, and then bites her lip, clearly on the verge of saying something.

I hold my breath and wait. For some reason, I feel like she's about to invite me to stay with her tonight.

I wait.

Finally, Tessa releases my hand, closes her eyes, and nestles her cheek into her pillow. "I'll see you at breakfast, Rum Cake. Sleep tight."

Chapter 43
Tessa

Okay, this is unexpected.

I'm on the phone with Charlotte, my half-eaten breakfast next to me as I sit on the patio attached to my room, looking out at the ocean, and my unpredictable best friend's just floored me by saying she wholeheartedly believes every word of Ryan's explanation, and, furthermore, that she thinks I should take Ryan up on his no-strings proposition and bang the hell out of him all week long.

"I'm thinking maybe I should quit while I'm ahead," I say. "If I keep going with him like this all week, I might develop genuine feelings for him. And then what?"

"And then... that'd be awesome."

"*No.* Even if Ryan's not a lying cheater like I originally thought, he's still a manwhore, *and* he's about to become Josh's brother. And all that makes him a nonstarter, even if he's as honest as Abe Lincoln."

"Why, again?"

"Because if I start something with Ryan, when we eventually break up, my *employer*, aka Ryan's brother-in-law, will feel like he needs to pick sides—and whose side do you think Josh will pick? Look at what happened with Stu: Josh never talked to him again."

"You're really putting the cart before the horse here, honey. If you're gonna quit the drug before you leave Maui, fine, but what's the difference if you quit the drug after banging the guy twice or ten times? Why not have fun this entire week?"

"But what if I develop feelings and get hurt?"

"I say risk it. Live a little."

I don't reply.

"There's always the chance you could develop feelings and *not* get hurt," Charlotte says.

"Not bloody likely," I say.

"By any chance, did Ryan say anything about what he's been up to these past couple months? I mean, like, did you two talk about how much you've both been thinking about each other since the night you first met?"

"Of course, not. Why would we talk about that? I'm sure Ryan didn't give me a second thought any more than I gave him one."

"Sweetheart, you thought about Ryan all the time after you met him. You imagined you saw him around every corner."

"Well, yeah, but only for about six weeks. After that, I didn't think of him hardly at all." I scoff. "And I know for a fact Ryan didn't think about me, even once. If he did, he would have told me so by now. To the contrary, I keep calling him a manwhore and he doesn't say a word. Obviously, that's a topic I don't want to know too much about."

Charlotte lets out a very long sigh. "Well, okay. Just keep me posted on what you decide to do. I vote you bang him all week."

"Your vote has been duly noted in the log. Oh, hey, I almost forgot: Kat told me to invite you to Maui. She wants to meet you."

"She does? Wow, that's so nice. But I can't. Remember? I've got that ten-day Mediterranean cruise with my parents for their anniversary starting the day before the wedding."

"Oh yeah. Crap. Well, can you maybe come for a few days and hang out and meet everyone?"

"Ooph. That'd be a lot of travel with the cruise on the other end of the world. I don't think I've got enough vacation days to do both trips. But I'll look at my work schedule and let you know."

"Okay, lemme know." I look at my watch. "Ooph. I gotta run, Nut Job. The wedding brigade is taking a bus to the top of Haleakala and then riding the whole way down on bicycles today. I gotta catch the bus."

"That sounds fun. You gonna ride with Ryan?"

"Yup. He texted this morning and made me promise to save him a seat at breakfast and then on the bus." Out of nowhere, my stomach flutters with a flock of butterflies at the thought of seeing Ryan this morning.

Charlotte sighs. "Oh, Tessa. Don't you hear yourself? Get out of your own way for once and just take a leap of faith."

"I'm thinking about it. You know I like to think things through."

"Thinking things through is the opposite of taking a leap of faith."

"I know. I'm just... He's too good to be true. I need to slow things down and protect myself."

"Okay, Crazy Girl. You do you. Have fun bicycling down a volcano. I love you."

"I love you, too, Nut Job. *Aloha.*"

Chapter 44
Tessa

When all two hundred of us return to the resort from our amazing bike ride down a huge, dormant volcano, we descend upon the massive swimming pool area to hang out and relax in the sunshine before it's time to get ready for the luau.

While one group floats on inner tubes around a lazy river, another one hops into the large pool to play a fierce game of water-volleyball (while wearing their spiffy colored jerseys, of course) and still another group cannonballs into the pool with no apparent agenda beyond making a gigantic splash. And what am I doing? Lying on a lounge chair at the edge of the pool in my black string bikini, a piña colada and smutty book both by my side, my body slathered in coconut-scented sunscreen. *Heaven.*

I pick up my book, but, despite my best efforts, I can't seem to focus on it, not with the impromptu "show" currently happening in the pool. Specifically, the Morgan brothers plus their honorary brother, Zander, are pretending to be dolphins under the deft command of their "trainer," eight-year-old Coco, who's standing on the ledge of the pool, directing her enthusiastic fleet with hand signals and chirpy, giggle-filled vocal commands.

Keane and Zander are definitely the "lead" dolphins (man, those boys are giving it their all), but Colby, Ryan, and Dax are no slouches in the dolphin-department, either. Oh my gosh, I can't remember the last time I laughed this hard. Oh, wait. Yes, I can. When Keane told me the preposterous story of how he met his best friend in a locker room. And when Dax told me the history behind his band's name. And when Ryan told me the story of how he wiped his shitty little five-year-old ass on his momma's prized Christmas hand towel. And when Kat told me she used to go into bars and pretend she'd just escaped from a cult. And this morning when Mr. Morgan pedaled playfully past Keane on his bike and yelled, "Eat my dust, sucker!" over his shoulder. And on and on.

My eyes widen.

Oh my God.

I just realized something: I'm totally and completely in love with the entire Morgan family. Every last one of them. Well, except for Ryan, of course. I'm not in love with Ryan. I scoff to myself. Of course not. He might not be a liar, but he's still a manwhore. And I'd better not forget it.

"Hey, Tessa," a voice says, drawing me out of my rambling thoughts.

I look to my left. It's Sarah with Henn's girlfriend, Hannah, both of them in dripping wet bikinis, motioning to two vacant loungers next to me.

"Are these open?" Sarah asks.

"All yours," I say.

The ladies make themselves comfortable.

"We were taking a bathroom-break from floating around the lazy river and saw you lying here all alone."

"Oh, I'm just hanging out, watching the dolphin show." I motion to the pool and both ladies check out the "dolphins" for a long beat.

"Who's the little girl?" Sarah asks, laughing.

"Coco. One of the Morgan cousins just married her dad."

"Aw," Hannah says. "Those boys are so sweet to make Coco feel so included."

"The Morgan boys are all really sweet like that," Sarah says.

"Their momma must have taught them well," Hannah says.

We all watch the show for several minutes, commenting and giggling about the boys' ridiculous (but strangely sexy) dolphin maneuvers, and, finally, when Ryan opens his arms to Coco and coaxes her to jump into them from the ledge of the pool, we all simultaneously gasp and swoon.

"Oh my God, that was hot," Hannah blurts. "Muscles and tattoos and pierced nipples and a leaping, laughing little girl? Jesus God, I suddenly wanna grab Henn and drag him to our room."

We all laugh.

"I used to have the biggest crush on Ryan," Sarah says matter-of-factly.

I stare at her, shocked.

Sarah shrugs. "Ryan's gorgeous."

Hannah scoffs. "How the heck did you pick just one Morgan brother to have a crush on?" She looks toward the swimming pool, her face etched with obvious appreciation for the men playing in the water. (The Morgan brothers are currently throwing Coco from man to man like a beach ball). "They're all freaks of nature, just like Kat," Hannah says. "Freaks, freaks, freaks. It's not fair how much hotness is contained within one family. I feel like I'm watching that volleyball scene from *Top Gun,* only *way* better."

Sarah and I both giggle and agree.

"So does Ryan know about your old crush on him?" Hannah asks Sarah, giving voice to the exact question I'm wondering myself.

"Hellz no," Sarah replies. "I never said a word. I did tell Kat about it at the time and asked her to find out if maybe he was interested in taking me out, but she refused."

"Why?" Hannah asks.

"Kat said Ryan would break my heart and then it would be weird at birthday parties and stuff."

My heart leaps into my throat. Oh, shit. Did Sarah just describe my future to a tee?

Sarah continues, "This was years ago, of course, and, apparently, Ryan had just gotten out of some relationship and was really sowing his wild oats. Total player. So Kat was like, 'Unless my brother's fully prepared to make you happy for the rest of your life—which he's *so* not—I'm not gonna let him touch you.' So that was that." She smiles broadly. "And thank God she refused, right? Or, heck, maybe Ryan wouldn't have been interested, anyway. But, seriously, imagine how weird it'd be now if we *had* gone out." She shudders at the mere thought.

Oh, Jesus. I'm suddenly reeling. What have I done? Have I ensured everything's gonna be weird every time I see Ryan from now on?

"Plus, think about the butterfly effect," Hannah says. "What if dating Ryan back then would have somehow kept you from meeting Jonas when you did."

"Ooph. I shudder to think about it," Sarah says. "Plus, nowadays, Ryan feels like a brother to me—the same as Josh or Henn. He's objectively gorgeous, of course—I mean, just look at him—but the minute I met Jonas, I instantly knew the difference between having a crush on a guy, even a massive one, and meeting the true love of my life. Once you've finally experienced true love, there's just no comparison."

"Aw," Hannah says. "You and Jonas are so amazing. Hashtag-relationship-goals."

"You and Henny, too," Sarah says. "I predict you'll be following in Jonas' and my footsteps before long."

"Oh, for sure."

Sarah squeals. "Really? Have you two talked about marriage?"

"Yeah, right after I caught the bouquet at your wedding, Henny and I talked about..."

I tune out, too freaked out to continue listening. When I met Ryan for the first time, it felt worlds different than any other time I've met a man—far, far different than when I met Stu or any other boyfriend. With all those previous guys, I'd felt sparks, sure, like I was meeting a crush, just like Sarah said, but when I met Ryan, oh, man, instantly, I felt something brand new, something otherworldly, like I was meeting... *No.* I can't even let myself think it. It's ridiculous. Preposterous. Out of bounds. *A recipe for a broken heart.*

"Hey, T-Rod," Hannah says, drawing me out of my thoughts. "I keep noticing Kat and Sarah and Mrs. Morgan calling you Tessa. And yet it seems like Josh and Henn and all those guys keep calling you Theresa. Do you have a preference?"

"Tessa, honestly," I say. "That's what my friends and family have always called me."

"Okay, then," Hannah says, smiling. "Tessa it is."

There's a shrieking giggle in the pool and we look over there to find Coco sitting atop Ryan's broad shoulders, battling Keane and Zander to the death in a game of chicken.

"Oh my God," Hannah says. "My left ovary exploded when the Morgan brothers played 'dolphin'—and now my right ovary's gone, too."

"He's so freaking hot," I blurt, without meaning to say it.

But neither woman seems at all fazed by my comment, thank God.

"A man who loves kids," Hannah says, sighing. "Gets me every time."

We all watch the battle for a long time, our tongues on the ground and our hearts throbbing, until finally, Coco pushes on Keane's gorgeous chest with all her little might and Keane and Zander topple backward dramatically into the pool, much to Coco's shrieking delight.

As Keane and Zander punch the surface of the pool like sore losers, Ryan guides Coco to stand atop his broad shoulders like a cheerleader, his strong hands gripping her calves, and takes her on a victory lap around the shallow end of the pool.

When Ryan and Coco's victory tour makes its way to our side of the pool, Sarah, Hannah, and I applaud and cheer effusively, attracting Ryan's attention.

Immediately, Ryan's eyes lock with mine. He smiles broadly at me, and I return the gesture, my heart beating wildly in my chest.

Ryan's not moving. Or looking away. And I'm glad. In fact, I wish this smiling, giddy moment would never end. *He's absolutely beautiful, inside and out.*

"Hey, ladies," a smooth male voice says.

Ryan's smile suddenly vanishes. His face darkens.

I look to my right.

Reed Rivers.

Chapter 45
Tessa

Reed pulls up a chair and sits down at the end of our threesome's lounge chairs, his dark eyes flickering over the length of my body before finally settling on Hannah's face with a congenial smile. He politely asks Hannah how she's liking her new apartment in L.A. and, when Hannah replies by profusely thanking Reed for the "amazing deal" he gave her on her place, it becomes clear Reed owns Hannah's apartment building.

Huh. Interesting. Reed seems to have his fingers in a lot of different pots.

As Reed continues talking to Hannah, I covertly study him. I've never seen him in his bathing suit before, and I must say, he's quite a specimen. But it's not just his beautiful body and rapidly growing business empire that makes Reed Rivers one of the world's most eligible bachelors—according to *TMZ*, anyway. It's that he absolutely reeks of animal magnetism. I knew that already, of course—swagger has always wafted off this guy, no matter what he happens to be wearing—but I suppose I'm getting a whole new appreciation for his appeal now that I'm seeing his bare torso for the first time. Wow. The man is absolutely stunning to look at. Not even close to as stunning as Ryan, of course, but who is?

Ryan.

I glance toward the pool to find him standing stock still in the shallow end all by himself, staring at Reed like an assassin, his muscled arms crossed over his chest.

I look away, my heart palpitating.

Shit. I swear I can see a little vein throbbing in his neck from all the way over here.

"And what about you, T-Rod?" Reed asks.

"Hmm?"

"You having fun so far?"

"Oh. Yes. I'm having a blast. I thought it'd be hard for me to relax and be a guest this week, but as it turns out, it's shockingly easy." I hold up my piña colada by way of explanation and everyone laughs.

"So, hey, T-Rod," Reed says, "I wanted to chat with you about the logistics for my surprise gift at the reception."

"Oh, yeah, I got your text," I say. "Having that musician play shouldn't be a problem at all. I've already got a crew coming for tonight's concert, so I'll ask them—"

I shut my mouth. Josh and Kat along with a large group of people are approaching and, obviously, we don't want them overhearing this particular conversation.

Sarah pops up from her lounge chair. "I'll drag them to the lazy river," she whispers. "Come on, Hannah Banana—help me lure them away."

And, just like that, I find myself sitting alone with the one and only Reed Rivers. In my bathing suit. Six inches from his tanned, muscled frame.

Reed smiles. "Looks like it's just you and me, T-Rod." His gaze scorches over my near-naked body again, pausing blatantly at my breasts, and then comes to a rest on my eyes.

"Who knows how long it'll last, though, so we'd better chat about this quickly," I say. I glance at Ryan again to find him staring at us, his jaw tight, his eyes like lasers—a sexy sight that sends blood whooshing straight into my cooch. I clear my throat. "So tell me what you need, Reed, and I'll make it happen."

Reed tells me he's arranged to have Josh and Kat's favorite singer-songwriter fly in from the UK to perform three of his songs at the wedding reception, including Josh and Kat's "first dance" song.

"Just put me in touch with the guy's management and I'll make sure everything's handled," I say. "I'll arrange hotels and accommodations for him and his team here, for as long as they need."

"Cool. But bill me for all that. Faraday can't pay for his own gift."

"Will do. And from a tech standpoint, it's not a problem—I've already got a great sound company handling both the wedding band and the 22 Goats concert tonight, so I'll ask them to add this guy's mini-performance to the job."

Reed smiles. "Perfect. The Mighty T-Rod's on it."

"Yes, sir. So, you're planning be at the 22 Goats concert tonight, right?"

"There's gonna be a 22 Goats concert tonight?"

"After the luau." I shoot him a snarky look. "And if you don't want me to break your legs, you'd better make sure you're there, Mr. Rivers, because I've got a strong hunch you're actually the guest of honor."

Reed smiles playfully. "Why on earth would I be the guest of honor?"

"Don't play coy with me. You know why."

Reed flashes me a panty-melting smile. "Are *you* gonna be at the concert, T-Rod?"

"Of course," I say, my pulse suddenly pounding in my ears. "I wouldn't miss it."

"Then I'll be there."

I smile and blush. Man, Reed Rivers is one attractive dude. Dark eyes. Brown hair. Strong jawline with stubble. Absolutely oozing confidence. "Well, you shouldn't go to the concert for *me*," I say. "Go because 22 Goats is awesome. I've watched their videos online and I can honestly say I think they're incredible."

Reed smirks. "I'm just playing with you. Josh sent me Dax's demo a while back, so I've already checked out all the videos. I'm actually pretty sure I'm gonna sign Dax—I just need to see him play live before I make my final decision."

"Oh, I really hope you sign 'em. I know Kat is crossing her fingers and toes, as well."

"Well, you're both sweethearts, but that doesn't affect my decision at all. I don't sign bands as a favor to anyone, not even Josh's lovely personal assistant or his stubborn but lovely future wife."

I blush. *Shit.* I'm so lame. "Oh, of course," I stammer. "You're running a business. Kat and I both realize that. I just meant..." I trail off. *Shit.*

"Too much goes into breaking a band to do anything half-assed,"

Reed explains. "I'm not in this for charity—I'm in it to make truckloads of money while introducing musical greatness unto the world."

I cock my head, assessing him, that last statement throwing me for a loop. "So if you knew a group would make you a mint but you thought their music was less-than-great, you wouldn't sign them?"

"I wouldn't sign 'em. I only sign bands I'm proud to put my name behind."

"But, say you had the chance to sign that 'Gangnum Style' dude, knowing in advance it would blow up like it did?"

"Even if I knew for a fact that dude would make me richer than God, I'd still say no fucking thanks."

"I'm impressed," I say. "That's very..." My eyes have involuntarily drifted over to the pool to check on Ryan again, but he's not there. I look back at Reed. *Where'd Ryan go?* Crap! Did he leave because he's pissed at me for talking to Reed? "Um. That's very... Uh. Sorry. I just totally lost my train of thought."

"I know the feeling. I keep losing my train of thought, too—thanks to that itty-bitty bikini you're wearing, T-Rod. *Damn.*"

Whoa.

Reed's flirted with me over the years now and again, but he's never said anything so blatantly sexual to me before. But, then again, we've never been sitting six inches apart in nothing but our bathing suits before. My eyes flicker over Reed's bare torso for a moment, taking in the unbelievable ridges in his abs and the bulges in his arms and the perfection of his round nipples. Sexy dude, I must say. Not as sexy as Ryan, of course, but who is?

"Seriously, you look mind-blowing in that bikini, T-Rod," Reed says. "T-Rod?"

My eyes snap up from blatantly ogling Reed's chest and he smirks.

"Looks like I'm not the only one feeling pleasantly surprised at the moment."

I clear my throat. *Shit.* "So you're seriously thinking of signing 22 Goats, then? That would be a dream come true for those boys. I talked to them last night and they're all really excited at the possibility."

One side of Reed's mouth tilts up, a sure sign he knows I've just pointedly changed the subject. "Dax Morgan doesn't need to worry about a damned thing," he says. "I've watched the band's YouTube videos with my entire team and we all agree: Dax is a star. Jesus Christ—have you seen the way that kid's face looks under the lights? If I could order a rock star from the Rock Star Factory, it'd be Dax Morgan."

I nod. "Yeah, he's stunning."

"Would you do him?"

I'm shocked. "What? No. Of course, not."

Reed laughs. "No, no. Not literally. Not you, *personally*—I mean, as a figure of speech—as a measure of his commercial appeal."

I flash Reed a snarky look. "I won't say I'd 'do' Dax Morgan. I already feel like the guy's my little brother. But I will say this: if you sign 22 Goats, I'd bet anything that armies of females, from tweeners to twenty-somethings, will be plastering Dax's face on bedroom walls across the globe."

"My thoughts exactly, T-Rod. That pretty little boy's gonna make me a fucking mint."

My heart rate spikes with excitement. "So you're sure you're gonna sign 22 Goats, then?"

"That's not what I said."

I look at Reed, confused. "What's your trepidation, if you don't mind me asking? I mean, I suppose if you were doubt-free, you would have picked up the phone the minute you heard their demo, right?"

"You're good, T. Hey, standing offer: if you ever get sick of working for Faraday, come work for me in L.A. I'm dead serious—no matter what, I'll find a position for you."

For a split second, I can't decide if Reed is being sincere, or if he means the phrase "I'll find a position for you" as some sort of sexual innuendo (because I'm pretty sure he was looking straight at my chest when he said those words).

"Why on earth would you say that?" I ask. "I know nothing about the music industry."

"Doesn't matter. You've got great instincts."

"Well, thanks, but you can't steal me away from Josh. No one can."

"Yeah, I figured. He'd kill me, anyway. And that's not a figure of speech—he'd literally kill me."

I laugh. "So what's your trepidation about 22 Goats? You didn't answer the question."

"The other two guys. From what I can tell, Dax *is* the band. He writes the songs, sings 'em, and plays guitar front-and-center. He's the one who makes all the girls wet their panties and the boys want to be just like him, not those other two. What value do the other two dudes bring? Honestly, anyone can play drums and bass on songs like these. The arrangements aren't particularly complex." He shrugs. "I'm just trying to decide if I should sign Dax as a solo artist and hire him a plug-and-play backing band."

My stomach clenches. "But, Reed, those three guys have been playing together since high school. You should have heard the way they were talking last night about their shared love of the band and each other and their dreams for the future." I suddenly feel breathless. "Reed, they're The Three Musketeers."

"That's always the story with young bands," Reed says calmly. "Doesn't mean it makes business sense to keep the band together." He leans back in his chair and his gorgeous eight-pack tightens and clenches with his movement.

"So that's what you're gonna do?" I ask, suddenly panicked. "Sign Dax and leave the other two guys out in the cold?"

Reed shrugs. "I haven't decided yet. But, to answer your question, that's why I didn't pick up the phone to make an offer. If it turns out I wanna offer Dax a solo deal, that's not the kind of conversation I should have with the kid on the phone."

"Reed," I say, my heart racing. "I know you know your business and I don't know a damned thing, but, *please*, keep an open mind here. From the little I've seen of Dax, he seems exceptionally loyal to his friends. They're like family to him. I'm positive asking him to choose between a record deal and his lifelong friends would be devastating to him, not to mention to the other two guys."

"I'll watch the show tonight and see what I think."

"*Please* keep an open mind."

"I will. But only because you're so passionate about it." He winks.

"Thank you." I breathe a sigh of relief.

A cocktail waitress walks by and Reed flags her.

"You want another one, T?" He points to my empty cup.

"Fuck yes," I say, my body wracked with stress from our conversation, and Reed laughs heartily at my unexpected reply.

Reed places our orders with the waitress and then leans back and smiles at me like a wolf. "I will say this about Dax Morgan: that kid could probably play with a couple monkeys backing him and still make it to the top of the charts."

"Then what's the harm in signing the whole band?" I ask. "Those other boys can't be any worse than monkeys."

"No harm, maybe, but felony-stupid for Dax. If he's a solo artist, he won't have to split the pot three ways."

"Maybe for Dax the pot's not worth having if he's gonna be sitting all alone at the top of the charts, feeling like the biggest asshole who ever lived," I say, my cheeks flashing with color. "Or, hey, maybe Dax only feels so comfortable onstage because he's got the safety net of being up there with his two best friends in the world. Maybe in that important, subtle way Fish and Colin contribute more to 22 Goats than you realize. Maybe, if Dax said yes to you and turned his back on his friends, he'd forever feel like he fucked them over—and then he'd start resenting you and the devil's bargain he made and he'd turn to booze and pills to numb the pain and, slowly but surely, or maybe quite quickly, the 'rock star' you signed would become a train wreck and a complete waste of your investment."

Reed throws his head back and laughs heartily.

"What?" I say.

Reed flashes me a massive smile. "So much *passion*."

"I poured it on too thick?" I ask sheepishly.

He nods. "Pretty damned thick. And yet it all rings true somehow."

I sigh with relief.

"Thanks for giving me some food for thought, T-Rod. It's nice to get bitch-slapped once in a while. It happens so rarely to me these days."

"Oh. I had no intention of 'bitch-slapping' you."

Reed waves dismissively. "I was being facetious. I just meant that nobody in my company ever pushes back with me anymore. Not like you just did, anyway."

"No?"

"No," he says. "If they push back at all it's always about dollars and cents and second-guessing the market—never about not being a total dick. Never about *passion.*"

"Reed, I wasn't calling you a dick. And I most certainly wasn't trying to be naïve about business. I was just offering a different point of view."

Reed flashes me a wicked smile. "No need to apologize, T-Rod. You're misunderstanding me. I'm telling you I *liked* it when you pushed back." His gaze turns decidedly sexual. "*I liked it a lot.*"

My crotch floods with blood all of a sudden. "Oh. Well... Okay."

We stare at each other for a moment, and there's no doubt in my mind he's imagining having extremely enthusiastic sex with me right this very minute. And I'm not gonna lie: I'm having the same mental image.

"So, T-Rod," Reed says, his voice low and intense. "What are you doing after—"

"Yo, Rivers," Josh says, out of nowhere, and we both lean back abruptly.

"Yo, Faraday," Reed answers smoothly.

"Jonas and Kat's brother, Ryan, just challenged me and you to a game of two-man volleyball." He looks at me. "Hope I'm not interrupting anything here, T?"

I shake my head like a little kid.

"Dude, gimme a minute. I just ordered a drink," Reed says, his eyes flickering across my body again.

"I'll bring your drink to you at the volleyball court when it arrives," I offer, happy to use Reed's drink as an excuse to watch Ryan playing volleyball in the sand.

"No, Miss Rodriguez," Josh says. "Tell the waitress to bring it to Reed at the court when she comes, okay? You go ahead and hang out here and read your book and relax." He looks at me pointedly. "*Just stay here and relax.*"

I nod. Damn. There was no mistaking the outright command of that last statement.

"Come on, man," Josh says, pulling Reed up off his chair. "Time to give my brother and soon-to-be brother a volleyball-beat-down as only the unstoppable duo of Faraday-Rivers can do."

Reed relents and stands, not taking his eyes off me, his muscles flexing and tightening as he does. "I'll catch ya later, T-Rod. It was nice chatting with you. Thanks for the advice."

"Nice chatting with you, too, Reed. See you later tonight—at the concert."

He winks at me. "Or maybe before then. You never know."

"Come on, Rivers," Josh says, physically pulling Reed away. "Goodbye, Miss Rodriguez. Wish me luck."

"Good luck, Mr. Faraday," I say. "You're gonna need it to beat Jonas."

"Gee, thanks for the vote of confidence. I'll be sure to tell him you said that, you traitor."

I giggle.

I watch Josh and Reed stride away from me toward the beach. Josh puts his arm around his dear friend's shoulders, leans into his ear, and says something to him—and not two seconds later, Reed turns completely around 'til he's walking backward in order to face me, lays his hands on his heart, and flashes me a shit-eating grin that makes me laugh out loud.

Holy hell.

Note to self, Tessa: stay the fuck away from Reed Rivers.

Chapter 46
Ryan

"Kat!" I shout to my sister. She's floating on an inner tube with Josh and his crowd down a circular lazy river, her adorable, bulging belly on glorious display in her white bikini. "Kat!" I call to her again.

Kat finally hears me and looks toward my voice.

I motion to her like, "Get the fuck over here!"

My sister says something to her group and paddles to the ledge and somehow manages to get her graceless body out of her inner tube and over to me.

"What's up, Rum Cake?" she asks, waddling up to me.

"You still dying to play matchmaker, Kum Cake?"

She smiles. "I really don't think that's necessary anymore, do you?"

I stare at her, holding my breath.

"I know all about you and T-Rod," Kat says, answering my unspoken question.

I exhale. "What do you know?"

"I know she's Samantha. And I know you've already slept with her." She snickers. "You devil, you."

I grab Kat's arm and drag her into a private corner by a fake waterfall. "How the hell do you know all that? Did Colby tell you?"

"Colby knows, too? Ha! Awesome. How'd he figure it out?"

"Because I told him."

Kat scowls. "Bastard! You told Colby and not me? What the fuck?"

"Jizz, you're a blabbermouth."

"*So.*"

"So, Tessa's afraid for anyone to know. She especially doesn't want Josh to know."

"Why? We've all been there. Or, at least, I have. Many times."

"She's not like you. She's, you know, *nice*."

Kat flips me the bird.

"How the hell did you figure it out?" I ask.

Kat tells me how she put two and two together last night when Henn mentioned "Charlotte McDougal," and then how she got Tessa to unwittingly give up the ghost without even realizing it.

"And Tessa still has no clue she told you everything?" I ask.

"Of course, not." Kat bats her eyelashes. "I'm a covert operative—you know that."

I let out a long exhale. "Kat, promise me you won't tell anyone, okay? Especially not Josh. He's already warned me off her and I don't want to piss him off."

"Josh warned you off her? When?"

I quickly tell Kat the story. "It's understandable," I say, "given that he thinks I've still got a massive boner for some Argentinian flight attendant named Samantha."

Kat bursts out laughing. "Oh my God. This entire situation is hilarious."

"No, it's not. It's horrible. Josh thinks I'm a fickle fucker whose only goal in life is getting laid by random Argentinians and it couldn't be further from the truth."

Kat giggles. "He thinks you're Keane with an Argentine fetish."

"Fucking Peen."

"Fucking Peen," Kat agrees. "So why don't you just tell Josh T-Rod is Samantha and he's got it all wrong?" Kat says. "Problem solved."

"I can't. I promised Tessa I wouldn't say a word to him or anyone. I mean, if I get my way, by the end of this week, everyone will know everything, but until then, it's nobody's business but hers."

Kat makes a face I can't decode.

"Please, Kat," I say. "Help me keep things on the down-low with her for a few days. Tessa doesn't make snap-decisions. She likes having plenty of time to process."

"I know. She's a Virgo." She rolls her eyes. "Don't worry—I know that kind of girl well. I'm best friends with Sarah, remember?"

"Speaking of which, whatever happened to you not wanting me to date your friends? When I wanted to date Sarah, you shut me down, and now you're gung ho to fix me up with Tessa?"

"That whole thing with Sarah was back when you were a little man-child, Rum Cake. You're a grown man now—a really, really good man."

"Thanks, Splooge. I always knew I loved you the most. Speaking of which, the reason I came over here is I need your brilliant, diabolical mind. Reed Rivers is sniffing around my girl right this very minute by the pool. I need you to go over there and get him the fuck away from her."

"I can't go over there. It'd be too obvious."

"Not as obvious as me going over there. Come on, Kat. Help a brother out."

"I think you're being paranoid, Ry. Reed might be hitting on Tessa, but he's not gonna make any headway. She's not the kind of girl who does two different guys in two days."

"Yeah, normally, but I'm worried as hell Tessa thinks she's on some sort of sexual-liberation bender." I explain how Tessa refused to commit to exclusivity with me last night. "If ever there was a moment in time when that girl would go completely off the rails, I think it's right fucking now." I run my hand through my hair. "Kat, please. I didn't come over here to debate this with you. I need you to get your preggers ass over there and get Mr. Music-Mogul-Fuckface away from my girl."

"Okay, take a chill-pill, darling brother—I've got this. One whisper to Josh that Reed's making the moves on his sweet and naïve personal assistant and he'll sprint over there and yank Reed back by the scruff of his neck. Josh loves Reed like a brother, but he's said more than once he doesn't want that guy within twenty yards of T-Rod."

"Well, good, because neither do I."

"You really like her, huh?"

"Kat, 'like' doesn't come close to encapsulating what I'm feeling. But we don't have time to talk about this. *You need to go.*"

Kat looks smug. "Maybe next time you'll listen to your little sister when she says she's got the perfect girl for you, huh?"

"Sweetheart, if things keep progressing the way I'm hoping they will, there won't be a next time."

Kat squeals and grabs my hand. "Okay, Rum Cake, let's go put a bug in my soon-to-be-husband's ear and get Mr. Music-Mogul-Fuckface away from my future sister-in-law."

Chapter 47
Tessa

"See how elastic our prejudices grow when once love comes to bend them."

All two hundred of us sitting in the audience at this private luau, including me, are cheering and laughing and basically experiencing death-by-adorableness right now. At the invitation of the professional dancers onstage, the few kids in our group have come onstage to try their hand at hula dancing, which means Coco and a few other cutie-pies are up there now, swiveling their little hips and making semi-hula-esque movements with their arms. Adorable.

When the kiddos clear the stage to furious applause, the emcee calls for ten to fifteen "lovely ladies" from the audience to come up and give the men a show. Well, of course, Kat pops up and drags Sarah and Hannah and several of her friends from college up there with her, and Keane stands and physically carries his mother up to the stage as she giggles and squeals her head off, which then prompts Ryan and Dax to grab Louise's two sisters and bring them up to the stage, too. And, ultimately, we're treated to a performance by the women that makes everyone cheer and applaud and laugh uproariously. Kat, especially, steals the show—man, does that woman know how to work that baby bump in a grass skirt!

Finally, the ladies leave the stage and the main event arrives—the moment we ladies have been waiting for since this little exercise in audience participation began: the emcee calls for a dozen or so gentlemen to come up and shake what the good lord gave them in a grass skirt. It's a suggestion that prompts every woman in the room to shriek and cat-call with a ferociousness that would put an audience at a Magic Mike show to shame.

It's interesting and funny to see which guys in our group leap up and which ones couldn't be dragged onstage by wild horses. Jonas, for instance, clearly won't be dancing for our enjoyment tonight, and neither will Dax or Colby. *Nope.* They've all crossed their arms over their chests and they're plastering their asses onto their chairs like they're Superglued onto them.

But, glory be, there's no such resistance from the more extroverted hotties in the audience, a group that includes Josh, Reed, Henn, Zander, Keane (of course), a few of Josh's fraternity brothers, and, thankfully, the one and only Ryan Ulysses Morgan.

The minute our gregarious men get onstage, an army of bare-chested male Hawaiian dancers descend upon them and, in no time flat, strip them of their shirts, and wrap them in grass skirts and other adornments.

As the audience looks on, hooting and hollering enthusiastically, loud drums begin thumping frenetically, cuing the professional dancers to break into a frantic and jaw-dropping display. After a few minutes of the dancers showing our men exactly what's expected of them, the professionals move aside and cue the drums again.

And that's when sheer pandemonium breaks loose.

Oh my God, our men aren't holding back up there. They're shaking and flexing and hopping around in their bare chests and grass skirts, each of them displaying their unique and full-throttled interpretations of the professional dancers' earlier moves. Okay, first off, this is just freaking hilarious. I'm pretty sure I just now peed a little from laughing. But, second off, *oh my God,* this is hot as hell. I mean, holy macaroni, that's a hot group of men up there! Especially Ryan. I mean, yes Keane and Josh have an obvious leg up on their competition from a "dance moves" standpoint—but, in my opinion, Ryan's got them all beat when it comes to sheer magnetism.

I bite my lip watching Ryan, my abdomen tightening with desire.

I want him.

Quickly, it becomes clear who the stand-outs onstage are, and, as if by design, the guys group themselves into two "teams" onstage—Josh, Reed, and Henn on one side versus Zander, Keane, and Ryan on the other—and we women cheer and scream, goading them into a fierce and funny three-on-three hula-off.

Oh my God, I've died and gone to heaven. I'm crying with

laughter. I glance down my long table and discover Kat, Hannah, and Sarah at the other end, all of them crying tears of laughter, too. By chance, Kat glances at me while I'm looking at her, and, without hesitation, she blows me a kiss before looking back at the stage.

And, just like that, I suddenly feel like I'm right where I belong in this world. With these people—a part of this wonderful family. A family who so obviously loves each other unconditionally.

Tears well up in my eyes and I wipe my cheeks, suddenly not sure if I'm crying tears of laughter at the performance onstage—or if, after this past year of shocking betrayal and heartbreak in my life, if, maybe, just maybe, I'm crying about something else entirely.

The dance-off is over.

Everyone in the audience resumes their seats, wiping their eyes from laughter, and the professionals prepare to resume their show.

But as our men put their shirts back on and begin walking offstage—Ryan bounds over to the emcee and whispers something in her ear.

She nods and hands Ryan the microphone.

"Hey, Keane," Ryan says into the mic. "Hold up."

Keane stops descending the steps of the stage and waits.

"Alooooha!" Ryan booms to all of us in the audience.

Everyone replies in kind, all of us already well trained how to respond to this greeting here in Hawaii.

"Before we let the show resume," Ryan says, "I think we should get the two best hula dancers of the night up here for a dance-off. What do you think?"

Everyone shouts and applauds their enthusiasm for the idea.

"Keane, come back up here, man." He turns to look at the line of professional dancers, standing off to the side. "Can we get my brother back into a hula skirt?"

A male dancer quickly descends upon Keane to dress him.

"And will our other stand-out dancer of the night please come on up here, too? Coco? Come on up here, honey!" Ryan finds Coco's little face in the crowd and his gorgeous face lights up. "Hello, beautiful. Come on up here, sweetheart. Time for you to beat Keane's booty in hula dancing."

The crowd explodes with excitement as Coco pops up and eagerly works her way toward the stage.

"Word on the street is my brother Keane challenged Coco to a hula-dancing duel on the flight over here," Ryan explains. "In fact, Keane's exact words were that he was gonna 'beat her booty in hula dancing.'"

Everyone boos loudly and Keane instantly assumes the body language of a villain-wrestler in the ring.

"Time for Keane Morgan to learn how to be humble, right, Coco Puff?"

As Coco ascends the steps of the stage, Keane rips off his shirt, crouches at the front of the stage like a lion in a hula skirt, and cups his hands to his ears like he's begging us to boo him even louder, which we do between fits of laughter.

Finally, Coco reaches the stage and walks across it timidly toward Ryan, obviously feeling a bit unsure. Ryan moves to her, bends down to her level, his body language gentle and attentive, and talks to her for a moment. Coco nods. Ryan puts his palm up and she high-fives it and he kisses the top of her head and rustles her hair.

And... I... just... died.

May Tessa Rodriguez rest in peace.

Ryan rises to standing and addresses the crowd, his face aglow. "Okay, folks, Coco says she's ready to kick some Keane-Morgan booty. Let's do this!"

The professional dancers descend on Coco, tying a grass skirt around her waist and slipping a flower lei around her neck, and, immediately, a ukulele-accompanied dance-off begins.

Oh my God. This is absolutely hilarious and lovely. Coco's moves are earnest and sweet. Man, that kid's really giving it her all up there! And Keane's moves are absolutely spellbinding, though not even remotely reminiscent of an actual Hawaiian dance. Side note? Holy hell, Keane Morgan can move! Even though he's obviously doing PG-rated versions of his moves for this particular audience, it's nonetheless very clear to me I should drag Charlotte to a Ball Peen Hammer show for her birthday next month.

But, as compelling as Keane and Coco are up there, my eyes quickly drift to Ryan. He's standing at the side of the stage, belly laughing and cheering Coco to her inevitable victory—and, for some reason, everything he's doing—everything about him—is making my ovaries vibrate and my heart physically ache for him. Oh my God, he's absolutely stunning up there. A work of art. *Beautiful. Inside and out.*

The dance-off ends and Ryan walks between the contestants, microphone in hand.

"Great job, guys," he says. "Okay, everyone, it's time to select our winner through applause. First, let me hear from you if you think Keane's our winner!" He raises Keane's hand into the air and a loud tidal wave of boos crashes onto the stage, followed by raucous laughter.

"Wow, Keane," Ryan says. "Not lookin' good for ya, bro."

Keane grabs the microphone. "You guys are lame."

More boos slam into the stage and Keane flexes every muscle in his body, yet again playing the part of the villain.

"Okay, okay," Ryan says. "And now... let me hear from you, nice and loud, if your vote is for... *Coco!*" He holds up Coco's hand and everyone explodes into enthusiastic applause and cheers.

Keane does a whole sore-loser thing behind Coco but ultimately shakes the victor's hand and rustles her hair and picks her up and takes her on a giggling victory lap around the stage. And, through it all, I still can't seem to take my eyes off Ryan Ulysses Morgan. The way he's smiling at Coco and his brother—the way he's laughing and so obviously enjoying this moment—the fact that he thought to engineer this shining moment for Coco in the first place... Oh my God, I'm so turned on right now, I'm gonna have to change my panties before I head to the 22 Goats concert later on.

Finally, Ryan, Keane, and Coco leave the stage and resume their seats and the professional show continues... and, the minute Ryan's seated at the other end of my long table, I steal a long, aching look at him, my cheeks blazing and my crotch pounding. Slowly, Ryan turns his face away from the show that's resumed onstage and looks straight at me, his eyes smoldering.

He smiles and my entire body jolts like I've been struck by a Taser gun.

I lick my lips.

And then return his smile.

And then, the same way Ryan did at the opening party last night, he taps the face of his watch as if to say, "It's only a matter of time."

Only this time, unlike last night, I nod, acknowledging the inevitable.

Chapter 48
Tessa

As I watch 22 Goats performing onstage in the resort's nightclub, I'm floored by how great they are. Seriously, who knew Dax and his two friends were this talented? Their videos are great, yes, but they don't come close to doing this amazing band justice. Just like Reed said, Dax Morgan is a needle in a haystack. Get that boy the right exposure and he's gonna be a mega rock star. And the other two guys in the band? Forget what Reed said: they're great, too. In their own ways, of course. I mean, obviously, Fish and Colin don't shine nearly as brightly as Dax up there, but who could? Dax is in a league of his own—otherworldly. I mean, thanks to Dax's showmanship and charisma, I feel like I've got the best seat in the house, and yet I'm at the very back of the club against a wall.

I scan the crowd, hoping to spot Ryan again, and, this time, when my eyes land on him, he's across the room, rocking out and singing along to every word in a happy cluster with his immediate family, all of them obviously enthralled with their beloved rock star.

My heart flips over.

God, I love that family.

"Hey, you," a voice says.

It's Reed, holding two drinks, smelling vaguely of cologne, and looking at me like he wants to fuck the living hell out of me.

"Hi, Reed."

"Mai tai?"

"Thanks. Great hula dancing earlier."

"Gee, thanks." He hands me one of the glasses. "You enjoying the show?"

"I'm *loving* it. 22 Goats is phenomenal—way, way better than I expected, and I had high expectations."

Reed nods and takes a sip of his drink.

"And you?" I ask. "You like what you see?'

Reed's eyes darken with heat. "Definitely."

Crap. I hadn't intended my comment as some sort of come-on. "I meant the band. You like the band?"

Reed grins. "I knew what you meant."

I swallow hard. "So do you think you're gonna sign them?"

Reed flashes me a sexy smirk. "What do you think I should do, T-Rod? Tell me your honest opinion."

"That's easy: I think you should sign them," I say, and it's the God's truth. "And not just Dax—the entire band. In fact, if you truly want my honest opinion...?"

"I do."

"I think if you don't sign the entire band, then you're a fucking idiot and completely devoid of a soul."

Reed bursts out laughing. "Aw, come on, T-Rod, tell me what you *really* think." He takes a sip of his drink as his eyes blaze a path from my face to my low-cut neckline and back up again. "You know what I'm gonna do, T-Rod? Just because you're so damned passionate about this? I'm gonna leave the decision up to Dax. I'll make him two offers: option one, a solo offer for X dollars, and, option two, an offer to the band for the same X dollars. I'll let the kid decide if he wants the whole pot to himself or if he wants to split the same amount of money three ways."

I jut my chin at Reed defiantly. "Suit yourself," I say, and then I shock myself by adding, "but there's no doubt in my mind Dax is gonna take the offer for the band."

"Oh, you know Dax pretty well?"

"No, I just met him yesterday. But he's a *Morgan*—and I know for a fact Morgans don't screw their friends."

A wide smile spreads across Reed's face—a smile that tells me he thinks I'm naïve.

My heart rate spikes. "Reed, listen to me," I sputter, all my bravado from a moment ago fading. "You gotta offer only one deal— the deal to the band."

"Why? If that's what Dax wants, then that's the deal he'll take." He looks at me sideways. "You afraid our boy's gonna take the money for himself and make you lose all faith in humanity?"

"No. My recommendation isn't for me—it's for you. If you play it the way you're saying, you run the risk our boy's gonna think you're a total prick for putting him in that horrible position—maybe even a prick with whom he has no desire to do business at all. And that wouldn't be in his interest or yours."

Reed looks thoughtful for a moment. "Have I ever mentioned you're a badass, T-Rod?"

"No."

"Well, let me fix that oversight now: T-Rod, you're a badass."

"Thank you. So are you."

"You want me to make one offer to 22 Goats?"

"Yes, I do. For your own good."

"And are you gonna break my legs if I don't?"

"Yes, I am. In multiple places. With a baseball bat."

Reed laughs. "God help me. Fine. Consider it done. I was just fucking with you, actually—just wanted to see what you'd say."

"That wasn't very nice."

"I'm not always nice." He flashes me a truly wicked smile. "Now, throw back the rest of that mai tai and put your glass down, hot stuff. I wanna dance with a smokin' hot badass to celebrate my brand new band."

I throw back the rest of my drink, as instructed, and then let Reed lead me by the hand toward an area that's become a makeshift dance floor.

"I'll dance with you, Reed," I shout over the music as we get closer to the blaring speakers. "But that's all you get. I've seen you on *TMZ*—I know exactly what you are."

Reed guffaws at that and pulls me to him. "Don't believe everything you see on the Internet, baby. I'm a pussycat, I swear."

Chapter 49
Ryan

I glance over to the spot where Tessa's been standing watching the 22 Goats show, the same way I've done at least ten times in the last thirty minutes, and, much to my dismay, this time, she's not there anymore.

I scan the small club, looking for her, only to find her in the middle of the crowd, doing the unthinkable: dancing with motherfucking Reed Rivers.

Oh, hell to the fucking no.

I disengage from my mother's arm and take two heated steps toward the happy couple, intending to physically shove that fucker away from my girl, and then stop short, suddenly remembering he's the man who holds my brother's rock-star dreams in the palm of his hand. Fuck!

I march back to my family, grab my sister's arm, and motion across the room to Reed and Tessa.

Kat looks over to where I'm indicating and, immediately, her facial expression matches mine. "Motherfucker!" she yells over the loud music. "Fuck no."

I lean into my diabolical sister's ear so there's no mistaking my words despite the loud music. "Get that fucker away from my girl, Kum Cake.

"I got this, Rum Cake," she says, her eyes narrowing. "Go out by the front entrance and wait. Your girl's gonna walk through that door in a minute."

I don't hesitate. Off I go.

I wait outside the front entrance of the club in the warm, fragrant night for what seems like for-fucking-ever, clenching and

246

unclenching my fists while forcing myself not to storm back inside the place and claim what's rightfully mine.

Thank God, just when I've decided to go back in there and handle things myself, Tessa comes out the front door of the club.

Immediately, I ambush her. I grab her by the arm and pull her around a corner, in search of a private spot where no one will see what I'm about to do to her.

"Wait," Tessa says, trying in vain to pull away from me. "I can't go anywhere with you. Kat asked me to get her—"

"Kat lied. Whatever my sister told you to get you to walk out that door, she was lying. She was sending you out here for me."

"You told Kat about us?"

"No. Kat's playing matchmaker, remember?" It's a true statement, technically. I didn't tell my sister about us—she figured it out on her own.

Tessa relaxes under my grip. "Where are you taking me?" she asks.

I spot a dark alcove surrounded by bougainvillea behind the club. "There." I drag her into the nook and, without hesitation, pin her against the back wall of the club. I grip her face, my heart racing. "No more 'thinking about it.' No more 'processing.' You're *mine*. All week long it's me and you and no one else and that's all there is to it. You got that?"

She nods.

"Say it."

"Me and you."

"You're mine. *Say it.*"

"I'm yours." She lets out a long exhale. "Oh, God, I want you, Ryan."

I'm hard as a rock. My heart is pounding. I pull up her dress and pull down her undies and slide my fingers inside her and she groans. "You want me or him?"

"I don't want him. I've never wanted him."

"Your body's mine," I say as I roll a condom onto my dick. "I own it. It's mine and no one else's—especially not *his.*"

She nods.

I grab her ass and pick her up and she wraps her legs around my waist as I slide myself into her, her back against the flower-covered wall. "Say my name."

"Ryan."

"Promise me it's just me and you."

"I promise."

"Say my name again."

She grips my face and looks into my eyes. "Ryan. It's just me and you. I'm yours. I promise..." She lets out a sigh of deep arousal. "*Ryan*."

Oh my God. I feel like my heart's exploding and melting, all at once, right along with my body. I kiss her passionately, relieved and thrilled and beyond turned on, my body moving in and out of hers, my palms gripping her ass as I hold her up, my chest on fire.

"Tessa," I whisper into her ear. "You own me, baby. You've owned me since before I laid eyes on you."

Just when I think I can't hang on any longer, she comes, hard, throwing her head back and stiffening in my arms—and, seconds later, I let go and come, too. *Hard.*

When we're both done growling and quaking with pleasure, we kiss for a very long moment in the moonlight, our chests pressed together, electricity coursing between us. There's no doubt about it—this thing between us is bigger than sex. And much, much bigger than one week in paradise. I want her and she wants me and that's all there is to it. Finally—fucking *finally*, we're both on the same page. From here on out, it's gonna be just me and her.

Tessa slides down my body, finds her undies in a bush and pulls them on, and then straightens her dress and her hair. "Okay," she says. "What happens in Maui stays in Maui—just like you said. We'll have some delicious fun on the down-low this week and, when we get back to Seattle, we'll both pretend it never happened." She holds up her palm for a high-five and I leave her hanging, feeling like she just slapped me across the face.

When it's clear I'm not gonna high-five her, she places her raised palm on my cheek, kisses my lips softly, and swipes the pad of her thumb across my lower lip—a maneuver that makes my heart physically pang for her.

"I'll go back into the club first," she whispers. "Wait a few minutes so nobody gets suspicious." She kisses me again and smiles. "God, this is gonna be fun. I can't wait." And with that, she turns and practically sprints into the club, leaving me standing with my mouth hanging open and my heart feeling like it's bleeding out.

Chapter 50
Tessa

After the 22 Goats concert ends, Ryan and I sneak back to my room, strip off our clothes, and eagerly begin exploring each other's bodies, inside and out. How is it every sexual encounter with this man makes me want him *more*, rather than *less*?

Finally, when our bodies are spent and satisfied, we lie in bed naked, nose to nose, on our sides, our fingers intertwined, and talk softly in the moonlit room, the relaxing sounds of the ocean wafting through an open French door.

We talk and talk—about our childhoods, religion, politics, music, and movies. We argue to near-death about the "secret ingredient" for great guacamole. Ryan swears by a pinch of cumin; I say it's a splash of Worcestershire sauce. Ryan calls the front desk and asks for a fitted sheet to be delivered by housekeeping and then proceeds to teach me how to properly fold a fitted sheet and then he promptly binds my hands with said sheet and fucks the hell out of me again.

After Ryan's finished showing me every sheet-related trick in his arsenal (holy hell!), I teach Ryan a trick of my own: I pull him out of bed and teach him the basic steps to the tango—and then we dance around the room naked for a while, accompanied by the one song I never seem to tire of hearing, "*Bailando*."

When we're done dancing, we flop onto the bed and Ryan asks me to translate the lyrics to "*Bailando*," line by line, so I pull them up on my phone and go through them.

"The lyrics are why I love the song so much, besides the obvious catchiness of the music and melody," I explain. "I love that it's about explosive, heart-palpitating physical chemistry, an attraction that takes Enrique's breath away. He says he wants to be with her, live with her, dance with her, have sex with her... He's just totally obsessed with her—completely under her spell. I dunno, the intensity of the lyrics just totally turns me on."

Ryan's eyes flicker with heat. "Ah, so a bit of obsession is a turn-on for you, huh, Argentina? Good to know."

"A little bit," I say, opening my index finger and thumb slightly to demonstrate, and we both laugh.

More laughing and talking ensues, and, eventually, the conversation flows to the backstories of each of Ryan's many tattoos.

"And what about your piercings?" I ask, running my fingers over the bars slicing through his nipples. "When and how did you decide to get those?"

"I got all three of my piercings when I was twenty-one, all in the span of a crazy three months," Ryan replies. "I went into this tattoo place in the University District with my buddies to get this one." He points to the bottle of rum on his left ribcage. "And, on a dare, I wound up asking the tattoo-artist out on a date. She was ten years older than me and really, really into the whole body-mod culture—both tattoos and piercings—and, unexpectedly, that first date led to this crazy, whirlwind, three-month relationship."

"She was ten years older than you?"

Ryan laughs. "Yeah. And a real wild child. We weren't compatible at all in any meaningful way, but, still, I got a lot out of the relationship: she wound up teaching me more in three months about how to please a woman than I'd learned my whole life up to that point." He smiles. "Within the first twenty minutes of our first date, I knew she wasn't gonna be a good fit for me long-term; but for three months, I was quite happy to let her poke needles into her horny young plaything's most sensitive flesh."

I ask a few more questions and he answers them openly and with astonishing self-awareness, and soon the conversation flows naturally to Ryan's lifelong dream of owning his own bar one day.

"Have you thought about what you'd call the place?" I ask.

"Captain's."

I roll my eyes at my own stupidity for not guessing that answer. "*Of course*. What would Captain's be like?"

Ryan's face lights up. "It'd be sophisticated and sleek, but people would feel at home there, too, like definitely not 'too cool for school.' I'd have foosball and pool tables but somehow still make the place feel like a high-end destination for people to hang out after work. Sophisticated but fun, that'd be my mission statement."

"So the place would be you, in bar-form."

He blushes. "Thank you."

I touch his gorgeous, chiseled jawline. "I love the whole concept. The only thing I'm wondering is how the foosball and pool tables would work out from a cost standpoint. They'd take a lot of space, which would increase your square-footage, which might make your rent on the expensive side, since you're gonna have to rent somewhere kind of trendy if you're targeting a sophisticated demographic."

"You're spot-on, baby. Wow. You're smart as a tack, you know that?"

"Thank you."

"Don't you worry, my pretty chickadee," he says playfully. "I've got a business plan all drawn up and I've been scouting locations for the past year. I think I've got the perfect solution."

"Oh, wow, I'd love to see your business plan, if you don't mind. I don't know anything about opening a bar, but I know a lot about logistics and vendor costs and stuff like that. Working for Josh for six years has given me a real education on some nuts-and-bolts things."

"I'll send it to you. I'd be thrilled to get your feedback."

"When do you think you'll be able to make Captain's a reality?" I say, pressing my naked body against his.

"A couple years, probably, depending on what commissions I manage to earn between now and then."

"You should ask Josh to put in a word with his friends about you being a commercial broker. Tons of Josh's friends are multi-millionaires and lots of them have real estate holdings."

"Sweet of you to think of that, but I don't want Josh to think I'm using him for his contacts list."

"No, no, Josh does favors for friends and family all the time. I'm sure he wouldn't think twice about floating your name to his circle of friends. Some of them are really loaded, Ryan."

Ryan shrugs. "I'm good. I wouldn't want Josh to question my intentions." He pulls me close to him and kisses me tenderly. "I wouldn't want *anyone* I care about to question my intentions, ever."

Warmth spreads throughout my body. I run my hand through his hair and nuzzle his nose. "I bet Kat will wind up saying something to Josh about you, regardless. If there's one thing I've gathered about the fearless Kat Morgan, it's that she looks out for the people she loves."

"She sure does. We all do. It's a Morgan thing."

"I love that about your family."

"And my family loves you."

My heart skips a beat.

Ryan nuzzles my nose. "So what are *your* dreams, my beautiful Argentinian whale?"

"You did *not* just call me a *whale*."

He laughs. "It's a reference to *Moby Dick.* I'm Captain Ahab and you're my whale. Never mind. Sorry. I'll never do it again. Tell me about your dreams, sweetheart."

I press my soft breasts into his hard chest and sigh contentedly. "I don't know, to be honest," I say. "Lately, I've been thinking I might like to spread my wings a little bit. Now that Josh and Jonas have launched Climb & Conquer and they're planning to expand aggressively, I was kind of thinking I'd maybe ask them for an official role in their new organization—you know, to help them grow it? I'm genuinely inspired by their mission statement. Did you know they donate to a whole bunch of charities as part of their business model?"

"Yeah, I know—I went to their grand opening party in Seattle and heard Jonas' speech."

I snicker. "I was at that party."

"No way!"

"Yep. I saw you there—from the back. I saw the back of your head and I thought, 'Wow, the back of that guy's head reminds me of Ryan from The Pine Box!'"

"Oh my fucking God!"

"When the speeches were over, I did a little loop around the place, looking for the guy—just out of curiosity, you know—but he was nowhere to be found. I guess you'd left by then."

Ryan looks thoughtful for a long moment. "Do you remember what song was playing when you looked around for me?"

"I sure do. My favorite: '*Bailando.*'"

Ryan shakes his head and chuckles. "Oh my God."

"What?"

He rubs his face. "Nothing. It's just funny we were in the same room and never ran into each other. So back to this idea of yours— spreading your wings. Does that mean you wanna stop being Josh's personal assistant?"

"Ooph. Just hearing you say that out loud makes my stomach hurt. I *love* being Josh's personal assistant. But, if I'm being totally honest, a part of me feels like I've been slowly outgrowing the job. And now that he's marrying Kat... I dunno. I just feel like it's maybe time for me to... I just don't know."

"You ever thought about starting your own business?" Ryan asks.

"I've thought about it. I've been saving well over half my income every year for the past six years, in case I maybe wanna start something one day—but then I just never know what that 'something' would be."

"You've saved over *half* your income for six years? Damn. You either make a shit-ton of money or you live like a mouse."

"Both," I reply. "I work my ass off for Josh, don't get me wrong, but, even so, he vastly over-pays me. I make probably thirty percent more than any other high-end personal assistant. The irony, of course, is that I don't give a shit about money and never have, other than when it comes to feeding my shoe addiction."

"So why does Josh pay you so much?"

"Because I gouge him mercilessly once a year for a massive raise."

Ryan laughs. "But why? You just said you don't care about money."

"I don't. Not at all. I gouge Josh for one simple reason: job security." I stroke Ryan's hair as I speak and he closes his eyes at my touch. "It didn't take long for me to realize this simple truth: when your boss has a closet full of two-thousand-dollar shoes and custom-made suits and a garage filled with vintage sports cars and he's never flown coach in his entire life, the man probably values things more when he pays exorbitantly for them. Hence, early on, the minute he hired me full-time, I started making him pay through the nose for my services, and it seemed like he continuously valued me more and more, so I just kept doing it. At some point, it got ridiculous, but I just figured, 'Why fix it if it ain't broke?'"

"You're a fucking genius, T-Rod," Ryan says, laughing.

"Oh, surely, Josh has figured me out by now, but he's just playing along."

Ryan flashes me a smile that warms my entire body. "I love the way your mind works," he says softly. "You're smart. Scrappy. Pragmatic. You see the finish line and you get there. I really love that about you."

My heart soars. I wrap my arms around him and kiss him, stifling my sudden urge to blurt something completely insane to him in reply—something only someone in a committed relationship would ever say—and, luckily, our kiss soon becomes heated, and, before I know it, we're in the throes of heated sex, yet again, an activity that makes me forget, at least temporarily, every single one of the ridiculous, fairytale-inspired thoughts threatening to fill my silly head.

Chapter 51
Tessa

It was the best day ever for the Faraday-Morgan wedding brigade: all two hundred of us toured Maui via helicopter today, five choppers, each holding six people, at a time. And when someone wasn't on an aerial tour, oohing and aahing about the island's jaw-dropping sights, they were back at the resort, engaging in activities ranging from jet-skiing to parasailing to kayaking to windsurfing to lei-making. And may I just say the time I spent kayaking and windsurfing and snorkeling with Ryan, along with varying other mix-and-match companions through it all, were some of the best times I've ever had in my life?

Best. Day. Ever.

The only thing that could have made my amazing day better would have been if I'd been assigned to ride in Ryan's helicopter. Unfortunately, though, when I checked the assignments, the activities director had scheduled Ryan to fly with his parents, Colby, and his aunt and uncle, and there was no way for me to switch up the helicopter assignments without it being *extremely* obvious that I'm now chomping at the bit to spend every waking moment with the Morgan family's beloved pirate.

Of course, if I couldn't sneak onto Ryan's helicopter, then I definitely got the best consolation prize: Dax, Fish, Colin, Keane, and Zander. That group of hilarious dudes would have been a fun group to tour the island with on any given day, for sure; but today especially, mere hours after the happy news broke that River Records had offered a record deal to 22 Goats, that ecstatic group of guys was pure joy to hang out with. Throughout our entire two-hour tour, whenever the six of us weren't marveling about the spectacular views outside the helicopter windows, we were collectively rhapsodizing about 22 Goats' bright future.

And now, after our fabulous day of helicopter-riding and fun-in-the-sun, a group of us is keeping the good times rolling with pre-dinner drinks in one of the hotel bars. And, although Ryan's not sitting next to me because I got skittish that we were becoming a bit too obvious, I'm thrilled he's sitting directly in my line of sight at the other end of our long table. It means we can easily shoot secret smiles and horny looks at each other without Josh or anyone else noticing.

Besides Josh, Kat, Ryan, and me, the squad for pre-dinner drinks is a bit of a mish-mash of Kat's and Josh's worlds: Henn, Hannah, Colby, Reed, Keane, Zander, and a mixture of Josh's and Kat's college- and work-friends, all of us at this point meshing like we're old friends.

At the moment, the energetic conversation around the table is about the "lost art of flirting" and how "kids these days," with their reliance on Snapchat and Instagram, have no idea how to pick someone up in-person.

"Josh and Kat gave me a brilliant tutorial on 'bagging a babe' not too long ago in Vegas," Henn says. "Those two could teach the ignorant kids of today a thing or two."

"That's revisionist history, Henn," Josh says, laughing. "It was Kat who was the true professor that night, not me."

Henn chuckles. "That's right. Kitty, what was that one rule of thumb you taught us? The one about how a guy who's talking to a very pretty lady knows if he should shut the hell up or keep talking?"

Kat giggles and raises her index finger. "Ask yourself this, gentlemen: 'Is what I'm about to say more or less likely to get me a blowjob?' If the answer is yes, then say it. If the answer is no, then shut the fuck up.'"

Everyone laughs uproariously.

"Now that's some advice to live by," Reed says. "I'll definitely keep that little gem in mind next time I'm talking to..." Reed looks straight at me. "A very pretty lady."

My skin pricks at Reed's unmistakable implication: the next time he speaks to me, he'll be wondering if his words are enticing me to give him a blowjob. I quickly look away from Reed's handsome face, my cheeks hot, and sneak a peek at Ryan, only to find him staring Reed down, his body language painting the stark portrait of a man plotting a murder.

"So what was Faraday's advice for 'bagging a babe'?" Reed asks Henn, apparently unaware the tattooed man to his right is thinking up ways to kill him. "I'm an old dog, but I'm always open to learning a new trick, especially from a world-renowned former playboy like Faraday."

Everyone at the table who knows Reed well simultaneously erupts with cruel mockery at the suggestion that Reed Rivers could possibly need to learn any "new tricks," even from someone as adept at picking up women as the renowned Playboy himself, Joshua William Faraday; and, quickly, the conversation spirals into a free-for-all of enthusiastic storytelling by every single one of Reed's college friends about Reed's "legendary" appeal to women "back in the day," and this from an era dating back before the man became rich and famous and known for having actresses and pop stars at his beck and call.

Blah, blah, blah. I don't give a rat's ass about Reed Rivers and his purportedly legendary appeal to women. I'm much more interested in staring at Ryan's blazing blue eyes and ridiculous jawline and thinking about all the utterly delicious things he did to me last night.

Sigh.

But after a few moments of daydreaming about last night's deliciousness with my very own manwhore of "legendary appeal," Keane's energetic voice draws me back to the present moment.

"It's true," Keane says emphatically to the group. "I've got mad skillz, brah."

"He does," Zander confirms. "*Mad.*"

"Give us an example," Henn says. "Something you'd say to bag a babe in a bar. Like, hey, pretend T-Rod's a random babe you wanna bag. Show us your magic."

"Okay," Keane says. He looks at me and flashes his ridiculous dimples. "*Hello.*"

"Hello," I reply, a smirk already dancing on my lips.

"What's your name, baby doll?"

"Tessa. And please don't call me baby doll."

"Hold up," Josh says loudly from the other end of the table, putting up his palm. "Theresa, why the *fuck* has everyone been calling you 'Tessa' all week? What am I missing?"

I smile sheepishly. "Tessa's actually the name I go by in real life. Not Theresa."

"In real life?" Josh asks.

"Outside of work. Everywhere else."

"See? I told you, babe!" Kat says triumphantly.

"What the fuck!" Josh says, laughing. "After six years, you finally tell me this little factoid about yourself for the first time?"

"I'm sorry," I say, laughing with everyone at the table. "For some stupid reason, I put my given name on my résumé, and when you started calling me 'Theresa,' I just never corrected you. But, yeah, I've never gone by Theresa in my life, ever, other than with you."

Josh shakes his head. "You're so lame, T."

I laugh. "I know. I'm sorry. Feel free to keep calling me Theresa. I'm totally used to it by now."

"Fuck *no*," Josh says, like I've just suggested he clean his toilet bowl with his tongue. "If family calls you Tessa, then that's what I'll call you, too." He smiles warmly at me.

I flash him a shy smile, but my heart is racing. If this isn't the best week of my life, I don't know what is. "Okay," I say. "Thank you."

Keane whistles like he's summoning a dog. "Um, excuse me, *Tessa*? Congrats on the Hallmark moment with your boss, but I believe I was in the middle of bagging a babe?"

Everyone laughs.

"Forgive me," I say. "Proceed with the babe-baggery."

"Thank you." Keane pauses for effect and then cartoonishly flashes me an unmistakable smolder. "*Helloooo*."

I giggle. "Hello."

"What's your name, beautiful girl?"

"Tessa."

"I'm Keane." He puts out his hand and I shake it. "It's a *pleasure* to meet you, *Tessa*." He flashes me his dimples for a long beat and then looks at Henn. "Okeedokey, she's good to go."

Everyone laughs.

"What?" Henn says, incredulous. "T-Rod, are you 'good to go'?"

"Not by a long mile," I say, and everyone laughs again.

Keane rolls his eyes. "Well, of course, *you're* not good to go, T-Rod. My charm won't work on you because we've already established a big-sister-little-brother thing."

My heart skips a beat. He feels it, too? Oh my God, I'm in heaven.

"Plus, you're a smart-girl," Keane continues, "and I never go for smart-girls. Ask anyone—way too much trouble. But, I'm tellin' ya, gimme a random, not-so-smart chick in a bar and what I just did would work like a charm. And you wanna know why? Because I sent you a subliminal message to the pleasure-center in your brain by using your name and the word 'pleasure' in close proximity. And *then*, I went in for the kill by flashing *these*." He smiles and points at his dimples. "Which means I've got my field sown, so to speak, and now, all I have to do is *this*." He crooks his finger in a come-hither motion. "And you'll follow me to the ends of the earth."

Everyone laughs and expresses outrage.

"Peenie's not exaggerating all that much, guys," Zander says. "I've seen him in action too many times to count, and all he has to do is smile and women pretty much throw themselves at him. The come-hither motion is a bonus."

"Yup," Keane says. "It's like pickin' chocolates outta box—pickles from a jar."

"Unfortunately, I can vouch for him, too," Kat tells the group. "Women blatantly throw themselves at Peenie, no matter what completely piggish or sexist thing he says or does. They have no self-respect or shame."

"Hey, I'm not a *pig*," Keane says defensively, and he sounds remarkably sincere. "I respect and admire women and that's the God's truth. The Motherboard would string me up by my balls if I didn't. It's not my fault I was born with *these*." Keane smiles and points at his dimples and everyone laughs.

"Ugh," Henn says. "You Morgan boys are living in the same alternate universe as the Faradays—a world I've never visited. Not that I need advice on 'bagging babes' these days, thank God..." He puts his arm around Hannah's shoulder. "But, if I did, I wouldn't ask any of you dudes. I mean, jeez, if I did *this* to a girl." He crooks his finger at Hannah. "She'd do *this*." He raises a stiff middle finger and everyone laughs.

"No, I wouldn't," Hannah says. "I'd do *this*." She grabs Henn's head like a bowling ball and lays a big ol' kiss on his lips, making everyone at the table laugh and swoon.

"So, hey, T-Rod," Reed says, smiling at me like a shark. "If cheesy pick-up lines like Keane's don't work on a smart-girl like you, what *does* work? I'm taking notes."

My chest tightens. Without meaning to do it, I glance at Ryan. If he was plotting Reed's murder before, he's now plotting a nuclear holocaust in which, somehow, Reed's body would simultaneously serve as both the bomb and the target.

I clear my throat. "I never said cheesy pick-up lines don't work on me. It just depends on the messenger. I remember this one time, a hot guy in a bar said a line to me that made me putty in his hands." I pause, suddenly feeling myself blush. "I'd mentioned to him that I speak Spanish because my dad grew up in Argentina, and we were talking about high school, and he goes, 'If I met you when we were both in high school, I would have been on you to tutor me like *blanco* on *arroz.*'"

I shoot Ryan a secret smile and his eyes blaze.

"*Blanco* on *arroz*?" Henn says, abruptly lifting his head like a Golden Retriever whose owner just threw a tennis ball. "A guy said that to you in a bar?"

I nod. "And I *loved* it." Again, I shoot a quick look and smile at Ryan.

Henn beams a huge smile at me. "You speak Spanish, T-Rod? I don't think I realized that about you."

"Mmm hmm. My dad's from Buenos Aires originally."

"That's so cool," Henn says. "You know, I just realized I know hardly anything about you. Like, for instance, how old are you?"

"Twenty-seven. And you?"

"Thirty. Where'd you grow up?"

"Los Angeles. You?"

Without warning, Ryan stands abruptly. "So, hey, you guys ready to head to dinner? Looks about time."

"Absolutely," Kat says, bolting up from her chair and standing alongside her brother. "Let's go. Right now. I'm starved. *Let's head to the restaurant right now.*"

Everyone gets up from the table and begins shuffling *en masse* out of the bar, but Henn's such a sweetheart, he lags to the back of the slow-moving group to walk with me and finish our conversation, instead of walking up ahead with his best friends.

"I grew up in Fresno, to answer your question," Henn says. "What's your sign, Tessa?"

"Virgo. Yours?"

"Sagittarius."

"I don't know anything about astrology," I say.

"Me, either. But Kat does."

Right on cue, Kat is suddenly walking alongside Henn and me. And then Ryan's right here with us, too, along with Colby, as the rest of the group walks ahead, chatting animatedly among themselves.

Now that Colby's walking with us, our small group slows down a bit to accommodate him, letting the rest of the group go on ahead.

"So you're a twenty-seven-year-old Virgo from L.A. who speaks Spanish because your dad's Argentinian, huh?" Henn says. "I feel stupid I didn't know any of that about you before. Hey, out of curiosity, have you ever—"

"Henny!" It's Kat, shocking the hell out of me by practically shrieking his name. She grabs Henn's hand. "Oh, my darling Henny! Can I talk to you for a second, love?"

"Sure."

As Kat pulls Henn away and begins whispering in his ear, my phone pings with a text from Charlotte.

"Shoot," I say, reading Charlotte's text. "Hey, Kat," I call to her. "Sorry to interrupt you. Charlotte just texted me: she can't make it to Maui."

"No?" Kat says. "Shoot. I was really hoping to meeting the legendary Charlotte McDougal."

Henn grins. "*Charlotte McDougal?*"

"Tessa's best friend," Kat says, grinning at Henn.

I nod. "I was hoping Charlotte would pop over here and be my plus-one for the rest of the week, but she's going on an anniversary cruise with her parents next week and she can't do both because of her work schedule." I look at Kat. "Charlotte told me to tell you and Josh congratulations and thank you for the invitation."

"Tell her we hope to meet her another time."

"What kind of work does your best friend Charlotte McDougal do?" Henn asks, sliding his arm around Kat's waist as we continue walking slowly alongside Colby and Ryan.

"She's a flight attendant."

Henn's smile broadens. "For what airline, out of curiosity?"

"Delta," I reply.

Henn's smile is absolutely beaming. "Charlotte McDougal of Delta."

We reach the entrance to the restaurant and the larger group walking ahead of us ambles inside.

"Hang on, guys," Kat says to our small group, making everyone halt. Kat calls ahead to Josh in the restaurant. "I'll be there in a minute, PB! Save me a seat!"

"You got it, PG!" Josh calls back.

Kat looks at me. "Oh, you can go ahead, too, Tessa. I just need to chat with Henny, Colby, and Ryan for a quick second about a birthday present for Keane. Henn's maybe gonna help us figure something out."

"Oh, cool," I say, feeling hugely relieved. For a split-second there, I had this weird feeling Kat wanted to talk to Ryan, Colby, and Henn about *me*. I look pointedly at Ryan. "I'll see you inside."

Ryan smiles warmly at me. "Save me a seat right next to you, okay?"

I feel giddy. I was hoping we'd sit together at dinner. "Ay, ay, Cap'n."

With that, I practically float into the restaurant, feeling like my decision to say yes to a weeklong, no-strings fling in paradise with a beautiful manwhore was a truly stupendous idea.

Chapter 52
Ryan

"How'd you figure it out?" I ask Henn, looking over my shoulder to make sure Tessa's firmly inside the restaurant.

"*Blanco* on *arroz*," Henn says. "You told me you said that to Samantha in the bar, remember?"

"Shit."

"Now please tell me how the fuck T-Rod is Samantha?" Henn says. "Because my gray matter is splattered all over those palm trees way over there."

I tell Henn the whole flippin' story and Henn seems absolutely astonished.

"So you *have* talked to Charlotte?" Henn says. "You said you called Charlotte and she hasn't called you back."

"What else could I say in front of Josh?" I say. "Tessa doesn't want Josh to know yet. Plus, he warned me off her on Day One."

"But you two already know?" Henn says to Kat and Colby.

"I figured it out," Kat says. She tells Henn the whole flippin' story of how she put two and two together.

"You're a genius, Kumquat," Colby says.

"Why, thank you, Cheese."

Henn snorts. "Dude, you'd better tell Jonas what's going on. At the opening party, when Jonas thought you were dropping 'Samantha' like a hot potato, he had a few not-very-nice things to say about you behind your back."

"Motherfucker," I say. "I don't want Jonas thinking I was being insincere about my soul connection with Samantha. But I can't tell him yet—I just need a couple more days with Tessa and then this whole thing will be out in the open."

263

"Why not just tell T-Rod everything *now*?" Henn asks.

I tell Henn the strange dichotomy that is Theresa "Tessa" Rodriguez: namely, that she wanted to "take it slow" when she thought there was real potential for a relationship with me, and yet she jumped right into the sack with me when she was positive we had no future. "If I tell Tessa everything before she sees a crystal-clear future with me, I'm worried she'll freak out and shut down on me."

"I used to do the exact same thing Tessa's doing here," Kat says. "I had a strict no-sex policy for first dates and I *never* broke my rule... *unless* I was sure my date wasn't boyfriend-material—in which case, if he was hot enough, I banged the hell out of him, made him fall in love with me, and then never saw him again."

Henn cringes.

"Ah, the ol' 'Dabble, Dash, and Destroy,'" I say, doing my best Keane impression, and we three Morgans crack up.

Henn looks appalled.

"Aw, come on, Henny," Kat says. "You've *never* pulled the ol' D, D & D?"

"*Never.*" Henn mutters something under his breath about us Morgans being another species of human, and then he shakes his head and says, "So, Ryan, my two cents? I wouldn't wait too long to tell T-Rod about the Search for Samantha. I think waiting could backfire on you."

"I'll for sure tell her before we leave Maui."

"Why don't you tell her at the wedding reception?" Kat suggests. "You know, dance the night away with her and then take her out for a walk in the moonlight on the beach and bare your soul to her?"

"But, dude," Henn says, "T-Rod might get pissed at you if you wait that long to tell her. She might feel like you lied through omission."

I feel anxious all of a sudden. I look at my brother and sister. "What do you guys think? Am I more fucked if I tell her too soon, thereby risking her freaking out and shutting down, or if I wait too long to tell her, thereby risking her getting pissed at me?"

"What does your gut tell you?" Colby asks.

"It tells me to wait 'til Tessa's fallen for me to hit her with the 'Search for Samantha.' But, hey, I'm the dude who dated Olivia, remember? My gut obviously can't be trusted."

Kat looks thoughtful. "I think your best bet is to wait a bit. Let's not forget you hacked into *nine* freaking airlines to find her. I mean, Holy

Stalker, Batman! If a girl doesn't trust a guy completely by the time she hears that cray-cray story, she's probably gonna feel more freaked out than romanced. Plus, the Virgo-Taurus love-compatibility info strongly suggests you gain her trust *before* dropping a bomb like that."

"All right, I'll bite," I say. "Tell us all about Taurus-Virgo's 'love-compatibility,' Kat."

Kat's face lights up. "Well, gosh, thanks for asking. Taurus-Virgo is one of the strongest love-compatibilities there is—both earth signs, so they innately understand each other. A female Virgo is tightly wound and extremely slow to trust, but that means her knight in shining armor is a male Taurus because he's the most patient guy on the Zodiac. The male Taurus doesn't simply know *how* to break down a female Virgo's walls, he *relishes* doing it. He absolutely adores the fact that, once he finally breaks down her walls and infiltrates her, he'll get to experience something hardly anyone ever does: her gooey-soft center. And since our female Virgo isn't someone who sleeps around or hops from relationship to relationship, once she finds the Taurus man who's willing to put in the time and effort to get to her gooey-soft center, she'll never, ever let him go and will make sure his efforts are well worth his while."

All three of us guys stare at Kat, speechless.

Kat shrugs. "It's just like *Pretty Woman,* only with the genders reversed."

"How do you figure?" Colby asks.

"Why do you think Julia was able to get to Richard's gooey-soft center in one week? Because Richard never for a minute thought he could develop real feelings for a hooker in thigh-high boots, so he didn't have his walls up—which is why she was able to infiltrate him. *She blindsided him.*"

There's a beat, during which Henn, Colby, and I look at each other.

"It actually makes a weird kind of sense," Henn says.

Colby nods. "It really does."

"I gotta hand it to you, Jizzy Pop," I say. "I'm constantly amazed at how many ways you're able to use *Pretty Woman* as a guide to life."

Kat shrugs. "Like I always say: 'Everything you need to know, you can learn from *Pretty Woman.*'"

Chapter 53
Ryan

"It sounds intriguing," Josh says—and my heart rate quickens with excitement.

While everyone else in the wedding brigade has traipsed off to the resort's nightclub for some post-dinner karaoke, Josh and I are sitting alone in one of the hotel bars, talking about my vision for Captain's—a conversation initially sparked at dinner, when it happened to come up that both Josh and I had been bartenders in college.

"So how far along are you in your planning?" Josh asks, sipping his Scotch.

"I've got a business plan drafted and I'm *this* close to having enough capital to get going," I reply. "I just gotta close a few big deals this year and I'll be off to the races."

"Well, if your only impediment to getting started right away is cash, I've got plenty of that. You interested in taking on a partner?"

My heart leaps. "Fuck yes," I say. "I'd *love* to partner with you, Josh."

"Fair warning, though: if I were part-owner of Captain's, I'd wanna get behind the bar and play bartender every once in a while. I recently did that at The Pine Box for a shift, and it reminded me how much I used to love it in college."

"You could play bartender at Captain's any time you like, Lambo," I say. "*Any time.*"

Josh laughs. "Okay, well, first things first. Shoot me your business plan and I'll take a look, and when I get back from my honeymoon in a week, we'll talk again."

"Fantastic. I'll send it to you the minute I get back to my room."

"Would you mind if I share it with Jonas? If I were to go in on Captain's, I'd wanna pull Jonas in on the deal, too. Don't worry, I'd cut Jonas in on my share—but I'd definitely want Jonas as a partner."

"Yeah, that sounds great. I heard Jonas speak at the Climb & Conquer party. He's one impressive dude."

"He's the smartest guy you'll ever meet, hands down. Seriously, I've got the brain of a toddler next to that guy. Make a point of getting to know my brother, if you can, Ry. There's no one like him. He's a prince among men and his business instincts are stellar."

"I will," I say, and, instantly, my stomach tightens. God, I hate the fact that Jonas thinks I'm a fickle little bitch. Fuck. I'm dying to shout from the rooftops about my feelings for Tessa, especially to clear my name with Josh and Jonas, but the rational side of my brain knows I've got to cool my jets for just a little while longer. I'm so close now with Tessa, I can feel it—why fuck it up by jumping the gun?

"Hey, you know who else I should show your business plan?" Josh says. "Reed. He's got a bunch of different business holdings besides his music label, including some high-end nightclubs he co-owns with an investment group. I bet he'd have some helpful advice for us."

My stomach clenches at the thought of Reed Rivers laying a pinky on my business plan. "Thanks for the thought," I say evenly, "but I prefer to keep this completely in the family. Plus, now that Reed's signing Daxy's band, I think I should keep the fate of my dreams completely separate from my brother's."

"Yeah, of course. I just meant I wanna pick Reed's brain—nothing more than that."

Okay, I'm being a jealous little bitch right now and I need to stop it. Reed's a kazillionaire-mogul for a reason—and Josh obviously trusts him with his life. "Sure," I manage to say. "I'd be grateful for Reed's thoughts about my business plan, of course. Thanks."

"Cool. The big thing I wanna ask Reed is how to possibly scale Captain's to other cities. If it turns out your concept works the way I think it will, why stop with Seattle? Maybe down the road, we could open Captain's in L.A. and San Francisco and who-knows-where?"

My entire body feels electrified. "That'd be amazing," I say, forcing myself to stay in my seat, even though I suddenly want to leap across the table and bear-hug Josh and tell him he's the answer to my fucking prayers.

Josh smiles. "The sky's the limit, Captain. But first things first: send me that business plan and we'll talk when I get home from my honeymoon."

"Will do. Thanks so much, Josh."

My phone pings with an incoming text and I look down at my screen. "Go to the bar near the main pool," the text from Tessa says. "Say hello to the brunette in the blue dress sitting at the bar. Introduce yourself as Ulysses."

I look up at Josh, my heart in my mouth. "So, hey, man, thanks again. I know you wanna head over to the nightclub and get your karaoke on with Kat, so I'll let you go."

Josh stands. "You're not coming? Kat told me you two do a mean 'Total Eclipse of the Heart' together."

"No, I think I'm gonna call it a night. I didn't get much sleep last night and I killed myself today doing every conceivable water sport known to man."

"Okay, sleep tight, Captain. Rest up for tomorrow. T-Rod tells me we're zip-lining and then going on some spectacular hike to a secluded beach for a picnic?"

"Yeah, she was telling me about that. Sounds incredible. I'll see you at breakfast. I'm just gonna sit here and finish my martini and then head off to bed."

I watch Josh leave and, the minute I'm sure the coast is clear, I pop out of my chair like a jack-in-a-box that just got cranked, and sprint at full speed out the door, straight toward the woman of my dreams.

Chapter 54
Ryan

There she is at the bar—the sexiest woman alive—looking particularly gorgeous in an electric-blue mini-dress that showcases her long, tanned legs.

I stride to the bar and stand next to her, my heart thudding in my ears and my dick tingling. "All right if I sit here?"

"Please do."

I sit down next to her and put out my hand. "Ulysses."

Tessa takes my hand. "Samantha."

I grin. *Excellent.* "Nice to meet you, Samantha. What brings you to Maui?"

"Work," she says. "I'm a flight attendant."

My smile broadens. "How long you here?"

"Just one night."

I motion to her near-empty glass. "Would you like a refill?"

"Thank you."

I order our drinks from a tattooed bartender who can't hide the fact that he's currently wishing me dead. Ha! *Fuck you, asshole. She's mine.*

"So what do you do for a living, Ulysses?" Tessa asks, coiling a lock of her silky dark hair around her finger.

"I own a chain of luxury hotels all over the world. I'm insanely wealthy, actually. I wipe my ass with hundred-dollar bills."

"Well, that doesn't sound pleasant. Aren't hundred-dollar bills kinda rough?"

"Rough feels good when you've got an ass as hard as mine."

"Oh," she says, raising her eyebrow. She leans forward, giving me a delicious view of her unbelievable cleavage. "Do you have a hard ass or are you a hard-ass, Ulysses?"

"Both."

"Tell me more."

"Well, my heart is as hard as my rock-hard ass. I care about nothing and no one but money and fucking."

"Tsk, tsk. Too fucked up to fall in love?"

"I don't know what love is. Fucking is my 'love.'"

"My, my, you *are* a hard-ass. And what about your hard ass?"

"I like having it gripped when I'm fucking. It gets me off."

She bites her lip. "How about a little bite on your hard ass? Does that get you off, too?"

I take a long sip of my drink. "Keep talking like that and I'm gonna be telling you about my hard dick."

Her eyes blaze. "Is your dick hard right now, Ulysses?"

What the fuck has gotten into her? She's on fire. "It's well on its way."

Her nostrils flare. "Well, let me know when it gets there."

"What will you do when it does?"

"It depends."

"On what?" I ask.

"On you—and your talents. There's nothing I hate more than a guy who only knows how to pound a woman without first applying a little finesse. I love a good pounding, don't get me wrong, but a guy's got to have a scalpel in his tool chest in addition to his hammer."

"Oh, I've got both in my tool chest, I assure you—and I know exactly how and when to use them both."

She leans forward and subtly widens her thighs. "*Prove it.*"

My cock jolts. "Right here and now?"

She nods, smiling wickedly.

Jesus Christ. Who is this woman? "It would be my pleasure, Samantha. Oh, and by the way?" I wink. "It's there."

She flashes me a wicked smile. "Glad to hear it. Let's see if you know how to use a scalpel. If so, then we'll move on to your hammer."

"Challenge accepted." I scoot my stool right up against hers, grab a menu off the bar, and place it over her lap—and then I slowly slide my hand up her smooth thighs, under the hem of her mini-dress, straight toward her undies..."One of my favorite things in the world is..." I stop talking. I was expecting to feel the cotton crotch of her underwear, but all I'm feeling is the sensation of bare flesh underneath my fingertips.

Oh, God, she's a fucking goddess.

She widens her legs and tilts her naked pelvis into my fingers, inviting me to finger-fuck her. "You were saying, Ulysses?" she breathes. She widens her legs again. "I'm wide open—all ears."

My cock is rock hard. I'm out of my mind—so turned on, I can barely breathe.

I clear my throat and slide my fingers inside her while pressing the pad of my thumb against her clit. "I was saying," I whisper, my fingers stroking her, "that one of my favorite things in the world is getting a woman off—in lots of different ways."

Her breathing hitches subtly. "Is that what turns you on the most?" she whispers.

Before I can answer, the bartender places our drinks in front of us on the bar, his jaw clenched.

"Anything else I can get you two?"

I stroke her swollen clit with more fervor. "Nope. I think we're good." I look at Tessa. "Anything else you need at the moment, sweetheart?"

Tessa shakes her head. "Nope. I'm good." A subtle moan escapes her throat. "Really, really good."

"Thanks," I say to the bartender, my fingers lodged firmly up Tessa's pussy, my thumb sliding up and down her swollen clit, and he stalks away, his eyes unmistakably raging with jealousy.

Oh, God, she's so fucking wet. Thank God there's overhead music pumping throughout the bar, or the whole world would hear the subtle sloshing sounds her pussy's beginning to make as I work her.

"You asked me what gets me off most?" I whisper.

She moans softly. "Oh, God... *Oh.*"

"Touching your wet, swollen pussy when another guy is looking at you, wanting to fuck you—that's high on the list."

I stroke her with increased fervor. "Touching your wet tip—feeling how swollen it is—how hard it is." I lick my lips. "Thinking about getting you alone so I can lick it and suck it 'til you're speaking in tongues."

"*Oh.*" She gasps.

"Thinking about spanking your round ass 'til it's bright pink—and how you're gonna come for me when I do."

"Oh, God." Her face contorts sharply like she's in severe pain, and a half-second later, pure ecstasy washes over her features and the flesh enveloping my hand begins squeezing and clenching rhythmically.

When she's done climaxing, I pull my fingers out of her, tug her mini-dress neatly down, place the menu back on the bar, and begin slowly licking every bit of her sweetness off my fingers, my eyes fixed on hers. "Was that enough 'finesse' for you, Samantha?" I ask politely.

She takes a long gulp of her drink, puts down her glass, and smiles wickedly. "You still hard, Ulysses?" she whispers.

"Rock hard."

"Then I'd very much like for you to show me some of the other tools in your tool chest now. Anything you want to do to me—anything at all—I'm all yours."

I grab her hand and kiss each of her fingertips, one by one, and then signal to the bartender at the other end of the long bar. "Check, please."

Chapter 55
Tessa

Ulysses bends my naked body over the chair in my room as he pounds me again and again, pausing only to spank my ass so hard, I stop breathing for a brief moment.

"You're gonna come again for me, Samantha," he growls into my ear.

I cry out, suddenly feeling like I can't hold my own weight anymore.

Without warning, he grips the back of my hair and pulls my head back as his shaft impales me. "You like getting fucked, Samantha?"

I let out a garbled sound, my body going completely haywire on me.

He spanks my ass again, this time even harder than the last time, and I come without warning. *Again.* Holy hell, this man is good.

He groans loudly with pleasure and reaches around my torso and fingers my clit, a move that sends spasms of pleasure ripping through me.

"You wanna suck my dick, Samantha?"

"*Yes.*"

"Say it."

"I wanna suck your dick, Ulysses."

"Call me Captain."

"I wanna suck your dick, Captain."

"Beg me."

"*Please* let me suck your dick, Captain, My Captain."

"You haven't earned the right yet, baby." He kneels behind me and bites my ass cheek so hard, my knees buckle—and the next thing I know, the dildo I retrieved from my luggage for him earlier at his

273

command is sliding deep inside me. He turns the vibrator on and I moan. I've never let a man see my vibrator before, let alone use it on me, but, I must admit, I'm enjoying how deliciously naughty this feels.

Still working the dildo inside me from behind, Ryan bends down, parts my cheeks, and tongues my asshole, making it clench and my entire body shudder with pleasure. A moment later, I hear the surefire sound of lube being squeezed out of a bottle, and then Ryan's slick fingers sliding up and down my ass crack.

Oh, God, clearly, he's getting me ready for his back-door entry. I tense. "I've never done this," I whisper urgently.

"I'll make sure you come hard."

I can't seem to relax.

"Do you trust me?" he whispers, his voice surprisingly earnest. "I promise it won't hurt."

"Okay."

"You trust me?"

I nod.

"Say it."

"I trust you."

Ryan flips a switch on my dildo, making the silicone "rabbit" at its base begin swirling rapidly across my clit and, just as my entire body begins jolting in response to this new stimulation, I feel Ryan's finger sliding inside my ass. Or, wait. That's not Ryan's finger.

I yelp.

"Breathe," Ryan says into my ear. "Take a deep breath."

I do as I'm told and he slides himself farther inside me.

One more deep breath and he's all the way in and gently moving inside me. Holy shit, I've never been this filled up before. Not like this. A vibrating dildo up my wahoo and a dick up my ass? Jesus God, I'm dying of pleasure.

I make a sound like a dying buffalo and clutch the table in front of me and, just when I think I can't take any more stimulation, Ryan flips the vibrator to "high."

"Good?" he gasps, his voice strained.

I open my mouth to reply, but a lightning bolt of pure ecstasy shoots through me, thwarting my words, and then an orgasm like nothing I've felt before shatters me—an orgasm so devastating to my system, it causes fluid to gush out of me and spray around the dildo. My thighs are covered in my own wetness. I'm a dam breaking. *And it feels so good.*

Immediately, Ryan pulls the dildo out of me, kneels behind me, and begins suckling every drop of fluid off my folds, clit, and thighs—licking and slurping and eating me with so much fervor, I truly feel on the verge of passing out.

My knees wobble and I clutch the table like a lifeline, moaning and baying at the outrageous pleasure he's gifting me. After a few moments of being eaten like I'm made of the finest chocolate, I come again, this time much more humanely than last time, though pleasurable nonetheless.

At the sound of my obvious climax, Ryan stands and scoops my sweaty, tortured body into his strong arms and carries me toward the bathroom. "I'm gonna let you suck my dick in the shower, Samantha. And after that I'm gonna tie you up and fuck your tits."

"Ay, ay, Captain," I breathe. I bite his pierced nipple. "Whatever you say, Captain. Anything. Everything. *I'm all yours.*"

Chapter 56
Tessa

I lie in bed next to Ryan, looking at his sleeping face in the moonlit room, the calming sounds of the ocean wafting through the window of my room.

When I texted Ryan to meet me in the bar and introduce himself as "Ulysses" this evening, I'd craved one thing: a wild night like nothing I'd experienced before. And, by God, that's exactly what Ryan delivered to me on a silver platter, without me needing to explicitly explain my desires to him. *He just knew.*

Oh my God, Ryan was on fire. The dirty-talk. The hair-pulling and spanking. The way he tied me up and commanded me like he owned me. All of it conspired to send me to erotic places I've never visited before.

I must admit, I never thought I'd be the kind of girl who'd get off on all that kind of stuff. Outside of the heat of the moment, I'd have thought being treated that way would upset me or at least make me roll my eyes, but, holy hell, in the moment, when Ryan and I were both feeling so uninhibited and free to explore our deepest fantasies, when we were both completely untethered from caring what society or anyone else might think, and instead cared only about ourselves and our deepest desires, I found Ryan's complete domination of my body and mind to be nothing short of electrifying.

And the cherry on top of our electrifying sundae? When Ryan untied me and held me close and whispered softly, "You're perfect, Tessa," which, of course, elicited my surprising but honest reply: "So are you."

And now, as Ryan sleeps, his beautiful face drenched in moonlight, I'm suddenly wide awake after only a few hours of sleep, body aching in the most delicious way... and my mind freaking the fuck out.

Holy shit. *No.* I'm suddenly realizing something rather disturbing: I think there's a very good chance I'll never again be able to have sex with a man without feeling deeply disappointed he's not Ryan Ulysses Morgan. What other man on this planet could *possibly* do me even half as well as Captain Morgan does? What other man would understand exactly what my body wants, even when I don't understand it myself?

For some reason, as I lie in this darkened room and stare at Ryan's beautiful face in the moonlight, I suddenly know in my bones Ryan Ulysses Morgan is the only man in the world capable of getting me off to my body's fullest potential. And that realization—that I might have bought myself an entire lifetime of sexual dissatisfaction with my future partners, all in the name of experiencing one short week in heaven—is a very troubling thought, indeed.

Chapter 57
Tessa

"So I guess it goes without saying you're gonna continue seeing Ryan when you get back to Seattle?" Charlotte asks.

I'm lying in bed naked and alone, my phone pressed against my ear, the ocean beyond my French doors glimmering in the late morning light, my body still humming from Samantha and Ulysses' delicious, filthy, unforgettable night. Of course, the minute Ryan left to shower and dress in his room this morning, I called Charlotte and gave her an update on the week, sexual and otherwise.

"No," I reply. "Seattle's not gonna happen. 'What happens in Maui stays in Maui.' That was our deal. It's the only reason I've been able to let loose with Ryan so completely—because I know there's no future for us."

"But... huh? Honey, haven't you been listening to yourself? It sounds like you're both falling in love."

"Because we're in paradise. We don't have a care or responsibility or stress in the world in this place. Of course, it *feels* like we're both perfect people and a perfect match, but it's not real."

"Oh my God. You're insane. There's a reason I've been calling you Crazy Girl since eighth grade."

"Charlotte, I'm perfectly sane. Ryan's gonna be Josh's brother in two days and he's a manwhore of epic proportions. He's a nonstarter."

"Why do you think he's a manwhore? You said yourself the pterodactyl's story about him was all bullshit."

"Yeah, he's not a lying *cheater* like I originally thought. But I've called him a manwhore multiple times and he's never corrected me. Babe, no man can screw like he does without *lots* of practice." I sigh.

278

"God only knows how many women he's made feel exactly the way he's making me feel this week—like I'm the most special girl in the world. Clearly, that's just what he does—and then he moves on."

"Oh my freaking God." Charlotte sighs. "Do me a favor, would you? Ask Ryan exactly how many women he's made feel 'like the most special girl in the world' and then 'moved on from' over the past three months. Would you do that for me?"

"Why on earth would I do that? I don't want to hear about Ryan's many conquests any more than he wants to hear about the number of times I've changed the batteries on my vibrator."

"Honey. You two need to talk. You're obviously falling in love with him."

"*No.* Look, Char, I totally get why you're worried, but I promise I won't let myself get too wrapped up in the fairytale, okay? I know Ryan *seems* perfect and it *feels* like we're falling in love—but I'm well aware it's all a role-play in paradise. Frankly, it's *good* he's an epic manwhore—knowing that is what's enabled me to let loose with him and have so much fun. But I've got my eyes wide open and my heart firmly guarded and I know what he is. Now stop worrying about me and I'll talk to you when you get back from your cruise. I've totally got this."

Charlotte exhales with exasperation. "If you say so, Crazy Girl. But if it turns out you're not quite as right about all this as you think and you need me for any reason while I'm on the cruise, email me. There's apparently no cell-phone coverage at all on the cruise, but I'll be able to log onto Wi-Fi every night."

"Thanks, but I won't need you. I'm having fun with a beautiful manwhore, pretending we're in a fairytale. And when the week's over, I promise I won't let myself get hurt. There's only two more days left of this fantasy. Surely, I can keep myself from falling in love with any man for that long. Don't worry—I've got this."

Chapter 58
Ryan

"How many cards?" Josh asks, looking at me.

"Two," I say, giving him my lame-duck cards in exchange for new ones. "And make 'em good ones, Lambo, for the love of God."

For the past hour, I've been sitting at a table in Josh's bungalow next to Zander, the two of us drinking Scotch and playing poker with Josh, Jonas, Reed, Henn, and a couple of Josh's old fraternity brothers.

Yeah, that's right: Zander and I are playing poker with Josh's brother and closest friends. It's a little random, I know, but the way it happened makes perfect sense: Keane, Z, Colby, and I were heading down to the beach for some kayaking when one of Kat's highly attractive friends from college sashayed past us in her barely-there-string-bikini and murmured something to Keane that made him turn on his heel and follow her, calling over his shoulder, "Go ahead without me, guys!".

So, Zander, Colby, and I wound up kayaking without Keane, and, afterwards, as we three were heading back in from the beach, we ran into Josh and his closest buddies on their way to play poker in Josh's bungalow, which is when they invited us to join in. Z and I accepted the invitation while Colby begged off, and, now, here Z and I are, the two of us smokin' cigars and drinkin' Scotch and hangin' like homies with Josh and his closest crew.

"How many cards, Z?" Josh asks, chewing on the end of his cigar.

"Three," Zander replies, tossing his cast-offs to Josh.

"So how you feeling on your last night as a free man, Josh?" Jonas asks his brother.

"Like a kid on Christmas Eve," Josh replies. "Oh, hey, by the way, Kat doesn't want me to see her on our wedding day 'til she walks down the aisle in her dress—so can she sleep with Sarah tonight and you sleep here?"

"Yeah, Sarah already told me," Jonas says. "It's fine. I mean, not sleeping with my wife tonight is a huge sacrifice, but I'll consider it one of my wedding gifts to you."

"It's your wedding gift to Kat and Kat alone. I don't want these stupid sleeping arrangements any more than you do, bro."

"Happy wife, happy life," Jonas says. "It's the key to the kingdom."

"No doubt."

"Yo, Henn, it's your bet," Reed says.

"Yeah, yeah, I know—I'm thinking," Henn says. "Why'd you have to deal me such shitty cards, Joshua?" He lays down his cards, facedown. "I'm out, thanks to your piss-poor card-dealing."

Josh chuckles.

Reed shoves a stack of chips into the pot. "Looks like Mr. Faraday dealt me all your good cards, Henny-Baby."

"Bah, you're bluffing," Josh says to Reed. "I can read you like a book, Rivers—and it's clear to me you've got nuttin'." He shoves a bunch of chips into the kitty to match Reed's. "You might have a Midas touch when it comes to selling music to the masses, but you're about to become my little bitch when it comes to cards."

"I guess we'll find out soon enough who's the little bitch, won't we?" Reed says.

"Hey, Reed," I pipe in. "Speaking of selling music to the masses, I've been meaning to thank you for signing 22 Goats. It's a dream come true for the guys."

"No need to thank me," Reed replies. "I didn't do it as a favor. I did it because I like making truckloads of money off of great music and your brother checks off all the boxes."

"Well, regardless, I still feel the need to express my personal gratitude to you. I would have hated to be stuck on an island for a week with Dax if you'd turned him down."

"Actually, Dax never had anything to worry about," Reed says. "I was always gonna sign him. The only question in my mind was whether to sign the other two dudes along with him."

My stomach clenches.

Josh pipes in: "Ah, that's why you wanted to see them play live before pulling the trigger?"

"Yeah. I wasn't sure if the other guys were gonna cut it."

My head is spinning. I can't imagine a more nightmarish scenario for my baby brother than Reed offering him a deal that didn't include his two best friends. I glance at Zander and it's clear to me he's thinking the exact same thing.

"You wouldn't really have cut out the friends, would you?" Henn says to Reed. "That seems a bit heartless, even for you."

"Sure, I would have," Reed says breezily. "I'm running a business in a cut-throat industry, not assigning bunk beds at summer camp. Honestly, I was leaning sharply toward a solo offer when I first got here, but then I fucked up by mentioning my dastardly plan to T-Rod and she slapped the motherfucking shit out of me until I cried mercy." He laughs.

Every hair on my body stands up, all at once. Reed talked to Tessa about Dax... *and she lobbied Reed on my brother's behalf?*

"Ah, T-Rod stepped on your neck, did she?" Josh says, chuckling. "God, I love it when she does that. She's so quiet and docile most of the time and then *bam*. Out of nowhere, if she feels strongly about something, she roars to life and lays down the motherfucking law."

"Yeah, she was pretty passionate about the topic, that's for sure," Reed says. "And she was right, actually. I must say, the girl's got good instincts."

My heart is exploding in my chest. Holy shit. Tessa fought for my brother and averted catastrophe for him? I clear my throat and force myself to sound casual. "What'd T-Rod say to you to change your mind, out of curiosity?"

"She said if I didn't sign the full band I was a 'fucking idiot' and 'devoid of a soul,'" Reed replies. He chuckles. "And then she went on to argue her point by smartly supplying every logical reason why signing Dax as a solo artist would turn out to be a stupid business decision." He shrugs. "At the end of the day, her points were valid so I decided to listen. Plus, I didn't want her to break my legs with a baseball bat, as she threatened to do. Yeesh."

Josh and Reed chuckle again.

But I'm not chuckling. I'm too stunned. Holy fuck, I can't believe my ears. When nobody was watching, when there was nary a Morgan in sight to witness her actions and give her props for her heroics, Tessa Rodriguez went to bat for my baby brother behind the scenes?

"T-Rod's damned smart," Reed continues. "And brutally honest, too. I never feel like she's bullshitting me—a rarity in my line of work."

"In mine, too," Josh says. "Hence, the reason I value her so much."

"Yeah, about that," Reed says. "Seriously, man, if you ever feel like you wanna cut T-Rod loose for any reason, send her my way. I'd hire her in a heartbeat. Not kidding."

"Nope, sorry, Old Man River," Josh says. "You can't have T-Rod, ever." He places his bet. "And, please, take that comment as broadly as I meant it."

Henn and I exchange a look.

Reed laughs. "Why you always gotta be such a hard-ass about your precious little assistant, Faraday? You're assuming I'd be a total dick to her. Maybe I wouldn't be. Maybe T-Rod would be the girl who finally slays my demons, once and for all. Maybe she'd *save* me, man." He chuckles again.

"Not bloody likely," Henn says, piping in. "And that's not a knock on T-Rod's demon-slaying capabilities, by the way, but a commentary on the virility of your particular strain of demon."

"Bah. I'm a total softie, deep down," Reed says, shoving some chips into the pot. "Raise you a hundred."

"You're not a softie, bro," Josh says. "A great guy? Yes. The best friend, ever? For sure. But a 'softie'? Hell no. Your bet, Zander."

Zander looks stressed. If I had to guess what's going on in his head, I'd say he's loving his cards but the stakes are getting too high for his measly personal-trainer-at-the-local-gym budget.

"I'll spot you whatever you need to stay in, Z," I say. "Bet as big as you want. If you wind up losing my money, pay me back with some personal training sessions. If you win, pay me back from the winning pot."

"Thanks, Captain. Much obliged."

"No, no, Captain," Josh says. "Zander's bets are on me tonight."

"No, I got him," I say. "He's my brother."

Josh waves me off. "Then he's mine, too. Keep your money, Ry. I've got him. I've had some massive poker losses to Reed over the years that I want to vicariously avenge." Josh slides a mammoth stack of chips over to Zander. "Get him, Z. Make him cry."

"Jesus, I'm getting it from all sides," Reed mumbles, but his tone is jovial.

Zander thanks Josh profusely and immediately shoves all his newly acquired chips into the pot to match and then raise Reed's bet.

"I like your style, Z," Reed says. "But, seriously, Faraday, why are you always so damned protective of T-Rod? She's a big girl. Let her make her own decisions. If I take a shot and it doesn't work out, I promise I won't leave her any worse for wear. In fact, even if her heart gets smashed into a thousand pieces, I promise she'll nonetheless thank me for the ride."

I clench my jaw tightly and focus all my energy on *not* leaping up and throwing a punch. I glance at Henn and he subtly shakes his head, warning me not to react.

Josh addresses Reed: "I'm not gonna risk anyone 'taking a shot' with her and smashing her heart, motherfucker. She's like a sister. Plus, on a selfish note, it's in my personal interest to keep that woman from getting her heart broken. Last time she did, it took months for her to fully bounce back, and I happen to like T-Rod running my world at full capacity."

"Speaking of T-Rod running your world, have you given her a raise lately?" Jonas asks. "You do realize you've had that poor girl doing the work of three people lately, right?"

"Dude, never worry about T-Rod getting herself paid—the girl's a fucking shark. The best negotiator I've ever met, besides you and Reed, and I'm not even joking about that. She squeezes me for more than any of my friends pay their personal assistants, by far."

"Oh, come on, Josh, T-Rod's not just a personal assistant anymore and you know it," Jonas says. "She outgrew that job description years ago."

"True."

"You know what we should do?" Jonas says. "We should find Theresa an official role at Climb & Conquer. Maybe put her on the sales team? Or, fuck it, maybe she should manage a regional team? I bet she'd kick ass doing that, she's so good at juggling a million things."

"No doubt T-Rod would kick ass at anything she tried," Josh says. "But I don't know. She's too valuable to me to give her up."

"Don't be a selfish bastard. You're not utilizing her to her fullest potential and you know it. T-Rod's no longer the naïve girl you hired six years ago—she's ready to spread her wings. Surely, you can see that?"

Josh looks thoughtful. "I'll think about it."

My heart is racing. Fuck. I don't know what to say here to help Tessa's cause—but I know I've got to say something. "I, uh, was talking to T-Rod the other day... by the pool," I begin. "And she was telling me how much she admires the mission of Climb & Conquer. She seemed excited about your plans to grow the company."

"See?" Jonas says. "T-Rod's obviously thinking about this kind of thing, too. Look, maybe the next thing for her isn't an official role at C & C, but all I'm saying is when you get back from your honeymoon, you should take a good, long look and think about ways to utilize her beyond making sure your fucking Lamborghini's washed."

"Yeah, maybe," Josh says. "I'll give it some serious thought, I promise. Thanks for putting a bug in my ear, bro."

"Hey, you've got the charm and I've got the brains, remember? I wouldn't wanna fall down on my job."

Josh looks at Reed. "And in the meantime, keep your paws off her, you fucking menace."

Reed laughs. "Fine. But only because it's you."

I breathe a huge sigh of relief.

Josh looks down at the cards in his hand. "From here on out, nobody goes near Theresa Rodriguez unless they're planning to make her happy for the rest of her fucking life, and that's final." He looks up from his cards, straight at me. "Got that?"

"Got it," Reed replies.

I subtly nod and Josh looks back down at his cards.

Oh my God, the hair on the back of my neck is standing up. I just realized something—something big. *I want to make Tessa happy for the rest of her fucking life.*

I look at Henn, my jaw hanging open, and he's already staring right at me, his eyebrows raised, a question on his face. Without hesitation, I nod decisively at him, answering his implicit query and Henn flashes me a broad smile in return.

Holy shit. *I want to make Tessa Rodriguez happy for the rest of her life.*

"Hey, can I ask you something?" Reed says to Josh. "I've always wondered: how come you never made a play for T-Rod yourself? I can't imagine withstanding the temptation, day in and out, for six fucking years."

Josh shrugs. "Because Jonas would have killed me."

Jonas laughs. "Fuck yeah, I would have. Josh was just coming off being a fucking train wreck back then. I told him if he hit on a single employee, whether his own personal employee or at Faraday & Sons, I'd fucking kill him."

"But, honestly, I wouldn't have touched T-Rod, anyway," Josh says. "I can't say the same about some of the women at Faraday & Sons—those women definitely owe their unblemished virtue to the iron hand of Jonas P. Faraday—but when it came to Theresa, I was never even remotely tempted. I know it's hard to believe looking at her now, but when T-Rod first started with me straight outta college, she was this sweet, naïve, sheltered little thing. Obviously intimidated as hell. She barely said a word to me, other than 'Yes, sir' and 'No, sir' and 'Right away, sir.'" He laughs. "Right off the bat, I felt totally protective toward her, like a big brother, you know? Of course, I could objectively see T-Rod was a strikingly beautiful woman, but there just weren't any sparks of that type for me. She walked through the door and, instantly, I felt like she was some kind of baby bird needing my protection."

"Well, your baby bird has grown into a badass swan," Reed says. "If you haven't noticed."

"Yeah, I've noticed. And, like I said, keep your fucking paws off my motherfucking swan, you fucking menace."

"Yeah, yeah," Reed says. "I heard ya loud and clear, sweetheart."

"Okay, what you got, Rivers?" Josh says. "Time for the rubber to finally hit the road, fucker."

Reed lays down his cards. "Three aces, son. Read 'em and weep."

Josh lays down his cards. "I got a pair of fours. I was totally bluffing."

Everyone laughs.

"What you got, Zander?" Josh asks. "Please tell me it's something that's gonna beat this fucker and make him cry."

Zander lays down his cards with a flourish and flashes a huge smile. "Full house, gentlemen. Read 'em and weep."

Everyone at the table cheers and laughs and hurls taunts at Reed as Zander rakes in his chips. I try to applaud and cheer, too—I'm thrilled for Zander, of course—but I can't seem to focus on the game at the moment. I'm too lost in my swirling thoughts. *I want to make Tessa Rodriguez happy for the rest of her life.* I know it to be true as surely as I know my own name: I love Tessa and I always will and I want to make her happy for the rest of her fucking life. *And that's exactly what I'm gonna tell her tomorrow night.*

Chapter 59
Tessa

I knock on the door of Josh and Kat's bungalow, my skin buzzing. I've only got a few minutes before I've got to meet up with the wedding coordinator to help her with a thousand things today, but I wanted to quickly stop by Josh and Kat's bungalow to give them my paltry attempt at a wedding gift to kick off their Big Day. But, to my surprise, it's Jonas who opens the bungalow door, not Josh or Kat.

"Oh, hi, Jonas," I say. "Good morning."

"Good morning, Theresa," he says.

I step into the room to find Josh sitting at a table filled with breakfast plates. "Good morning, Mr. Faraday," I say. "Where's your almost-wife?"

"Kat swapped places with Jonas last night. She didn't want us seeing each other today until the moment she's walking down the aisle."

"Aw, she's so cute."

Josh offers me food, but I decline while plopping myself down on a chair next to him. "How are you feeling?"

"I've never been so excited in my life."

I swoon just a little bit. I can't believe how far this formerly commitment-phobic boss of mine has journeyed in the time I've known him. Although, wait, come to think of it, I *can* believe it. Now that I've spent so much time with Kat and her family this week, I can plainly see nobody, not even a world-renowned playboy like Joshua William Faraday, not even the most thick-skulled, thick-skinned, stupidest person in the world, could possibly resist the chance to become a permanent member of the Morgan clan.

"So what's up, T-Rod?" Josh asks, munching on a piece of bacon.

"I just wanted to come by and tell you and Kat how thrilled I am for you both and give you my wedding gift."

"We told everyone no gifts, remember?" Josh says. "'Your presence is our present.'"

"Fuck that. I'm not 'everyone.'"

Josh and Jonas both laugh.

"T-Rod lays down the law," Josh says, smiling.

"I'm just saying—you've been so generous with me over the years, I wasn't gonna let this occasion pass without some attempt at showing my gratitude, however pathetic it may be. Can I just say you're *impossible* to buy a gift for, Mr. Faraday? You're truly the man who has everything."

"Not quite yet, but I will in approximately"—he looks at his watch—"five hours and thirteen minutes." He grins.

"Okay, so don't expect too much, but I just wanted you and Kat to know how happy I am for you. So, drum roll, please..."

Jonas gives me a drum roll on the table.

"I've arranged for you and Kat to have twelve ballroom-dancing lessons in the privacy of your home."

Josh laughs. "Wow, T. That's awesome. Thank you."

"But, wait, there's more. During each lesson, a chef will be hard at work in your kitchen, making you a five-star meal to be enjoyed when you're finished dancing."

"Amazing. Kat's gonna be thrilled."

"Plus, I've already chatted with Kat's parents and Ryan and Keane and Colby and Sarah, and if you wind up taking some or all of the lessons *after* Gracie Louise arrives, they all said they'd be thrilled to watch the baby while you and Kat dance and dine the night away."

"Put me on the list of babysitters, too," Jonas says. "I wanna cement my spot as Little G's favorite uncle early on."

"Oh, man, don't let the Morgan boys overhear you saying that, Jonas," I say. "At the pool the other day, all four of them almost got into fisticuffs about which one of *them* was gonna be Gracie's favorite uncle."

"Shit. I forgot about those bastards," Jonas says. "It's gonna be awfully tough to compete in the Uncle Olympics with those motherfuckers. They've definitely got me beat in the goofy department." He laughs.

My body floods with sudden warmth. "Those boys have *everyone* beat in the goofy department, not just you, Jonas," I say, my cheeks rising with color. "I just *love* that about them."

Josh and Jonas exchange a look.

"Well, thanks, for your incredible gift," Josh says. "And, hey, as long as you're here, and Jonas happens to be here, too, there's something I want to talk to you about. I was gonna wait 'til I got home from my honeymoon to talk about this, but now that we're all here..." He sighs. "I'll just get right to the point, T-Rod: you've grown a lot in the time I've known you. And, lately, it's clear to me I'm vastly underutilizing your talents, solely out of selfishness."

I'm speechless.

Josh looks at his brother, gets an encouraging nod, and looks back at me. "T, I'm gonna ask you a question and I want you to answer me with complete honesty, okay?"

I nod.

"Do you still feel like being my 'executive personal assistant' is enough for you, or do you have aspirations beyond that role?"

I pause. I didn't expect to be having this conversation today, if ever. I take a deep breath. "I love being your personal assistant with all my heart—I really do. But, yes, if I'm being completely honest, I do have aspirations beyond that role. I mean, what I mean is..." I swallow hard. "I just feel like I could maybe delegate and oversee some of my more mundane tasks to free me up for tasks that require a bit more... high-level thinking?"

"Precisely my thoughts," Josh says. "I couldn't agree more."

I exhale with relief. "Really?"

"One hundred percent."

"For what it's worth," Jonas says. "I agree, too. Not that I have any say in the matter—I'm just a bystander. But I've watched you grow and blossom exponentially from the sidelines, and I think it'd be a crying shame not to acknowledge and foster that growth. Excellence isn't magic—it's habit, the by-product of doing something over and over and striving to be the best at it. Visualize the divine original form of yourself and then strive to become it. The sky's the limit for you, Theresa."

I feel my cheeks bloom. "Thank you, Jonas."

"And thank you, Plato," Josh says dryly. "So, okay, it's settled, then. We need to think about how best to utilize you. It's not something I want to figure out today—no offense, but I've got bigger fish to fry today."

We all chuckle.

"But we'll definitely put our heads together on this when I get home, okay?"

"Okay. Great. I'm excited."

"I do have one idea I'd like to float past you now, though," Josh says. "A little something for you to think about while I'm gone this week."

"Okay."

"The other night, Ryan sent me his business plan for this bar he's planning to open. Captain's."

My stomach tightens with excitement.

"Jonas and I were looking at the plan together last night and we were both impressed at how good it is. We both feel confident it's something we want to invest in and be a part of—and, if Ryan's on board with the idea, maybe even grow it beyond Ryan's initial vision to something really big."

My skin is buzzing. My heart is racing. "Mmm hmm," I say, trying very hard *not* to let my body language betray any of the following facts: one, I've already devoured Ryan's business plan and was thoroughly impressed; two, I'm *dying* to be a part of Ryan's dream, in any teeny way he might let me be (and, in fact, I've already got a thousand ideas of ways I might contribute); and, three, I've been fucking Ryan Ulysses Morgan to within an inch of his life all week long.

"Don't say anything to Ryan yet, please," Josh continues. "Jonas and I need to talk to him when I get home from my honeymoon, so this is purely hypothetical at this point, but what would you say if Jonas and I were to partner with Ryan and bring you on as a member of the team to help us launch? I mean, surely, helping launch a new business venture would be a better utilization of your time and talents than ensuring my Lamborghini is shiny and my suits ordered from the latest Anthony Franco show." He grins at Jonas.

I feel like my head's exploding. "I think that sounds awesome," I say evenly.

"Perfect," Josh says. "Jonas and I won't be able to commit a whole lot of time to Captain's—we're gonna be crazy-busy with our plans for Climb & Conquer, so having you be my eyes and ears on the project will be a win-win. Plus, to be honest, now that I'm getting married and having a baby, I think there's a good chance I won't need the same kind of personal attention you've always given me anymore. I could be wrong—I've never been married with a kid before—but I figure, whatever I might need from a personal assistant going forward, you could hire someone to do it, teach him or her exactly what I like, and then manage them for me so I never need to talk to them."

I laugh. "Absolutely."

"Cool. So, yeah, all in all, I think it's a natural progression for you—and me—and this new, amazing life I'm embarking on—if you become my proxy in some new, expanded ways. And I can't think of a better project to sic you on than Captain's. It's like the stars were aligned." He takes a deep breath. "So, in concept, that all sounds good to you?"

I feel like I just won the lottery, but I try to keep my cool. "It sounds great," I say. "I'm actually thrilled about the idea."

We share a smile.

"So, cool, Jonas and I will talk to Ryan when I get back, and let you know if he's equally thrilled with the idea, too."

"I think he will be." I swallow hard, stuffing down my impulse to tell Jonas and Josh everything about Ryan and me. "I, uh, I've actually had a chance to spend a little time with Ryan this week, and we get along very well," I say lamely.

Josh and Jonas exchange another look, this one even more loaded than the last.

"Look, T, as long as we're talking about Ryan and thinking about you possibly working closely with him as my proxy," Josh says, "I feel the need to say something I wouldn't otherwise say."

My stomach clenches. Something tells me I'm not gonna like whatever words are about to come out of Josh's mouth. "Okay."

"There's one source of trepidation I have about this whole idea, to be honest." Josh exhales. "I've noticed sparks between you and Ryan. I don't know if it's a two-way street, but it seems pretty clear to me he's interested in starting something with you. I don't know if you're open to that or not, or even if I'm right about that—and, frankly, it's none of my business; but just, you know, in case I'm right, I'd kick myself later if I didn't give you a heads-up about something I've observed."

I wait, my pulse pounding in my ears.

"Just do yourself a favor and proceed with caution if you're gonna get involved romantically with Ryan, okay? Ryan's a great guy—I already love him like a brother. I genuinely think he's loyal and honest and funny and smart as hell, and Kat sure thinks the world of him. I have no doubt he's gonna make a spectacular business partner or I wouldn't even think of doing a deal with him, brother-in-law or not. But when it comes to the way I've seen him interact with women, I think he might be a diehard 'something shiny' kind of guy, if you know what I mean."

My chest is tight. "Why... do you say that?"

Josh and Jonas exchange yet another look.

"For a couple months now," Josh says, "Ryan's been losing his shit over this one particular woman he met a while back. I'd even go so far as to say he's been totally obsessed with her. And I know for a fact he was still feeling that way about her the day everyone arrived at the resort because, at the opening party, he was talking about how he'd been trying to contact her that very day."

I feel like I've just been punched in the stomach. *That's* what Ryan was talking about with Jonas and Josh and Henn and that group at the opening night party while I stood there giggling about Keane's and Zander's imaginary dick-tattoos— some woman he's "obsessed with"? And he was doing it *after* he'd already fucked my brains out? Well, shit, if he's so obsessed with her, why the hell didn't he bring her to Maui? Did he decide not to bring her precisely because he was anticipating having a vacation-fling behind her back?

What happens in Maui stays in Maui.

Oh my God. I feel physically ill.

"Maybe you... misunderstood him?" I offer, clinging to hope maybe some of the amazing things Ryan said to me this week—and the feelings he's made me feel—have been real. "Maybe Ryan isn't as into this other woman as you thought?"

"Oh, he's not," Jonas says. "That's the part that's confusing. Right before the party, he was totally into her, no doubt about it, and then, all of a sudden, at the party, he was saying he was ready to turn the page and move on. It was so weird—and it pissed me off, to be honest. He was really, really into this woman for quite some time, Theresa—I won't go into detail about how I know that to be true, but just trust me: a while back, he was talking about them having a 'soul connection.' And then, for some reason, the minute he got here, that other woman was yesterday's news and he was ready to drop her like a hot potato. I mean, sure, a dude can move on. *Of course.* Sometimes, that's the healthiest choice. But the way he was able to do it so fucking *fast* after being obsessed with her right before he got here is what was so weird to me."

"Well, let's not be disingenuous, Jonas," Josh says. "We both have a strong hunch the reason Ryan was so willing to drop the other woman like a hot potato is that he met you. I saw the way Ryan looked at you in the lobby the first day—everyone did. And, hey, that's great. I mean, if Ryan's attracted to you and has a sincere desire to start something serious with you, then more power to you both. Who the fuck are Jonas and I to say a damned thing about it? All we're saying is this: keep your eyes wide open, okay? If and when Ryan makes a move on you, which I personally predict is inevitable, take it slow and feel things out before you get in too deep with the guy because, as great as he is, it seems like he's got a shockingly short attention span with women. Especially if you're gonna be working with him on Captain's, it's gonna be important you don't rush into something with the guy and then have things go to shit on you. I'd hate for you to get hurt. Plus, I'm not gonna lie, I'd also hate for our business dynamic to get fucked up."

There's a long pause, during which I'm smashing my lips together so damned hard, they hurt. Oh, fuck. This is a nightmare. I was so damned excited to work on Captain's a moment ago, and now I feel like it's an absolute impossibility.

Ryan swore to me he'd jumped from Psycho Barbie to "Samantha" in lightning speed as some sort of aberration—because he simply couldn't resist our incredible connection. But now I see he jumps from woman to woman pathologically. He's ping-ponged from Psycho Barbie to Samantha to this Mystery Woman to me. Jesus, how many "soul connections" can one guy claim to have in three fucking months? *Samantha,* he called me while screwing me on our first day here—and now it makes perfect sense. The man is addicted to fantasies and role-plays—nothing is ever fucking real for him.

"To be clear: Jonas and I love and respect the guy," Josh says. "Or else we wouldn't even consider investing in his bar. But after what happened with Stu, I wouldn't be able to sleep at night if I didn't warn you about what I see as a potential red flag in the romance department. What you do with the information is totally up to you. You're a big girl."

I manage to stuff my emotions down deep enough to speak in a calm, clear voice that, hopefully, betrays nothing of the hurricane of emotion suddenly swirling inside me. "Thanks for the heads up," I say. "I appreciate it. But, honestly, your warnings aren't necessary because I have absolutely no intention of starting anything 'in the romance department' with Ryan Morgan." I clear my throat. "None whatsoever."

Chapter 60
Tessa

Kat is breathtakingly beautiful as she floats down the sand on her father's arm toward Josh, and it's not because of the lovely way her simple white dress floats like a cloud over her baby bump or the way the large jewels dangling from her ears are glinting in the pre-sunset light. It's because she's the embodiment of pure joy and love itself.

I look at Josh, biting my lower lip, trying to keep tears from my eyes. He's standing in the sand, mere yards from the glittering ocean, dressed in a sharp black-and-white tuxedo, an expression of unadulterated elation on his face. To his right stands his best man, Jonas, who, in turn, is standing next to Josh's groomsmen, Henn, Reed, and Uncle William, all of them looking sharp in tuxedoes, all of them smiling broadly.

When Mr. Morgan and Kat reach Kat's future husband, the proud father kisses his beloved daughter, guides her gently to Josh, and takes a seat next to his teary-eyed wife; and the officiant—a large Hawaiian guy in a white linen suit, sunglasses, and a lei—commences the ceremony.

The whole scene is utterly perfect. Touching. But I'd be lying if I said I was completely in the beautiful moment. In truth, I can't stop thinking about Ryan, seated on the other side of the audience.

I knew exactly what I was getting into when I agreed to be Ryan's secret fuck buddy this week, didn't I? So why the hell do I feel so utterly rejected to find out he was obsessively fixated on some other woman the day he stepped foot on the resort grounds—mere moments before he screwed me so passionately in his room? Okay, yes, I realize the guy probably screws a different woman every week of his life, but I guess I'd convinced myself the way he screwed *me* had brought out a whole new kind of passion in him.

Oh my God. I'm such a fool. *What happens in Maui stays in Maui.* It's what I agreed to, right? In fact, it's exactly what I wanted. Or so I thought.

"And now, Josh and Kat have prepared vows for each other," the officiant prompts. "Kat?"

Kat takes a deep breath. "Josh," she begins. "*Joshua.* You once asked me if I believe in fate—and I said, no, that I believe in kicking ass."

Everyone in the audience chuckles, including me, despite the panging of my heart.

"But now I know I was wrong about that," Kat continues. "You're my fate, my love—my *destiny*. I truly believe that every minute of my life up 'til now was engineered by a greater power to bring me to this moment—to *you*—so that I could become your devoted wife."

At Kat's words, tears prick my eyes. I want to believe in fate, too. *I want to become a devoted wife.*

"Josh?" the officiant prompts.

Josh takes a deep breath and cups Kat's gorgeous face in his palms, making every woman in the audience, including me, swoon. "My beloved Kat. Good God, you're evil."

Kat chuckles and everyone in the audience joins her.

"And not just evil," Josh says. "Stubborn as hell, too. But you're also hilarious. Compassionate. Honest. *Passionate*. Baby, you're hell on wheels. And, most of all, you're loving and kind and beautiful. *And I love it all—every single thing about you.*"

Okay, that's too much: I can't control myself anymore. A sob lurches from my throat and I cover my mouth to muffle it. I want a man who loves me, for exactly who I am! I don't want a fuck buddy! I don't want a fling! Why on earth did I think screwing Ryan all week long with no commitment or feelings involved was a good idea?

Josh continues his vows: "And, most of all, my beloved Kat," he says, "I vow to you, right here and now, in front of God and all the people we love, which includes Keane, by the way, just to be clear—"

Laughter erupts from the Morgan area of the audience, and I steal a quick glance over there to find Ryan throwing his head back, laughing with Keane and Colby.

And that's it: the final straw. I'm suddenly feeling so utterly heartbroken, I can barely stop myself from running out of the ceremony to the bathroom to sob in private. I didn't expect Ryan to fall in love with me this week—and I certainly knew he'd been seeing and screwing other women before he got here, but now it's clear Ryan's pattern of veering sharply from one woman to the next isn't a phase or a circumstance or a one-time thing—it's simply who he is.

The sun is setting behind Josh and Kat, rendering the sky a tapestry of oranges, purples, and yellows over a sparkling ocean. This moment is sheer perfection in every way. So why the hell is it making me feel so sad?

"YOLO, Kat," Josh says to Kat, his tone playful—and Kat smiles broadly in response. "Damn, I'm a lucky bastard that I get to live my one and only life with you." He touches Kat's chin. "I. Will. Always. Love. You. I promise to make every day of our life together better than any fantasy, baby. *Forever.*"

They kiss and the officiant pronounces them husband and wife—and, suddenly, amid all the clapping and cheering around me, I'm bone-certain about something: I'm not a weeklong-no-strings-fling-in-paradise-with-a-manwhore type of girl. I thought I'd be able to play fuck buddy and come out unscathed, but I was fooling myself. I want something real. I want what Josh and Kat have and I'm not going to settle for anything less. I don't care how good the sex might be with Ryan—or if I never find sex that good again with another man; great sex simply isn't enough for me to disrespect myself and disregard my core values. I want someone to make love to me, even if he happens to be fucking and spanking me on any given occasion. I want a man to love me, all of me, for better or worse, 'til death do us part, no matter how crazy and uptight and over-thinking and guarded I might sometimes be. *And, by God, I'm not gonna settle for anything less.*

Chapter 61
Tessa

"When Josh asked me to be his best man," Jonas says, holding a microphone in one hand and a flute of champagne in the other, "the first thing I thought was, 'Oh, shit.'"

Everyone seated at tables in the reception room laughs.

"Because I immediately realized I'd have to give this fucking speech—excuse my language—and anyone who knows me will tell you I absolutely *hate* giving speeches, almost as much as I hate hip-hop and One Direction and talking about my fucking feelings—excuse my language again."

Oh my God, I'm dying. So far, I've managed to avoid Ryan throughout the entire wedding reception, but I feel like the jig is gonna be up soon and he's gonna force me to talk to him. And when he does, I still don't know what the hell I want to say to him—or if I'll be able to stomach whatever lies he tries to tell me in reply.

Jonas raises his glass. "To Josh and Kat. Hear, hear."

"Hear, hear," everyone says, including me.

I take a long sip of champagne and flag a roaming waiter for another flute.

"Kitty Kat," Sarah begins her speech, smiling. "My best friend and now my *sister*—oh, I just gave myself goose bumps saying that." She giggles and everyone joins her.

I feel like I'm gonna explode. All throughout dinner, I could feel Ryan looking at me, willing me to look at him, but I didn't do it. Actually, I was supposed to sit with Ryan at his table tonight, along with Keane, Zander, Colby, Dax, Fish, and Colin—a table I would have given my left boob to sit at yesterday; but the minute I left Josh's bungalow this morning, I headed straight to the wedding planner and immediately requested she re-assign me to Uncle William's stodgy table.

But, obviously, I can't avoid Ryan forever, especially now that dinner is finished and toasts are underway and dancing is about to begin.

Sarah raises her glass. "To Josh and Kat. May you always inspire everyone around you to scan for emergency exits and fire extinguishers. Hear, hear."

"Hear, hear," everyone in the room says, raising their glasses.

Josh kisses Sarah's cheek and takes the microphone from her.

"Thank you, Sarah," he says. "Thank you, Jonas. We love you guys so much. We Faradays are pretty effing cool, I gotta say. I want to thank you all for joining us, not just for today's celebration, but for this whole past week in paradise. I know you all have busy lives so we thank you for taking so much time to celebrate and party with us this whole week. It's been incredible, hasn't it?"

Everyone claps and cheers.

Josh proceeds to make a long speech, which he's been known to do a time or two. While he speaks, I can't resist covertly peeking over at Ryan's table, ever so briefly, just to see if... *Crap.* Ryan's looking right at me.

I look away, my cheeks hot.

Shit. The minute this speech is over, he's gonna corner me—I can feel it. I'd better get myself ready. When we talk, I just have to be calm and clear. I'll tell him I don't want to continue this—that it's been fun and I'm grateful for the time we've spent together, but I have no interest in moving forward because, frankly, I just don't feel like I can fully trust him. And I'll just leave it at that. Why say more than that? If I tell him my suspicions, he'll just deny any wrongdoing *again,* the same way he always does, and I'm likely to believe his bullshit *again.* Oh, God, I'm such an idiot.

"I'd like to say a special thanks to my great friend Reed for that incredible surprise earlier," Josh continues. "Wasn't that amazing?"

Everyone claps and cheers wildly, including me.

"Amazing" is the right word for Reed's surprise, I gotta say. Thanks to Reed's connections, Josh and Kat danced their first dance to their favorite song, performed live by the original artist himself— James Bay—after he surprised and thrilled everyone by gliding into the reception with an acoustic guitar strapped to his chest.

Josh raises his champagne flute to Reed. "Thank you, bro. We'll never forget that moment as long as we live."

Josh pulls Kat out of her chair and slides his arm around her. "And one last thing," he says into the microphone. "With my beautiful wife by my side, I wanna say a few words of thanks to my new family, the Morgans. There's been a lot of talk about Kat becoming a Faraday today, but, trust me, I got the better end of the bargain. You know that expression 'The apple doesn't fall far from the tree'? Well, that's especially true when it comes to Kat." He raises his glass to Kat's family at their various tables in the large room, and they all return the gesture—and, just for a second, my heart physically pangs with unfathomable envy and yearning. *I want to be part of the Morgan family, like Josh.*

"To Tom Tom Club, Momma Lou, Cheese, Captain, Peen, and Baby Brother," Josh continues, his champagne flute in the air. "And to all the Morgans I've met this past week, too—" He raises his glass to the various pockets of Morgans seated around the large room. "Thank you for your part in making Kat the incredible woman she is today and for letting me be part of your hilarious and fucking awesome family. Hear, hear."

"Hear, hear," everyone in the room says in unison.

My eyes are filling with tears. I quickly wipe them and down my champagne.

Josh whispers something to Kat and she shakes her head.

"So, okay," Josh says into his microphone. "Mrs. Faraday says enough talking about our fucking feelings—it's time to *dance*."

Chapter 62
Ryan

As Josh gives his toast to the rapt audience, I look longingly at Tessa across the reception room, the same way I've done countless times tonight, but, still, she won't look at me.

Clearly, she's been avoiding me today and I can't figure out why. I mean, okay, I fully understood when she said she needed to help the wedding planner with a bunch of pre-wedding preparations today and therefore couldn't hang out at the beach with my family and me. Cool. No problem. And, during the ceremony, when she didn't sit next to me, but instead sat on the other end of the seating at the end of a row, I figured she wanted to be able to pop up, just in case the wedding planner unexpectedly needed her. And when she steadfastly stared at Josh and Kat during the entire ceremony without even a cursory glance in my direction, I told myself I was being paranoid.

But then came the reception and I couldn't explain away her aloofness anymore. I mean, seriously, why didn't she sit at my table for dinner? For fuck's sake, she's been sitting with me and my family at dinners all week long—and, now, at the biggest dinner of all, she's suddenly gotta sit with William Faraday and a bunch of Josh's boring work friends? Yeah, I know that's what the official seating chart said (what the fuck?), but surely Tessa of all people could have defied the seating chart and sat with me and my brothers at our table? Or, fuck it, she's The Mighty T-Rod! The Woman Behind the Curtain! Couldn't she have gotten herself assigned to any table of her choosing in the first place? I just don't get it.

I stare at her across the room for a long beat, and to my surprise, she looks over at me, meets my eyes... *and instantly looks away.*

302

Fuck!

So, I'm not imagining it. The look on her face just now told me everything I need to know: she can't even stand to look at me.

What the fuck is going on? This entire night feels like a train coming off the tracks and I can't understand why. When I imagined tonight, I pictured us having a blast together, celebrating and laughing and dancing the night away, and then, finally, when Tessa and I were high on life and champagne and dying to maul each other, I planned to lead her to the moonlit beach, take her into my arms, and *finally* bare my soul to her, without holding back. But how the fuck can I do any of that now, when she's been giving me the cold shoulder all day?

"So, okay," Josh says into the microphone. "Mrs. Faraday says enough talking about our fucking feelings—it's time to *dance*."

Josh cues the band and off they go, loudly kicking off their first song of the night (a dance-remix-cover of Whitney Houston's "I Will Always Love You"), and, immediately, almost everyone in the room beelines to the dance floor.

I get up from my table, my heart pounding and my mouth dry, and stride around the edge of the bustling dance floor toward her. I don't know what the fuck's going on in her head—or if I truly want to find out—but there's no turning back now.

Right before I reach her table, Tessa rises from her seat, wipes her eyes, and turns on her heel like she's planning to get the hell out of Dodge and never come back, so I pick up my pace and, thankfully, reach her before she's gotten too far. In a flash, I've got her elbow firmly in my grasp and her trembling body pressed into my side.

"We need to talk," I say, gripping her fiercely. "Let's take a walk."

Chapter 63
Ryan

Tessa's body language is tight and closed off as I pull her past the dancing bodies on the dance floor, out the front doors of the reception hall, and straight into the warm, starry night, and then, on a sudden impulse, wordlessly continue walking with her toward the private beach about a hundred yards away.

When we reach the entrance to the beach, Tessa kicks off her heels and marches onto the sand without looking back. "I don't know why you led me all the way out here," she mutters. "We don't need to take a moonlit walk on the beach to say, 'Thanks for the memories.'"

I take two loping strides to catch up to her, grab her by her arm, and force her to stop marching away from me. "What the fuck is wrong with you?" I bellow, panic welling up inside me. "'Thanks for the memories'? Is that what you think is on the tip of my tongue tonight? Tessa, I'm not your prick of an ex-boyfriend, okay? *I'm not him*. This has been the best week of my life and all I want is to keep going when we get back home."

"Keep going? What would be the point when all you're gonna do is telepathically break up with me the minute some other woman makes your dick hard?"

"Jesus, I thought we were past this. I told you I'd broken up with Olivia by the time I met you and that—"

"This isn't about Psycho Barbie," she grits out. "And this isn't about my stupid ex-boyfriend, either. This is about you and the woman you've been dating for the past few months—the woman you've been 'obsessed with' right up until you arrived in Maui."

The starry night buckles and warps around me. *Shit.*

"Tessa, I don't know who you've been talking to, but they gave

304

you some wrong information. There's no other woman but you and there hasn't been since the moment I laid eyes on you. I haven't even touched another woman since I met you that night at The Pine Box."

She looks at me like I'm scum. "Stop with the bullshit, Ryan. I talked to Josh and Jonas. They told me everything."

"What did they tell you? Whatever it was, they've got it completely wrong. Tessa, the woman I've been 'obsessed with' for months is *you*."

"Yeah, everyone's always got it 'completely wrong' when it comes to you, huh? You've always got a nifty explanation."

I grab her shoulders, practically hyperventilating with panic. "What did Josh and Jonas say to you? *Tell me.*"

"Let go of me," she commands.

I release my grasp.

Her eyes are wild. "Josh and Jonas saw sparks between us. They have no idea we've gotten together, but they felt the need to warn me that, if I'm possibly gonna start something with you, I should be careful because, although they generally think you're the greatest guy ever and they love and respect you, when it comes to women, you seem to hop from one to the next at breakneck speed. Case in point, they told me you'd been obsessed with some woman for months prior to coming here, right up to the very day you arrived at the resort, and that, in fact, the afternoon you arrived—*the same day we fucked for the first time*—you were still totally into this other woman, which they knew for a fact because at the opening night party you were talking about how you'd desperately tried calling her that afternoon." She crosses her arms over her chest. "So I have a question, Ryan: did you break up with this woman before you fucked me, or did you just do it *telepathically,* like you always do when you're ready to move on to your next conquest?"

"Oh my fuck." I sigh. "Sweetheart, Josh and Jonas meant well, but they were completely clueless. Baby, look at me. When they told you about that other woman, they were talking about 'Samantha.' *That's* who I've been obsessed with for three months. *Samantha.*"

She looks utterly flabbergasted.

I take her hands in mine and, thankfully, she doesn't resist my grasp. "Baby, after everything went to shit at The Pine Box that night, I went straight to Josh and Kat's house and we hung out with Jonas and Sarah, and I told all of them about this amazing woman I'd met that night—Samantha the Flight Attendant. I told them we'd had a soul connection—that I couldn't stand the thought of never seeing her again, that I couldn't stand the thought of her being out there in the world, thinking I was a lying, cheating scumbag. And that's when the Faraday brothers hooked me up with Henn to help me track Samantha down."

Tessa puts her palm to her forehead. "Oh, Jesus."

"Baby, Henn hacked into the employee databases of *nine* fucking airlines to find Samantha for me. Of course, Henn ultimately came up empty, despite his best efforts, but it wasn't for lack of trying."

"Oh, shit. Oh my God. *No.*"

I squeeze her hands. "Do you know how long it takes a world-class hacker to hack the databases of *nine* airlines to find a twenty-seven-year-old, Virgo flight attendant named Samantha? Well, I do: it takes him approximately three months."

Tessa puts her palms on her cheeks. "This is insane."

"Baby, I've loved you from the minute I laid eyes on you." I swallow hard. "You're my fate. My destiny. And I knew it the minute I saw you." A lump rises in my throat. "Tessa, my love for you is involuntary. You're my 'kick' when the doctor bangs on my knee with a hammer. *I've got no choice but to love you.*"

She furrows her brow and drops my hands. "But Josh and Jonas said you'd called this other woman the day you arrived here. If that woman was *me*, then... Who did you call?"

Oh my God. No. I feel sick. I promised Charlotte I wouldn't say her name. *I swore.* But, fuck my life, if I *don't* tell Tessa about my calls to Charlotte, I'm toast.

Tessa's entire body visibly tenses. "Who'd you call, Ryan?"

My mind is reeling. I can't string coherent thoughts together. Shit. It seems like the best plan is for me to call Charlotte and get her permission to tell Tessa about our conversations. Otherwise, I'm simply gonna trade one problem for another here. It's not that big a deal, right? I'll call Charlotte tonight, get her permission, and head straight to Tessa's room to tell her everything.

"Ryan?" Tessa says, her eyes hardening. "It's a simple question: who's the woman you called the day you arrived?"

I take a deep breath. "Baby, I can't answer that right now—you just need to trust me that it wasn't anyone I was romantically interested in. Look, I know you're a 'just gimme the facts' kind of girl—I know that about you—but I really need you to take a leap of faith here and trust me. I promise I'll answer your question—"

She throws up her hands, grunts in frustration, and begins marching back toward the entrance to the beach. "Goodbye, Ryan. 'What happens in Maui stays in Maui.' Let's just leave it at that."

I chase her and lurch in front of her, impeding her forward progress.

"Did you not hear me? I told you I love you, Tessa."

"I heard you. Let me pass."

"What the fuck happened to you to make you this jaded about love? I know the soccer-douche cheated on you, okay? I know he broke your heart. *But I'm not him.* Haven't I shown you who I am this week? Hasn't my entire *family* shown you?"

Tears flood her eyes. "I don't know what to believe anymore, Ryan. Every time I let down my guard with you, nothing is ever what it seems. You've obviously omitted telling me certain things in order to manipulate my feelings and make me fall for you. And guess what? It worked. I fell for you. Hard. But now I don't know if my feelings are real or the result of some sort of manipulation."

I grab her shoulders. "Your feelings are real. We're perfect together, and you know it."

"I don't know it. I can't trust my own feelings. Clearly, I have horrible judgment."

"Okay, then, if you can't trust yourself or me, then trust my family. Do you know how many members of my family came up to me this week and told me we're perfect for each other? And not just my mom and Kat, baby—*everyone* wants us together because they can see we're made for each other."

She looks like she's about to pass out from the stress of this situation. Clearly, her brain and heart are waging a fierce battle inside her. "Everything's happened so fast," she stammers. "I haven't had time to process. How could anyone fall in love in a week, especially like this—when it turns out they're being lied to? We're in a bubble—it's just a fantasy."

"Baby, no. We fell in love for real. You like facts? Okay, then look at my parents. In college, my dad saw my mom in a lecture hall on the first day of school, sat down next to her, and they fell in love right then and there. That very night, my dad told his roommate he'd met the woman he was gonna marry. Or, fine, fuck my parents, you want more facts? Then look at your own parents." My voice is edged with barely contained panic. "Remember what you told me? Your dad knew your mom was rightfully his the minute she walked into his studio and, to this day, he still thinks she 'hung the moon.' Well, that's you and me. I saw you in that bar and, instantly, I knew you were rightfully mine. And, I promise, thirty years from now, a hundred years from now, a thousand years, I'll still think you hung the moon. Baby, we could have it all, just like your parents."

She throws her hands over her tear-streaked face and shrieks, "Stop! Please, Ryan, just stop!"

"Tessa, I'm not gonna stop. Your parents have it all and we could, too."

"Stop!" she shrieks, clearly distressed. Tears flood her eyes. "My parents don't have it all, Ryan! Not even close!"

I press my lips together, rendered completely speechless.

For a long beat, the sound of crashing waves fills the awkward silence.

"Tessa?" I prompt, my heartbeat pounding in my ears. "What happened?"

She takes a deep breath. "He cheated on her," she whispers, her entire body trembling. "My dad says my mom 'hung the moon' but he cheated on her and broke her heart."

The hair on the back of my neck stands up. "When?"

"It happened twenty-something years ago, but I only found out about it this past year." She takes a deep, shaky breath. "I was looking through boxes of old photos to make an anniversary present for them, and I found a stack of old letters in a box—letters that shattered everything I thought I knew about love and marriage and the ability of any man on this planet to stay faithful."

I'm too shocked to speak.

She takes a deep, shaky breath and wipes fitfully at the hot tears streaming down her cheeks. "They separated for six months, but I was too young to realize it. She kicked him out and wouldn't return any of his calls, so he wrote letter after handwritten love letter, begging for forgiveness, pleading with her, swearing it had been a one-time, drunken, stupid moment of weakness with a dance partner. So finally, after six months of letters and begging and pleading, she finally took him back." A sob lurches out of her throat. "A year ago, I found out the man I'd thought I loved for two fucking years, a man who said he loved me and wanted to marry me and start a family with me, had been cheating on me throughout our entire relationship—and then, three months after that, I found out the father I worshipped had cheated on my beautiful mother and, by extension, on me and our entire family and everything we were raised to believe, because, apparently, getting laid by some nobody was more important than honoring his sacred vows."

I open my mouth and close it.

"I gripped that handwritten letter in my hand and looked at my dad's familiar, sloping script, and I just couldn't believe my eyes. If I hadn't read his words with my own eyes, I never would have believed them possible. I would have defended my father's integrity to my dying breath." She swallows hard. "I confronted my parents about it, and they told me it was a lifetime ago, that it ultimately made them stronger, that it was actually a blessing in disguise and opened up lines of communication and blah, blah, blah. They said marriage is hard and people are flawed and nobody's perfect—that to forgive is divine and so many other platitudes; but, golly gosh, I'm sorry if I can't so easily move past it and pretend it never happened when my whole life I've worshipped the ground my father walks on and idolized my parents' marriage and based my entire conception of marriage and what I'm looking for in a man on my father." Tears are gushing out of her eyes. She's a dam breaking. A rambling mess. "My whole life, whenever anyone else was jaded or skeptical about love or marriage, I was *always* the one who said, 'But fairytales really do exist!' Because, no matter what, I always knew my dad thought my mom 'hung the moon' and that my mother was worthy of his undying devotion—which gave me hope that *maybe* that kind of love might one day be possible for a mere mortal like me—that maybe *I'd* find a man who thought I hung the moon one day." Her chest is heaving. "Their marriage is what I've always aspired to have, Ryan, my whole life—but now I don't know what the fuck I'm aspiring to anymore."

"Tessa," I say softly, taking a step toward her, my arms open, but she lurches backward, her eyes glinting with fury and hurt.

"You lied to me," she hisses. "If you're willing to hide certain facts from me to create an optimal environment for me to fall in love with you, then how the fuck can I ever fully trust anything you say or do—let alone trust my feelings for you when your plan eventually works?"

I can't fathom how she's blowing up my slight omissions this past week into a betrayal of this proportion, especially when the only thing I failed to tell her is that I moved heaven and earth to find her because I fell in love with her at first sight. "Tessa," I say. "Calm down. I was scared the hacking thing would freak you out right outta the gate, that's all. I always intended to tell you before leaving Maui."

She wipes her eyes and looks out at the ocean. "It's exactly what Stu did—he showed me some perfect version of himself—a version he wished he could be, I suppose—but that version never really existed."

"Babe. *No.* This is nothing like that. I'm not Stu. Everything I showed you this week was exactly who I am. I told you the complete truth; I just didn't tell you a few things at first, for the greater good."

She narrows her eyes. "If your definition of telling the truth is hiding certain things from me 'for the greater good,' then you're not someone I want to be in a relationship with."

My heart feels like it's shattering and gushing blood onto the sand. Tears prick my eyes. "Please, baby. I haven't been with anyone else since I met you. I couldn't stand the thought of touching another woman since I laid eyes on you. I saw you and fell in love with you and knew you were rightfully mine. You own me, Tessa. Mind, body, heart, and soul. Please, you gotta believe me."

She puts her hands over her face. "I don't know what to believe. This is too much for me to process. I need time, Ryan. You're Josh's brother and you two are going into business together and Josh is thinking about having me work with you guys and—"

"Josh wants you to work with us on Captain's? Oh my God! That would be a dream come true. Tell him yes."

"It's not that simple now. What if I give this a chance and we don't work out? I don't want to fuck things up for you or for Josh and Jonas. And I certainly don't want to fuck things up for myself, either."

I put my hands on her wet cheeks and, thank God, she doesn't pull away. "Stop thinking so much, love. Get it through your head: *I love you.* That's not gonna change. Ever. Come to my room with me right now. Let me make love to you. Let me show you how much you mean to me. And then we can lie in bed and talk things through calmly and I promise all your worries and concerns will melt away."

She looks deeply into my eyes for a long beat, and, for a split-second, I think she's gonna throw her arms around me and declare her love for me. But she doesn't. "Who'd you call that day, Ryan?" she whispers.

I open my mouth and close it.

She smiles wanly. "I thought so."

I sigh loudly. "I tell you what, my love. I'll come to your room first thing in the morning to answer that question. We'll talk then. Okay? You just need time to think and process. So go back to your room and I'll come see you in the morning. Spoiler alert, though—no matter what you say to me tomorrow, I'm not leaving 'til I've convinced you we're meant to be."

She shakes her head. "I'm gonna need more than a night to get my thoughts straight. I need to go back home and get back to real life and see how I feel about things then."

I exhale with relief. If she's negotiating the number of days she needs to work through her shit, as opposed to my underlying assumption that I'm ultimately gonna convince her to be mine, that's a very good sign. "Fair enough. How much time do you need, sweetheart?" I ask gently, stroking her cheek. "We can take things as slow as you need."

"I don't know. As it turns out, I've been having sex with a crazy stalker all week. Who knew?"

I laugh, despite myself.

She smiles—which I take as another very good sign. "I need a week," she says. "When I get home, I'm gonna be slammed with work while Josh is on his honeymoon. Plus, I'll want to talk to Josh about me working on Captain's. Things could get dicey from a business perspective for him if things don't work out romantically for us and he and Jonas deserve to know exactly what they're getting themselves into."

"Baby, are you not listening to me? There's no way things won't work out for us. That's what I'm telling you. I love you. You're The One. We're gonna have it all, baby. You and me."

She fidgets.

I sigh. "Okay. Here's what we're gonna do: You're gonna take eight days to think things through in the 'real world' because you're a fucking loon. That gives you a week on your own plus one day to talk to Josh when he gets back to Seattle. And then, the afternoon of the eighth day, no matter what the fuck you *think* you've decided about us, I'm gonna hunt you down and do whatever the fuck I have to do to convince you to be mine. Sound good?"

She nods. "Okay."

Warmth spreads throughout my body. Oh my God. This woman's a fucking bunny-boiling loon. Truly. And, oh my fucking God, I love her more than life itself.

Chapter 64
Ryan

"Is he mad? Anyway, there's something on his mind, as sure as there must be something on a deck when it cracks."

I'm insane. It's official.

It's been four days since I've been home from Maui and I'm most definitely not right in the head. Why the fuck did I tell Tessa I'd give her eight fucking days to "process"? When I said that bullshit, I thought for sure I was actually gonna speak to Charlotte that very night, get her permission to tell Tessa the truth about our phone conversations, and then head straight to Tessa's room to tell her everything and make sweet love to her all night long.

But it's been four fucking days and Charlotte still hasn't called me back—and I can't understand why she's ignoring me. All I can think is Tessa must have called Charlotte and told her everything that happened... and Charlotte misunderstood and thought I threw her under the bus? Or maybe Charlotte confessed everything to Tessa and the two of them got into a big fight? I just don't know. Either way, Charlotte's radio-silence is driving me mad—especially when I haven't talked to Tessa, either.

I've texted Tessa every day since I got back to Seattle, of course, just to tell her I'm thinking about her and can't wait to talk to her and can we maybe speed things up a bit here, despite what I said in Maui? But she's replied to insist she needs to talk to Josh about the Captain's thing before she has "full clarity."

Fuck! If only she'd trust me, or, fuck it, if not me, then my entire family. Because, oh my God, if I'd had any doubts about how perfectly Tessa and I fit together (not that I ever did), those doubts

313

would have been laid to rest during my flight back to Seattle, when at least fifteen members of my family berated me, telling me "not to be an idiot" and to "close the deal on that girl."

"I'm with you, guys," I told everyone. "You're preaching to the choir. But she's a tough nut to crack."

"Well, crack that dang nut," Mom said emphatically. "I swear, Rum Cake, if you don't have babies with that girl, I'll never forgive you as long as I live."

"I'll do my best, Mom."

And now, here I am, lying on my couch in sweats and bedhead, just back from a particularly grueling workout at the gym, feeling too sorry for myself to do a damned thing except lie here and flip channels.

My phone rings and I quickly grab it, hoping it's Charlotte—or, better yet, Tessa. But, unexpectedly, the name on my display screen says "Josh."

"Yo, Lambo," I say, answering the call.

"Yo, Captain."

"Aren't you and Kat still on your honeymoon?"

"Yeah. We're still here, having a blast. I'm calling because I was just telling my lovely wife about Captain's, and I mentioned I've got this fantastic idea to cut T-Rod in as a part-owner—out of Jonas' and my share, don't worry. I want T-Rod to have some skin in the game, but only if that's something you'd be comfortable with, you know."

"Yeah. Great idea. Do it."

"Great. So, anyway, I was telling Kat about all that and..." Josh sighs. "Ryan, Kat spilled the beans. She told me everything."

The hair on my arms stands up. "Everything?"

"That T-Rod's Samantha and you two were having a torrid love affair all week in Maui. And that you love her."

My stomach ties into knots.

"Ryan, I owe you a huge apology," Josh says. "Jonas and I really torpedoed everything for you. So, I'm calling to find out if there's any way I can help make things right. Dude, let's figure out how I can help you get your girl."

Chapter 65
Ryan

"Hello?" a male voice says into the phone.

"Mr. Rodriguez?" I ask.

"Yes."

"Hi, Mr. Rodriguez. My name is Ryan Morgan. You're familiar with Josh Faraday, your daughter Tessa's employer?"

"Of course, yes," he says—and, for the first time, I'm making out his slight accent when he speaks.

"Josh is my brother-in-law," I say. "He married my sister, Kat, last week."

"Yes, I heard about that. Congratulations to all. Tessa said the wedding was beautiful."

"Yes, it was." I clear my throat. "Sir, I'm calling because I just spent a week in Hawaii with your daughter, along with Josh and Kat and my entire family, and now, sir, I'm in love with her. Deeply, totally, and completely in love with her. Sir."

"*Oh.*"

"Tessa and I had met prior to the Hawaii trip—about three months beforehand, just by random chance—and the minute I saw her back then, I felt like I'd been struck by a lightning bolt. I've never felt that way before with anyone, but the minute I saw your daughter, I instantly felt like she was rightfully mine and I didn't want anyone else."

Mr. Rodriguez pauses and then says softly, "I know the feeling well."

"So, fast-forward three months after that initial lightning bolt, and I've had the good fortune to spend an entire week with your daughter in paradise, getting to know her well, hanging out with her

315

and seeing how she interacts with my family—they all love her, by the way—and those initial love-at-first-sight feelings I had for her have grown exponentially, and now I can confidently tell you, sir, without equivocation or a shred of doubt, your daughter's the one I want to spend the rest of my life with. The woman I want to raise a family with." I clear my throat. My heart is racing so fast, I feel like I'm gonna faint. "I know it's been a short amount of time, sir, and that marriage is hard and not a fairytale, but I'm positive I want to make a life with Tessa and no one else." I inhale and exhale a shaky breath, emotion suddenly overcoming me. "Sir, I want Tessa to be my wife and the mother of my children, if God blesses us that way."

"Wow," Mr. Rodriguez says. "This is... wow."

"So, I'm hoping to ask Tessa to marry me as soon as possible; but, before I do that—I know you're a traditional man and that Tessa shares your values, sir; so, before I ask her to be my wife, I'm well aware I've got a question to ask of you first, as her father—actually, a question I'd like to ask you and Mrs. Rodriguez both. It's a very important question, sir, a very traditional one, and I don't want to ask it over the telephone, and especially not before you and your wife have met me and had ample opportunity to look me in the eye and assess the depth of my sincerity and feelings for your daughter." I take another deep, steadying breath. "So I'm hoping you and your wife—and your two sons, too, if they're available—would be willing to meet me for dinner in the next day or two? I live in Seattle, but I'll fly down to L.A. to take you all out to a nice dinner." I let out another shaky breath, my chest tight and my head throbbing.

"That sounds wonderful. What did you say your name was, son?"

"Ryan Morgan."

"Thank you, Ryan. One moment." He speaks to someone on his end of the line for what seems like forever. "My wife says she's very excited to meet you. How does tomorrow or the day after work for you?"

"Tomorrow's perfect. But, um, sir, fair warning? It won't be just me coming down for dinner. I hope this doesn't seem too crazy, but my entire immediate family wants to come with me—my parents, Thomas and Louise Morgan, and my three brothers, Colby, Keane, and Dax. My sister Kat would have joined us, too—she really wants to meet you—but she's still on her honeymoon with Josh, so she made me swear to FaceTime her from the restaurant so she can say hello to your family, face-to-face."

Mr. Rodriguez laughs. "Well, why don't we wait until Josh and Kat return from their honeymoon and include them? I've always wanted to meet Josh—Tessa has told us wonderful things about him over the years. In fact, maybe our family can come up to Seattle, instead of you coming down here. We've been meaning to see Tessa's new place in Seattle, anyway."

"No, um, actually, that won't work, sir. I'm sorry, but..." I take another deep breath. "Tessa doesn't know I'm calling you, sir. And, although I've told her I love her, she doesn't know I'm planning to ask her to marry me." I take another deep breath, trying to keep my voice from shaking. "I'll tell you more about it when I see you in person, but suffice it to say, your daughter's kind of a tough nut to crack so I wanna do this right."

Mr. Rodriguez sighs. "Oh, Tessa. She's her own worst enemy sometimes."

"Yeah, she is, God bless her."

We share a chuckle.

"But, it's okay," I say. "I love that about her. I love everything about her."

"Your patience will be well rewarded. Our Tessa's a rare jewel once she finally lets down her guard."

"Yes, she is. I know that about her. So if you're willing, sir, I'd appreciate it if we could keep our dinner a secret for just a couple days, until I've popped the question, which I'll do very soon after our dinner, assuming things go well when our families meet."

"Ryan, I can already tell things are going to go very, very well when we meet. But, yes, we can certainly honor that request for a few days. Of course. We look forward to meeting you and your family."

"Thank you, sir. I can't wait to meet you, too—and to introduce you to my family." My entire body feels electrified. "Thank you so much, Mr. Rodriguez," I blurt, suddenly overcome by adrenaline. "I'll see you tomorrow."

Chapter 66
Tessa

"Welcome home, Josh," I say, settling myself into a chair opposite Josh at his desk. "You and Kat had fun?"

"So much fun," Josh says. He leans back in his desk chair and absentmindedly twirls the wedding band on his finger. "Thanks for holding down the fort while I was gone."

"My pleasure. It was quiet. So, now that you're back, are you and Kat in full nesting mode?"

We chat for a moment about the baby's expected arrival in about six weeks and what remains on their To Do List, and then Josh places his forearms onto his desk and says, "There's something I want to talk to you about, T-Rod. It's about Captain's."

My chest tightens. "Yeah, I want to talk to you about that, too," I say calmly, but the truth is I'm about to burst into tears.

When I first got home to Seattle, I convinced myself for about two days I'd made a good call by throwing on the brakes with Ryan—that taking things slow never hurt any situation and usually helps it significantly, especially since he *still* hasn't told me whom he'd called the day he arrived at the resort; but on the third day, I woke up feeling like I'd most definitely fucked up in a big way, even if Ryan never winds up telling me whom he called. On the third day, I woke up feeling like I'd made the most catastrophic mistake of my entire life by not throwing my arms around Ryan's neck right then and there on the beach and declaring my undying love for him. And on the fifth day, I woke up feeling like I could barely breathe. And that's how I've felt ever since.

So this morning, I picked up the phone to call Ryan, wanting to tell him I love him and can't live without him—that I don't give a crap what anyone else says or thinks, not even Josh and Jonas—that I

318

don't care if he's Josh's brother. I wanted to tell him I reacted that night out of fear—that's all it was, stupid fear—and that I've decided I'll go to therapy or do anything else I need to do to work through my issues, but please, please don't give up on me because I promise my love will be well worth his patience and understanding.

I wanted to tell him all of that... until I realized two things: one, if I'm being honest, I still want to know who he called that day; and, two, I still want to talk to Josh about Captain's.

Whether I like it or not, I simply can't embark on a relationship with Ryan *and* work with him to launch Captain's at the same time. What if something happens and he breaks my heart? I'm certainly never planning to leave Ryan, but can he say the same to me? Of course, he can't. Not after one week in paradise together. Even if I'd be willing to pledge forever right here and now, I can't rationally expect that of Ryan in return. Which means we absolutely shouldn't mix business and pleasure—not this soon, anyway, not when what's at stake is his lifelong dream.

So, I'm here today at Josh's office to tell him I don't wish to work on Captain's, despite our prior discussions, but that I'll be happy to work on anything else he likes, including whatever role he might have for me at Climb & Conquer. And then, right after I've spoken to Josh, I'm gonna call Ryan and tell him I love him and I'm sorry and throw myself on his mercy—and, hopefully, when I tell him all that, he'll feel comfortable enough to finally break down and tell me whom he called that day.

"So, about Captain's," Josh says. "Jonas and I are for sure gonna invest."

"Wonderful. I'm thrilled to hear it."

"I've had a chance to talk to Reed and some other friends of mine with expertise in the bar industry, and I've gained some valuable insights and an even greater appreciation for Ryan's vision and knowledge. The guy definitely knows what he's doing. So Jonas and I are thinking we want to expand Ryan's initial idea to five or six more locations beyond Seattle over the next three to five years—and, thankfully, Ryan's totally on board with that idea."

"Great," I say, my heart panging. Damn, that sounds like something I'd give my right arm to be a part of. "The thing is," I begin, but Josh cuts me off.

"Hang on, T," Josh says. "Lemme just get all this out, and then you can put in your two cents, okay? Thanks."

I lean back in my chair, my body trembling.

"Jonas, Ryan, and I have talked about it and we'd all like to make you an equity partner in Captain's. You wouldn't hold an equal share with the three of us—your share would probably be settled at around twelve percent, based, in part, on capital contributions I'd personally make on your behalf, and also in consideration of the sweat-equity we all expect you to contribute. Basically, you're gonna be the person with nuts-and-bolts oversight as we give birth to this thing. But those are details we can hammer out later. The main point is this: we'd like you to be our partner, not just a hired employee. And, in recognition of your six years of valuable service to me, during which time period my portfolio has grown exponentially, in part because I've had you holding down the fort for me in a thousand ways, not to mention providing a steadying influence on me when I've needed it most, I'd like to contribute your share to the business as my gift to you."

I can't believe my ears. Oh my effing God. This would have been a dream come true if I weren't in love with Ryan. "Josh, thank you," I say. "But you can't do that. If I were going to invest in the business, I'd do it with my own money. I've got plenty saved, thanks to the ridiculous salary you pay me."

"T, I'm talking about, like, a quarter-mill here."

"I've got that sitting in the bank and then some."

"You've got a quarter-mill sitting in the bank?"

I nod. "I've been saving."

Josh laughs. "I'll be damned. Well, I tell you what. I'll pay the initial two-fifty as a gift, like I was planning to do, and you can add however much as we start to expand."

I rub my forehead. What the hell am I doing? I shouldn't be negotiating my partnership share in Captain's—I should be telling Josh I can't be part of this venture at all, due to my feelings for Ryan. That was my plan coming in here, after all. Why am I going off plan? "Josh," I say. "Thanks for the offer, but I can't do this."

"Sure you can," Josh says. "Jonas and I will be far too busy with Climb & Conquer to be hands-on with this, so we're gonna need you and Ryan to pick up the ball and run with it together."

I bite my lip. Oh my God. That sounds like heaven on earth—working alongside the man I love to build something together from the ground up?

"So what do you think, T?" Josh asks. "Does this sound like something you'd like to do or what?"

I open my mouth and close it, suddenly feeling like I'm going to burst into tears. I swallow hard and gather myself. And then promptly burst into gigantic, sobbing tears.

"Tessa?" Josh says, looking stricken.

"I love him!" I blurt. "I love Ryan! He's the love of my life, Josh!" Oh, God, I'm crying like a shaken baby. "Ryan and I secretly got together all week in Hawaii—all week, Josh!—and now I *love* him! But he doesn't know that because I'm a fucking idiot with major trust issues!" I continue babbling incoherently for a long moment, ultimately confessing I'm Samantha the Flight Attendant.

Josh gets up and walks around his desk and opens his arms and I throw myself into his embrace and sob my eyes out.

"Why haven't you told him how you feel yet?" he asks.

"Because I wanted to talk to you about Captain's first. And because I still don't know who he called that day. He said he'd tell me and he still hasn't and I don't understand why he's keeping that from me. I shouldn't care. I love him. I should just trust him, but that last little thing is holding me back."

Josh is looking at me like I'm a little, injured bird in his palm. And I don't blame him. I've never once cried in his presence, or shown any kind of vulnerability, as far as I know. "Sit," he says simply.

I sit.

Josh walks around to his side of the desk again, offers me a tissue, and then places his muscled forearms on his desk. "T, I already know about all of that. Kat told me everything on our trip, even the Samantha thing."

I put my hands over my face. "Oh my God. Ryan swore he didn't tell Kat."

"He didn't tell her. She figured it out on her own, thanks to something Henn said."

"Henn knows, too?"

Josh nods. "Ryan didn't tell Henn, either, by the way. Henn just figured it out."

"Shit."

Josh laughs. "Tessa, nobody cares about the Samantha thing. Do you have any idea how crazy Kat is? The girl's one brick short of a wall."

I laugh.

"Look, the only reason Jonas and I warned you about Ryan was to protect you—because we both want you to be with a guy who loves and respects you, a guy who's gonna treat you right." He smiles. "And that guy is Ryan."

I feel the weight of the world lifted off me. "But Ryan called some other woman the day everyone arrived at the resort. If he'd been obsessed with 'Samantha,' who'd he call?"

Josh bites the inside of his cheek, looking guilty as sin.

"You know, don't you? Kat knows and she told you?"

Josh nods. "I'm not supposed to tell. But, fuck it, I'm gonna do it, anyway, because you having any remaining doubts about Ryan over something this stupid is a fucking tragedy." He sighs. "It's your best friend, T. The flight attendant with the leprechaun name." Josh tells me the whole story, exactly as Kat told it to him.

"Holy fuckburgers," I breathe. "So Ryan decided to keep his promise to Charlotte rather than clear his name with me?"

Josh nods. "Kat says that's a total Ryan move. The guy never breaks a promise. He's just like Jonas, I guess. His word is his bond, maybe to a fault."

I feel light-headed all of a sudden. "I thought you'd be pissed about me dating your 'brother,' especially after your falling-out with Stu. Every time Reed comes near me, you chase him away."

"Oh, you've noticed that, huh? And here I thought I was being so subtle."

"You were as subtle as a flying brick, Josh."

"I just didn't want you dating a prick."

"Okay, that explains Stu. But you didn't want me dating Reed, either—and he's like a brother to you."

"Yeah, my brother the prick. At least when it comes to women. They love him for it—so whatever works for him—but that shit's not gonna fly when it comes to my T-Rod." He smiles broadly. "But none of that applies to Ryan. Not that you need my blessing, of course, but as far as I'm concerned, the greatest thing that could ever happen would be for you to be sitting with Kat and me, right next to Ryan, at Morgan-family dinners."

Tears flood my eyes. I swallow hard and rub them, completely overwhelmed. I've known Josh for years and we've never once had a conversation like this before. "Thank you so much," I squeak out.

"Kat's been trying to get you and Ryan together since the first time she met you. It's been her mission from God."

I laugh. "God help anyone who comes between Kat and something she wants."

"Amen."

"I really love her, you know."

"Yeah, I know. That makes two of us. And she loves you. She couldn't stop talking about you and telling me how badly Jonas and I fucked up. So what do you say, T-Rod? You gonna help me get myself out of the doghouse with my wife and agree to be a partner in Captain's?"

"I'd love to—if me being a partner is okay with Ryan."

"I already talked to Ryan about it and he loves the idea."

"But what if things don't work out between Ryan and me?" I say. "Ryan shouldn't have to be stuck with an ex-girlfriend as a partner on his dream business." A horrible thought seizes me. "Or what if Ryan's feelings have cooled since Hawaii and he doesn't want to start a relationship with me anymore?"

"T-Rod. Stop being a fucking freakazoid. Ryan warned me you're a loon. Dude, I had no idea."

I laugh.

"How have you kept your crazy hidden from me all this time?"

"It hasn't been easy."

Josh chuckles. "Ryan *loves* you. He wants you to have his babies. Do you think he's stopped loving you in a week's time, just because you're acting like a nutcase?"

I shrug, but I can't help smiling.

"Take a chill-pill, woman. I've talked to Captain Morgan and he's anything but 'cooled' on you. To the contrary, he's more determined than ever to lock you down."

My heart leaps with joy.

"But, okay, hypothetically, if things ultimately don't work out for you two and you decide leaving the partnership is for the best, then I'll personally buy you out at a number that's insanely awesome for you, okay? Above-market valuation. And, furthermore, any such buy-out will come out of my own personal pocket, not the business's and not Ryan's, so there won't be any protracted negotiations or hard feelings."

I cock my head to the side. "Why would you agree to that? It's sweet and generous and I'm grateful, but from a business standpoint, that's just plain stupid, Josh."

Josh laughs. "You've just answered your own question. I'm not doing Captain's for business reasons—I'm doing it because life is short. *YOLO*. Let's have some fun with the people we love the most and maybe make some money while we're at it."

"'The people we love the most'? You're already talking like a true Morgan."

We share a smile.

"Honestly," Josh says, "I'm happy to risk a stupid business decision if it means putting an end to your present stupidity. Plus, it's only gonna be stupid on my part if I actually have to make good on my promise one day—and I've got a strong hunch I won't." He winks. "Now, come on, Miss Rodriguez, enough yapping and talking about our fucking feelings. I told Ryan I'd be talking to you about the partnership proposal and then we'd come meet him for drinks to celebrate and discuss next steps."

My eyes widen. "You want me to come with you to meet Ryan for drinks?"

"Correct."

"When?"

"Now. So wipe the snot off your face. You're a mess."

My chest tightens. "But Ryan and I haven't spoken since Maui. I need to talk to him in private. I need to..." I put my hands on my cheeks, suddenly feeling anxious. "I haven't told Ryan any of the stuff I just told you."

"All right. So you and Ryan will sit at the bar alone for a bit while I'll go to the coffee place a few doors down. In fact, I'll text Kat right now and have her meet me there so I'm not feeling lonely." He flashes me a beaming smile. "You and Ryan can talk as long as you need—no rush—and whenever you two are done with your declarations of undying love and you feel ready to talk business, you'll text me and Kat and we'll come to the bar."

I let out a long exhale and shake out my arms.

"T, there's nothing to be nervous about. I spoke to Ryan. He still feels the same way he did in Hawaii, even more so."

"He said that?"

Josh nods. "And wouldn't shut the fuck up about it."

I laugh. "Thank you, Josh."

"My pleasure." He stands. "Now, come on, Miss Rodriguez. Time to bag yourself an amazing dude."

I stand. "Okay, Mr. Faraday. Let's do this."

Josh's phone beeps and he looks down at it. "Oh, speak of the devil. Ryan says he's already at the bar, waiting for us. I'll tell him we're on our way." He punches out a message as we walk toward the door of his office.

"Where are we meeting him?"

Josh grins. "The Pine Box."

Chapter 67
Tessa

Josh parks his Lamborghini in a paid lot across the street from The Pine Box (and, of course, pulls a total "Josh" by slipping the attendant a hundred bucks to park it in a spot far away from any other car) and the two of us walk toward the bar. When we reach the front entrance, Kat's already standing on the sidewalk in front of it, a huge smile on her gorgeous face, her hair glittering like gold in the late afternoon sun, her slender palms resting on her bump.

Kat and I exchange hugs and kisses and chat breezily for several minutes about the honeymoon and the baby and about how Kat knew "the second" she met me I was "perfect for" Ryan. Finally, when I feel like I'm gonna explode if I don't get my ass inside that bar and throw myself at Ryan, Josh puts his arm around his chatty wife's shoulders, guides her bulging frame toward a coffee place a few doors down, and leaves me to my mission.

I step inside the bar and pause for a half-second to let my eyes adjust to the dim light—and when they do, I'm shocked to find there's nobody inside the place except for two stark figures: a bartender dressed in black behind the bar and... the man I love. *Captain Ryan Ulysses Morgan.* He's sitting on the same stool he occupied when I first beheld his heart-stopping image three months ago, and looking even more perfect to me today than he ever did that night.

When Ryan spies me standing inside the door, his gorgeous face breaks into a beaming, wide smile. He stands and motions to the stool next to him—and I stride toward him, feeling like he's pulling me on a string.

When I reach Ryan, I wordlessly throw myself into his open

arms, press my aching, yearning body into his, and kiss his magical lips like I've never kissed any man before.

"I love you," Ryan murmurs into my lips, his warm breath tickling my skin.

"I love you so much," I reply, my heart leaping, my tears flowing. "I'm sorry. Please forgive me. I love you."

Ryan tightens his grip around me and presses his body firmly into mine. "There's nothing to forgive. Oh, God, baby, I've missed you so much."

It's easily the most electric moment of my entire life.

"I was just scared," I gasp, my entire body trembling. "I'm a loon."

He chuckles and nuzzles his nose into mine and his stubble rubs softly against my chin. "It's okay. If you're a loon, I don't care. I love it all."

"I'm not scared anymore," I whisper. "I trust you. I love you. I want to be with you."

He cups my face in his palms, his blue eyes blazing. "I'll never hurt you, Tessa—I promise I'll always be worthy of your trust. I can't live without you."

"Me, either," I agree, tears streaking out of my eyes.

Ryan's face lights up. "You mean that?"

I nod.

He kisses me deeply, his body quite plainly telling me what's in his heart, his lips devouring me, our physical connection more powerful than any words could ever be. After several moments of passionate, elated kissing, we somehow manage to peel our lips apart and sit our bodies down onto our stools, our fingers interlaced, our chests heaving, our faces on fire.

"I just needed time to process," I explain. "It's my Achilles' heel: I make snap-decisions at work every day, but when it comes to my emotions, I can't do it."

"I understand," he says. "I mind-fucked you. I justified it in my head as the end justifying the means, but the bottom line is I wasn't completely honest with you. I won't do that again. I'll always tell you the whole truth from now on."

"I understand why you did it," I say. "Honestly, you played me exactly right. If you'd told me everything right up front, I probably would have freaked out."

He laughs. "You definitely would have."

We share a smile.

He sighs. "Babe, that phone call. I still can't—"

"I know it was Charlotte," I say, cutting him off.

"She told you?"

"No. Charlotte's on a cruise with her parents—no cell phone service."

Ryan palms his forehead.

"Josh told me about Charlotte after Kat told him."

"Oh my God, my sister is such a fucking blabbermouth!" he says, shaking his head. "Please don't be pissed at Charlotte. I sweet-talked her."

"Oh, I'm sure you did. I'm not mad. Obviously, my best friend knows me better than I know myself. Oh my God, I've missed you." With that, I grab Ryan's beautiful face and kiss him again and again, until the bartender comes over and politely asks if we'd like to order drinks, which we do.

"Isn't it weird nobody else is here?" I ask as the bartender walks away, looking around at the empty bar.

Ryan shrugs. "It's a weekday, middle of the afternoon."

"Yeah, but shouldn't there at least be a couple other people here? Whatever they're doing at this place for marketing, let's do the opposite for Captain's."

"Does that mean you're on board to be a part-owner?"

I nod enthusiastically. "You'd be okay with that?"

"Baby, I wouldn't have it any other way. As far as I'm concerned, we're a team, me and you, from now on."

We kiss again, elation flooding us—and when the bartender returns with our drinks, we disengage again, laughing at ourselves.

"You know, the last time we sat on these exact stools together, we weren't properly introduced," Ryan says. "I think we should do it now, you know, to get off on the right foot this time."

I giggle and put out my hand. "Hey, good-lookin'. My name is Tessa Rodriguez. I'm a personal assistant to this guy named Josh Faraday. I live in Seattle and I'm most definitely *not* a flight attendant."

Ryan takes my hand. "Ryan Morgan."

"*Morgan*? Any relation to Kat Morgan?"

"Why, yes. She's my little sister."

"Oh my gosh. What are the odds? My boss is marrying your sister!"

"Imagine that!"

We both laugh.

"Can you imagine if our first conversation had gone like that?" Ryan says. "Would have saved me a whole lot of time."

"No, it would have been the end of us. If I'd known you were Kat's brother right off the bat, I would have run like hell."

"Nah. We're fate, baby. We would have found our way to each other, regardless."

I feel myself blushing.

"So, hey, Tessa Rodriguez, it's nice to meet you," Ryan says, resuming our little role-play. "Why don't you tell me a little bit about yourself?"

I take a sip of my drink. "What would you like to know?"

"Oh, I dunno." He smiles playfully. "How about you just give me a brief overview?"

"*A brief overview?*" I say, matching his playful tone. "Dang it! The *one* time I didn't bring a Power Point presentation with me to a bar and the hottest guy in the place asks me for a 'brief overview'? I knew I should have brought my laptop with me today."

Ryan bites his lower lip. "Shoot. I sound like I'm conducting a job interview, don't I? Sorry."

"It's okay. It happens."

"You know what?" Ryan says. "As long as I'm conducting a job interview here, why don't I ask you one of the all-time, classic job-interview questions?"

I take a happy sip of my drink. "Hit me."

"Where do you see yourself in five years, Tessa?"

I smile. "That's easy. Co-owning a fabulously successful bar named Captain's with multiple locations."

Ryan's cheeks flush. "And... in your... personal life?"

My heart lurches into my throat. I know exactly where I see myself in five years in my personal life—married to Ryan with a baby or two—but there's no effing way I'm gonna say that after such a short amount of time together, no matter how enthusiastically the man just declared his love for me. "Um, you first," I choke out.

Ryan chuckles to himself. "Damn, I love how predictable you are sometimes, Argentina—it's like we choreographed this conversation." He takes my hands and looks into my eyes. "In five years, I see myself married to you. I see us changing two sets of diapers with more babies on the horizon. I see us sitting down for Thanksgiving at my parents' house and going to football games on Sundays and soccer games on whatever-the-fuck-days they play soccer. And I see us making love every night, sometimes as me and you, sometimes as Ulysses and Samantha—and maybe sometimes as characters we have yet to create—but always, always lighting the world on fire. I see myself loving you, and protecting you, and making your happiness in life my top priority. And, most of all, I see myself as the luckiest man alive."

My jaw is hanging open. My heart is medically palpitating. My eyes are full of tears.

"Do you see any of that, too?" he asks softly.

I nod.

"How much of it?" he asks.

I can barely speak. "All of it."

Ryan exhales like the weight of the world has just been lifted off him. "Thank God." He takes a deep breath. "Then, in my opinion, we shouldn't wait to get this show on the road. Do you agree?"

I open my mouth and close it, not quite sure what he means. Because if he means he's gonna... Wait. *No.* Please, God, don't let him do it now. I haven't even introduced him to my family yet! I couldn't possibly say yes to Ryan without my family's blessing, no matter how much I love him! Shit, shit, shit! "Ryan," I gasp. "*Wait.*"

Ryan touches my cheek. "Ssh."

"But Ryan," I persist. I want to tell him my ultimate answer is going to be yes—*of course*—but that my father is traditional and I don't feel comfortable leaping into any kind of official arrangement without certain respects being paid. I want to tell him not to ask me yet because I never want to say no to him—Oh, God, never!—but that I can't possibly—

"*Tessa*," Ryan says. "I can see your mind is racing, baby." He chuckles. "It's *okay*. I'm not gonna ask you right now. I'm not stupid."

I exhale with relief.

"I know certain things have to be done before we get there, don't worry."

My entire body relaxes.

"And I also know you're probably gonna need some time to 'process' before you can say yes to me. So, just to get you mentally prepared for when I eventually pop the question, whenever that's gonna be in the future, no rush, I've prepared a little Power Point presentation to help you with your ultimate decision-making."

"A *Power Point?*" I ask.

"A Power Point," he says matter-of-factly. "Now, come on, have a seat over here and watch my presentation and hear me out."

I freeze, suddenly worried he's gonna ask me now, even though he just said he isn't.

"Sweetheart," he says, pulling me up and guiding me toward a chair near a white wall. "I'm not gonna ask you anything yet. I'm gonna show you a silly little Power Point, just for fun. Okay? Now, please, have a seat and keep an open mind."

Chapter 68
Ryan

Tessa looks around at the empty bar as she takes a seat. "You rented this place out, didn't you? I can't believe it could possibly be this empty by chance."

I wink. "I thought we could use a little privacy. Hey, let's get you a drink while I get my Power Point set up."

"You're seriously gonna show me a Power Point presentation *here?*"

"Yup." I signal the bartender and he comes over to take Tessa's drink order, and as he gets her situated, I quickly set up my laptop and a projector, and place two previously stowed bowls on the bar.

Once everything's all set up, I grab the small remote for the projector, position myself like a professor next to my "screen" (a white wall I've cleared of framed posters), and turn to face Tessa. "Okay, sweetheart," I say. "Please watch my presentation without commenting. Any thoughts, questions, objections, or stressed-out reactions may be offered at the end. Okay?"

"Okay."

"Promise?"

She leans back, smiling. "Promise."

I take a deep breath and click the button on my remote control, and the title slide projects onto the wall next to me: "The Top Ten Reasons Why You Should Say 'Hell Yes!' When I Ask You to Marry Me."

Tessa lets out a little yelp. "*Ryan.* Wait."

I put my index finger to my lips. "This is just getting you primed and ready for my *eventual* proposal, okay? I know how much you like having time to 'process' before making major decisions, so I'm getting your gears turning nice and early." I'm lying about that, of course—I'm not walking out of this place without a fiancée. But I swear it's the last little white lie I'll ever tell her.

Tessa's shoulders relax. She nods.

I hit the button for the first slide and up it comes: "Reason One: If you marry me, your family will be thrilled."

Tessa looks at me quizzically, her lips parted in surprise.

I tell her about my recent dinner with her family in L.A., scrolling through photos of our smiling families together as I do. "And when I asked your parents for their blessing," I say, "they said that, although the decision is yours, of course, they'd be 'thrilled' to welcome me and my entire family into yours."

Tessa opens her mouth like she's going to speak and then, without warning, bursts into tears.

Damn, I'm good. Do I know my girl or what?

I move to her and stroke her back and kiss the top of her head as she cries and thanks me profusely for doing that, my heart melting and leaping, all at once.

"You ready for the next slide, love?" I ask. "That was just my opening salvo."

"They're not all gonna make me sob, are they?"

"I make no promises." I bring the next slide up: "Reason Two: If you marry me, my family will be thrilled." I grin at her. "Do you have any idea how many times in Hawaii members of my family *ordered* me to make a move on you? Oh my God. They must have thought I had absolutely zero game the way I kept putting them off."

She laughs.

"Tessa, seriously, everyone *desperately* wants you to be a part of our family, through any means necessary. Worst case scenario, I truly think they'd be willing to pair you off with Keane, if it would mean bringing you into the fold."

She laughs again.

I click the remote control and bring up the third slide: "Reason Three: If you marry me, I'll make you my world-famous guacamole any time you like."

"*Wow.*"

"Of course, you can't appreciate the enormity of this promise until you've tasted my guacamole. So..." I grab two bowls off the bar—one filled with tortilla chips and the other with my famous guacamole. "I made you a batch. I promise, once you've tasted this guac, you'll understand what I'm offering you here."

Dutifully, Tessa dips a chip into the bowl of guacamole and pops it into her mouth—and her entire face lights up. "Nirvana," she gushes. "Best guacamole I've ever tasted. You were right about the cumin."

"Now, just imagine being *married* to the guy who made that—and then imagine him making it for you any time you want. That'd be a truly happy life, wouldn't it?"

"It'd be the happiest life I could possibly imagine."

Oh my God. My heart leaps. Did she just tell me she's gonna say yes? Holy fuck, I think she did!

I click to the next slide, my heart racing: "Reason Four: Based on objective facts and figures and numbers, you should definitely marry me." I quickly scroll through a series of slides riddled with pie-charts, graphs, and figures, all of them extolling the scientifically supportable benefits of marriage from social, health, and economic perspectives, plus a whole bunch of ridiculous numbers having to do with me, personally (things like my height, weight, IQ, street address, and SAT score).

"The night we met right over there," I say, pointing toward the stools, "you told me guacamole alone wouldn't be enough to make you fall in love with me. You said you'd also need facts and figures, in order to satisfy your pesky left-brain. Well, here you go, my love—and, as you can see, the numbers don't lie. Marriage is the only logical thing for us to do, objectively.'"

"Oh, Ryan," she says, her eyes sparkling, her smile beaming.

I click to the next slide, a lump in my throat: "Reason Five: If you marry me, you'll receive a lifetime supply of Morgan-family perks."

"Where do I sign up?" she blurts, making my heart leap.

I clear my throat. "Said perks include, but are not limited to, the following: one, lifetime tickets to *any* 22 Goats show, anywhere in the world, including backstage passes. Two, Momma Lou's famous cooking at frequent family meals, including, but not limited to, her famous lasagna, spaghetti and meatballs, and turkey chili. Three, fishing with my dad and Colby, any time you'd like. Asterisk: not to exceed one day of fishing per month."

She laughs.

"Four," I continue, "for the next year, Kat says you can borrow any item of clothing in her closet at any time, no need to ask permission, since none of it fits her, anyway. Five, I'll expertly fold all our fitted sheets—I promise."

"*Wow.*"

"I know. Life-changing. And, six—and this is by far the most valuable perk—Ball Peen Hammer will shake his ass *for free* at Charlotte's next birthday party!"

Tessa hoots with laughter.

"Now, do you *really* wanna be the one to tell Charlotte you turned down a lap-dance for her from Ball Peen Hammer?"

"Hell no," she replies. "Actually, Charlotte's birthday is next month. I'm thrilled to be able to get my shopping done so far in advance."

Oh my God. Did Tessa just tell me she's prepared to say yes to me *today*? Holy fuck! I think she did.

I move to the next slide, my pulse quickening. "Reason Six: If you marry me, I'll take ballroom dancing lessons."

She flashes me an adorable smile. "Really?"

"Really. I wanna be able to lead you and not embarrass myself."

She clutches her heart. "I can't wait."

My heart is gonna break my sternum. Why, oh why, did I write ten fucking reasons into this presentation? The ring box in my pocket suddenly feels like it's on fire.

I click on the next slide: "Reason Seven: If you marry me, I promise the sex will always be fucking amazing."

"This one is self-explanatory," I say. "But lemme just say, I'm gonna worship your body every night of my life, I swear to God."

She shoots me a sexy smile.

I move to the next slide: "Reason Eight: If you marry me, the universe will be happy. We're fate, baby," I say. "You think it's *coincidence* I met you in a bar in Seattle, hacked nine airlines to find you, and then *happened* to run into you on a tiny island in the middle of the Pacific Ocean? Bah. There's no such thing as coincidence. We're meant to be. Clearly, the universe wants us to be together, Tessa."

"Well, gosh," she says. "I wouldn't want to disappoint the *universe.*"

I feel like I'm gonna pass out. I click to the next slide, leaping out of my skin with excitement: "Reason Nine: If you marry me, I promise to make you happy."

I swallow hard. "Tessa, to be clear, I don't actually believe one person *can* make another person happy long-term—true happiness is something a person's gotta find for him or herself. But I sure as hell promise to give you everything humanly possible to allow you to find your happiness. I promise I'll be the best husband and father I can be. I'll support and protect and love you with all my heart and soul. I'll worship your body and cherish your heart and nurture your soul. I promise I'll never do anything to hurt or betray you. *I promise*. We'll be a team, love. A *family*. Me and you. You'll never, ever have reason to doubt me."

She looks deeply moved. Speechless. She presses her lips together, obviously trying not to cry.

I click on the final slide, my entire body quaking: "Reason Ten: If you marry me, you'll get to wear this fucking awesome rock on your finger 'til the end of time."

Her eyes widen. She inhales sharply.

Quickly, I kneel before her, pull the burning ring box out of my pocket, and open its lid to reveal the big-ass, sparkling rock my momma helped me pick out (with the help of Tessa's momma via FaceTime)—and, just as I hoped she would, Tessa instantly morphs into a gasping, trembling, sobbing mess.

"Tessa Rodriguez," I say, tears in my eyes, my voice breaking. "I think you hung the moon, baby, and I always will. *I love you the most*. So, please, for the love of God and all the reasons outlined in my Power Point presentation, will you *please* say 'hell yes' to becoming my wife?"

Tessa nods furiously. "Hell yes."

I slide the ring on her trembling finger with a whoop and leap up to kiss the living hell out of her. After a few moments of kissing and gasping and whispered promises, I disengage from her and pull out my phone. "Let's get Josh and Kat over here to celebrate."

"Oh my gosh," Tessa exclaims. "I totally forgot they're at the coffee place!" She looks down at the ring on her hand. "I can't wait to tell them."

"Hey, Tim!" I call through a door behind the bar. "Crank the music and pour the champagne! We're getting married!"

The bartender enters from a back room and Tessa holds up her hand, displaying her sparkling rock. "Make it champagne for four, Tim!" Tessa shouts happily. "We're gonna have ourselves a little party."

"No, baby, we're having ourselves a *big* party." I call to the bartender: "Make it champagne for twenty, Tim!"

Tessa looks at me quizzically.

"You'll see," I say.

Two seconds later, just as my chosen song (*"Bailando"* by Enrique Iglesias, of course) begins blasting overhead, the front door swings open and our engagement party bursts in: Josh, Kat, my parents, Colby, Keane, Zander, Dax, Fish, Colin, Jonas, Sarah, and Tessa's family (her parents, brothers, sister-in-law, and niece).

Hugs and tears and kisses and high-fives abound and Tessa happily shows off her ring as champagne is passed out. Various introductions to Tessa's family are made. Lots of chatting and laughing. And all the while, my hand is firmly clasped with Tessa's, my heart bursting with joy.

Kat comes over to tell me Henn and Hannah sent their love, but couldn't make the party due to Hannah's little sister's birthday dinner.

"Henn's my brother for life," I tell Kat, my arm around Tessa. "He didn't find my girl for me, understandably, but that guy, more than anyone else, helped me keep the faith and listen to my heart."

"Well, cheers to Peter Hennessy, then," Kat says, raising her glass, and Tessa and I clink it.

"That reminds me," I say. I turn to the party. "Hey, everyone! A toast!" I raise my glass, my arm snaked around Tessa's waist, and everyone raises theirs, too. "First off, lemme just say, 'Thank God this is a surprise engagement party, as planned, and not a 'Consoling Ryan' party."

Everyone chuckles.

I aim my drink at Tessa's family. "To the Rodriguez family: thank you for welcoming my family into yours."

The Rodriguez family salutes me.

"To the Morgans," I say. "You rock. You know it. Nothing more needs to be said."

My family cheers.

"Thank you, Bob Gaskins, the man Wikipedia says is the inventor of Power Point. You rock, Bob, wherever you are—thanks for the dog and the wife."

Everyone laughs and cheers.

"And, finally..." I look at Tessa. "Thank you to my beautiful fiancée for saying yes. In *Moby Dick,* Herman Melville asks, 'Where lies the final harbor, whence we unmoor no more?' Well, Tessa, for the first time in my life, I know exactly where my 'final harbor' lies: with you—wherever you happen to be."

Everyone claps and cheers and then descends upon us, offering hugs and kisses and congratulations. But after a few minutes, I can't resist pulling Tessa into a corner for a celebratory kiss.

"You good?" I ask, nuzzling my nose into hers.

"I've never been better," she whispers. "This is the best day of my life."

"Mine, too. I can't wait to—"

"Excuse me, Ryan," Kat's voice says behind me.

I disengage from Tessa and look toward Kat's voice.

My stomach drops.

Olivia.

Kat's got a fake smile plastered across her face and her arm around Olivia's shoulders. "Look who texted me thirty minutes ago to complain you haven't been returning her texts," she says. "Look who begged me to tell her where she could find you so she could 'pretend to run into you' and 'try to win you back.'" Kat turns to Olivia. "Oh, crap. Now that you're here, honey, I just remembered a small detail I forgot to mention when I replied to you: Ryan's at this bar for his *engagement* party. Olivia, meet Tessa—my brother's future wife. Oh, wait, that's right—you two have already met, the night you called my future sister a 'cunt.'" Kat's smile is sweet but her eyes are blazing with unmistakable menace. "Do I have that right, Tessa sweetie? Did Olivia here call you a 'cunt'?"

"Why, yes, she did, Kitty Kat," Tessa says, her tone as sweet as Kat's.

Olivia clenches her jaw. "Fuck you, Kat. You ambushed me."

Kat laughs.

"Olivia, I'm sorry," I say, glaring at Kat. "I didn't put Kat up to this. You should go."

"I didn't do this for you, Rum Cake," Kat sniffs. "I did it for Tessa." She smiles at Tessa. "Anything you wanna say to Olivia, honey? Now's your chance."

Tessa pretends to yawn and puts her hand over her mouth, blatantly flashing her diamond. "Nope, not a damned thing."

Olivia shoots daggers at Kat. "Fuck you."

Kat laughs again. "You're all class, Olivia. Come on. I'll show you out."

"Don't bother, bitch." Olivia jerks away from Kat's touch and stalks straight out the door in a huff.

"Kat, what the fuck?" I say. "I never wanted to see Olivia again, especially not today."

"I couldn't resist. I wouldn't have *instigated* vengeance, but when I saw her text, I thought, 'It's fate.'" She shrugs. "If it were me, I'd sure as hell want that bitch to see my big-ass ring." She looks at Tessa. "Did it feel good showing her your big-ass ring?"

"It felt *great*," Tessa says, shocking the hell out of me.

They high-five and giggle.

"Welcome to the family, sister," Kat says, putting her arm around Tessa's shoulders. "I just wanted to make sure you know: you're not just getting a husband who loves you, you're getting the Morgan Mafia, too."

Chapter 69
Ryan

"I felt a melting in me. No more my splintered heart and maddened hand were turned against the wolfish world."

Tessa and I can't rip our clothes off fast enough. As fun as our engagement party was this evening, for the last hour of it, the only thing I could think about was bringing Tessa to my house for the first time and, finally, *finally*, getting to make love to her in my own fucking bed.

I lay her down on my sheets, kissing her and pulling down her G-string, the tip of my hard-on already wet with pre-cum. I suck on her nipples and gently stroke between her legs, my entire body trembling with excitement, and she writhes and moans her appreciation.

"You're so wet," I whisper, my fingers slipping in and out of her.

"I've been crazy-wet since you opened the ring box," she whispers back, and I laugh.

"Is it wrong I got turned on when you wordlessly bitch-slapped Olivia?"

"If I could have fucked you right in front of her, I would have," she says.

"Oh my God, you're so fucking hot."

I trail kisses down from her breasts over her belly and then lap and suck at her pussy 'til she's gripping the sheet and rippling in my mouth. In a flash, I'm on top of her, my balls tightening with my intense arousal, my wet hard-on nudging at her entrance, my heart exploding.

340

"I'm clean," I whisper, my body trembling, my cock aching to get inside her. "Are you on the pill?"

"No," she whispers, but when I move to grab a condom from my nightstand, she grips my arm, indicating I should stay. "We don't need it," she says. She widens her legs and tilts her hips up, rubbing herself against my aching tip. "Make love to me." Again, she tilts her pelvis, rubbing herself against me, making me crazy.

"Are you sure?" I gasp, my dick throbbing. "I'm so turned on, I can't think straight. That'd be crazy, right?"

"Do you love me?" she breathes, her slick, wet pussy gliding up and down against my tip.

"With all my heart," I choke out.

"You're gonna marry me?"

My heart is exploding. My soul is on fire. My dick is straining. "I swear to God, no matter what," I reply.

She moans. "And you want babies with me?"

Oh, God, my entire body's practically convulsing, I'm so fucking turned on. "More than anything," I gasp.

"Then make love to me. We'll let fate decide."

Without a single reservation or doubt, I pull her arms above her head, clasp my fingers in hers, and burrow inside her, groaning loudly as I do—and, the minute I get all the way inside her, I feel a sensation like nothing I've experienced before—a melting inside me—a fusion of our bodies and souls. "I love you," I say, euphoria slamming into me. "Oh my God, you feel so good."

She mumbles something incoherent underneath me, squeezing my fingers in hers. I begin moving inside her, kissing her voraciously, my body telling her everything my words can't convey. Oh, God, I've never felt so good, so fucking *sure* about anything in my life. Every splintered part of me has been made whole. She's the one I've been waiting for my whole life—the one who makes this crazy, fucked-up world make perfect sense. "I love you," I choke out as I come inside her, spilling my seed into her, taking a leap of faith. "Oh my God, Tessa, I love you."

Tessa stiffens as her body climaxes underneath mine, a declaration of love on her lips.

After a moment, we unclasp our fingers and she embraces me tightly.

When I look into her eyes, I'm worried to find tears in them. "What's wrong?"

"Nothing's wrong. Literally, nothing." She chokes up. "I'm euphoric."

I roll off her and put on some music ("Marry Me" by Jason Derulo), pull her to me, and kiss her. "This is gonna be a great life, my pretty chickadee."

"The best life."

We listen to the music for a moment, both of us lost in our thoughts—but, after a moment, I chuckle to myself.

"What?" she asks.

"I was just picturing us at the movies with Josh and Kat and you telling Josh to get his own fucking popcorn."

She giggles.

I squeeze her. "So do you think we just made a baby?"

"Probably not—I don't think the timing is right. But if we did, it was meant to be."

"You wouldn't freak out if we did?"

She smiles. "No. I mean, yes, I'd totally freak out, but not because I'd be second-guessing anything—only because getting pregnant is gonna freak me out, no matter when it happens. What about you?"

I consider my answer for a long beat, not wanting to say anything short of the whole truth. "I'd be absolutely elated if we just made a baby."

She considers that answer for a moment. "Growing up, I thought walking down the aisle with a baby bump would be the worst possible thing. But after watching Kat do it so joyfully, and seeing Josh morph into a husband and father before my eyes, I don't think there are any one-size-fits-all rules about love and marriage anymore."

I stroke her face, marveling at how beautiful she is. "I couldn't agree more."

I kiss her softly, my heart melting.

"Hey, guess what I just realized?" she says, her lips an inch from mine. "Congratulations, Romeo—you finally executed your 'master plan.'"

A wide smile spreads across my face. "Yeah, but not in the way you mean. My 'master plan' wasn't getting you into my bed. I lied."

"What?"

"I mean, yeah, that was *step one* of my master plan—but not the full plan. I just said that so I'd seem sane and wouldn't scare you off."

She laughs. "Yet *another* lie? Jesus, dude, you're pathological."

I laugh.

"So what the hell was the actual 'master plan,' then?" she asks.

I grab her hand and touch the sparkling ring on her finger. "*This.*" I place my palm on her flat belly. "And *this.*"

She visibly melts.

I sit up and lean onto my elbow, looking down at her gorgeous face. "So when do you want to get married, Argentina?"

She shrugs. "Next week? Next month? Three months? Whenever won't conflict with the arrival of Gracie Louise because I certainly don't want to..." Something in my facial expression makes her trail off, mid-sentence. "What?"

I can't form words.

"What?" she asks again. "Are you okay?"

I nod. "I just had a premonition."

"Of what?"

"Of us. The future."

"Really?"

I nod. "It was crystal clear."

"What did you see?"

"I saw you and me and a bunch of kids. And Captain's kicking ass. It was you and me against this crazy, fucked-up, wonderful world. And we were *happy*." I squeeze her hand and press myself into her naked body. "Tessa, don't worry about a thing, baby. I just saw the whole thing. And I'm one hundred percent positive: we're gonna have a truly beautiful life."

Epilogue
Tessa

"Hey, everyone," my gorgeous husband says to the small assembled crowd of our closest family and friends, our newborn daughter strapped to his broad chest, his blue eyes twinkling. "Thanks so much for coming out this afternoon to celebrate the opening of our *fifth* Captain's location."

"And our second in Seattle!" Josh shouts, raising his beer.

Everyone cheers.

I'm watching Ryan and Josh from the back of the room (the same way I always prefer to observe events such as this); but this time, unlike the last four times I've stood at the back of a Captain's grand opening event and swooned over my husband, it's the middle of the afternoon, the place is riddled with kids, and I'm seated rather than standing, thanks to a precious (and very tired) little human (who bears half my DNA) who's draped over my chest.

Ryan places his palm on Claire's tiny, sleeping head against his chest and continues: "Tessa had the idea for us to have a little family-friendly gathering with our closest friends and family before tonight's adults-only soiree." He looks directly at me at the back of the crowd. "And I gotta say, babe, it was a great idea." He winks at me and I wink back.

Oh my God, I love my husband. There's nothing like seeing him with our baby strapped to his broad chest while hearing him talk so passionately about the business he's worked so hard to make successful. And that cute little wink he just gave me was the cherry on top of the sundae. Wooh! I'm suddenly feeling the distinct urge to give my sexy husband a highly enthusiastic blowjob at my first opportunity.

"Honestly," Ryan says, drawing me out my fellatio-themed reverie, "I never once imagined in my wildest dreams we'd be opening our *fifth* location at all, let alone this quickly—or that we'd be having this much fun along the way." He shoots me a massive smile that melts my heart and makes my ovaries quake like rockets just before lift-off. "So I want to thank my partners, especially my wife, for..."

"Mommy?" my son, three-year-old Zachary Hennessy Morgan, says, abruptly lifting his sleepy head off my chest.

I smooth his tousled hair out of his dark eyes. "What's up, bubba?"

"I gotta go pee-pee, Mommy," Zac says, his little voice edged with unmistakable urgency.

I spring into action. "Good boy. Come on, buddy. Good boy!"

I quickly lead my little potty-trainer through the crowd toward the restrooms, smiling and nodding at the friends and family we pass along our route: Keane and his fiancée, Maddy (a documentary filmmaker who happens to be Hannah Banana Montana Milliken's little sister); Colby and his pregnant wife, and Henn and Hannah and their brand new daughter, Hazel (who looks so much like Henn, Hannah keeps accusing her husband of sneaking their combined genes into a centrifuge and somehow extracting every characteristic having to do with her).

Finally, Zachary and I reach the bathroom door, just as my mother-in-law emerges with Kat's four-year-old mini-me, Little Miss Gracie Louise Faraday (aka "Little G" aka "Mademoiselle Terrorist").

"Hi, Zacky," Louise says. She looks at me. "Do you want me to take him?"

"Oh, thanks, Momma Lou. I don't wanna miss Ryan talking about Captain's. You know how much I love hearing him gush."

Louise winks at me. "I know. Just do me a favor and take Little G back to Kitty. Come on, Zacky-baby. Show me what a big boy you are."

"Will you give me a candy like Mommy does, Gramma Lou?"

Louise looks at me, a question on her face, and I nod.

"Of course," my mother-in-law replies. "Where do you think the mommies in this family got the brilliant idea to give their kiddos

M&Ms for pee-pees in the toilet?" She winks at me and guides my baby through the bathroom door.

I escort Gracie to her mommy and daddy and brother and then stand off to the side, listening with rapt attention to the tail end of my husband's speech, my heart swelling with pride and joy and love of a magnitude I truly didn't know existed before this gorgeous man came into my life.

"...which is why I'm so thrilled to own Captain's with the people I respect and love the most," Ryan is saying, his face aglow. "So thanks again to my partners—Josh, Kat, Jonas, Sarah, and, most of all, my beautiful wife—for making this journey, and this crazy life, so much fun, and thanks to all of you for dropping by this afternoon to celebrate with cupcakes and lemonade before we ditch the kids and come back tonight to celebrate with lots and lots of booze. Hear, hear!"

Everyone laughs and clinks glasses of lemonade.

Josh assumes the microphone to say a few quick words about an upcoming fundraiser Captain's will be hosting for a children's charity we all support, and Ryan immediately strides across the bar to me.

"Hey there, Mrs. Morgan," he says. He wraps me in his strong arms and pulls me close, gently smooshing the tiny human we (brilliantly) made together (because we're super smart like that) between our warm bodies.

"Hey, Baby-Daddy," I reply, looking down at the top of Claire's fuzzy head between our chests. "Is C-Dog still sleeping down there?"

"Like a baby," Ryan says. "Where's Z-Dog?"

"With your momma in the bathroom. He woke up and told me he had to pee-pee."

"Awesome. The power of M&Ms. You're so damned smart, woman."

"I can't take credit for that little trick. Kat told me about it— although, I just found out she got the idea from the Grand Dame."

"Of course, she did. All good parenting tricks originate with my mother. I mean, yeesh, if changing *two* kids' diapers at once is nuts, I can't imagine how my mom simultaneously changed diapers for *three*."

I laugh. "You don't get to complain about changing shitty diapers, babe. You're the one who kept begging me for a second human. You don't get to beg for 'em and then complain about having to change their diapers."

"Oh, I'm not complaining about a damned thing and you know it. I love it all, including changing shitty diapers." He chuckles and kisses me and his stubble slides roughly across my chin, making my nipples harden at the memory of his stubble between my thighs last night. "I'm the last guy in the world who's got anything to complain about," he whispers, his lips skimming mine. "In fact, just puttin' it out there: I'm ready to change a third human's diapers any time."

"Dude. I just popped Claire out three months ago. Gimme a minute to catch my damned breath. We've got plenty of time. I'm not going anywhere."

"No pressure. I'm just letting you know, I'm totally on board, whenever you're ready. Let's make a soccer team. *Viva La Banda Morgana!*"

I giggle and he nuzzles his nose into mine.

"I've heard you loud and clear, Romeo," I whisper. "But let's just slow it down a tad, shall we?"

"I can't help it, baby. You're just so damned sexy when you're pregnant. And when you're not pregnant. And when you're sleeping. And awake. And talking. And not talking. And when you're reading. Or cooking. Or *breathing.* Oh my God, and don't get me started on what a turn-on it is when you hold our babies—oh my God—I'm seriously getting hard right now, just thinking about it."

I laugh. "You're not normal, Captain Morgan."

"I'm pretty sure that particular cat leaped out of its bag a long time ago." He lets out a loaded sigh. "Holy shit."

"What?"

"I knew we'd have a great life—I really did. *I saw it.* But I had no idea it'd be *this* great. Thank you for saying yes."

"It was the Power Point. I couldn't resist the effing Power Point."

He laughs. "Dogs and wives. I'm telling ya."

"And school dances. But just to be clear, I made a huge sacrifice saying yes to you. *Huge.*"

Ryan chuckles. "How about I work off my debt again tonight?"

"You better. Right I after I have my way with you, Captain."

"Oh, yeah?"

"You know how much it turns me on when you've got one of our babies strapped to your chest."

"Why do you think I do it all the time?"

I laugh. "Because you love having a baby strapped to your chest."

Ryan smiles. "True. But I also do it because I know it turns you on."

"Well, it's working." I lower my voice. "I'm thinking Samantha and Ulysses should come out to play tonight."

Ryan skims his lips across mine. "Oh my God, woman, you turn me on."

"*Captain, My Captain,*" I whisper.

"Are you trying to torture me?"

"Daddy, I made pee-pee in the toilet!" Zachary says, appearing out of nowhere with Louise.

Ryan smiles wistfully at me and bends down to pick up his beloved son with one of his muscular arms, taking care not to smash Claire's little body against his chest as he does.

As my husband learns the exciting details of Zachary's hard-earned M&M, I stand, frozen, watching him, my heart bursting.

I don't know why Ryan loves me so passionately. I don't know why he thinks I "hung the moon" and regularly brings home little "moon" gifts to remind me of that fact (like the cow-jumping-over-the-moon salt-and-pepper shakers he got at a flea market not too long ago and a charm bracelet featuring a dangling diamond moon he gave me for Mother's Day this year). I don't know why this beautiful man's attraction to me never seems to wane but, instead, only seems to grow and strengthen with each new day.

I don't know why Ryan seems convinced I'm perfect, when, in fact, I'm so obviously flawed in a thousand annoying ways.

I truly don't know how I managed to stumble into this wonderful life, whether it was just dumb luck or fate; but, either way, the end result is the same: I'm married to the man of my dreams.

And that's why, after much thought on the topic, I've finally decided to stop trying to analyze his unflagging devotion and instead focus my energies on deserving it, to the best of my abilities—trying, on a daily basis, to do whatever I can to make sure my beloved husband feels as worshipped and adored in this marriage as I do.

As Ryan continues chatting with Zac, Claire stirs against his chest and makes a little yelping sound, signaling she's hungry.

"Hang on a minute, buddy," Ryan says calmly to Zac. He puts our son down, deftly pulls Claire's tiny body out of her carrier, and gently hands her to me, no words necessary.

"Are you hungry?" I coo to Claire, sticking my fingertip into her mouth and heading toward a quiet corner.

"Sorry, buddy," Ryan says behind my back to Zachary. "Finish your story. I'm listening. And then what happened?"

I turn back around. "Babe?"

Ryan looks at me, his eyebrows raised.

"I love you so much," I say. I swallow hard, suddenly feeling overcome with emotion. Those words are so paltry. So insufficient. But they're all I have. "I love you more than words can say."

Ryan shoots me a beaming smile. "And I love you—the absolute most."

We smile at each other for a beat, until Claire jerks free of my fingertip and lets out a screeching noise that tells me I'm playing with fire if I make her wait any longer.

But I still haven't managed to convey everything I'm feeling. "I just wanna thank you..." I choke out. "For..." I don't even know what the hell I'm trying to say to this beautiful man. "For loving me the way you do."

The look that overtakes Ryan's features is pure love and patience. "Baby, I have no choice but to love you—you're my 'kick.'" He flashes me a beautiful smile. "Don't ever thank me for loving you." He kisses Zachary on the cheek and winks at me. "Loving you is what I was born to do."

Music Playlist for *Captain*

"Bailando"—Enrique Iglesias
"Use Somebody"—Kings of Leon
"Sex on Fire"—Kings of Leon
"Shape of You"—Ed Sheeran
"Beneath Your Beautiful"—Labrinth ft. Emeli Sandé
"Marry Me"—Jason Derulo

Acknowledgments

This book is dedicated to The Love Monkeys, my devoted and wonderful readers. Thank you for loving my characters as much as I do. Thank you also to my team: Melissa, Sophie, Alicia, Judi, Sarah, Jill, Andrea, and Kevin. Thank you, as always, to my beloved family. I could not write the Morgans were it not for my own awesome family members, immediate and extended, who show me every day what it means to love and be loved. And, finally, thank you to Damon for telling me an old joke over dinner one night that inspired the Keane Morgan inside me. I have researched and not been able to find the author or origin of the old and quite famous "Welcome to Jamaica" dick-tattoo joke, but let me thank and credit that person or persons here and note that Keane's story about his matching dick-tattoo with Zander was inspired by and an homage to that old joke. It has many iterations out there, but the core of it always remains a dick-tattoo with a lengthy welcoming message on it as the punchline.

Author Biography

USA Today and internationally bestselling author Lauren Rowe lives in San Diego, California, where, in addition to writing books, she performs with her dance/party band at events all over Southern California, writes songs, takes embarrassing snapshots of her ever-patient Boston terrier, Buster, spends time with her family, and narrates audiobooks. Much to Lauren's thrill, her books have been translated all over the world in multiple languages and hit multiple domestic and international bestseller lists. To find out about Lauren's upcoming releases and giveaways, sign up for Lauren's emails at www.LaurenRoweBooks.com. Lauren loves to hear from readers! Send Lauren an email from her website, say hi on Twitter or Instagram @laurenrowebooks, and/or come by her Facebook page by searching Facebook for "Lauren Rowe Author."

Additional Books by Lauren Rowe

All books by Lauren Rowe are available in ebook, paperback, and audiobook formats.

The Morgan Brothers Books:

Enjoy the Morgan Brothers books in any order:

1. *Hero.* Coming March 12, 2018! This is the epic love story of heroic firefighter, **Colby Morgan,** Kat Morgan's oldest brother. After the worst catastrophe of Colby Morgan's life, will physical therapist Lydia save him ... or will he save her? This story takes place alongside Josh and Kat's love story from books 5 to 7 of *The Club Series* and also parallel to Ryan Morgan's love story in *Captain.*

2. *Captain.* A steamy, funny, heartfelt, heart-palpitating insta-love-to-enemies-to-lovers romance. This is the love story of tattooed sex god, **Ryan Morgan**, and the woman he'd move heaven and earth to claim. Note this story takes place alongside *Hero* and The Josh and Kat books from *The Club Series* (Books 5-7). For fans of *The Club Series,* this book brings back not only Josh Faraday and Kat Morgan and the entire Morgan family, but we also get to see in detail Jonas Faraday and Sarah Cruz, Henn and Hannah, and Josh's friend, the music mogul, Reed Rivers, too.

3. *Ball Peen Hammer.* A steamy, hilarious enemies-to-friends-to-lovers romantic comedy. This is the story of cocky as hell male stripper, **Keane Morgan**, and the sassy, smart young woman who brings him to his knees on a road trip. The story begins after *Hero* and *Captain* in time but is intended to be read as a true standalone in *any* order.

4. *Rock Star.* Do you love rock star romances? Then you'll want to read the love story of the youngest Morgan brother, **Dax Morgan,** and the woman who rocked his world, coming in 2018 (TBA)! Note Dax's story is set in time after *Ball Peen Hammer.* Please sign up for Lauren's newsletter at www.laurenrowebooks.com to make sure you don't miss any news about this release and all other upcoming releases and giveaways and behind the scenes scoops!

5. If you've started Lauren's books with The Morgan Brothers Books and you're intrigued about the Morgan brothers' feisty and fabulous sister, **Kat Morgan** (aka The Party Girl) and the sexy billionaire who falls head over heels for her, then it's time to enter the addicting world of the internationally bestselling series, *The Club Series.* Seven books about two brothers (**Jonas Faraday** and **Josh Faraday**) and the witty, sassy women who bring them to their knees (**Sarah Cruz** and **Kat Morgan**), *The Club Series* has been translated all over the world and hit multiple bestseller lists. Find out why readers call it one of their favorite series of all time, addicting, and unforgettable! The series begins with the story of Jonas and Sarah and ends with the story of Josh and Kat.

The Club Series (The Faraday Brothers Books)

If you've started Lauren's books with The Morgan Brothers books, then it's now time to enter the world of The Faradays. *The Club Series* is seven books about two brothers, Jonas and Josh Faraday, and the feisty, fierce, smart, funny women who eventually take complete ownership of their hearts: Sarah Cruz and Kat Morgan. *The Club Series* books are to be read in order*, as follows:

-*The Club* #1 (Jonas and Sarah)

-*The Reclamation* #2 (Jonas and Sarah)

-*The Redemption* #3 (Jonas and Sarah)

-*The Culmination* #4 (Jonas and Sarah with Josh and Kat)*
  *Note Lauren intended *The Club Series* to be read in order, 1-7. However, some readers have preferred skipping over book four and heading straight to Josh and Kat's story in *The Infatuation* (Book #5) and then looping back around after Book 7 to read Book 4. This is perfectly fine because *The Culmination* is set three years after the end of the series. It's up to individual preference if you prefer chronological storytelling, go for it. If you wish to read the books as Lauren intended, then read in order 1-4.

-*The Infatuation* #5 (Josh and Kat, Part I)

-*The Revelation* #6 (Josh and Kat, Part II)

-*The Consummation* #7 (Josh and Kat, Part III)

In *The Consummation* (The Club #7), we meet Kat Morgan's family, including her four brothers, Colby, Ryan, Keane, and Dax. If you wish to read more about the Morgans, check out The Morgan Brothers Books. A series of complete standalones, they are set in the same universe as *The Club Series* with numerous cross-over scenes and characters. You do *not* need to read *The Club Series* first to enjoy The Morgan Brothers Books. **And all Morgan Brothers books are standalones to be read in *any* order.**

Does Lauren have standalone books outside the Faraday-Morgan universe? Yes! They are:

1. *Countdown to Killing Kurtis*—This is a sexy psychological thriller with twists and turns, dark humor, and an unconventional love story (not a traditional romance). When a seemingly naive Marilyn-Monroe-wanna-be from Texas discovers her porno-king husband has thwarted her lifelong Hollywood dreams, she hatches a surefire plan to kill him in exactly one year, in order to fulfill what she swears is her sacred destiny.

2. *Misadventures on the Night Shift*—a sexy, funny, scorching bad-boy-rock-star romance with a hint of angst. This is a quick read

and Lauren's steamiest book by far, but filled with Lauren's trademark heart, wit, and depth of emotion and character development. Part of Waterhouse Press's Misadventures series featuring standalone works by a roster of kick-ass authors. Look for the first round of Misadventures books, including Lauren's, in fall 2017. For more, visit misadventures.com.

3. *Misadventures of a College Girl*-a sexy, funny romance with tons of heart, wit, steam, and truly unforgettable characters. Part of Waterhouse Press's Misadventures series featuring standalone works by a roster of kick-ass authors. Look for the first second of Misadventures books, including Lauren's, in spring 2018. For more visit misadventures.com.

4. Look for Lauren's third *Misadventures* title, coming in 2018.

Be sure to sign up for Lauren's newsletter at www.laurenrowe books.com to make sure you don't miss any news about releases and giveaways. Also, join Lauren on Facebook on her page and in her group, Lauren Rowe Books! And if you're an audiobook lover, all of Lauren's books are available in that format, too, narrated or co-narrated by Lauren Rowe, so check them out!

11345545R00211

Printed in Germany
by Amazon Distribution
GmbH, Leipzig